D0271365

THE HOLMES INHERITANCE

*Brian Freemantle titles available from
Severn House Large Print*

Dead Men Living
Ice Age
Two Women

THE HOLMES INHERITANCE

Brian Freemantle

COMMUNITY INFORMATION LIBRARIES	
H453457536	
Bertrams	09.02.08
	£19.99

Severn House Large Print
London & New York

This first large print edition published in Great Britain 2005 by
SEVERN HOUSE LARGE PRINT BOOKS LTD of
9-15 High Street, Sutton, Surrey, SM1 1DF.
First world regular print edition published 2004 by
Severn House Publishers, London and New York.
This first large print edition published in the USA 2005 by
SEVERN HOUSE PUBLISHERS INC., of
595 Madison Avenue, New York, NY 10022.

Copyright © 2004 by Brian Freemantle.

All rights reserved.
The moral right of the author has been asserted.

British Library Cataloguing in Publication Data

Freemantle, Brian
    The Holmes Inheritance. - Large print ed.
    1.   Intelligence officers Great Britain - Fiction
    2.   Illegal arms transfers - Fiction
    3.   Spy stories
    4.   Large type books
    I.   Title
    823.9'14 [F]

ISBN 0-7278-7458-6

To my three daughters, Victoria, Emma and Charlotte
With the love that only they know.

Except where actual historical events and characters are being described
for the storyline of this novel, all situations in this publication are
fictitious and any resemblance to living persons is purely coincidental.

Printed and bound in Great Britain by
MPG Books Ltd, Bodmin, Cornwall.

To my three daughters,
Victoria, Emma and Charlotte.
With the love that only they know.

Author's Note

The Holmes Inheritance is quite obviously a total work of fiction, although my efforts throughout to avoid offending the thousands of worldwide devotees of one of the greatest and best known characters in modern English writing constantly imposed upon me the research required for a non-fiction book. I am unaware of a fictional legend other than Sherlock Holmes upon which an entire encyclopaedia* has been compiled.

There are, however, factual references upon which I have liberally drawn and I apologize for any even more liberal interpretation. The foundation charter for Winchester was granted in 1382 and pupils first entered the still uncompleted buildings in 1394, making it Britain's oldest collegiate school. Over that 600-year history the school has evolved its own unique language, called Notions, comprehensive enough to support a

*The Encyclopaedia Sherlockian. Jack Tracy. New English Library. 1977

7

319-page dictionary**. Notions – which I have employed as a code for Sherlock Holmes's hitherto unknown son engaged upon his first inherited investigation in the United States of America – is supplemented by *ziph*, the disguising of a word by doubling its vowels and inserting a medial 'g'.

The brash, self-publicizing political buccaneering of Winston Churchill is a matter of public record, although less well recorded is his connection as First Lord of the Admiralty with the German U-boat sinking on May 7, 1915, of the Cunard liner *Lusitania*, resulting in the loss of 1,198 lives. Or how, in its aftermath, a well-concealed decision by Churchill on the conduct of naval warfare might have contributed to that disaster.

Also now publicly acknowledged is that in the officially neutral United States of America in the immediate years prior to the inevitable outbreak of the First World War there were among the industrial pirate kings and robber baron entrepreneurs of the period those who saw – and gained – enormous profit supplying war materiel to either side. Or both at the same time.

Winchester, 2004

**Winchester Notions. The English Dialect of Winchester College. Charles Stevens. The Athlone Press. 1998.

Acknowledgements

For their unstinting help resolving what to them must have seemed totally bizarre queries I thank Drs David Ceiriog Hughes and Julian Havil and Lachlan Mackinnon. I also wish to thank Richard Symons, of the department of private books at the Imperial War Museum, London, Paul Keogh, of the Liverpool Library Records Office, and the entire and tireless staff of the Winchester Reference Library.

Prologue

'It's making our Americans nervous,' said the man who had sought the meeting. 'They're frightened of being publicly identified.' The German intonation was soft, Bavarian.

'Then it has to be stopped. At once,' decided his superior. There was a contrasting harshness in the Prussian tone.

'Easily achieved,' assured the small man, whose function it would be and who was eagerly anticipating it.

'But if we remove him we remove any chance of discovering his source,' warned the Bavarian.

'Which we've been seeking – but failing – to do for the past month,' complained the Prussian.

The small man inferred the criticism. 'Whoever they are, they're being cautious. We've even got someone into the Capitol building itself without being able to discover a name.'

'And there's always the risk of someone else taking up the campaign,' the Bavarian pointed out.

'Through whom it might prove easier to locate the source,' said the Prussian. 'I want

11

to resolve the immediate problem.' He looked directly at the assassin. 'It has irrefutably to be an accident, of course.'

'Accidents don't act as deterrents,' insisted the small man.

'Don't become a liability yourself by starting to enjoy your work,' cautioned the Prussian. 'An accident. Understood?'

'Understood,' accepted the man. 'There's very little he can do without our knowing about it in advance.'

'Except meet with his source,' sneered the superior. 'There are to be no mistakes.'

'There won't be,' said the small man.

'If there are, you'll be the sufferer.' The smile was totally devoid of humour. 'The first casualty of the war, you might say.'

One

Sebastian Holmes pulled himself into the drawing-room shadows cast by an exhausted, early summer sun, wanting to study unseen the head-slumped, heavily breathing figure of his near-stranger father on the outside verandah. Sebastian was bewildered by the wicker bath chair and the heavy tartan rug over Sherlock Holmes's lower body, recognizing from the accounts of the diligent Dr Watson only the ornate red Persian slippers visible below the covering. There had been no warning of infirmity in any correspondence, either from his father or from his uncle, whose summons had brought Sebastian so curiously from Germany. Such frailty, he conceded, was entirely understandable after the extremes – as well as the damned narcotics – to which his father had exposed himself on his way to becoming the world's foremost consulting detective, but the deterioration since their last encounter, six months earlier, was a shock.

Was he, regarding the very reason for the summons back to England, here to bid farewell to a dying father he scarcely knew?

13

Standing, as he was, the unsuspected observer of someone once so active, Sebastian was abruptly swept by sadness, despite knowing the man so little. And just as quickly knew from anecdotes rather than experience that it was a sympathy to be kept hidden from a person of such fierce independence. Better, in fact, to withdraw as silently as he had entered and have the attentive Mrs Hudson announce him, to give his father time to awaken and collect himself.

Sebastian was half turned, tensed against the slightest footfall, when a far-from-frail voice rasped: 'Don't you think you've skulked there sufficiently, sir!'

Sebastian physically jumped, the fading sadness quickly turned to irritation at once more being caught out. 'I believed you to be resting, sir.'

Sherlock Holmes had straightened, contemptuously throwing aside the rug and disparagingly thrusting the wheelchair backwards unattended across the verandah. Sebastian accepted he had witnessed firsthand the astonishing ability to perfectly take on the mien of another that Dr Watson had so often commented upon when his father chose to adopt a disguise. Holmes said: 'Come! Let's see you.'

Sebastian advanced on to the low, brick-walled verandah, savouring the perfume of the roses that had become one of his father's several hobbies since his supposed retirement. The rose garden was lit by an orange-

14

gold sun perched precariously upon the furthest fold of the Sussex Downs, but night fingers were already feeling out over the intervening countryside. There was still more than sufficient light upon the verandah, too, for Sebastian to see there was none of the tiredness or dissipation in the older man's features that he'd earlier imagined. The grey eyes were as intense as always, subjecting him to examination in return, and the narrow, beak-nosed face was remarkably unlined. It was difficult to detect any fading in the swept-back hair, either. The suit was country tweed but muted and dark, predominantly green, for which the emerald tiepin personally presented by Queen Victoria was a perfect complement. The only incongruity was the scarlet slippers. Sherlock Holmes became aware of it at the same time as his son, deftly balancing from foot to foot to replace them with burnished brogues in readiness just inside the drawing-room door. As he did so, he said: 'Not in my dotage yet. But don't forget preparation in advance is never wasted.'

It was difficult to remember all the axioms presented by his father since their belated and still uncertain reunion. 'In fact you appear very well, sir.'

'As fit and able as I have ever been.'

His drawing-room detection had to be acknowledged: there were always rules. 'I didn't think you were aware of me.'

There was the briefest of smiles. 'Your train

15

was scheduled at Brighton at five thirty and it takes the worthy Mr Wright, whom I assigned to meet you, twenty-three minutes to bring his carriage here. The doorbell didn't sound until seven minutes past six, so your train was late. And no matter how light the tread, the three boards surrounding the drawing room are excellent warnings against being crept up upon: intentionally allowing floorboards to rub one edge against its neighbour is a security I adapted from the palace of the Kyoto shogun. The Japanese liken it to the trilling of the nightingale.'

Sebastian was unaware of his father having journeyed to Japan during the long lost years in Tibet and beyond, after the final confrontation at the Reichenbach Falls with his arch foe Professor Moriarty. But there had been no faithfully recording Watson, Sebastian reminded himself, as always far more eager to discover his own early and still unknown history, little of which had been offered by either his father or his uncle, Mycroft Holmes, into whose care he had been placed in infancy. 'Having now finished my education, perhaps I might take time to hear for myself such Japanese nightingales.' But then again maybe not, he reflected. He still needed to discover why he was here.

'What of Heidelberg?' the other man said dismissively. 'A graduation equalling that of the Sorbonne?'

'Just so,' confirmed Sebastian. It hadn't always been his belief but Sebastian now accepted that his father's insistence upon such varied schooling was not the abandoning of an unwanted boy who had caused his mother's death in childbirth but the determination of a man whose own university education had been incomplete to ensure his son had every advantage. And he'd surpassed even his father's exacting expectations. Mathematics had such an obvious logic to Sebastian Holmes that he'd gone up three years early from Winchester to King's College, Cambridge, and graduated as the youngest ever Senior Wrangler, the highest possible mathematics accolade that quaintly sounded more like an occupation in America's newly explored cowboy West. The designation had been different but he had continued to graduate top of his year at the Sorbonne and again, two weeks earlier, from Heidelberg.

There was another brief smile. 'Well done.'

Sebastian acknowledged that those two perfunctory words were as close as his emotionally limited father could ever come to allowing what his tutors at every school had openly ascribed to be unprecedented prodigiosity. But their judgement had never matched up to the admiration he'd so anxiously sought but never received. With objective hindsight Sebastian knew his never-admitted, even self-embarrassing insecurity – the naively formative need to prove himself *better* than the infallible Sherlock Holmes – stemmed from the infant imagination of having been foresaken. From his arrival at Winchester his always attained goal had been to excel at everything to gain his absent father's approval, never that of the always offering and praising Mycroft. Reminded, Sebastian said: 'I had expected to encounter my uncle on the train.'

'He has acquired an automobile, along with leather travelling cloak and goggles,' said Sherlock Holmes, disdainfully. 'Today is to be his most adventurous expedition.'

'His summons is intriguing.' Sebastian was irked at mistakenly imagining he'd been called to his father's deathbed.

'The life of the government's Permanent Cabinet Secretary is one of perpetual intrigue,' said Sherlock Holmes.

'Am I to be forewarned?'

'I no longer care to consider my brother's mysterious schemes.'

'A scheme that involves me!' demanded Sebastian. Surely the God of fortune had not anticipated him!

'Never forget the virtue of patience,' said Sherlock Holmes, slightly putting his head to one side. 'Which won't have to be strained much longer.'

Sebastian heard the car's arrival too and followed his father through the drawing room – detecting the birds' chirp as they crossed the intentionally loose boards – to be confronted in the driveway by Mycroft Holmes, majestically seated, goggled and leather-clad as promised, in a black, canvas-canopied vehicle large enough to diminish even a man of his size. Mycroft stepped regally down from the vehicle, announcing as he did so: 'It's a Rolls-Royce Silver Ghost, built by two engineers I predict to have a brilliant commercial future. Got up to fifty, just before Brighton. Give you both a spin over the weekend...' He looked beyond the two men, to the formidable figure of Sherlock Holmes's devoted housekeeper. 'And you, too, Mrs Hudson.'

'You'll not get me in that contraption, sir,' refused the woman. 'The good Lord never intended his flock to move like that.' She was dressed, in ankle-length, high-necked black, not a single white hair escaping from its ridged and pinned perfection.

Against his father's aesthetic, sharp-boned leanness the observant Watson's description of Mycroft having an uncouth body was very apposite. Yet, remembered Sebastian, again according to Watson, his father believed Mycroft possessed far greater powers of observation than himself, though lacking the ambition to utilize the faculty. Yet how could a man acknowledged the éminence grise of successive British governments, someone whose authority was often said to be greater than that of an incumbent prime minister, lack ambition?

It was Sherlock Holmes who somewhat curtly ended the Rolls-Royce inspection, leading the way back into the house for Sebastian to help his uncle with his luggage,

19

declaring as he preceded them that there was an hour to dress for dinner, with drinks strictly limited to thirty minutes for Mrs Hudson's beef to be served precisely at the time she insisted.

Sebastian was first down in the drawing room, where bottles, glasses, ice and a shaker were already set out on a silver tray by the ever-efficient housekeeper. After a moment's hesitation, Sebastian decided upon the American-imported dry martini that had been the rage at the Sorbonne, but was disappointed by his attempt. He had, Sebastian decided, been too easily distracted in its making by the unaccustomed normality of his surroundings: a lived-in room of comfortable furniture and tasteful paintings and prints far more homely than Baker Street even. He supposed it again stemmed from his inherited childhood misconception but his college rooms had always seemed transitory, little more than convenient refuges from the elements, never places in which he'd ever felt settled: never ever a home. Neither had he during his vacation stays at his bachelor uncle's rooms in Pall Mall's Diogenes Club: his recollection there had been that Mycroft Holmes could have one day walked out never to return, leaving the constabulary insufficient personal effects ever to discover who'd occupied the premises.

Throughout his reflections Sebastian had been closely studying everything around him, idly testing the nightingale cheep underfoot,

20

but abruptly he stopped, intent upon a so-far-unseen pole-table near the hearth. Every other bureau or console was close to being overwhelmed by memorabilia but this one was quite clear apart from its pristinely white damask covering upon which stood two silver-framed photographs of a woman. One was a ski-slope snapshot, the laughing subject bundled obscurely in coat, voluminous skirt and incongruous pert bonnet, dwarfed by the skis and single control staff upright beside an earlier pioneer of the sport. The other was a studio portrait of a more serious-faced, although slightly smiling girl of about twenty-five, naturally waved blonde hair a cascade to her shoulders, her ingenuous face unlined, pale-coloured eyes – a light blue, grey perhaps – open and honest towards the camera. The studio portrait ended at shoulder level and the protective clothing of the snapshot made it impossible to judge any stature, although from the comparable length of the skis Sebastian guessed she would have been middle height, maybe 5' 5". He reached to pick the portrait up, for closer study, but halted at the bustled entry into the room of his dinner-jacketed father, immediately followed by the brother. At Sebastian's gesture, both asked for whisky and soda. Sebastian mixed himself a second martini, more conservative this time with the vermouth.

'The toast must be to another excellent graduation,' announced Sherlock Holmes.

'And now what of the future?' asked Mycroft, as they touched glasses. His voice, like everything else about the man, was big.

Tread cautiously, Sebastian warned himself: test those whose pastime was all too often testing him. 'Until your summons I'd intended shaking off the dust of academia with a little travelling. France, certainly. The galleries and architecture of Florence and Venice.' He was curious at the look that passed between the two brothers.

'Let us talk about Europe,' invited Mycroft.

Sebastian frowned. '*About* Europe?'

'The unrest there,' prompted Mycroft.

He shouldn't resent this test, Sebastian decided. 'Serbian nationalism will be the tinderbox, in the Balkans. And if it is, the conflagration will ignite the Triple Alliance of Germany, Austro-Hungary and Italy.'

Mycroft raised his glass again, this time in silent toast. 'Were more than half the British Cabinet so succinct.'

Before another question could be put, Sebastian said to his uncle, 'Hardly a major summation, after so many recent wars and skirmishes among Turkey and Greece and Bulgaria and Serbia. But then you, more than most, are in a position to have knowledge and opinions upon such events?'

Sebastian did not set out to pose his remark as a question and was surprised at his uncle's response, as he was at the exchanges that immediately followed. Momentarily Mycroft Holmes hesitated, looking between father

22

and son. Then he said: 'Aware as you both are of my position, I'm trusting myself entirely to your integrity and discretion.'

'Which in Sebastian's case you always intended,' said Sherlock Holmes, sharply. 'I hardly imagine you have reason to doubt mine. It's your choosing whether to continue.'

Mycroft looked just as sharply at his brother. 'Do we have a change of heart here?'

'What we have is the need for considerably more thought!'

'Could I be included in this conversation instead of being talked over, as if I do not exist?' protested Sebastian, irritated afresh.

Mycroft smiled at the outburst. 'The Cabinet – Asquith particularly – thinks the Home Rule Bill will lead to civil war in Ireland. He's probably right. But it's preoccupying all but a few. I'm not usually an advocate of Churchill. I think he's too impulsive and enjoys his own headlines too much, but he's been outstanding as First Lord of the Admiralty, one of the very few with a proper perspective of the dangers of the future.'

Both Sherlock Holmes and his son had discarded their drinks, conscious of the political thinking to which they were being admitted. It was Sebastian, ahead of his father, who said: 'What danger of the future?'

'The benefits of war,' replied Mycroft, simply.

'To be gained by whom?' questioned Sebastian.

'America,' declared Mycroft.

'America is isolationist,' argued Sebastian, eager to show political awareness.

'I confidently expect Woodrow Wilson legally to declare their neutrality,' agreed Mycroft.

'Who then are the beneficiaries?'

'America is *the* land of the entrepreneurial barons like J. P. Morgan and the Astors and the Vanderbilts, men – groups – quick to take advantage of every opportunity. At the moment Great Britain dominates world trade: the global economy, in fact. America is close to challenging that supremacy. Germany's our other commercial challenger. If, because of our European alliances, we have to go to war with Germany the true winners will be the already poised industrialists of America.'

'Already poised?' picked out Sebastian.

'Our ambassador in Washington believes there already exist industrial cabals – virtually secret societies – of American businessmen establishing trading links with Germany in the event of war,' disclosed Mycroft.

Why was he being allowed the innermost intelligence of the British government? There was an obvious inference but Sebastian refused it, despite the excitement stirring through him. 'Aren't there American cabals offering links with us?'

Mycroft shook his head. 'Nothing of the scale we suspect to exist supporting Germany.'

The responses he showed over the next few minutes could resolve his unknown future in a way he'd not dared to speculate, Sebastian decided. 'If such German supporting groups were exposed, it could greatly change America's attitude towards neutrality, couldn't it?'

'Very greatly,' smiled Mycroft.

'But we have no official intelligence apparatus to which such exposure could be entrusted,' said Sherlock Holmes.

'Even if we did, we'd risk alienating American neutrality in Germany's favour if Great Britain were exposed attempting any sort of intervention,' warned Mycroft. 'Any attempt would have to be unofficial, with no provable government backing whatsoever. It would require a stalwart and patriotic volunteer.'

'I put myself at your complete disposal,' offered Sebastian, quite sure it was the response expected by his uncle at least.

'We're not talking of schoolboy adventures here,' said Sherlock Holmes.

'And I am no longer a schoolboy,' retorted Sebastian, determining to prove it. Determining, in fact, to prove many things.

Two

Sebastian anticipated hearing at dinner specific details of what was expected of him but the disappointment at not doing so was brief, replaced by an awareness of what was to be gained by listening, observing and deducing, which were the ingrained tools of his father's craft.

His deep-voiced uncle dominated the conversation, drawing a map of European political affiliations in the event of war, balancing the strengths and weaknesses of Germany's Triple Alliance against those of Great Britain's treaty partners, questioning whether they could present a deterrent to Germany's expansionism. The current French government was weak and despite the fledgling democracy forced upon Tsar Nicholas II by the 1905 revolution the country was still riven by unrest, with revolutionary leaders plotting in exile. A Russia torn by civil war would be ill equipped to honour an agreement to confront aggression outside its borders.

'It's a strategy worthy of von Bismark himself,' judged Mycroft. 'Imagine our alliance splintered in such a way and Germany with supply links firmly established in the United

States. We could be starved as well as shelled into submission.'

'It's a clear enough danger,' said Sebastian. This was the first time he'd experienced his uncle working – thinking – professionally and he was impressed.

Brandy, port and a humidor were laid out in readiness for their return to the drawing room. The two older men kindled cigars. Sebastian didn't smoke. There was for several minutes an uncomfortable silence which appeared to Sebastian to be oddly rehearsed. But then, abruptly and directly addressing his son, Sherlock Holmes said: 'Our relationship is not of the ordinary. Because of which I owe you an apology.'

Mycroft's frown reflected Sebastian's surprise. 'I don't understand your remark, sir.'

'Your being called here today was against my better judgement,' declared Sherlock Holmes. 'And the more I hear of it, the less I am persuaded you should become involved.'

Before Sebastian could respond, Mycroft said: 'I thought we had an agreement?'

'This is work requiring long experience,' insisted Sherlock Holmes. 'The slightest mistake could cost Sebastian his life.'

'It cannot be you,' refused Mycroft. 'Von Bernstorff knows you, from his posting as ambassador to London. You'd be recognized within an hour. You acknowledged as much when we first spoke of it: even evolved a subterfuge against any foreign surveillance upon you here in England.'

27

'Stuff and nonsense! Von Bernstorff and his spy nests are easily avoided,' replied Holmes. 'And I've changed my mind about being pushed around in that confounded invalid carriage!'

It cannot be you. The man wasn't motivated by concern for his safety. His father either did not think him capable or was jealous. Perhaps, even, a combination of both. The realization hardened Sebastian's earlier conviction that he could actually do better than the supposedly omniscient Sherlock Holmes. 'I regret you do not consider me worthy of the task!'

'The stakes – and the penalty for failure – are too high.'

'You *know* there'll be the need to circulate in Washington at von Bernstorff's level,' persisted Mycroft. 'This late objection serves no purpose! There is no one else but Sebastian in whom such complete trust can be placed. The telegraph is already installed in Baker Street. Sebastian will be your surrogate as we always intended.'

They might intend it but Sebastian was damned if he did. But this was not the moment to make his feelings known to either man. To his father he said: 'You've schooled me in your art, these last few years. Has that all been for nothing?'

'Instinct can't be taught. Nor experience.'

Confrontation or cajoling, wondered Sebastian. Persuasion first, before openly declaring that if he didn't have his father's blessing he'd

28

go without it. 'If there is to be such close communication, the instinct will be yours. And the experience.'

'It cannot work that way.'

'Some way has to be found,' demanded Mycroft. 'Your personal doubts must be secondary to national needs and by your own admission that is what we are discussing here.'

Sebastian's annoyance at his participation once more being discussed between the two men as if he were not in the room was compounded by the awareness that in some previous conversation his father *had* expressed doubts about him, which reduced all the lectures and instruction on the art of detection to condescending play-acting. Would he be sacrificing so very much alienating his so long absent father by announcing that he was going to America whatever the older man's feelings?

'I am not personally shirking from national requirements,' Sherlock Holmes defended himself.

'We're too far advanced to change course: Winston won't ally himself to any other proposal,' insisted Mycroft, his voice matchingly loud.

Sebastian decided the suggested personal involvement of Winston Churchill was a disclosure to be explained later. He moved at last to defy his father but before he could Sherlock Holmes once more turned directly to him and said: 'If I agree, I insist upon there being daily exchanges between us.'

'Of course,' agreed Sebastian, easily. Saved by a second, he thought.

'And at the slightest suggestion of your coming under suspicion, you are to withdraw.'

'I understand.' With the stakes this high, Sebastian doubted if he'd be allowed to withdraw.

'I hope more than I've ever wished anything that I don't regret this weakness,' finally capitulated Sherlock Holmes.

The tension went almost visibly from Mycroft Holmes. 'Let's agree that there will be no further questioning.'

'I have a question,' announced Sebastian, addressing his father. 'Who is the skier whose photograph is displayed so prominently on the hearth table?'

'I have no part of this conversation,' said Mycroft, rising from his chair. 'This is the moment for me to retire.'

For a long time, so long that Sebastian feared his father would continue to refuse, Sherlock Holmes remained slumped as he had earlier on the sun-warmed verandah, his head forward on his chest. It was a contemplation from which the man did not appear properly to emerge, even when he eventually began to speak.

'Her name was Matilde Huber and she is the person to whom I owe my life and an apology impossible ever to make,' Sherlock

Holmes answered, his voice, like his mind, distant in memories. 'She was the mother you never knew and the wife I never had and for whom I have grieved for too many years...'

The older man lifted his brandy goblet to his lips but seemed unaware it was empty. Sebastian rose quickly to fill it. Sherlock Holmes appeared equally oblivious to the gesture although almost at once he sipped.

'I was so nearly done for in that struggle with Moriarty. The ledge was wet, from the spray. Moriarty slipped and lost his footing: released me in his panic to snatch out for a purchase that did not exist. Had wc still grappled, he would have taken me with him...' The man paused. 'I managed to scramble to a higher ledge, to escape Moriarty's henchmen, who I well knew would finish me off. I have no proper recollection of how I reached Meiringen and the clinic there. Matilde later told me I was delirious from total exhaustion and the injuries I sustained, a cracked head and two splintered ribs, as well as the blood loss from a wound to my side. Matilde's was the first face I saw when I recovered consciousness...'

There was another pause, this time for a faint smile, and Sebastian realized he was hearing an account not even imparted to Dr Watson. But then Sherlock Holmes had a secret to keep that had only ever been shared with his brother: at every school, academy and place where records were necessary Sebastian had always been acknowledged the

31

son of Mycroft Holmes.

'I remained much weakened for many weeks. My recovery was impaired by too many years of self-medication, against which Watson so often argued. Matilde was appointed my permanent nurse, whom I saw several times daily...'

Sherlock Holmes positively stirred for the first time, turning to focus upon his son, but lapsed into silence again. Sebastian knew that the wrong intervention, just one misplaced word, would forever end this confession.

'I have never been a man comfortable with female companionship,' took up Sherlock Holmes at last. 'Lying as I was, for so many weeks, I made decisions about my future. Perhaps the most important, now that the world was rid of the despicable Moriarty, was that I would give up the profession I had chosen to follow. That same world believed it to have been me who perished at the Falls and I was content to let that misconception be. My thoughts were of another life and Matilde became an important part of such thinking. When I was sufficiently recovered to leave the clinic I took a small set of rooms with a distant view of the Haslital, and Matilde, who was the freest spirit I have ever encountered, defied convention to join me. I can truly say that those first months of our being together were the most contented I have ever known. Marriage would have completed it and of course I sought her hand, all the more so when she disclosed her condition. Anyone but Matilde would have accepted at once for the sake of propriety. Instead she called me bourgeois: said that being with child was neither a cause, reason nor enforcement to get married and that a ceremony to comply with convention could wait...'

He'd slumped once more, retreating into the past, but Sebastian was aware of his father's throat moving with tightly curbed emotion.

'But there wasn't time to wait,' continued Sherlock Holmes, his voice uneven. 'There was an internal weakness no one at her former clinic anticipated ... a haemorrhage that couldn't be stopped. I held her, as she died. Promised to bring up a son of whom she would be proud...' The man's throat began to work again, making him stop. 'I didn't know how ... didn't want to learn ... I entrusted you to Mycroft and others better able than me while I wandered off to lose myself the only way I knew how. And for so many years remained lost...'

'I'm sorry,' broke in Sebastian, finding difficulty himself in choosing the words. 'I was not aware of the pain ... I should not have made this demand...'

'Of course you should!' recovered Sherlock Holmes. 'You should not have had to wait until now ... mine really is the apology that has to be made to you ... And to Matilde, for not being the father she would have expected of me.'

Three

After the reunion with his father Sebastian's vacation visits to England had been divided between 221b Baker Street and guest accommodation at his uncle's Pall Mall club. It was clearly Sherlock Holmes's expectation that on this occasion Sebastian should return to London with him, but Mycroft argued that were his brother under foreign surveillance it was obviously impossible for father and son to be together. Sebastian sided with his uncle's logic, anxious to limit any further debate that might prompt Sherlock Holmes's renewed opposition to his going to America. Sebastian suspected Mycroft shared his thinking when the Cabinet Secretary announced an early return to London with the suggestion that Sebastian accompany him in the Rolls-Royce.

'You know now about the circumstances of your birth?' Mycroft drove with fierce and unwavering determination and, even though the canvas hood was secured, wore his driving goggles.

'A great deal more than I did.'

'Then you can understand your father's concern for your safety.'

'I think so.' Sebastian was sure he concealed

34

his lack of conviction. Probing for more about his background, he added: 'Did you meet my mother?'

The hesitation was brief. 'A few times. It was Matilde, at Sherlock's request, who summoned me to Meiringen with the news that he had survived the battle at the Falls. He was in a desperate condition, mentally as well as physically. His only rational demand was that the world should continue to believe him dead.

'We did not meet again until after they set up home. The summons then was for me, as his next of kin, to settle the necessary matters of his estate and arrange its undisclosed transference to Switzerland to secure their future. Matilde was a truly remarkable woman, totally unconventional, with attitudes and ideas unacceptable for a woman of that – or indeed *this* – time. Her wish had been to become a doctor – a surgeon even – but such a profession was denied even the most committed female. So instead she became a nurse sufficiently gifted to restore to health people like your father, who without her would most surely have died.'

'I wish, in the future, to visit her resting place,' decided Sebastian.

Mycroft nodded. 'It's at Meiringen, of course. The headstone acknowledges her as your father's companion, by name. And your birth. You should also know that you are the sole beneficiary of his will, in which he is acknowledged your biological and rightful father. There is also a trust fund, established at the time of your birth, that has compounded over the intervening twenty-four years into a considerable fortune.'

'Set up by my father? Or you?'

Mycroft broke his driving concentration for the quickest of sideways frowns. 'I necessarily had to put it all in place, here in London. Every instruction and wish was your father's.'

Sebastian had occupied his allocated guest quarters at the Diogenes Club on previous occasions and they remained as sterile as always. Recalling the car-journey revelation, Sebastian supposed he was well enough off to purchase a London home of his own but he found the prospect – and the opportunity – strangely unexciting. Having known nothing but a rootless, moving-on existence, Sebastian Holmes was not even sure that London – any city, in fact – was where he wanted to make a permanent home.

He and his uncle dined that night at Rules off steak-and kidney pudding and a well-laid claret and afterwards Mycroft insisted they walk awhile along the Strand beyond the hearing of other diners.

'You offered yourself in this matter with an alacrity I expected but did you really have no thoughts of future employment?' asked Mycroft.

'From the first meeting with my father I always had the impression of being trained, just as I was always conscious of your promptings in other directions.'

'Do you *want* to be a consulting detective, like your father?'

'I'm attracted by the thought,' allowed Sebastian. Because at the moment I have no other and I've seen Florence and Rome, he thought.

'Which isn't an answer to my question.'

Was his uncle belatedly having the doubts of his father? 'I believe myself capable of what's being asked of me, as you must by putting me forward for it.'

For several moments Mycroft walked unspeaking in the direction of a fog-cloaked Trafalgar Square. There were far more hansoms than automobiles plying the thoroughfare and Sebastian wondered how long it would be before the imbalance reversed. He supposed with his newly found wealth he could afford to buy such a vehicle. It appealed to him far more than considering a permanent place to live.

'We none of us know each other as well as most families,' said Mycroft. 'I won't repeat the warnings of the past weekend save one. From my part in your upbringing I'm aware of an impulsiveness of which your father himself has sometimes been guilty and which you may well have inherited. Don't let haste be your undoing...'

There was more, anticipated Sebastian. 'A trait you complain of in Churchill...'

'Against which danger,' continued Mycroft, ignoring the interruption, 'I have had installed a dedicated telegraph, for my eyes and

37

attention only, at the Diogenes.'

Verbally tiptoeing upon such fragile ice had to be unnerving even for a man of diplomacy. Sebastian guessed that possibly for the first time ever the man's awkwardness came from seeking to circumvent his famous brother. It was important he show Mycroft he recognized the approach for what it was. 'The balance between uncovering conspirators and avoiding political pitfalls is going to be a fine one.'

'Quite so.'

'A diplomatic embarrassment would be worse than failing to discover a pro-German cabal?'

'I'm glad you appreciate that. It is why communication between us has to have priority.'

Mycroft had demanded this gas-lit promenade to avoid his seeing any physical discomfort, Sebastian decided. 'With copies of anything I transmit to my father?'

'I have to have the complete picture. But your father's excellent guidance will be limited to his unquestioned expertise, for which he will not need the distractions of diplomacy.'

He was now embroiled in family as well as international intrigue, Sebastian accepted. Which would be the most demanding?

With the following day free, Sebastian wandered the streets of an unfamiliar London, admiring some of the Mayfair and Belgravia mansions but seeing nothing to change his lack of interest in having a residence there. He studiously avoided the Baker Street vicinity and was back early at the Diogenes Club to prepare for the eagerly anticipated evening.

The venue was a mahogany-panelled club, in a set of private rooms served by its equally discreet private staircase leading from a corridor with its own street level, heavy-doored entry quite separate from the building's main entrance. It was guarded from within by an anonymously uniformed attendant who closely scrutinized every arrival through a sliding hatchway. It was within easy walking distance of the Diogenes Club so Sebastian and his uncle made the journey on foot, despite their formal dinner attire of white tie and tails. It was much colder than the previous evening, although the day had been warmer, and the contrasting temperature was already bringing a flitting mist to mingle with the persistent night-time fog of London.

Sebastian missed the exchange between Mycroft and the hatchway sentinel but from the quickness of their admission and the sureness with which his uncle unerringly led the way to the third stairway along the communal corridor the man was evidently a regular visitor. The door at the top of the gas-lit stairs gave directly on to a salon, also gas-lighted, in which a fire already blazed in a hearth around which were grouped heavy, button-backed Chesterfields of maroon leather. On a white-clothed table to one side a selection of bottles and glasses were arrayed, with Laurent Perrier already cooling in its ice-packed silver container. Almost at once the sound of ascending footsteps heralded the arrival of Sherlock Holmes. He was formally attired and cloaked, too, but with the addition of the silver-topped malacca swordstick that Sebastian identified from previous evening outings with his father. Sebastian again appointed himself butler and that night joined the other two in whisky after Mycroft's warning to delay the champagne as a courtesy to Churchill, whose favourite it was.

'Any unwelcomed attention here in London?' asked Mycroft.

'None that gave me cause for concern. But I did not come by direct route or single cab.'

Sebastian remained silent, bemused that two men, neither of whom he regarded as fantasists, could seriously discuss even the possibility of being under surveillance in the very centre of England's capital. He was at the side table, replenishing the two older men's drinks, when the door opened to admit the plump, smiling figure of Winston Churchill.

As he discarded his cloak among the others on an unneeded side chair, the politician said: 'My apologies for lateness. Delayed at the House by another question over the confounded Home Rule Bill.' A fresh-faced youthfulness made the man appear younger

40

than his thirty-nine years although the voice was thick, sonorous with the timbre of an orator. At their introductions, he said to Sherlock Holmes: 'I'm most honoured to meet a man of such stature and fame, sir.' To Sebastian he said, as they shook hands: 'One of the slight disadvantages of such clandestine occasions as these is the necessary absence of attendants but I see you've appointed yourself strategically.'

It was quickly apparent that both Churchill and Mycroft Holmes were well accustomed to such meetings from the politician's immediate suggestion that they get the food ordering out of the way as soon as possible and his uncle's instant production of cartes. Sebastian was delayed in completing his order by having to replenish Churchill's glass, and by the time their orders were placed in a rope-hauled delivery conveyance in the corner of the salon, half the champagne had been consumed.

There was one commanding carver chair at the already set, circular table of immaculate damask and candle-sparkling crystal and Churchill hesitated, deferring to Mycroft. He in turn deferred to the First Lord of the Admiralty. As he sat, Churchill gestured Sherlock and Sebastian Holmes to be either side of him with Mycroft directly opposite.

The encounter unfolded to be the most unique and memorable of Sebastian's experience thus far. Apart from the brief seating hiatus there was no deference to title, reputation or rank. Although Sebastian did more than most, each fetched food from the bell-summoned dumb waiter – Churchill commenting that serving himself was a lesson well learned soldiering in Cuba and the Transvaal – and poured wine for the others. It was, however, Churchill who dominated the conversation, although the Admiralty minister was always ready, sometimes poised, to give way to Mycroft.

It was from Mycroft to Sebastian that Churchill turned, halfway through the meal. 'Now to the business at hand. Great demands are being imposed upon you, sir.'

'I am fully aware of that, sir.' Let there not be second thoughts!

'Are you?' challenged Churchill.

'I believe so.'

'I don't. You're being cast adrift.'

'To perform a service for which I am proud to offer myself.'

'My concern is not your valour. It's your capability.'

'Would I be here, having this conversation with such a person as yourself, if my capability were in question?' demanded Sebastian, affronted once more.

Winston Church examined the contents of his glass. 'A forceful rejoinder.'

'I do not consider that...' Sebastian hesitated, deciding upon using the response to address more than one listener. 'I do not consider this a schoolboy adventure. I know all its implications. And dangers.'

Churchill said: 'It's most certainly not a schoolboy adventure.' He went to his other side. 'And you, Mr Holmes? Are you satisfied your son can, in this instance, take up your mantle?'

Sherlock Holmes hesitated and Sebastian lifted his own wine glass to hide his concern at the suggestion that he was positively taking over from his father. Mycroft concentrated upon the quail he was dissecting, similarly concerned.

Sherlock Holmes said: 'I have attempted, in a regrettably short time, to pass on to my son an expertise in a craft that has taken me a lifetime to acquire...' There was a further pause. Almost steadfastly refusing to look towards Sebastian, the older man continued: 'I am confident that he will be able to translate much-repeated theory into effective practice.'

Now it was Churchill who hesitated, his face betraying nothing as he digested the response. He returned to Sebastian, gesturing around their covert quarters. 'You accept that if ever called upon to do so, I shall personally deny this encounter ever took place; that I have any knowledge of you whatsoever?'

'I have already made it clear that I fully understand all the implications, have I not?'

'There will also be a total denial by the British government of your having any official function or approval whatsoever?'

'Which I also understand and accept.'

'You are under no circumstances to make

43

any approach to the British embassy in Washington,' persisted the politician.

'I know that.'

Winston Churchill pushed the wine decanter towards Sebastian. 'You will need to be among the highest and richest echelon of American society. Have you any thought of the guise you will adopt?'

'An entrepreneur of matching wealth, seeking to increase his fortune, would be acceptable in such surroundings, don't you think?' The disguise had come to him in a flash and Sebastian was impressed with himself.

There was a smile from the rotund man, who broke the conversation to fetch another decanter, this time of brandy, from a small sideboard. As he returned he said: 'Within the Admiralty there is a contingency fund to which I have later accountability. There's finance available for such deception.'

Had the need for such financial provision been the reason for Mycroft informing him of his personal wealth? wondered Sebastian. 'I will not call upon it lightly.'

'Nor will it be made available lightly,' warned the politician. 'The withdrawal will be upon your uncle's recommendation, no one else's.'

'An arrangement I acknowledge,' said Mycroft, at once.

The acceptance was so quick that Sebastian guessed there had been previous conversation upon the subject between the two men. The slightest miscalculation or mistake upon his part would lay open his uncle to a criminal charge of embezzlement and corruption.

Sherlock Holmes said: 'You are setting a heavy burden upon the Holmes family, sir!'

'An imposition I believed you willing to bear,' came back Churchill, brusquely.

'We are,' insisted Mycroft, before his brother could retort.

Winston Churchill took a folded, unevenly edged sheet of paper from inside his tailcoat and for several uncertain moments tapped it against his teeth. Abruptly he slid it to his left, towards Sebastian. 'My mother is American, which provides me with family connections. Julius Hemditch is a personal friend to whom I will provide an introduction and in whom you can put your complete trust. He is a man of considerable substance whose fortune comes from steel mills in Pittsburgh. He can certainly be your communication link. But from him I have heard the suggestion that the American transatlantic cable at White Plains might have been penetrated by German intelligence, rendering it unsafe. Have you any thoughts of a cipher?'

Sebastian hadn't but at once said: 'Notions would be incomprehensible.'

Churchill frowned. 'As it's incomprehensible to me!'

'Brilliant!' enthused Mycroft.

'I'm sure it will be, when it's explained,' Churchill continued to protest.

'I went up to Cambridge from Winchester.

Within the college, Notions is a traditional vocabulary – a language – understood only by Wykehamists...'

'Of whom I am one,' interrupted Mycroft. 'Sebastian went to Winchester because it was my alma mater. He and I will be able to talk with perfect clarity in what will be gibberish to all others.'

Churchill nodded. 'Brilliant indeed.' He smiled towards Mycroft. 'Take care not to mislay any correspondence: our current Foreign Secretary is also a Wykehamist.' The smile went as quickly as it had come. 'We will need more than enciphered messages. I shall personally arrange with Sir Alfred Booth, Cunard's chairman and another convenient friend, for his ships' captains personally to carry sealed reports from you ... You, Mycroft, will make the collection arrangements: return despatches, too.'

Sebastian at last took up Churchill's offered sheet. 'I go with no official support or position: I am, in your words, being cast adrift. Yet you provide me with introductions to people my approach to whom surely implicates you!'

Churchill carried another decanter of brandy from a sideboard. 'I am not a scoundrel. Sometimes there are distasteful necessities, one of which I come upon now. It disturbs my conscience that you are being asked to perform this duty so totally alone. This help is as far as I am able to go and even then it has to be a blackguard's gift.'

46

'That confuses me still further,' protested Sebastian.

'Your name was recorded on the visitors' log at the Admiralty this day. A personal address ledger has been reported missing from a junior secretary's office where I carelessly left it. The ledger will be located tomorrow. That sheet you hold, of little significance of itself, will be discovered torn from it.'

At last the enormity of what he was embarking upon registered with Sebastian Holmes. He waited for the apprehension but none came. He hadn't expected there to be.

Four

They met not in Winston Churchill's official, civil-servant thronged rooms but in the smaller set of chambers that were his preferred work place, atop Admiralty Arch with its unobstructed view down the broad expanse of The Mall to the still-incomplete memorial to Queen Victoria against the backdrop of Buckingham Palace. When Mycroft entered, Churchill was already standing, legs apart, cigar in hand, gazing at the symbol of British imperialism. It was still several moments before Churchill acknowledged Mycroft's presence.

'I was reflecting that it was Kaiser Wilhelm himself who cradled our dear Queen in his arms at the moment of her death. Now he's intent upon destroying the very monarchy of which he is part!'

'Not destroying it,' argued Mycroft. 'Usurping it.'

Churchill turned at last. 'I'll die before I see this country a vassal state of Prussia. My flesh crawls at the memory of having officially accompanied the popinjay on inspections of the Grand Fleet. He would have been planning even then: actually *spying* upon what his navy was likely to encounter!' In his anger, Churchill's sibilance became even more pronounced.

Uninvited, showing the intimacy of long professional if not personal association, Mycroft sat in one of the expansive leather chairs that gave him, too, a view of the palace. 'Let's pray there could still be an eleventh-hour reversal to avoid those plans ever having to be put to the test.'

'Pah!' dismissed Churchill, even more vehemently, jabbing his cigar to extinction in a dottle-filled ashtray. 'The die's cast, in all but formal declaration. And I'll not have you turning pacifist on me!' He jerked his head towards the palace. 'I know of three direct, personal appeals the King himself has made, cousin to cousin, imploring the Kaiser not to make the mistake of moving against Russia or France. The intelligence from the Berlin embassy is that the Kaiser believes we will remain neutral if he does.'

'We have treaty obligations.'

'Which he dismisses as being worthless pieces of paper.'

'Then he's poorly advised.'

'There's a very personal subject upon which our own king may need advice.'

'What?'

'The name Saxe-Coburg.'

Mycroft stirred, alerted to a further, unwarned reason for this unrecorded meeting. 'What about the name?'

'Don't you think the British public will be uneasy, having such a reminder of the King's German descent?'

'Are you suggesting the monarchy should change its family name?' Mycroft demanded.

'What's your feeling?' responded Churchill, avoiding a direct answer.

So politically respected a figure was Mycroft Holmes that it was not uncommon for ministers privately to sound him out on proposals in advance of their being formally discussed, even in Cabinet. 'In the event of an outright war there could indeed be public unrest at the royal family's ancestry,' he allowed.

'And let us not forget the tide of republicanism sweeping Europe: the civil insurrection of British strikers that we've had to call out the army to quell,' Churchill reminded him.

'You're not seriously suggesting an overthrow of the King!'

'I'm pointing out there are at work strong political forces in whose favour the King's German antecedents would play.'

Mycroft remained momentarily silent, sure now that this discussion was not a secondary reason for his being summoned but its primary cause. Cautiously he said: 'It would be a profound step for the monarch to take.'

'You're for it then?' pressed Churchill.

'It would greatly influence public morale. Is it your intention to propose it?'

'Taking soundings,' avoided Churchill, again. 'It's a matter of the utmost delicacy.'

The man would ensure it came from someone else in the Cabinet, to avoid his personally becoming associated with an offence to the Palace, guessed Mycroft.

'I've discussed it with no one else.'

It was important that Churchill, who too often acted prior to sufficient thought, realized he would not jeopardize the respect in which he was held by associating himself with an idea that some might even construe to *be* revolutionary. 'Show care, Winston, with whom you take your soundings. At this stage such a proposition is premature. Dangerous even. And most certainly not what you supposedly invited me here to discuss.'

Winston Churchill gave no verbal response but the slight stiffening was indication enough that the man had taken the rebuke. 'Quite so. You've been able to study the Declaration of London?'

'To remind myself of it,' qualified Mycroft.

'The rules of naval engagement are well enough defined but I acknowledge the need to re-examine it now. The Declaration was agreed in 1909. Even in the short time that has elapsed since then science and technology have made great advances. If it breaks out, this will be a war different from any we've known before.'

'A fact of which I am more aware than most,' insisted Churchill. There was a brief, private smile. 'So, what about armament limitation?'

'None that are applicable to battleship classification,' replied Mycroft.

Churchill's smile widened. 'During his tour of the Grand Fleet, the Kaiser wasn't shown the fifteen-inch guns that have been fitted to twenty-two of our battleships: the gun that's been described to me by our ordnance experts to be the modern equivalent of the longbow at Agincourt!'

Mycroft stirred again, uncomfortable with the analogy. 'Equally there's nothing specific about the German *Unterseeboots*.'

It was an intended deflation and it succeeded. 'Our naval attaché in Berlin understands the German navy has virtually a fleet of them. If that is true they could cordon off every supply route we have. And until they're on the surface, where our ships can see them, we have no way of detection or defence.'

It was the first time Mycroft could recall Churchill acknowledging a weakness in naval preparations.

Seemingly aware of the admission, Churchill hurried on: 'I intend blockading the contiguous neutrals of Denmark, Sweden, Norway and Holland.'

'Which will position our battleships like ducks on a pond for the German *Unterseeboots*,' Mycroft pointed out. He was worried Churchill saw himself as the battle strategist as well as the Admiralty's political controller.

'We'll still have firepower supremacy against them,' argued Churchill, ineffectually. 'This will be a war of short duration, over in months when the Kaiser confronts the strength of his opposers. I'm advocating a secret weapon every bit as impressive as their *Unterseeboots*. An armoured landship.'

'A *land*ship?'

'What protection do our troops have against the machine gun apart from a trench, to be cut down the moment they raise their heads or attempt to advance! The landship is a...' Churchill pawed the air, as if the proper description hung there to be grasped. '...a tank fortified to resist bullets, propelled not on wheels that can too easily be obstructed or punctured but tracks that can defy holes – trenches even – and low barriers. It is, if you like, a totally secure machine-gun emplacement that can advance against the enemy, its occupants immune from injury.'

'Winston!' protested Mycroft Holmes, his concern increasing at the other man's warlord ambitions. 'Apart, perhaps from its ill-chosen name, a landship does not come within your Admiralty remit. It's military, the responsibility of the War Office.'

'Mycroft!' exclaimed Churchill, protesting in return. 'You have not an hour ago described the forthcoming conflict as a war like no one has known. Do you really think ministers should cocoon themselves, each within his own departmental chrysalis?'

'No, sir, I do not!' came back Mycroft. 'I believe that in the event of such a conflict there should be a war cabinet composed of government ministers and Sea Lords and army chiefs and commanders of the air corps who consider with the benefit of their joint professional expertise the planning and execution of engagements.'

'I do not believe I was advocating anything other,' retreated the politician.

'That's gratifying to hear. If I misunderstood then you must accept my apologies,' said Mycroft, diplomatically allowing Churchill the exchange, in which both knew there had been no misunderstanding.

'What's your assessment of last night's encounter?'

'Everything fairly put. No misunderstanding there,' said Mycroft.

'I was personally caught by the physical and facial similarity between father and son,' said Churchill. 'The likeness is astonishing: two peas from the same pod.'

'There's sufficient dissimilarity,' insisted

Mycroft.

'I pray you're right,' said Churchill.

Mycroft Holmes made his way on foot the short distance back to Downing Street unsettled by the conversation of the previous hour. From his unique, inner-circle position within Downing Street he knew there was a lack of focus upon the American danger, which was why he'd responded without hesitation to Churchill's initial approach. But now he suspected he might be inveigled into some far wider and more complex intrigue. He would have to be extremely careful that he did not become an early casualty in Churchill's impetuosity-spurred determination personally to conduct a war. He had, with hindsight, allowed some extremely dangerous personal concessions last night. It could be disastrous if he had misplaced his trust in Sebastian.

Sebastian's resented instructions were to arrive free of the pursuit warned of in advance for a meeting with his father at the Ritz hotel, which he was sure he achieved by establishing a relay of hansoms for a circuitous journey from the Diogenes Club. He was taking tea in the lounge when his father arrived and spent the first five minutes recounting in detail every failed twist and turn Sebastian had attempted.

'It was a practice,' defended Sebastian, burning with embarrassment.

'Practice is supposed to make perfect,' said

Sherlock Holmes. 'It's clear from your countenance you'll not forget this lapse. Carry always in your mind something the good Dr Watson recorded several years ago, about my method of working. Good detection is founded upon the observation of trifles.'

Of which this lecture was the most trifling of all, decided Sebastian. To move on from it he said: 'Earlier today I booked passage aboard Cunard's RMS *Lusitania*. There's little else that needs attending to. I brought all my belongings back from Germany and have scarcely unpacked.'

There was a long silence before Sherlock Holmes said: 'I *was* acquainted with Count Johann von Bernstorff when he was ambassador here in London. He's a Prussian Junker of the old school, a brilliant diplomat totally dedicated to his country. Mycroft is right. Von Bernstorff will be the spider in an intricate web of spies. Stray too close and you'll become entangled.'

Why, wondered Sebastian, had his father stopped short of completing the metaphor by describing him as a hapless fly? 'If I am to penetrate the intrigue then I must penetrate the web.'

Sherlock Holmes sighed, deeply. 'Just heed the warning.' From a valise his father took a cardboard-protected package. 'I have something that should be yours.'

Sebastian guessed what it was before opening it to gaze down at the skiing photograph of his mother.

'The single pole has long since been discarded in favour of two sticks,' said the older man, his voice once more low in reverie. 'She would have laughed at the need for so much help to stay upright. It was Matilde's nature to be adventurous.'

'I think I know the depth of this gesture,' said Sebastian. 'Appreciating it as much as I do I am reluctant to take it.'

'It should be yours,' insisted Sherlock Holmes.

'Let's agree it shall be mine but that it remains in your safe keeping.'

'Diplomacy befitting your uncle!'

'Practicality befitting yourself,' suggested Sebastian.

There was no hesitation in Sherlock Holmes retrieving the offered snapshot. 'I would that there had been more time for us to become better acquainted, beyond the sterile correspondence and occasional meetings.'

'There will be, when this episode has past.'

Sherlock Holmes moved as if to reply but changed his mind. Instead he said: 'Over the years I have so frequently been consulted by Scotland Yard I have formed many friendships, a few well beyond these shores...' In the same gesture of returning the photograph to the valise the man extracted a folded square of paper pinned to a sealed envelope. 'I performed a service a few years ago for a certain Captain O'Hanlon, of the New York Police Department: he is in my debt. This is a letter of introduction. I'm annoyed at that damned man Churchill avoiding every risk but poised to take every credit. If a situation becomes difficult don't hesitate to present this letter. O'Hanlon won't be found wanting and the consequences can go to hell.'

Accepting the papers, Sebastian said: 'I don't intend to be found wanting, either.' Or ending up in hell, he thought...

Five

In his unanchored, peripatetic life Sebastian Holmes had journeyed through most countries in Europe but apart from the uninterestingly flat countryside of Cambridgeshire he knew little of England outside London. Travelling by train to Liverpool was the furthest north he had ever been and he found the experience unexpectedly depressing. There was none of the grandeur of the alps of Germany and Switzerland and France, nor the river sweeps of the Danube or the Rhine or the Seine demanding a painter's palette. There were occasional touches of Wordsworthian beauty but all were overwhelmed, sometimes literally, by an industrialization of truly dark, Satanic mills, worsened by an unremitting, wind-driven rain that didn't lessen from his moment of departure. The predominant feature of practically every city and town through which he passed was smoke-belching, sky-staining chimneys. There was a pervading blackness, too, to the buildings and even the unsmiling people who jostled the platforms at intervening stations.

The dining car was well enough appointed and the linen starchly crisp but the luncheon beef was overcooked into greyness and the claret thin. Sebastian had been prevented catching the boat train by his father's insistence upon a final farewell and when his express arrived not at Liverpool's Riverside terminal but at the city's Lime Street station there were initially insufficient porters for his cabin trunks, portmanteaux, hat boxes and walking-stick case and then difficulty finding a hansom big enough to carry it all as well as himself. As he led the head-turning procession along the concourse Sebastian reflected the irony that the demanded meeting – which had been little more than a warning never to relax his guard, emphasized by the parting gift of the malacca swordstick – had brought about the contravention of another warning, never to attract unnecessary attention.

His slower, meandering progress through the Liverpool streets heightened Sebastian's earlier impressions of a land of mono-chromed greyness. The first smiles Sebastian saw – although of hope, not happiness – were on the faces of the shoeless street urchins running escort to his cab, hands outstretched for coppers, which mistakenly he dispensed through the lowered sash to a screaming, punching mêlée.

Sebastian's spirits lifted with his arrival at the *Lusitania*'s berth alongside the floating Prince's Landing Stage of the Riverside terminal. The huge, four-funnelled liner dominated a rain-sagged, bunting-bedecked quayside upon which a uniformed brass band energetically defied the downpour to perform an appropriate but to Sebastian unrecognizable marching tune. A loadmaster immediately took control of Sebastian's baggage and at the top of the gangway he was assigned a personal reception cadet to escort him to his starboard stateroom overlooking the landing stage and its indomitable band.

The waiting steward, who with a slight inclination of his body introduced himself as Denning, was a balding man with an Irish accent and the imperious demeanour of a butler, which from his quick but pointed reference to 'my staff' the man regarded himself to be. He even affected butler's white gloves, which Sebastian had not seen other stewards wearing as he passed along the corridors. There was a proudly conducted tour of the apartment, which consisted of an expansive, easy-chaired drawing room and a separate double bedroom to the side of which was a fully equipped, en suite marbled bathroom. The decor of the drawing room was walnut and mahogany and there was already a fire burning in the marble-surround fire-place. Denning had held back from arranging flowers until learning Sebastian's preference. He had similarly withheld from stocking Sebastian's liquor cabinet. He drew Sebastian's attention to the invitation on the mantelpiece to sit throughout the voyage at the captain's table. It was optional to dress for dinner on the first night of the voyage, Denning advised. Sebastian's evening clothes would be pressed and ready every night of the voyage. Also pressed by each evening would be any other garment Denning felt needed attention when he unpacked Sebastian's clothes. His personal linen would be laundered daily.

Sebastian's immediate stateroom neighbours were an American mining magnate and his wife, a Grand Duke of the Imperial Russian court travelling with his daughter and an unchaperoned princess of European royalty. That last intelligence came with the slightest frown of disapproval. Their names, against their stateroom numbers, were on Sebastian's writing bureau. Denning suggested the morning, around eleven, was the most favourable within the ship's timetable to present an introductory calling card, if Sebastian felt so inclined. Engraved cards could be printed within two hours if Sebastian chose to give a reception, for which rooms larger than his personal drawing room could be arranged. Denning also offered a seasickness remedy far more effective than that offered by the ship's surgeon.

Sebastian willingly quit the stateroom for Denning to unpack. He disdained the fila-greed-metal lifts between the deck levels for the elegance of the reproduced fifteenth-century Italian grand staircase. The design for the first-class dining salon was drawn from the Petit Trianon of Versailles and furniture strewn like dropped pebbles in placid ponds throughout the public salons were recogniz-ably Adam and Sheraton and Chippendale. The barrel-vaulted stained-glass ceiling mural in the first-class lounge depicted the twelve months of the calender. The marble fireplaces were green like that of his state-room but here were twice the size of a man. Another domed stained-glass ceiling ad-mitted natural light to the grey and cream silk-brocaded library where fires burned, here in fireplaces of white marble. The huge book-case, which extended along one wall, held many volumes – some in French and Ger-man, as well as English – with which Sebas-tian was unfamiliar, and the prospect of reading them at uninterrupted leisure, in such surroundings, reminded Sebastian of country-house weekends as a guest of univer-sity colleagues in France and Germany.

Denning was waiting when Sebastian returned to his stateroom, the immaculate choice of white or black tie in readiness. The rest of his clothes were as faultlessly arranged in their cupboards and closets, with no evidence of trunks or cases, and there were three vases of roses – red, shading into pink and finally into tinged opal. Denning drew Sebastian's attention to the invitation card to that night's captain's reception, already on the mantelpiece alongside his seating reservation.

As Sebastian thanked the man Denning said: 'I am sorry, sir, but your malacca cane became disconnected when I was unpacking it. I reassembled it without difficulty.' The remark ended just short of being a question.

'It's normally quite secure,' said Sebastian.

'A useful device, in uncertain surroundings.'

'Quite so.' Sebastian wondered how long it would take for his father's gift to be gossiped among his neighbours and beyond: indeed, it was probably already in circulation. Sebastian was unperturbed.

In London the rain had stopped, although the clouds remained sullen and the improperly laid pavements and even older and more unevenly set cobbles were puddled, in some places into miniature lakes. Very shortly after leaving Baker Street Dr John Watson stopped bothering carefully to manoeuvre his wickerwork craft, propelling Holmes directly through the water.

'This is a difficult machine to navigate, Holmes!' They were not yet at Oxford Street but Watson, permanently disabled by injuries sustained while seconded as army surgeon to the Berkshire Regiment in the battle of Maiwand in the second Afghan war, was feeling the strain, despite the outward appearance of stalwart good health.

'An absurd invention,' complained Sherlock Holmes.

'Your choice, as I understand it.'

'My misjudgement.'

Rarely, in all the years of their association, had Watson heard Sherlock Holmes so openly – or quickly – confess a miscalculation. 'Am I to be acquainted with this enterprise, to record it?'

'Not my decision.'

'Not *your* decision!' In his astonishment Watson made an awkward turn towards the park, surging a puddle over Sherlock Holmes's no longer burnished brogues.

'Sebastian has been entrusted with it.'

Watson held back from any quick response, propelling the invalid chair steadily towards Marble Arch, grateful for the pavement's width, splashed from the dangerous, competing confusion of snorting horse and hooting automobile. There were, however, inevitable muddied splashes negotiating the crossings before Watson got them to the comparative safely of Hyde Park. There other invalid carriages were being pushed by nurses in a gentle, sympathetic cavalcade parallel to Park Lane. As Watson moved to join it, Sherlock Holmes hissed vehemently: 'Don't imagine for a moment to include me in such a sorry procession!'

'It's precisely the backdrop your subterfuge demands,' insisted Watson, easing them into the procession, returning and offering nods of acknowledgement to the other carers.

'I won't easily forget this humiliation, Watson!'

The doctor ignored him once more. 'Am I to meet Sebastian?'

'Perhaps, in the future.'

'You're being damnably mysterious, Holmes.'

'Sebastian is not in this country.'

'Am I allowed to ask *where* he is?'

'No,' refused Sherlock Holmes, shortly.

'Nor what he is doing?'

'No.'

They kept their place in the slowly paced parade for several moments before Watson said: 'This certainly seems a strange one.'

'In which we are scarcely involved!'

'What, then, is the purpose of what we are doing now?'

'Laying false scents for slavering hounds ... hounds, my dear Watson, far more fearsome than that of the Baskervilles.'

'You unsettle me, Holmes.'

'Not for the first time.'

Watson awkwardly turned the mobile chair to return in the direction of what, before the transfer there of the March Arch, had incongruously been the Tyburn site for hangings and even earlier additional drawing and quartering. 'Tell me, what sort of boy is Sebastian?'

'Certainly not a boy, as he so forcefully reminds me.'

Watson waited.

'A fine young man,' resumed Sherlock Holmes, after several minutes. 'A son of whom a father could be proud.'

'*Could* be proud?'

'I've not been the father I should have been, Watson,' admitted the chair-bound man. 'There is too little...' There was a searching pause. '...too little feeling between us, which I deeply regret.'

'You must at least have sufficient confidence in him to entrust whatever this undertaking is.'

'Would that, but for some identifying association in the past, it could have been myself and not Sebastian.'

Watson began, 'Then we must...' before being urgently interrupted.

'Watson, I asked you to carry sal volatile.'

'I have it, Holmes!'

Sherlock Holmes was suddenly convulsed by an apparent paroxysm of coughing that reduced him to slumped collapse, despite which he managed to demand, sotto voce, that it be observably administered. Holmes's recovery was equally visible but frail, the gestured insistences to be wheeled back to Baker Street the most obvious of sign languages. As they rounded the corner from Oxford Street, Watson said, quiet-voiced himself, 'I was looking, every moment we were talking. I saw no one.'

65

'Two men, Slavic-featured, fell into step upon our emergence on to Oxford Street and very professionally remained parallel throughout, effectively using the public entrances and exits of the Grosvenor House hotel,' isolated Sherlock Holmes. 'They stayed with us, all the way back to Oxford Street. They are no longer in attendance.'

'So there's good reason to spread false scents?'

'Something I'd hoped wouldn't be confirmed.'

'Where does that leave you?'

'As far as public awareness is concerned, confined to this confounded invalid carriage!' complained Sherlock Holmes.

'If the hounds are sniffing you, they're not tracking Sebastian,' Watson pointed out.

'Which is the only reassurance I have,' said Sherlock Holmes, as they arrived at the doorway of 221b. 'I've never before had so little to do to achieve so much.'

Six

Sebastian timed his arrival to the second, after most of the other guests had assembled but insufficiently late for his entry to attract attention or cause offence to his host. Captain Geoffrey Dow, an imposing, flushed-faced man, was attended just inside the salon by an eager pack of senior officers who, after the formal, welcoming handshakes from the ship's master, detached themselves with practised social ease to take guest to guest and group to group, introducing and reintroducing, never forgetting a name or a title before eventually rejoining their captain's side, ready to start again after integrating their earlier charges. Sebastian's escort was a fresh-faced first officer named Hughes who quickly linked him to a solitary American called Ansberger and just as quickly propelled both into a previously arranged gathering of a dour husband and timid wife and two elderly sisters, who were bird-like thin and responded to conversation in appropriate chirps, one beginning the sentence, the other finishing. All were American. Hughes assured them that the weather forecast was good and that the crossing should be smooth. He very pointedly said they were taking a southerly route and as far as he knew there were no plans on this voyage to try to recover the Blue Riband from their sister ship *Mauretania*. With the smile of a man hinting a secret Hughes added that there was, though, always the possibility. Each day there would be a sweepstake to estimate the number of nautical miles travelled.

There were champagne-bearing stewards permanently within arm's reach but Sebastian used the excuse of exchanging his glass to disentangle himself, wanting undistractedly to study the people with whom he had to share the next five days. He kept, however, casually in motion against being corralled by the attentive Hughes or one of his fellow officers and reassigned to another group.

Sebastian was sure he isolated Russian Imperial Grand Duke Alexei Orlov, whose name had been inscribed on Denning's list. The Russian was a towering, deep-chested bear of a man with a full but neatly clipped deeply black beard in the fashion of Tsar Nicholas himself. Sebastian had compromised this first night, to Denning's approval, with black tie, but the Duke was resplendent in white tie and even – overly ostentatious, Sebastian thought – a magnificently jewelled Order at his left breast. If Denning had explored Orlov's belongings, which Sebastian suspected the man might well have done, Sebastian mused a more likely discovery would have been a fully loaded, heavy-calibre pistol. The man's daughter was as arresting as her father but for entirely different reasons. Princess Irena Orlov was tall and shared her father's deeply black hair, which she wore long, practically to her shoulders. It was held perfectly in its face-framing place by a diamond band that matched a double-strand necklace that was her only other jewellery on a sheer, high-necked black dress that accentuated the slightly rouged paleness of a flawless, fine-boned face with only, again, the lightest of lip-colouring. It was not, however, the princess's outward appearance making her the focus of several women as well as men within the room. It was, Sebastian decided, her inherent ambience of absolute, undisturbable calmness, a totally serene inborn sureness about herself, her position and unchallengeable acceptance that were so naturally ingrained as to have nothing of disdain or superiority about them.

Sebastian briefly paused between concealing clusters of first class guests, turning back almost at the end of the small salon towards the captain at the precise moment of the second royal arrival. Princess Anna Boinburg-Langesfeld wore a floor-sweeping gown of shimmering gold to provide the perfect background for the three ropes of superbly matched black pearls, for which there were matching earrings equally well set off by the rich blond colour of an unusually short, almost mannish hairstyle cut tight into the nape of the neck. She was narrow-faced but prominently featured, her full mouth a darkly coloured red.

Almost instinctively obvious to Sebastian was the immediate awareness of one woman of the other in the same room, despite neither, as far as he could see, even looking in a direction to acknowledge her challenger. Which, he acknowledged, had nothing to do with royal training – contravened it, in fact – but everything to do with simply being women.

The contemplation brought Sebastian up short, a mixture of surprise and recognition. *You know my method. It is founded upon the observation of trifles.* One of his father's most persistent aphorisms, not just quoted by the scribbling Watson but oft repeated by his father himself. Echoing in Sebastian's mind came another legend. *Instinct: definitive, deducing observation must never be that of conscious thought, but of easily recalled instinct.* Which was what he had been doing, operating instinctively, not consciously observing. It would please his ... With conscious determination Sebastian stopped the thought. He was alone now, with only himself to impress. Briefly, he met the unresponsive gaze of the Austrian princess and thought, maybe not only himself to impress.

Hughes, more deferential than the captain, had appointed himself an anxious male duenna to the blonde princess, although it was she who appeared to guide their perambulations. Never once did Anna Boinburg-Langesfeld look in the direction of nor acknowledge the presence of Irena Orlov and never once did Irena Orlov betray the slightest awareness of Anna Boinburg Langesfeld. There would, Sebastian supposed, be an understood protocol according to longevity and superiority of one royal lineage over the longevity and inferiority of the other. To Sebastian it looked more animalistic, territory-establishing, and he enjoyed the ritual. There could, he thought, be a lot to enjoy, although that was a reflection lacking any protocol.

Because of the lateness of the Austro-Hungarian's arrival it was a short minute before dinner was announced and Sebastian at once noted a reversal to the dance, Princess Anna accepting Captain Dow's escort almost at once – before, as far as Sebastian was aware, even taking any champagne – with the Duke and his daughter showing no inclination to leave. When the salon was noticeably emptied and still the Russians had not moved, apparently oblivious to the departure, Sebastian attached himself to the slow drift along a corridor so conveniently close to be a private access into the high-vaulted dining room. At its principal table only three places remained empty. One was his, adjoining the other two. Captain Dow and the Austro-Hungarian princess were talking animatedly, but the five others already at the table were clearly looking for guidance, which came almost at once when, at the unobtrusive signal from First Officer Hughes, they stood at the

Russians' arrival. So conveniently – and discreetly – close was the entrance from the private reception salon that the Grand Duke and his daughter were at the captain's table practically before anyone further into the huge public room was aware of their presence: certainly there was no awkward public attention. At Captain Dow's formal introduction Anna Boinburg-Langesfeld dipped in respectful curtsy to the Russian royalty, to the Grand Duke's slight bow of acknowledgement, and Sebastian accepted the woman was according the Grand Duke and Princess Irena their order of precedence.

Apart from the two ship's officers and the royals there were in addition to Sebastian the American, Walter Ansberger, to whom he had been introduced in the salon, mining magnate John Morganstein and his wife, Rebecca, who were on Denning's close neighbour list, and another American husband and wife, James and Henrietta Paterson. Princess Olga's limitation with English quickly became apparent with Captain Dow's attempt to guide the general social exchange and at once Sebastian went into the French of the Russian Imperial court, to her obvious gratitude and the Grand Duke's curt head nod of appreciation. It was, admitted the Russian, her first visit to America and she hoped to see as much of the country as possible, although her father's affairs were concentrated in Washington DC. Anna came easily into the conversation, her French as fluent as Sebastian's, recommending that for comfort the other woman should restrict her tour to the east coast and not venture too deeply westwards, where a lot of the country, apart from its major cities, remained undeveloped. With he and Anna able to alternate as conduits, the conversation around the table became comprehensibly bilingual and at the translation of Anna's travel warning Paterson emerged as the owner of an east-to-west-coast railroad company who at once brashly offered the Russians his personal carriage, equipped with sleeping accommodation and its own chef and staff. Rebecca Morganstein insisted San Francisco, where they had a mansion on Nob Hill, was as attractive and sophisticated as either New York or Washington but her husband conceded the gold rush of sixty years ago – and after that the silver mining with which he was still associated – had badly scarred the countryside of southern California. Sebastian found strange the easy readiness of the Americans so openly to discuss their businesses – unprompted, Walter Ansberger volunteered himself a venture capitalist underwriting the sort of cross-continent railway expansion from which Paterson had clearly benefited – and guessed that the other Europeans, particularly the aristocrats, would be just as bemused. There were several opportunities – indeed one inferred invitation from Ansberger – for Sebastian to declare himself, all of which he ignored.

With apologies that his duties demanded his return to the bridge, Captain Dow prompted the rising and departure from the table of the Russian royal couple, which was not, however, strictly formal. As he passed the standing Sebastian the Grand Duke Orlov paused and quietly thanked him for his consideration. In the momentary hiatus of their disbanding Captain Dow also hesitated, also murmuring his gratitude for Sebastian's social aptitude. The double delay made Sebastian the last to leave the dining room along their short corridor and, as he emerged into the outside passageway, Princess Anna Boinburg-Langesfeld approached from the opposite direction, the shimmering gown now covered by its matching cloak.

She said: 'I would welcome an escort, to walk outside upon the deck.'

'I would be honoured,' volunteered Sebastian. If a cat could look at a king, a rat catcher could gaze upon a princess.

In abrupt reversal to the day they had left it was a totally still and undisturbed night, the moon a perfect white globe in an unclouded sky. The sea was unrippled by any wind and the seasonal warmth had returned. There was a sound – a hum – from the liner's engines far below but little sensation of movement beyond the faintest tear through the unbroken water, the hiss of a razor parting silk. The far more obvious noise was of people promenading around them. Anna formally took

Sebastian's offered arm, resting her forearm above his, but properly kept a distance between them and for several moments there was no talk, a curious Sebastian still observing the royal etiquette of waiting to be spoken *to*.

Which Anna did, continuing in French. 'I *am* a princess.'

'I accept you to be.' Sebastian was bewildered.

'An elevated title descending from the birth of my grandfather to his accommodating although already minor-titled mother, who was bricfly a favourite of a grateful, honour-granting emperor with landless princedoms to bestow as bedchamber rewards.'

'I am at a loss,' protested Sebastian. But intrigued, he admitted.

'I have a title but little position. With me, alas, the title dies: much to the chagrin of my family I was born a girl, not a boy to carry on the title.'

'I remain at a loss,' said Sebastian.

'After tonight's social feat I look upon us as companions in arms. One should have no secrets from one's companion in arms.'

Another invitation to declare himself, accepted Sebastian, enjoying the encounter but surprised at what was surely flirtation. Cautious against embarrassing misunderstanding but hopefully responding to the mood, Sebastian said: 'Am I to be d' Artagnan to your Athos? Or Porthos to your Aramis?'

'D' Artagnan was the most impoverished of the musketeers. I want someone of more substance.'

'Porthos then,' chose Sebastian, continuing the game. 'Who's role will you take?'

There was enough brightness from the moon for Sebastian clearly to see the inviting smile when she turned to him. 'My own, I think. I do not imagine myself comfortable playing a male part. We will have to invent our own story.'

'We seem to be doing that quite well.' Surprisingly so, he decided.

'Do I shock you?'

'No,' lied Sebastian.

'I think there are others – the Grand Duke most of all – who cannot understand my lack of a chaperone.'

The lightness was going out of the exchange. Trying to recover it, Sebastian said: 'But now you have a companion at arms.'

'For which I am grateful. I found Mr Ansberger too pressing. The officer, Hughes, was close to being impertinently attentive as well.'

'You really *do* wish me to be your protector?' He had come close to misunderstanding, Sebastian thought, disappointed.

The smile came again. 'I don't believe myself in actual physical danger! But there are several more days of close proximity. I want to avoid any misapprehensions or difficulties.'

'A true musketeer, to the rescue of two

princesses in one night!' Sebastian tried again.

'This princess's name is Anna.'

'To address you by which in public would compound misapprehension upon misunderstanding.'

'We are not now in public.'

'There are people all around.'

'None of whom know who we are. We'll lead double lives of double standards.' Anna led the way to the deck rail, taking her arm from Sebastian's. She gestured to a faint smudge of deeper blackness on the far horizon. 'Is that Ireland: Queenstown?'

'I'm not sure.'

'How far away do you think it is?'

'Twenty miles, perhaps.'

'I'll ask Captain Dow, tomorrow.'

'Why is that so important?' He was enjoying her closeness, their arms touching far more intimately as they stood side by side. Her perfume was of musk, mixed with other fragrances he couldn't identify.

Instead of answering, she said: 'Did you receive the too obviously reassuring lecture from Hughes, about this ship not attempting the recovery of the Blue Riband?'

'Yes.' Sebastian was intrigued by the sudden, almost mournful seriousness.

Anna was silent for several moments. 'I was booked on the *Titanic* for its maiden voyage last year: should have been aboard when it went north, to gain the crossing record. My mother became ill: later died. Her death – my

77

cancelling, which of course I did – saved my life.'

'Are you frightened now?'

She shook her head.

'It was fate,' he insisted.

'Or God. Do you believe in God, Sebastian?'

'I have difficulty.'

'I don't. Not after that.'

'I don't imagine you do.'

Anna turned abruptly away from the rail, although not from him. 'I've taken the bubbles out of the evening, haven't I: made everything go flat?'

'We can get the bubbles back.'

'We'll complete the walk to the end of the deck!' she announced, enthusiastically, taking his support again but no longer formally, crooking her arm fully through his to bring herself close to him, their bodies touching as they walked. 'And then it will be time to retire.'

The number of people on deck had thinned to the occasional couple. Sebastian sought something to say but then stopped bothering, realizing that Anna didn't need conversation. He was sure there was some floral element in the perfume. He regretted their approach to the barricading rail separating the passenger and crew area. The collision was so sudden and unexpected that Anna almost pulled Sebastian down with her. He only managed to prevent their both falling by snatching out and luckily grabbing the securing rope of a

lifeboat tarpaulin. She was teetering peril-
ously on her right leg, the left drawn up protectively beneath her, whimpering through
tightly clenched teeth.

'What is it?' Sebastian demanded, balancing himself to steady them both.

'I don't know ... I struck something ... my
foot!'

Sebastian half carried her to the nearest seat
but even kneeling the moon was no longer
sufficient for him to see what she had done. 'I
must get you to the hospital.'

'What was it?'

'It doesn't matter.'

'I want to know!' Her voice was uneven in
anger or near hysteria and he guessed she was
crying.

Sebastian hurried back to where she had
stumbled, more carefully prodding out with
his own foot at a raised dais for which he
couldn't see any purpose but even less able to
see what it was in the dark shadows of the
decking.

'A platform of some sort. Let's get you
inside.'

He had almost completely – but unpro-
testingly – to support Anna's weight with his
hand around her waist as she limped to the
door back into the ship, which was fortunately close to a metal-grilled elevator. He
said: 'I can't remember which deck the
hospital is on!'

She said: 'My rooms. They can come to
me!'

Her eyes were red but the tears had stopped and Sebastian guessed she had insisted upon his examination of whatever she had stumbled into to compose herself. There were no other people in the lift, nor in the corridor to their staterooms. Hers was almost directly opposite his. He eased her on to a blue velvet chaise longue but then hesitated. 'May I look?'

'Please!'

The slipper on her left foot, the silk so perfect a match to her dress that it had to be of the same material, was scored along its entire outside length, actually ripped for almost an inch. Cupping her ankle, Sebastian tried as gently as possible to prise the shoe off her already swollen foot. Above him she whimpered again. The discoloration began below her toes but, more gently still, he moved them, to her twitched stiffening at each tweak. Finally, looking up, Sebastian said: 'Nothing's broken but there's a bad bruise. We'll get the surgeon to apply a compress.'

'It's easier, without the constriction of the shoe. There's ice and towels conveniently here.'

'I'm not a doctor.'

'I don't think I need one.' Their eyes held. 'You really have been called upon to be the gallant tonight, haven't you?'

'I'll get ice.' Sebastian did so, from the vacuum-sealed container, and wrapped it in a hand towel which he pressed against the swelling.

'Would it be better, do you think, if I removed my stocking?'

'Perhaps.'

'You'll have to help me to the bedroom.' She leaned heavily against him, barely touching her left foot to the ground for the short distance between the two rooms.

'I should withdraw.'

'I have not asked you to withdraw.'

She'd turned, fully to face him. He held her with both hands to her waist, conscious of her body beneath the thin silk. She had both hands along his arms, unprotesting.

'You shouldn't put any more weight upon that foot than is absolutely necessary,' he said.

'No. It should be rested in bed. There are buttons, at the back of the dress.'

'I have them.'

'Please hurry. My foot is aching so.'

There was eagerness but no frenzy. They explored and tested and made their mutual discoveries and found no barriers. They kept the lights burning, each enjoying the sight of the other's total nakedness and Sebastian, who had lost his virginity in the best and most professional houses of Paris, thought Anna's arcing, thrusting body was the most beautiful he had ever seen. So perfect were they together that Sebastian coaxed Anna to orgasm first and held back for her to climax with him a second time. They lay entwined, in utter fulfilment, the wetness of their heat drying upon them.

Anna said: '*Now* admit you're shocked!'

'Delightfully so. And want to go on being shocked.'

'Denning will be even more disapproving.'

'Denning won't know.'

'Denning knows everything.'

'Butlers are to be seen but not heard.'

'Tell me something,' Anna demanded, pulling slightly away from him.

'What?'

'Why do you have a swordstick?'

'To fight off predatory princesses.'

'I'm glad you weren't carrying it tonight.'

'So am I.'

They were carelessly aware that the omniscient Denning did know, although Sebastian was confident he was never observed crossing from Anna's suite to his own. Ansberger stopped pressing his suit and the overfamiliar Hughes returned to officer formality. Sebastian did help her to the hospital the day after the accident, for the foot to be bound, but otherwise there was no treatment. She needed Sebastian's stoutest walking cane to begin with but demanded the malacca swordstick on the third day. Captain Dow expressed his gravest concern at the accident but couldn't understand how they had passed through a previous barrier which should have been secured. It was to Sebastian, not Anna, that the captain revealed the obstacle to be the mounting for one of twelve six-inch rapid-firing guns for which provision had been made during the *Lusitania*'s Clydeside construction, in readiness should the ship be commissioned into naval service. The revelation came when Sebastian was invited to visit the bridge, an experience which Anna's incapacity prevented her sharing. She was appalled when Sebastian told her, although it prompted her admission she was going to America for an extended vacation because Europe had become, as she put it, 'Too frightening, full of strutting, loud-voiced men in uniforms.'

More important to Sebastian during his bridge visit than learning of gun mountings was Captain Dow's further disclosure that there had been a personal message from Sir Alfred Booth warning all his captains that they were to make themselves available to Sebastian whenever called upon to convey letter packets to England.

At each meal Anna and Sebastian continued to provide the linguistic conduit and on the third night of the voyage the Grand Duke Orlov hosted a reception in the same private salon in which the captain had greeted them on sailing night. Orlov insisted upon vodka, served numbingly cold, to accompany the beluga and imbibed too much himself, drunkenly hinting his visit to Washington involved Russian government affairs and even more indiscreetly talking about an Imperial court cancered by a mad, debauched monk, all of which Sebastian decided was interesting enough to pass back to Mycroft, despite it being outside his specific remit.

That night, in her bed, Anna said: 'I believe even Princess Irena suspects us. But she more than anyone knows that princesses can do as they like.'

Upon the advice of the ship's surgeon Anna rested her foot and leg for at least two hours a day and the windless, sun-warmed weather enabled her to do so outside, on a deck lounger alongside which Sebastian invariably joined her. Once, in daylight, she insisted on examining the gun mounting for herself, through its now firmly chained and pad-locked grill, and afterwards insisted it defaced the ship.

On the afternoon before their arrival, her eyes closed against the brightness as they lay side by side on the sun-facing deck, Anna said: 'We'll become infamous, by the stories they'll tell.'

'Does that distress you?'

She laughed, without looking at him or bothering directly to reply. 'And what about your reputation?'

'There isn't one.'

'It's been blissful.'

'Absolutely.'

'But tomorrow it will all be over.'

'Yes.' Believing he could gauge her thinking, Sebastian said: 'No souvenirs, no addresses.'

'No souvenirs, no addresses,' Anna agreed. 'Thank you, my musketeer.'

'Thank you, my princess.'

'Kitchener for War Minister! Can you believe such absurdity!' protested Churchill.

'It remains a rumour,' cautioned Mycroft.

'He's clearly Asquith's choice. It has to be opposed: let him stay ruler of Egypt, out of everybody's way!'

Mycroft realized he was being sucked into another whirlpool of political intrigue. 'I keep needing to remind you, Winston, that I cannot become part of any of this.'

'Kitchener is a devious, over-promoted quartermaster who'll go down in history for losing the Boer Wars and for the genocide of Boer women and children in his concentration camps and blockhouses,' declared Churchill. 'He kept our troops in bright red and put them into battle in the same side-by-side squared formation that Gage and Howe used in America's independence war. And with the same result. The Boer guerrillas picked them off hidden safely behind trees and rocks, just like the Americans did almost one hundred and fifty years before! And Kitchener complained they weren't fighting fairly! When are the field and naval commanders of this damned country going to realize war hasn't got anything to do with fairness or rules but everything to do with winning!' Churchill gulped at his brandy after such a diatribe.

'Kitchener reconquered the Sudan,' Mycroft pointed out.

'British solders and their commanders

reconquered the Sudan, *despite* Kitchener.'

Mycroft had momentarily forgotten how it had been Churchill's bed-conquesting mother who had needed to use her influence to get her son an army position in the Sudan, against Kitchener's opposition. Mycroft wondered how much Churchill's antipathy stemmed from personal slights and offences, imagined or otherwise. It was true, though, that Kitchener's aloof, abrasive obduracy had made him unpopular, most infamously of all when his argument with Lord Curzon over the control of the Indian army, of which he had been commander-in-chief, led to Curzon's resignation as viceroy. Reminded, Mycroft said: 'You'll have allies far more influential than me.'

'It's your counsel I seek, Mycroft.'

'That's easily provided. Don't dissipate your objectives by fighting on too many separate fronts.'

'It's not my objectives that are being dissipated. There's only one. Being ready.'

Anxious to move their meeting on, Mycroft said: 'My brother is convinced he is under observation.'

'All the better for our purposes.'

'Sebastian reaches New York tomorrow.'

'I've already telegraphed Hemditch,' disclosed Winston Churchill.

'I understood the traffic with New York over this matter is to be shared fully between us,' frowned Mycroft.

'It is,' insisted Churchill. 'Mine was quite

simply a message reminding a personal friend of Sebastian's arrival, following upon my letter of introduction, which Hemditch will by now have received.'

Mycroft didn't believe the too-easy assurance.

Seven

There had been general farewells at the previous night's dinner and he and Anna had made no plans to meet before Sebastian slipped out of her stateroom before dawn. He had expected to see her at the rail, as he was, but she was not among the crowd for the *Lusitania*'s passing of the Statue of Liberty. No souvenirs, no addresses, he remembered: his own edict. It had been an uncommitting, brief interlude of exquisite memories and several unanswered but unimportant personal questions. Now he had to devote his every thought and concentration upon an enterprise which, in the considered judgement of one of his country's major political figures, could truly be vital to Great Britain's very survival, awesomely unreal though such a cataclysm seemed. From this day there would be little place or time for interludes. His mind totally refocused but, prompted by

87

the huge, star-crowned figure that had been France's fraternal gift to the United States, Sebastian recalled another of Winston Churchill's strategy predictions, that it would be against the traditional enemy of France that the Kaiser would initially direct hostilities. If that forecast were fulfilled surely the ties between Paris and Washington would quickly bring America by formal declaration into any war on the side of a French-allied Britain and resolve Churchill's apprehensions. Speculation outside his commission, Sebastian at once acknowledged, although perhaps something to discuss with his uncle. But not yet. He would, however, relay the alcohol-spurred indiscretion of the Russian Grand Duke.

Confident that Denning would be packing his belongings, which required the man having the space he'd needed to unpack upon the Liverpool embarkation, Sebastian remained on deck until the actual docking at Cunard's Hudson River pier, able from the elevation of such a high deck to get a bird's-eye view of the approaching city. It was another sunlit, cloudless morning and therefore an unfair comparison but New York appeared a much more favourable city than the Liverpool he'd left. The buildings looked cleaner – and, oddly, he had the impression of their being set out in a more orderly fashion – and although he was too far away properly to judge, the people on the quayside seemed to be moving with more purpose, a vibrancy almost.

As he turned to go back into the ship Sebastian saw from his dockside viewpoint officers and baggage loaders attending the autocratically flustered departure of the Russians, far below, and realized he had lingered too long. The white-gloved Denning, waiting outside his suite, reported with the familiar hint of reproach that Sebastian was the last of his stateroom charges to leave and that all Sebastian's luggage had been removed to the main disembarkation deck, there to await his instructions. Despite their understanding, Sebastian looked surreptitiously around his sitting room for a departing communication from Anna. There wasn't one. Denning accepted and pocketed Sebastian's gratuity envelope with a sleight of hand Houdini himself could not have bettered. Denning's final service was to provide Sebastian with the dated New York sailings and arrivals of Cunard liners. Sebastian's response, to Denning's hope to have him as a passenger again, was interrupted by a commotion in the outside corridor, culminating in a shouted demand for Sebastian by name and a flurried arrival at the door of a stocky, grey-haired man of about his father's age in black silk frock coat complete with a hunter-chained waistcoat enclosing an expansive stomach clearly accustomed to three, if not more, full meals a day. The black cane had a filigreed gold top and there was a heavy gold signet ring on the hand that held it.

'Hemditch, Julius Hemditch,' said the man,

other hand outstretched. 'At your service, sir!'

Sebastian's instant thought was that more people were expected to be at Hemditch's service than he at theirs. Accepting the man's hand, Sebastian said: 'I was not expecting to be met. I have kept you. I am sorry.'

'Of no consequence,' dismissed the American. 'You are ready?'

Sebastian fell into hurried step with the other man, who walked as fast as he talked, a machine-gun delivery of welcoming pleasantries and rhetorical hope that Sebastian had enjoyed the outward voyage, to which Sebastian broke in that it would have been difficult to have enjoyed it more. Sebastian's initial suspicion of Hemditch's feigned humility was confirmed by the authority with which the man organized the baggage train of handlers to convey his luggage down the gangway, directly at the bottom of which, to the exclusion of all others, was a dark-green carriage embossed on both doors with the intertwined, curlicued initials JNH, the custom-built conveyance quite unlike any Sebastian had seen or could identify from anywhere in Europe. At the rear was an enclosed luggage box sufficient for all Sebastian's cases with capacity to spare. Their stowage was supervised by a green-liveried coachman in control of two superbly matched black stallions. All the horses lacked were plumed headdresses, which Sebastian was sure existed in their equipage. More seriously he decided that even though he had no cause yet to be apprehensive, such flamboyance scarcely qualified as an inconspicuous arrival. The contradiction came at once. The disguise he intended – an investment-seeking entrepreneur – did not demand discretion. The contrary. From his American shipboard companions he already knew that wealth and success were not things to hide but to be openly displayed and freely discussed. Hemditch's coach actually contributed more than it detracted from the masquerade: perhaps the horses should have been plumed after all. Sebastian glanced along the assembled transport behind, coaches outnumbering cars, but could not see Anna.

Hemditch gestured him into the green-leather-upholstered carriage and followed to settle himself in the facing seat. He said: 'There's been correspondence from Winston. And a telegram of your arrival to bring me here today.'

Sebastian hesitated. He should have been advised of Churchill's message: of how much this recommended stranger knew. 'I am indebted.'

Hemditch gave a sparse smile at the limited response. 'I have been asked to effect some introductions.'

'For which I would again be even more indebted.' When was the coachman going to be told to move on?

'Winston and I were at Harrow together: I preferred Oxford to Sandhurst and the soldier's life he chose.'

Sebastian became aware that Hemditch's accent was less pronounced than other Americans he'd encountered on the voyage. 'In which he served valiantly before entering politics.' The flattery was necessary, decided Sebastian. And true, according to accounts.

'He passed through here on his way to Cuba for his first overseas assignment with the 4th Hussars. It was a memorable reunion. His mother's American, you know. The Jeromes are New Yorkers.'

'He told me, in London.' Why were they just sitting there?

'Did you also know that his mother – Jennie Jerome – is my mother's sister, which makes us related?' The American sat with his stick supported between his legs by both hands resting upon its gold handle and with his chin, in turn, judgementally atop that.

Sebastian allowed a polite smile. 'No, I did not.'

'You have my confidence, by my cousin's guarantee.' It was, oddly, an accusation.

What reply was expected? 'I am entrusted with a matter of the greatest delicacy. Were there to be misfortune I would not want to bring embarrassment upon you.'

Hemditch's smile broadened. 'A remark I appreciate.'

'I want us to understand – to trust – each other.'

'Winston has made me aware of the purpose of your visit. The only one who is. I

92

will make the introductions, to people who might lead you further, but I will not be their guarantor. Their integrity is for you to decide. My advice is that you continue the same caution with which you've greeted me.'

He'd correctly responded. 'I sincerely hope my caution has not caused offence.'

'The absolute opposite,' insisted the American. 'Impressed by the reticence. I am now at your service ... all the more so.'

Now, picked out Sebastian. What would have happened if he'd failed Hemditch's probing? Would he have been pitched out of this still-unmoving carriage? Or perhaps merely conveyed to a convenient hotel, to be abandoned to his own unaided devices? There was no benefit in retrospection. And Julius Norton Hemditch still had to pass *his* test. 'I am interested in freight traffic. This, I know, to be the Hudson River port. What about the East River?'

Hemditch reversed his stick against the overhead sounding board finally to mobilize the driver, and as the carriage moved off said: 'The Hudson has the deep-water anchorage. What you're concerned with would go from here. But there's a lot of ports along the eastern seaboard.'

Hemditch had very obviously anticipated his needs. The American maintained a guiding commentary as they headed downtown but keeping as long and as near as possible parallel with the river, for Sebastian to be shown the division between passenger-liner terminals and the larger-capacity warehouse supplying freighter anchorages, with their more powerful, heavier cranes. Everywhere was a maelstrom of milling, often shouting people and as they eventually turned inland, away from the water into the Battery area to go uptown, the cacophony grew with their entry into the raucous, vendor-yelling street markets, as strident and traffic-blocking as any Sebastian had ever known in Europe. Which, he at once acknowledged as his ear picked up the different accents and words, was hardly surprising: he guessed the majority of the people shouting their wares all around him had learned their trade doing exactly the same, perhaps selling the same, in France or Spain or Italy. He was intrigued as they went through what Hemditch identified as SoHo that many of the buildings had cast-iron frontages, which he had never seen before, and decided the numerically graduated south-to-north, east-to-west grid system in which the streets were laid out could be partially responsible for his deck-view impression of buildings being set out in an orderly fashion.

As they passed the Fuller Building, at Broadway and East 23rd Street, Sebastian said: 'They really do seem to scrape the sky, don't they?'

'That's more commonly known as the Flatiron Building because that's exactly what it looks like. Buildings can go that high – and will go higher, mark my words – because of the quirk of Manhattan's geology. The entire island is one giant slab of solid, unending granite. It'll support anything.'

It was at the Fuller Building that they turned properly uptown, along Fifth Avenue, and at once Sebastian recognized it was New York's equivalent of the Champs-Elysées of Paris or the Regents Street of London or the Brandenburgische Strasse of Berlin, the boulevard of the rich and powerful and the castles from which they ruled their domains. Which, more aptly than Sebastian first envisaged, described the difference between this and most of the European citics with which he was comparing. In Paris and London and Berlin or Rome those same mansions built for the same reasons – the majority far larger than those Sebastian was passing at that moment – had a conformity, size rather than dissimilarity governing their architects' pencils. The mansions of Fifth Avenue had no rigidity of type or design: there was even one in the manner of a ruler's fortress, its roof surround castellated and turreted. Most had manicured garden fore-fronts, several with matching closely coif-feured trees. It was almost incongruous finally to turn at Central Park into the most European-appearing property – with front-ing, tree-pruned and grass-cropped garden – that Sebastian had so far seen, a preference understandable from Julius Hemditch's English schooling. There was an extensive ostler's yard immediately beyond an inner

95

gate, in the middle of which gleamed an automobile as large as Mycroft's, although in black and not a Rolls-Royce.

As they descended from the coach, Hemditch gestured up to where the coachman still sat and said: 'Johnson's practising how to drive. I'll miss the coach. But that's progress. If this country were to have a motto that's what it would be – to progress.'

Sebastian was sure of a woman's presence from the profusion of flowers and the pastel softness of the furnishings but the house appeared to be empty apart from obvious servants. After the proud, landmarking tour of the city Sebastian – believing himself to be adapting to American openness – expected to be invited to survey the grand house and doubtless its even grander contents. Instead of which Hemditch stumped across an echoing marble entrance hall into a more traditional, mahogany-panelled library with its requisite, solitary-lamped desk, button-backed Chesterfields with their matching, solitary seated offspring and bottle-supplemented tantalus, its decanter cover already unlocked. But still, initially, he did not stop, continuing on into an expansive but matchingly furnished study and then further, into a side office where Sebastian immediately isolated the telegraph.

'Your quarters,' Hemditch announced, gesturing as he spoke. 'There's space cleared on that desk for you to work, alongside the telegraph. And I've cleared that cabinet in which you can store whatever material you choose. The only key is that already in its lock.'

'You have been uncommonly generous,' thanked Sebastian.

'I'm a man of my word,' insisted Hemditch, leading the way back out through the study into the library, where he gestured towards leather. 'Are you apprehensive?'

'Alert to the difficulties. But not frightened.' Had he sounded bombastic? He hoped not.

Hemditch's flicker of disbelief was brief but sufficient for Sebastian to discern. 'I believe there's benefit for you in my discussing America,' the man announced. 'Five years from now one, maybe more, of those vendors downtown selling berries for three cents a pound could be building a house bigger than this on the other side of the avenue. America is the land of the always possible. OK, so my money is old, being multiplied into new. So is that of the Astors and the Vanderbilts and the J. P. Morgans. All of whom – me included – would three hundred years ago have probably been pirate captains, plundering every ship carrying whatever had already been plundered from the Americas or the Indies. Pirates, entrepreneurs, the words – the attitudes – are interchangeable. The philosophy is the same. It's only the trade that's changed, become acceptable if not always legitimate.'

Sebastian passingly thought he was fortunate to have read at his various universities such a pure science as mathematics. 'The glitter of gold?'

'Don't despise or denigrate it!' demanded Hemditch, almost irritably. 'The British Raj was founded upon the trading ability of the East India Company, which fought wars to establish its stranglehold on trade: your country made a hero of Clive of India, who as a boy ran a protection racket in his English birthplace and carried on exacting tribute from every merchant he ever encountered when he became governor of Bengal. It was trade that demanded the tobacco and cotton fields of the American south and the unfair tax demands – *trade* tariffs – upon American businessmen, which lost Great Britain its North American colony. After it gained its independence, this country fought a civil war between north and south to free slaves from the plantations of the south: slavery in this country – snatching Africans from four thousand miles away – was spawned by the kidnapping of their African forefathers to work British sugar plantations in the Caribbean. Trade. Always trade.'

'I'm well enough aware of Germany's envy of Great Britain's supremacy in world business,' said Sebastian, curious at Hemditch's diatribe.

'Envy shared – and a supremacy to be competed for – by the industrialists and pirate businessmen of this country,' insisted

Hemditch. 'And with better chances of success if all the forebodings of Germany going to war are correct. The United States will remain very much on the sidelines, unless unpreventable circumstances provoke them otherwise. Because it makes sound business, trading sense to do so. The sufferers of war are only ever those involved in its fighting. Everyone else benefits.'

'I understand your argument – accept, even, its relevance – but I can't see its conclusion.'

'Events in Europe are yet too uncertain to predict a conclusion,' said Hemditch. 'I'm going no further than to make a point I believe essential always for you to bear in mind. America – Americans – are enemies of neither Great Britain nor Germany. By which I'm not talking about the neutrality decreed by President Wilson. I'm advising you not to approach this affair on the basis of good or bad, friend or foe. If the price is right and the material is available an American will as readily trade with London today as with Berlin tomorrow. And with London again the day after.'

Sebastian was unsure whether he was being given a highly selective, postage stamp history of earlier British imperialism or of current North American business ethics. Perhaps it was an offered balance between the two. Which wasn't his to make: not even to consider. A doubt wisped into Sebastian's mind. Or was Julius Hemditch trying to establish his integrity in advance by inferring he had trading contacts in both countries? 'In London there is talk of clandestine groupings: cabals, even.'

'You are in a great hurry, sir!'

'Perhaps with good cause.'

'Perhaps indeed. And hurry we shall, although I doubt in the way you anticipate. Your baggage has been deposited in your rooms. You only need to have sufficient for an overnight journey.'

'This moment!'

'Yours is the urgency. There's time enough for you to wash up: the departure is still three hours away.'

Chamber can, translated Sebastian at once, easily bringing to mind the closest Winchester College dialect phrase for the facility or means to wash. 'I'd like to telegraph London of my arrival.' Could he utilize *chamber can*? he wondered. Sebastian hoped his uncle would be able to understand the improvisation he'd already decided was going to be necessary.

'It's gibber!' protested Sherlock Holmes, to whom the inability to resolve any conundrum was unthinkable. 'Pure gibber.'

'Which is what it is intended to be,' reminded Mycroft. He'd broken away from deciphering Sebastian's first telegraph, surprised by the unexpected, demanding arrival of his brother at his Diogenes lodgings. 'Are you sure this visit is safe?'

'You know I can move unseen when occasion demands,' dismissed Sherlock Holmes. 'Watson is at this moment perambulating the somnolent, heavily swathed image of myself, complete with cloak, shawl and my oldest deerstalker, around the perimeter of Hyde Park's bridle path. Much to the disgust of my substitute, Mrs Hudson.'

Mycroft resented the intrusion. 'I have an appointment with Winston in an hour.'

'You'd better hurry then,' said Sherlock Holmes, peremptorily. 'I think I need to learn this confounded language.'

'It takes years,' avoided Mycroft, who had anticipated the demand. 'Sit patiently while I work.'

Sherlock Holmes did not sit. In his impatience he wandered the room, subsiding into a chair only when Mycroft protested a second time at the distraction of the constant movement. Even in his chair the man shifted constantly, scribbling his own deciphering efforts on the duplicate of the message to Mycroft his son had sent. It was a further thirty minutes before the Cabinet Secretary finally leaned back in his chair, stretching the cramp from his shoulders.

'Well?' demanded Sherlock Holmes, at once.

'Notions by itself is not going to be easy,' said Mycroft, more to himself than to his brother. 'He's had to rely upon ziph, although I think I've got it.'

'What in Heaven's name is ziph?'

'A somewhat despised precursor to Notions proper: a slang in which the vowels of a word are repeated and a medial "g" is inserted,' provided Mycroft.

Sherlock Holmes at last stopped fidgeting, spreading out on Mycroft's desk his own copy of Sebastian's message, which read: *Buck crima duucgaal carthage fogor chamber can taaglkspeetgeerspoogiint*. After only minutes he said: 'Still gibberish.'

'It needs interpretation as well as translation,' insisted Mycroft. '*Buck* and *crima* are simple Notions: a dandy, someone who's good-looking or important, and *crima*, which is Crimea, a derivation that entered the school's language in the 1854 war between Russia and the British and French. Now comes the ziph. *Duucgaal* is ducal. *Carthage* is a Notion again, a debating society, but I'm guessing he wants me to stretch that definition, which I've done, to mean debate or talk. I think I've also got to stretch *chamber can*, too. It means a washing bowl. But I'm reading it as washing *can*, phonetically close enough to be Washington. Now we come back to ziph, which Sebastian has intentionally joined, for confusion. Separated as it's obvious he intended *taaglkspeetgeerspoogiint* comes out as "to talks Peter's point".'

'So what's your full translation?'

'He's only arrived today: a few hours ago,' reminded Mycroft. 'So it must refer to something that he learned during the crossing. An important Crimea – Russian – duke was a fellow traveller, heading for washing can – Washington – to debate or talk upon Peter's – St Petersburg's – point or behalf.'

For several moments Sherlock Holmes was finally unmoving, looking down at the previous jumble. 'Yes,' he allowed, reluctantly. 'That makes sense. Did you know that the Russians were treating separately with America?'

'No, we did not,' said Mycroft.

'Then Sebastian has already done well.'

'Indeed he has,' agreed Mycroft.

Which was Winston Churchill's assessment when Mycroft, an hour late, finally relayed the message and his translation of it to the First Lord of the Admiralty in his hideaway office within sight of Buckingham Palace.

'It's something that needs urgent consultation with our Russian ambassador,' said Churchill.

'How do we disguise our knowledge of it?'

'Washington gossip,' replied Churchill, at once. He took several moments coaxing his Havana cigar into life, smiling up over its smoke plume. 'You tell me that a boy at Winchester could read this?'

'The interpretation might not be as easy.'

Churchill chuckled. 'Asquith's just sent his son to Winchester! Imagine a boy being able to make partial sense of something that his prime-minister father wouldn't be able to understand!'

Eight

The carriage was much more easily identifiable, a calash with its folding hood, on this excursion, erected against outside observation, in the same deep green colour of the earlier customized model and again with Hemditch's initials intertwined upon its door panels. There was no meandering orientation but very effective proof to Sebastian of the benefits of New York's street system in bringing them to Pennsylvania Station from Fifth Avenue in less than ten minutes. It was fortunate that there were no intervening street markets. The geography of the city was already sufficiently imprinted upon Sebastian's mind for him to estimate that they were within a very few minutes of the Cunard berth at which he'd arrived. Strangely, that arrival seemed longer than just hours ago. He hoped everything would continue as quickly. There was no delay, either, once they reached the rail terminal: blue-uniformed guards at the two-lane private entrance saluted as they opened the restricting gates for them to descend to the exclusive section of a platform – also gated against the intrusion of normal fare-paying passengers – at which Hemditch's personalized green and once more initialled railroad car waited, already hitched to the rear of the scheduled Pittsburgh express. The greeting from the black, white-gloved chief steward at the top of the embarkation steps was without the attempted intimidation employed by Denning.

Sebastian actually found the Victorian grandeur of the car reminiscent of the *Lusitania*. In addition to the decorative curtains withheld by tassled ropes there were Venetian blinds already tilted against outside curiosity. The coach area was deeply carpeted in maroon to match the burgundy leather, button-backed Chesterfields and easy chairs that ran the length of both sides. At each seat were conveniently arranged small wine tables and a working desk, with a Tiffany-shaded lamp and study chair near the entrance. At the opposite end was a bar, glittering with socket-held crystal and decanters, which divided the car between sitting and dining areas. The decor was the familiar, brass-mounted mahogany. All the shades were miniature copies of that of the desk lamp. The curlicued JNH motif was woven into the carpet and headrest covers.

'There's sleeping accommodation beyond the dining car, although we're sleeping at the Pittsburgh house,' announced Hemditch. 'But there's a telegraph aboard, if you need it.'

'I don't imagine that I will.' But he hadn't imagined this excursion, either. And wanted not just the acknowledgement from Mycroft

105

that his uncle had received the communication but that he'd understood it. Immediately to change his mind would make him appear ineptly unsure, which he didn't want to do. There was no hour-to-hour – even day-to-day – urgency about the Russian intelligence. Sebastian wondered if the Grand Duke had accepted James Paterson's private railroad car for a westward expedition: unlikely if the man's visit were an official although covert one.

'We are to be joined on the journey,' disclosed Hemditch.

'By whom?'

'The sort of people to whom Winston wishes me to introduce you. But before I do, how are you – and your presence here – to be described?'

I must stress that I am not their guarantor, Sebastian remembered: from Churchill's avoidance at their London meeting, he didn't for a moment believe the First Lord of the Admiralty was pledging the integrity of whoever he was going to meet, either. 'Someone with substantial finance to invest in high-return business proposals.'

Hemditch nodded, smiling. 'Good for the purpose. Oscar Lepecheron's my banker.'

Sebastian hoped his mathematical prowess would obscure his ignorance of arcane banking procedure. But then, he reassured himself, why should he, as an independently wealthy man, be required to have any esoteric banking knowledge at all: that expertise was what bankers were engaged *for*. All he needed was the ability to convert a supposed rate of interest return upon a supposed figure of investment and he was more than able to calculate that. 'And the other?'

'Lowell Smithlane. Has one of the biggest freighter fleets on the Eastern seaboard: carries out of Boston as well as New York.'

'You've put yourself to some inconvenience, arranging an encounter entirely for my benefit.'

'Not entirely for your benefit,' denied Hemditch. 'Not entirely at all. Oscar's coming to look over some mill-expansion plans I need financing. Lowell's a longstanding customer with a business interest.'

Yet the man would not guarantee them, thought Sebastian. Although he had only been on American soil for a matter of hours and needed the contact Churchill had provided, Sebastian was uncomfortable at being so quickly swept along by events rather than initiating them himself: at least being able to discuss them before they were instigated.

'I am...' began Sebastian but their travelling companions arrived, together, before Sebastian could finish, or more importantly be further briefed about either travelling companion on their journey to the steel-producing centre of America.

Oscar Lepecheron was a saturnine, dark-haired, melancholy faced man of slow, considered movements and speech who actually appeared to examine Sebastian, as if deciding whether he approved, before offering his hand. Sebastian's linguistic ear at once detected an accent. Lepecheron wore the immaculate attire of his profession, black frock coat and striped trousers, with a black, diamond-pinned stock at his throat.

Lowell Smithlane was in total contrast, by every comparison. His striped brown short-jacketed suit was modern American, with no deference to any European style, a motif-adorned club tie beneath a hard-collared shirt. He was pinkly fresh-faced with white, close to albino blond hair and unhesitatingly, almost exuberantly, pumped Sebastian's hand up and down between both of his, and with the familiarity of previous privileged Hemditch expeditions addressed the steward by name – Cowling – and in mock severity demanded to know why he was being made to wait so long for his first drink.

He wasn't.

Cowling was already approaching with champagne so well balanced in crystal flutes that none was spilled by the abrupt jolt of the train getting underway. Having delivered the drinks, the man distributed individual menus with choices from five offered courses. They selected in a leisurely fashion, the other three men spreading themselves expansively, Lepecheron and Smithlane side by side. Sebastian chose his own territory in a single, red-leather barrel chair. Hemditch smoothly directed the conversation on to Sebastian's recent arrival from England, which just as easily initiated the discussion about the political uncertainties in Europe.

At once Sebastian moved hopefully to guide the talk, anxious to gauge the sympathies of the first two men recommended by Churchill's emissary, and at once believed there was something to be interpreted from Lepecheron's opinion that if Berlin did declare war upon France – the bait with which Sebastian floated his allegiance-seeking hook – the assault would be through Lepecheron's Belgian homeland.

'Germany is equipping and recruiting its armed forces at an unprecedented pace,' coaxed Sebastian.

'That's well enough known,' agreed the banker, sombrely.

'Do you believe Belgium could resist?'

'No,' said the Belgian, unequivocally. 'But there is a non aggression pact with your country.'

Hemditch came to Sebastian's assistance. 'Will England make such a fateful commitment, if called upon to do so?'

His function was to lure, not to answer, Sebastian reminded himself. 'You're right: it might be a fateful commitment.'

'Not to do so would ridicule Great Britain internationally, the more so in the eyes of those countries who have placed their trust in it!' protested Lepecheron.

The train had long ago emerged from the river tunnel and was now attaining its maximum speed and for several moments

Sebastian looked out at the blurred, passing countryside, building the pause to imply he was unsure. Cowling's arrival to replenish their glasses provided a further, unwitting delay before Sebastian said: 'England's current government is greatly exercised by unrest in Ireland.'

'A province!' protested Lepecheron, anew. 'We're discussing sovereign *countries*!'

'We are indeed and I'm not proposing comparison between the two,' said Sebastian. 'I am a private person with no reason to doubt the integrity or intention of my government.'

'I'd like you to be my guest at my place outside New York during your visit,' invited Smithlane, abruptly.

Sebastian was bewildered by the intrusion, so momentarily nonplussed that he stumbled his reply. 'That would be very kind ... delighted to accept ... but I am altogether unsure of my movements, and...'

'I have a hobby, a passion,' broke in the American again. 'I collect everything I can about the original Pilgrim Fathers. Did you know, for instance, that they did not embark on their epic voyage to the New World from Plymouth, as everyone supposes, but from Southampton?'

'No, I did not,' encouraged Sebastian, fully recovered and knowing this was a deliberate change of subject.

'I have traced my forefathers among those original settlers.'

'Something of which I am sure you're very proud,' said Sebastian. Was it something as simple as Smithlane setting out which side he was on?

'I am,' agreed Smithlane. 'I'm an American who likes to think of himself as an original Englishman. My ancestry is Suffolk.'

'Then you must look upon the uncertainties in Europe with greater concern than most other Americans?' riposted Sebastian.

'Very much so,' countered Smithlane. 'And you, sir! How much is your mind occupied by those same uncertainties?'

'Quite obviously, even more greatly.'

'I have not discerned that from your hesitations.'

The directness was almost becoming aggressive, thought Sebastian: there was no longer the first-encounter bonhomie. Sebastian wasn't sure he was any longer in control of the debate nor that he had been for some time. He shook his head against Cowling's wine-offering return. Setting a test of his own, Sebastian said: 'Believe me, Mr Smithlane, I will not be found to be a sunshine patriot shrinking from the service of his country in its hour of crisis.'

There was an immediate and obvious identification from all three men of the paraphrase of the Englishman who so much influenced the very wording of America's Declaration of Independence.

'Tom Paine also wrote: "My country is my world and my religion is to do good",' reminded Smithlane, quoting back with absolute accuracy.

Sebastian acknowledged that as well as being a freight line owner Smithlane was also very clearly the well-versed amateur historian he claimed to be. 'A philosophy to which I just as readily ascribe.'

'Very philosophical,' broke in Hemditch, rising to Cowling's return. 'Let's talk while we eat.'

The blinds were raised in the dining car, giving Sebastian an unbroken view of a flat New Jersey landscape, far beyond which the blue-black mountains never seemed to get any closer but rather to retreat ahead of them. There were, he remembered, several inter-connected mountain chains. There appeared more settlements than towns on the plain across which they were still travelling, isolated outcrops of two or three houses, far more built of shingled wood than brick. Sebastian made out very few surfaced highways. All the side roads and tracks were hard-packed dirt or aggregate and he didn't see an automobile until Newark and then only two, parked on the main street, visible from the train as if on display.

Sebastian decided the lounge discussion had too quickly become intense, even by the standards of the newly recognized forceful-ness of American exchanges, and the moving from one section of the railroad car to another gave him a brief opportunity to search for every definition for every word that had passed between him and the other men. Certainly the conversation had been specifically channelled by Julius Hemditch but from the quickness with which first Oscar Lepecheron and then Lowell Smithlane took up the baton – the cargo-ship owner intervening at precisely the moment he had – it could have been inferred they had been prepared in advance. Or could it? Wasn't it understandable that a worried Belgian-born banker and an Anglophile freighter owner should become so ardently animated with someone so recently arrived from England about the prospect of a major European conflict? Why had Julius Hemditch, whom Churchill trusted sufficiently to confide the reason for this mission, so positively refused to offer the same assurance for his personal banker and a long-time business associate? Sebastian didn't have an answer but accepted he was demanding too much too soon. If he gave way to impatience he was throwing into the wind all the caution that had been impressed upon him in London.

Sebastian decided it was time to recommence the discussion although more in the direction of his choosing. 'In the event of hostilities your own government has indicated it will be strictly neutral. Do you believe that will remain its firm stance?'

'As far as I am aware there are no intervention or alliance treaties with any European nation,' said Lepecheron.

Looking more to Smithlane than the

banker, Sebastian said: 'Aren't there traditional alliances of original nationality?'

It was Lepecheron who answered the question. 'Since the beginning of this century it is calculated that the United States has accepted twelve million immigrants from Europe, a substantial proportion of them German: already the number of first-generation naturalized German-Americans is way up into the millions.'

'And America is a trading nation,' said Lowell Smithlane. 'Its icon is John Jacob Astor...'

'Who was born at Waldorf, near Heidelburg, until recently my university,' cut off Sebastian. What would that disclosure prompt?

'Does a German education create a loyalty problem for you?' demanded Lepecheron, bluntly.

Damn the need for the social graces! 'You come close to offending me, sir! Heidelberg – Germany – was but one of several countries in which I was fortunate to study. My interests there were academic, not political.'

'But you were exposed to the politics?' persisted Lepecheron.

'Given an opportunity to know at first hand the rising militarism.'

'And how formidable a challenge to your country do you judge such militarism to be?' asked Smithlane.

Sebastian conceded the conversation had yet again been taken from him. 'Considerable. Which makes worrying suggestions in London that some American industrialists are already making provision greatly to benefit from their country's isolationism.'

'Businessmen anticipate their markets,' said Lepecheron.

'Individually? Or as a caucus?' demanded Sebastian.

There was almost imperceptible movement, quickly stopped, from each man to look to the other. Once more it was Lepecheron who spoke. 'I am unsure I've fully appreciated the purpose of your visit here.'

'My oversight,' hurried in Hemditch. 'Mr Holmes is a financier of some sound standing, seeking investment potential in a country growing as fast as the United States is growing. And as you know personally, Oscar, I'm seeking investment for the further expansion I have in mind in Pittsburgh.'

Sebastian held back the startled look towards Hemditch. Without warning the American was presenting him as an alternative financial source to Lepecheron. They were clearly talking in millions and whatever the capacity of Winston Churchill's private contingency fund Sebastian was sure it didn't run to a private investment in steel manufacture, which meant Julius Hemditch, for all his outward assistance and bonhomie, was manoeuvring advantage through him. Or did it? It was an ill-fitting comparison but just as Benjamin Disraeli's share purchasing in the Suez Canal had proved so strategically

115

worthwhile, couldn't Britain secretly financing an American steel mill be a hugely wise anticipation in the event of war and a more than worthwhile, profit-returning investment if Europe remained at peace? Sebastian wished there had been more time – or that time had been made – for he and Hemditch to have discussed such a possibility in advance of this encounter. Among people in whom he'd hoped, perhaps naively, to discover likemindedness, Sebastian felt he was playing blind man's buff with the bandanna too tightly around his eyes.

Lepecheron's vision did not appear to be so obscured. He stared fixedly at Sebastian for several moments before saying: 'Are you capable of providing two million or three million dollars, Mr Holmes?'

Further testing time, Sebastian accepted. 'More than capable of creating a consortium to provide such a sum. Singly to advance it – committing too much capital to one enterprise – does not in my judgement make sound business sense. Gamblers – which I regard myself to be and which I hope I do not offend you by suggesting you might be as well – spread their wagers, wouldn't you agree, Mr Lepecheron?'

'I don't gamble with clients' money!'

'Neither, sir, do I. Which is why I spread my investments. Those that succeed compensate for those that do not.'

'And how averages your luck?'

'Luck is not something in which a com-

petent gambler trusts. He properly examines
form and track record and puts his money on
to as near a certainty as possible.' Sebastian
felt he was in charge of the exchanges again.
They were deeply into the mountains now,
lights needed in the dining salon because of
the premature darkness cast by the high-
sided clefts and tunnels through which they
were passing.

'I think I detect a personal compliment
deeply hidden there somewhere,' said Hemditch. 'Let's take our coffee, brandy and
cigars in greater comfort.'

They automatically took the same seats
back in the lounge. The Venetian blinds had
been raised but lights were on, as well. Only
Hemditch and Lepecheron smoked.

Smithlane said: 'What other enterprises are
you interested in, Mr Holmes?'

'My visit is an exploratory one,' easily
avoided Sebastian. 'In that respect I am, of
course, seeking introductions.'

'In which I might be able to assist you.'

Wouldn't Oscar Lepecheron, a financier
who was obviously much better known to the
freight line owner, be the more obvious
person to whom to make such an offer? wondered Sebastian. The banker himself showed
neither surprise nor offence. Sebastian said:
'That would be extremely kind of you.'

'Do you regard Germany as your country's
enemy?' Smithlane demanded.

Sebastian needed the pause but assured
himself the hesitation befitted such openness.

Was the man testing the loyalty that had already been questioned? Or challenging his business determination? His response would be a gamble. 'Potentially. But there has been no formal declaration of hostilities, so no, I do not regard Germany as Great Britain's enemy.'

'What are your movements to be, after Pittsburgh?'

'I return to New York.'

'I am on an invitation list for a reception to be held shortly at the German embassy in Washington,' disclosed Smithlane. 'Would you have me attempt to extend that invitation to include you?'

'I would indeed,' accepted Sebastian. Surely not this quickly, this easily?

The deluge was unaccustomedly heavy for the time of year and Dr John Watson was delayed at the entrance to 221b Baker Street, divesting himself of coat, hat and umbrella for Mrs Hudson to dry. He remained unpleasantly wet around his feet and lower legs, conscious of the squelching as he ascended the stairs. He entered the drawing room as Sherlock Holmes emerged from his bedroom on the other side, comfortable in curly-toed slippers and dressing gown in place of a jacket.

'No walk in the park today, Holmes.'

'It was never the intention.'

With a flicker of foreboding, Watson at once detected the timbre in the other man's voice and looked with medical expectancy through the still-open bedroom door, easily identifying the discarded syringe. Staring very obviously at it, the doctor said: 'This is appalling, Holmes! Absolutely and utterly appalling. You'd agreed with me – cooperated with me – in curing you of this wretched dependence!'

'I never conceded to being ill.'

'You accepted my treatment.'

'I need clarity of thought,' insisted Sherlock Holmes.

'We've talked long enough about this not being the way to achieve it,' argued Watson, as forcefully as he knew how. 'Clarity inevitably becomes clouded by such stimulation. You're discarding what took us so long to achieve!'

'Your treatment is unendangered,' insisted Sherlock Holmes, impatiently. 'Today's clouds are concern, nothing more.'

'Concern about what?' Confrontation was not the approach. Would it be as difficult as before?

'Hare and hounds,' said Sherlock Holmes. He was sitting in his customary chair, chin reflectively on his chest, his high, brittle voice the only indication of the aid to which he had succumbed.

Watson took his equally familiar place opposite, dismissing the first thought that the remark was a reference to the Baskerville case, content with this return to the old habit of his being the sounding board for Sherlock Holmes's ruminations. 'In which role have you cast Sebastian?'

'Initially I considered him the hound, but I am no longer sure.'

'The hare then?'

'It could be the role in which others have put him, for them safely to identify pursuing hounds.'

'But that accuses Mycroft of complicity against someone he treats as a son! It's unthinkable to imagine he would be part of such a scheme!' protested Watson.

Sherlock Holmes shook his head. 'The scheme is not Mycroft's. It's Churchill's, as Sebastian's contact is Churchill's also.'

Watson was silent for several moments. 'I don't think we should forget Mycroft's influence, in inner government. Can you really contemplate that Churchill would risk deceiving a person of such power!'

'Mycroft's influence and power is the guarantee for the whole enterprise. By his own admission Mycroft regards the man as an opportunist.'

'Shall you voice your concerns to Mycroft?'

'My first priority is to learn this confounded language by which Sebastian is communicating so that I may caution him without interference.'

'To communicate with Sebastian without Mycroft's knowledge!' challenged Watson, at once.

'My brother may be bound by integrity on his part to share everything with Churchill. I will not compromise Mycroft. We're off to Winchester, Watson. There must be an account of the language somewhere!'

'A worthwhile expedition,' accepted Watson. He needed to be in close and constant proximity to Sherlock Holmes to stop and hopefully reverse this worrying relapse.

Nine

There were dark Satanic mills as far as Sebastian could see, their gouting stacks in sentinel lines filling the sky with permanent half night, and inside the one Hemditch chose to show him there were the fires and heat and smell and noises of hell. Sweat-glistened men worked stripped to the waist, a few even discarding trousers for improvised loincloths, everything black and grimed except the orange-yellow molten ore milking from their smelting furnaces to be flattened into glowing tongues of hissing, spitting metal. Managers and supervisors from this and adjoining Hemditch factories trailed dutifully behind their owner, eager with shouted production figures and output targets when the louder yelling Hemditch proudly demanded them. The bedlam was too great for any proper exchanges until they emerged into the better but still obscured light of the outside day. It was still a thicker fog than any Sebastian had suffered in

London, the grit positive against his skin, the fumes snatching at his throat.

'That's toil indeed!' exclaimed Sebastian, the words gasping from him. He was waistcoated as well as suited and not a part of his body was free from soaking, prickling perspiration. He felt as dirty as the wretched men inside although he knew he wasn't – couldn't possibly be – anxious to bathe for the second time that morning.

'Those are good conditions, by comparison,' insisted Hemditch. He waved his arms generally to more mills, to his left. 'They were Carnegie's, before he sold out to J. P. Morgan. Carnegie had his people work seven days a week, every week of the year except Christmas. My workers get the sabbath and I employ sufficient to provide shifts. And the beer they need to replace the water they sweat is free.' He looked pointedly at the acolytes around him. 'Thank you for your attention, gentlemen. I'm sure you've matters to attend to.'

Hemditch shook his head against the mill manager's invitation for refreshments and as the man led the group's dispersal Hemditch gestured again, this time towards the mill they had so recently left. 'You just witnessed the secret of American industry, sir: what's going to make this country the manufacturing leader of the world. Production lines. Raw material at one end, finished product at the other...' He smiled. 'Essential experience for a potential investor.'

Sebastian seized the opportunity, the first offering any private conversation between himself and Hemditch since the shared railway journey and the previous evening's house party at Hemditch's northside Pittsburgh mansion, at which the magnate's daughter, Laura, had been the unexpected but perfect hostess in the absence of Hemditch's consort. That morning, obviously from the experience of earlier conducted mill tours, Lepecheron and Smithlane had both forcefully declined a reprise. Lepecheron's additional excuse was that he wanted to examine the new mill site alone, before doing so with Hemditch. Sebastian said: 'I would have welcomed prior awareness that I was to be presented as a potentially alternative backer to Lepecheron.'

'It justified your presence, without further explanation. And until a few moments before they joined us at the station I had no foreknowledge of your intended subterfuge,' said Hemditch.

That was true, allowed Sebastian. But then Hemditch had said he had been fully acquainted with everything by Winston Churchill, who most certainly had known the disguise. 'What of the risk of Lepecheron withdrawing from your negotiations?'

Hemditch's smile towards Sebastian was sympathetic. 'That's not the American way, Mr Holmes. You're imagined to be competition to be faced, not run from. Oscar will be all the more determined to involve himself.'

123

So he *had* been made use of, Sebastian accepted: but on an objective balance, he was equally making use of Julius Hemditch.

The mill was intentionally close to the Ohio River, down which barges still carried a proportion of the steel production that was not moved by the rail spur that came right into the foreyard. What had been a welcome breeze when they had first left the mill was now drying Sebastian's wetness, chilling him. 'Were you aware of Smithlane's connection with the Germans?'

'No,' said Hemditch. 'It's likely to provide you with a convenient entry, don't you think? The Washington embassy is the very centre of activity mustering support to the German cause. There's an irony that von Bernstorff was born in London, although of a Prussian Junker dynasty. Did you know that?'

'I was aware of his having served as ambassador to England, not of his being born there,' said Sebastian. How, he wondered, had Hemditch gained such intelligence? 'Do you not find further irony too in the fact that someone so proud of his English heritage as Lowell Smithlane should be on an invitation list to the German legation?'

'Not particularly.'

'Might he not belong to the sort of group I'm seeking to penetrate?'

'I told you, Mr Holmes, that I'll not stand guarantor. If he is, it is for you to discover.' Hemditch looked irritably towards the bordering road. 'Where are they?'

Sebastian took his hunter from his waist-coat pocket, which felt damp, and said: 'We're five minutes ahead of the time you stipulated.' The coach that had brought them to the mill had returned to collect the banker and the freight line owner.

'I prefer people to be early for me,' said Hemditch.

'We are exploring ironies,' prompted Sebastian.

'You were,' corrected Hemditch. 'I don't see a serious dichotomy in an *American* accepting such an invitation. I've had two myself and taken up both. How else would I be able to report the nationalistic activity there?'

'Report to whom?' he quickly rejoined, as the suspicion came to him.

Hemditch turned away from the road outside and his search for their transport to look fully at Sebastian. 'I did communicate it to Winston,' admitted the man. 'I'm sure I was only repeating what was already well known to your Washington embassy.'

Would Hemditch report to Churchill upon him? wondered Sebastian. The First Lord's admitted anxiety at embarrassment was sufficient to make such monitoring more than possible. And easily achieved with his being Hemditch's constantly observed house guest.

American directness once more, Sebastian decided. 'Were business approaches made to you after your embassy visits?'

'Of course.'

'By someone outside the embassy?'

Hemditch appeared to consider the question, mentally debating his reply. 'By the Trade Counsellor, whom I told I was considering building additional mills to expand my production capacity, which I am...' There was the sudden appearance of the coaches on the bordering road. 'And here they are, at last!'

'Precisely on time,' Sebastian pointed out, heavily.

Sebastian envied the newcomers the crispness of their attire and obvious cleanliness. He naturally withheld his analogy to hell and instead admired the innovation of production lines, which instantly brought from Oscar Lepecheron a demand for his investment assessment. Sebastian evaded the question as impossible to answer upon the basis of an hour-long tour of one mill, as well as pointing out that unlike the banker he had not yet had the advantage of seeing where the development was intended. The intervening distance to the planned expansion site was so short that Sebastian thought they could have easily walked it.

Even to Sebastian's inexperienced eye Hemditch's new location was a natural extension, the cargo-navigable river still conveniently close and requiring little more than half a mile of augmentation to the rail spur already serving the other mills. The only obvious drawback was the narrowing of the land available by a rock escarpment big enough to be considered a mountain foothill and Sebastian doubted the clearance, construction, plant installation and provision of transportation facilities could be achieved within Lepecheron's $2,000,000 to $3,000,000 estimate. Carefully avoiding the straightforward challenge to those figures, Sebastian suggested the cost of levelling and preparing the land would be substantial, to Hemditch's assurance that it had been costed into the business proposal on the basis of two independent geological surveys. There was a limited exploration of the land, Hemditch leading them to the river bank to illustrate how the construction of the mill would complete his empire. It was only from a riverside remark by Lowell Smithlane about the ease of a water route to Lake Erie and the Great Lakes complex that Sebastian appreciated the business reason for the freight owner's presence. What, he wondered, had his own been?

Sebastian expected that Laura's presence in her father's private railroad car the following morning would have precluded any further business discussion but in less than half an hour of its departure for New York Oscar Lepecheron manoeuvred a separation from the others.

'What do you think of the proposal?' Lepecheron demanded at once.

There was also room for manoeuvre available to him, Sebastian realized. 'It would seem to be an altogether sound, logical proposition, although, as I said on site, for a cost greater than the figure you suggested earlier.'

'How much greater?'

'I've not yet had the chance to submit the independent geological reports to even further independent analysis,' Sebastian easily parried. 'Until I do – and balance the business plan against it – I wouldn't risk estimating a budget.' He was conscious of Laura's attention, further along the car.

'Is your consortium already comprised, the finance available?' asked the Belgian-born banker.

Sebastian at once discerned an escape from Julius Hemditch's entrapment while at the same time maintaining his entrepreneurial charade. 'I thought I'd just made it clear I'm not yet able to estimate the necessary finance.'

'You surely know the extent – the individual commitment – to which each is prepared to go?' challenged Lepecheron.

Not as easy an escape as he'd imagined. Feeling himself nevertheless still in control, Sebastian said: 'We are potential rivals in this! I'm unsure of the propriety of this conversation.'

'Need we be rivals?'

The rejoinder tilted Sebastian. Candidly he complained: 'You confuse me.'

'Consider committing your resources to my already bonded and audited group,'

Lepecheron invited.

Sebastian's confusion was momentarily complete, his recovery – and his assessments – matchingly quick. The cost of Hemditch's expansion *was* far greater than Lepecheron anticipated and the banker was apprehensive of his imagined competition. What better way for Lepecheron to nullify that competition – as well as securing his additional extra funding – than by absorbing it within his own consortium? Sebastian did not halt the evaluation. For Lepecheron to advance such an approach had to mean that the banker – and presumably Lowell Smithlane – accepted upon Hemditch's introduction his bona fides as a financial backer to be taken seriously: that he'd satisfactorily passed the scrutiny of his business-orientated peers. Sebastian said: 'I represent a group of people who have put their trust in my integrity, just as they are prepared to accept from thousands of miles distance my judgement on business opportunities. I am flattered by your offer but in no way feel I can honourably accept it.'

'I have surprised you with such an approach,' apologized Lepecheron. 'You will need an opportunity to reflect.'

'I don't consider so,' insisted Sebastian. 'I am honour-bound to keep faith with the colleagues I represent.'

'The offer remains open, should you change your mind.'

It was Mycroft Holmes's function, among so

many others both official and unofficial, to be first in the Cabinet Room to ensure everything was in readiness, which of course it was because Mycroft always supervised every preparation. Having done so, he remained at his appointed place at the table, although not sitting in advance of the ministers. Winston Churchill was predictably and impatiently first, slightly ahead of Viscount Haldane, the Lord Chancellor and a close Churchill ally, although not as intimately so as David Lloyd George, who came in slightly ahead of Sir Rufus Daniel Isaacs. Sir Edward Grey came in alone, appearing deep in thought, having so long occupied the position of Foreign Secretary that his approach to his accustomed place was automatic. Reginald McKenna, the minister for Home Affairs, entered into conversation with Colonel Jack Seely, the War Minister. David Lloyd George entered alone. The Prime Minister was the last to arrive, waving everybody down as he did so.

'I have only scheduled one item for discussion today,' announced Herbert Asquith without any preliminaries. 'It is time to talk fully about Germany.'

'It is indeed,' rumbled Churchill, disrespectfully.

Asquith ignored the aside, looking to Haldane. 'With the benefit of time for reflection, what's your feeling?'

In Mycroft's opinion – for which, rarely, he had not been consulted in advance – it had been a mistake taking part German-educated

Haldane from the War Office to be Lord Chancellor. As War Minister Haldane had created a much needed and long overdue army general staff and inaugurated a Territorial Army as well as an officers' training corps. Mycroft suspected the transfer had been pique, now regretted, on Asquith's part at Haldane's failure, the previous year, to persuade the Kaiser's government to halt the naval armaments race during a specific peace mission to Berlin.

'My feeling is unchanged from what it was when I returned from Germany,' said Haldane, for once speaking with a clarity unlike his usual philosopher's metaphysics. 'The Kaiser is intent upon aggression. There's no dissuasion remaining.'

'There's surely room for one final peace initiative?' urged the Foreign Secretary. It was Sir Edward Grey who had six years earlier personally concluded the entente with Russia, with which he later negotiated an alliance to include Belgium and France.

'A waste of time and effort,' rejected Haldane.

With consummate timing, Churchill said: 'Russia could be treating independently with the United States.'

Grey's head came up in startled surprise. 'Where does that intelligence come from?'

'Rumours, reported from the naval attaché in St Petersburg,' said Churchill.

Mycroft was better able to conceal his reaction but he was as startled as the Foreign

Secretary at Churchill actually introducing Sebastian's telegram.

'I know nothing of this!' protested Grey.

'The ambassador must quite rightly be waiting for more than diplomatic gossip,' said Churchill. 'I'm not for a moment proposing we regard it as any more than a rumour. I am just introducing it into this very necessary discussion as a possibility, although you, Grey, might care to contact St Petersburg upon the suggestion.'

'I most certainly will,' said Sir Edward Grey. At once he went on: 'We have treaty obligations to Belgium.'

'A major consideration in having this discussion,' reminded Asquith.

'We are also aligned with Russia by treaty,' said the Foreign Secretary. 'If St Petersburg were to forge some alliance with Washington it would, by reason of our alliance, put the United States in our sphere of influence. Our position would be so strengthened as to face down any German aggression before it began!'

'We all know well enough your feelings at the prospect of war, which we all share, but I fear you are being over-hopeful on nothing more than gossip,' said Haldane.

'I propose a demonstration of force,' declared Churchill. 'Apart from submarines, about which I've been too long opposed by our Sea Lords, I believe we have matched German cruiser and dreadnought provision ton for ton, vessel for vessel. I intend withdrawing my Mediterranean fleet to our waters, for exercises in the North Sea.'

My Mediterranean fleet, isolated Mycroft. How quickly – and how conveniently – Churchill was able to forget how strongly he and Lloyd George had opposed only three years earlier the expenditure of £36,000,000 to build up the dreadnought fleet he now seemed to consider his personal property.

'Isn't there a risk in such concentration, on Germany's doorstep?' queried Colonel Seely, damning himself from his own mouth as War Minister.

Churchill showed no pity. He permitted the astonished silence to build, but let Haldane be the executioner. The former War Minister said: 'Seely, the entire purpose of such an exercise would be to demonstrate our naval might on Germany's doorstep, as a deterrent! We wouldn't let them be there if war *was* declared...' The philosopher politician came back to Churchill. 'But isn't there another risk in that strategy? If it fails as the deterrent it's cleverly intended to be and there are hostilities, Turkey will most likely commit to Berlin. Which will expose Russia's underbelly with our fleet in the wrong place.'

'By the time of any actual declaration our Mediterranean fleet will be back on station,' promised Churchill. 'And I'm already formulating a scheme to maintain an open Mediterranean supply route to Russia.'

Seely was a disaster, Mycroft concluded. Kitchener could only be an improvement,

133

despite Churchill's opposition.

'We're clutching at straws here,' declared Lloyd George. The emphasized Welsh lilt was always an indication of the Chancellor of the Exchequor's satisfaction at Asquith letting a Cabinet meeting get out of his control. 'Let's confront reality. There's going to be a war that has to be paid for.'

'David, David!' said Asquith. 'Let's not get into another discussion about a super tax on the rich. We fought a war of our own with the Lords over that and had to concede the lowering of a parliamentary term to five years in exchange for getting the financial veto from the Upper House. We'll consider the need for taxes when the time comes. Which is not now.'

'What about mobilization?' demanded Reginald McKenna.

'I put in place a system for rapid mobilization when I was at the War Office,' reminded Haldane. 'It can be initiated in two weeks.'

'Then it would be premature, at this time,' decided Asquith. 'I do not consider, however, that we should ignore the Irish problem. If there were to be internal conflict it would make strategic sense for Berlin militarily to support Irish secession and by so doing provide itself with a base from which to attack our flank.'

'What positive action are we going to take?' demanded Lloyd George.

'The Mediterranean fleet should be withdrawn, for North Sea exercises,' demanded

Churchill.

There were gestures and nods of assent from around the table. Asquith said: 'Then we're agreed on that. And let's try to find out from St Petersburg what the Russians are up to, if anything.'

'I don't think I shall confine that enquiry to St Petersburg, either,' said Sir Edward Grey. 'I'll see what Washington can tell us.'

'America is the direction in which we should be looking,' insisted Churchill. 'Instead of wasted journeys to Berlin an emissary of the Foreign Secretary's stature – you, even, Prime Minister   should go to Washington personally to put a case to Woodrow Wilson that the United States cannot remain neutral.'

'The problem is that they can,' said Asquith. 'Such a journey would be as wasted as another to Berlin.'

'So we wait?' said Churchill, scarcely bothering to disguise the contempt.

'We can do nothing else,' said Asquith.

Sherlock Holmes waited on the platform to greet Watson from the London train. Ebulliently he said: 'Welcome to Winchester, the original capital of England!'

Watson frowned, in worried recognition.

Ten

Sherlock Holmes's continued ebullience rose in contrary measure to Watson's deepening depression.

Effusively Holmes declared that Winchester was a city of much character easily explored and Hampshire was a county as pleasing, if not more so, than his country-house choice of East Sussex. A commemorative statue of King Alfred the Great graced the High Street and legend had it that the circular board displayed in the great hall of Winchester Castle was the very Round Table at which King Arthur himself held court with his twelve chivalrous knights, all of whose names adorned it according to their rank: the deceiving Lancelot was at the King's right hand.

Holmes had secured excellent lodgings at a coaching inn but a short and easy walk away and was impatient to discover a source or lexicon for the hidden language of the college. He had already located a tavern, appropriately called The Wykeham Arms, frequented by college dons. All this voluble information was delivered with the briefest of pauses for breath and considerable, emphasizing hand movement.

'Tell me, Watson. How did Mrs Hudson

adapt to taking my place in that confounded bath chair?'

'Uncomfortably. She complained greatly of the heat, bundled as she necessarily had to be in rugs and shawls. You watched our progress along Baker Street?'

'For as long as I could, from the window.'

'And?'

'I was not alarmed by any obvious observation but my view was severely restricted,' conceded Sherlock Holmes. 'I'm satisfied, though, that my later departure was undetected and am exhilarated to be here, beyond any unwanted scrutiny, with work to do.'

Watson transferred his valise from his left to right hand, hoping there was not much further to walk at the pace his companion was forcing. 'I fear, Holmes, that the prospect of work is not the only cause of your exhilaration.'

The walking slowed. 'I've had a lot to achieve in a very short time: I'm only in advance of you here by little more than three hours. St Peter's Street: we're here!'

The registration requirements interrupted the conversation, which was as much to Watson's satisfaction as to that of Sherlock Holmes. Their rooms adjoined and the linking door was open.

'Let's be off!' urged the detective, from his own room. 'It's but another short walk.'

'No, Holmes,' refused Watson. 'There's a personal priority greater than mastering a schoolboy language.' It had been his misjudgement, Watson acknowledged, insufficiently to gauge Holmes's frustration at having to remain on the periphery of an investigation. But then he'd believed, obviously now wrongly, that after the initial, sometimes agonizing episode, Holmes had been scoured of his narcotics dalliances.

'Don't confront me, Watson!'

To demand that Holmes cross the dividing room barrier, to come to him, would appear an admonishment. The symbolism of his going to Holmes was practically as bad. Each remained in his own territory, staring through the open doorway. 'I most definitely will confront you, sir! For as long and as many times as it takes me to restore an equilibrium. For a man of your intellect and strength – physical as well as mental – to give way to such weakness defies belief! You have in me a friend versed in medical matters. That's what got this damnable addiction business out of our lives the last time. And so we shall again.'

'I am not addicted!'

'Why then do you need artificial stimulus and support?'

'To take my mind that extra inch.'

The opportunity could not have been better presented. 'The mind of the great and renowned Sherlock Holmes needs to be taken an extra inch to learn the slang of schoolboys! You gravely disappoint me, sir!'

'As you do me, by the insolence of this exchange.'

Watson extended the silence, wanting his

138

response hopefully to show his astonishment at the petulance. 'Could the words you have just uttered not better illustrate the effect upon your reasoning of the morphine or the cocaine or whatever else you have chosen this time for experiment? You are not meeting insolence. You are being offered the concern of a true and concerned friend for a weakness that has to be conquered.'

'There's work to be done,' stubbornly refused Sherlock Holmes.

'There is most certainly,' agreed Watson. 'You were a match for it once. I am unsure whether that remains so.'

'Am I expected to rise to such offence!'

Watson could not recall a dispute of such words vehemence in all the time he had been chronicling the activities of Sherlock Holmes and was unsettled by it. 'I speak such words in the hope of concentrating your mind by honesty, not by the method you choose.'

'You have been my sounding board, Watson.'

'So you have often told me in the past.' Where was this direction taking them?

'Perhaps it is a function you no longer wish to fulfil.'

Once more Watson intruded a silence, wanting the other man to hear the echo of his own voice. Then he said: 'Has it truly come to this, Holmes?'

'That must be for you to judge.'

Watson's head-shaking refusal was positive: internally he was in turmoil. 'Most definitely not, sir! It is for you to judge – to decide – if our long friendship shall end thus. I will not – I will *never* – walk away from you! I never envisaged a situation from which you might walk away from me.'

Watson's later impression was that in the space between the two of them, each in their separate, door-framed rooms, a gulf almost visibly opened, a chasm of earthquake proportions. The face of Sherlock Holmes, as always, remained totally inscrutable, not even an eye blink. Watson hoped he remained similarly impassive but was unsure if he did. The hotel – all around – was silent, as if waiting.

Sherlock Holmes said: 'We've delayed too long! Let's not waste any more time!'

Watson turned to his still-unpacked valise to hide the exhalation of pent-up breath and by so doing failed to see the similar burst of relief from Sherlock Holmes.

It was a warm, even balmy evening. From inside the cathedral, which Watson resolved to visit before their departure, came the perfect harmony of a superb evensong choir unmarred by the equally harmonious practice peal of bells from the square, flag-staffed Norman tower. Couples, families, enjoyed the fading sun on the greensward of the Outer Close. Tottering babies, screaming, jostled with mortal intensity for possession of disputed balls and playthings.

'Imagine, Watson, the threat to such

tranquillity by what's unfolding so few miles across the English Channel.'

'It takes little imagining.' The pace had slackened as they traversed the cathedral grounds and the earlier effervescent travelogue had lessened. Watson identified the slip into the aftermath depression of whatever it was in which Sherlock Holmes had indulged. They reached the Inner Close through a flying-buttress-supported walkway which encouraged the detective to recount the turn-of-the-century salvation of a professional deep-sea diver named William Walker who for more than two years, helmeted and suited, worked in the total blackness of the slimed bog upon which the endangered church had been built 900 years earlier to create a concrete foundation to replace the rotted-away logs upon which it had originally been built and through which it was sinking. Within the inner close there was, added Sherlock Holmes, a garden supposedly laid out by a queen displaying the most excellent roses, far better than those he had been cultivating in East Sussex.

'I well remember our brief visit to this city in the case of Miss Hunter, which I recorded as the matter of the Copper Beeches,' reminisced Watson. 'But to be as well acquainted as you appear, you must have spent more time than that here.'

It was not until they came in sight of Cheyney Court and its yellow-washed Elizabethan buildings that the other man replied. 'Not a

141

visit I am minded to recall and the memory of which caused me to seek the support that so much disturbed you earlier.'

'Better for us to have talked of the matter, which I am glad we are now doing,' encouraged Watson. Sherlock Holmes, personally the most secretive of men, would not be making this confession had he not still been affected by whatever drug he had misused.

'Sebastian's first exeat from school. I knew, of course, that Mycroft would be coming to collect him, to provide me with a marker to a son I did not know. Mycroft was the most dutiful of guardians. He was unaware of my presence that day, concealed as I was in the shadow of one of the original city gates which we shall come upon shortly. It was my first sight of my son, since the day he had been born to my beloved Matilde thirteen years earlier...'

'You watched but held back!' said the astonished Watson.

'Of course. What else was there to do? Mycroft was the parent he knew. I was a stranger then, a mystery figure. At such a formative age I did not dare risk the confusion my sudden appearance would have caused him.'

'And by so doing – or rather not doing – you put yourself in equal confusion?' guessed Watson. Could Holmes's despair over his early treatment of Sebastian be the root cause of the man's narcotic dabbling?

'To relieve myself of greater agony,' said Sherlock Holmes. 'For too long I had stupidly regarded Sebastian as the culprit for Matilde's death: denied him, in my mind, as my own flesh and blood! Can there be a more shameful admission for a father to make than that?'

This could be cathartic, Watson decided: the purging of the narcotic demon. 'You came again?'

'Not for a long time. Difficult though it might be for you to envisage, knowing as intimately as you do the experiences I have undergone in my chosen profession, I found that first occasion almost too harrowing to bear: more so, perhaps, than that final, fateful confrontation with the despicable Moriarty. Guilt was my burden, the recrimination I strove to avoid and I tried to succeed in that by retreating into denial once more. I determined never to acknowledge Sebastian as my son: to let him always regard Mycroft as his only relative.'

'What changed your mind?' persisted Watson. Guilt clearly remained a burden.

'The simple wish to see my son again: to find in him, even from afar, something of Matilde. Which I did, that second time. There is an annual cricket match, between Winchester and Eton. I attended and watched him, in the crowd, and several times felt my heart would burst so many were the memories of Matilde the mere sight of Sebastian brought to me.'

'When did you effect your first meeting?'

'Not for a period of years. The absurdity of

blame still had its place in my mind. I buried myself in the distraction of my profession. You'll call to mind the adventure of the Six Napoleons ... the Golden Pince-Nez and Abbey Grange and the Second Stain and so many others...?'

Watson stopped walking, bringing Sherlock Holmes to a halt beside him. 'I call every one to mind as clearly as if I recorded them yesterday. But I am truly bewildered that throughout them all, knowing as you did of Sebastian, you kept his existence from me!'

'Please don't be offended, old friend. I am confessing, for the first time, an abject personal cowardice. And it is not easy for a man such as myself to admit to being a coward.'

'I don't see cowardice in this. Nor am I offended. Indeed, I am honoured you are giving me this account.'

'Which must never be chronicled!' warned Sherlock Holmes, sharply.

'It won't be, not by me,' assured Watson. 'But tell me, how did you effect the eventual encounter?'

'By keeping as close to the truth as possible and waiting until I felt he'd achieved the maturity of young adulthood. Mycroft prepared the ground with some of your very excellent chronicles of my activities and with a loose retelling of my being brought to the point of death and mental collapse after the Reichenbach business, which you know to be the case. I appeared before him in Paris, a

144

man scarcely restored to health. I gave no clear account of the death of his mother until a few weekends ago, despite his urging. He resents me, Watson. Dislikes me, even. With every good reason.'

'You can't suddenly present yourself, as you say you did, and expect instant acceptance.'

'I acknowledge that readily enough. Often I have reflected that it would have been better for me not to have declared myself at all.'

'You can't truly believe that!' They were at the main, heavy wooden gate of the road entrance to the cathedral grounds. Watson was vaguely aware of noise beyond.

'I try not to. I think much of our future relationship depends upon the outcome of this current affair.'

Kingsgate, one of the two remaining original arched entries into the city in its walled medieval past, was to their left as they departed the cathedral precincts and as they passed beneath it Sherlock Holmes identified the very spot from which he'd first observed his son. The noise of roistering was much louder now and Canon Street, upon the corner of which their intended hostelry was sited, was surprisingly crowded, a greater proportion of the men in uniform.

'This is a garrison town,' provided Sherlock Holmes. 'In that street alone, which is little beyond half a mile, there are two very obviously active houses of ill repute and five taverns, in addition to the object of our immediate interest.'

'So close to a college and a cathedral of such magnificence!'

'My dear Watson, there has always been between the secular and the churches of every denomination the most practical compromise: for your own faith, do not forget the profession of Mary Magdalene ... the leases of the very brothels of which we talk were once – maybe still are – held by the church authorities.' There was a momentary blockage, a confrontation with four arm-linked, slurred singing soldiers by whom they were jostled aside. 'You've served at a war front, Watson, albeit briefly. I remain eternally grateful that the maladies you contracted there, rather than a more fateful bullet, enabled our association to be formed. Again I come back to the matter in hand. Those boisterous youths who have just pushed past you will be cannon fodder if there is no way found to avert the impending catastrophe. Would you deny such unwitting heroes their proud moment of manhood?'

'Of course not, although I have some medical reservations.'

'A comment that marks you as a man of the world.'

'I like to think so,' said Watson.

'Someone prepared to accept its setbacks?'

'I like to believe that, also.'

'Well and truly spoken, Watson! I've rarely seen a wallet lifted as yours was by the young, fair-haired private who shouldered you aside not five minutes ago. I trust there was enough

146

to provide the four of them with sufficient entertainment, whatever their choice.'

Watson belatedly clutched his breast, feeling the emptiness of his inner jacket pocket. 'Holmes! We could have apprehended the villain.'

'Soldier, about to die,' corrected the other man. 'At this moment he and his doubtless celebrating companions have more use for your money than you. And you know I will make good your loss...' There was a pause, refreshingly playful. 'But I must admit disappointment that after so long an association as ours you so easily fell such an unsuspecting victim.'

Watson felt the warmth of his colouring. 'You have allowed me to be humiliated, Holmes!'

'Only by your own assessment, the same measure by which you judged me. Your loss will not become my anecdote.'

'I believed I had already sufficiently assured you of my integrity!'

'You misunderstand, my dear Watson. It's not integrity that is the lesson. It is fallibility.'

'I do not believe I needed that instruction, either!'

'That's good to hear. You doubtless left your watch and its chain in our lodgings, giving no cause for concern at their absence.'

'Damnation!' erupted Watson, both hands now clutching his empty waistcoat pockets.

'It was an inferior timepiece that it will be my pleasure to replace. But please remain

147

more alert. There would seem to be nothing further to lose but your clothes themselves.'

The Wykeham Arms hummed with the excited anticipation of a nest from which eager, fertilizing bees were about to set flight. The green and khaki of military uniforms were everywhere and there was a constant pitch of bravado laughter which Watson unthinkingly likened to sharp explosions and just as quickly wished he had found another analogy for. It was a dark place, ill served by its outside windows, and heavy with the smoke from pipe and cigarette. Obvious, open-bloused touts from the bawdy houses further along the street circulated among the appreciative throng with promises physically difficult to fulfil. A man dull-eyed by familiarity stood by the door, a club-like baton ready for the inevitable conclusion of the night.

So thick was the crowd that only those immediately around Sherlock Holmes and Dr Watson displayed any interest – and that quickly past – at the entry of such obviously well-attired gentlemen, and therefore even more obviously men of stature and financial well-being. Watson at once recognized that such acceptance was helped by the apparent accustomed ease with which Sherlock Holmes made his way towards the beer-swilled bar, Watson himself in tandem with his arms tightly around himself, although unsure what there was left of his property to be purloined. Sherlock Holmes's command proved as influential at the bar itself, a bar-man at once attentive and two tankards produced ahead of other demands all around. Those demands were further ignored in the brief, head-lowered and gestured conversation with which Sherlock Holmes persisted before turning back to his companion.

'Good fortune, Watson. A regular attached to the college itself is in residence in the back parlour.'

'In residence?' queried Watson, curious at the expression.

'The barkeep's words. More resident here than in his own home with his long-suffering wife.'

'A don?'

Sherlock Holmes shook his head. 'Its chief carpenter and handyman, more important in the scheme of things than the headmaster himself. I even have a name. Nutbeam, Colin Nutbeam. A strong old Hampshire name. Let's make his acquaintance.'

Watson again followed his taller companion through the jostle, quickly relieved at the sudden release of pressure in the rear of the establishment. The man they sought hunched isolated on a stool in the corner of the bar, gazing in lost contemplation into a pewter pot grasped between two calloused work-man's hands. His two exposed arms held a gallery of faded tattooes and there was still wood dust clinging to his shirt and rough hessian trousers.

'I don't see such a man as someone of

influence, Holmes. I fear you've been misled.'

'It's a primary mistake to judge by appearances alone, my dear Watson.'

'I wait to be convinced.'

'I pray you will be.'

It had been a long time, more than two years, since Dr Watson had been able to observe at such close proximity Sherlock Holmes actively conducting an investigation and he was at once irritated at himself for how quickly he had forgotten the great detective's expertise. Sherlock Holmes allowed them to be drawn closer and closer by the ebb and flow of custom until finally their quarry was even further isolated, Holmes at the man's right, against the bar, Watson virtually filling the remaining space behind. Nutbeam continued his clairvoyant study of his tankard's reflection.

'The porter's well kept,' opened Sherlock Holmes, savouring his own tankard.

'What do you want?' demanded Nutbeam, not lifting his gaze from his own pot.

'Want?'

There was a near-imperceptible nod, through the serving gap into the larger bar. 'Nathan said you were asking questions.'

'We seek someone with local knowledge.'

'You're not the law. I know the law.'

'We do not represent the law,' confirmed Sherlock Holmes.

'You've got the smell. I can always get the smell.'

'For once, sir, your nose betrays you.'

Nutbeam lifted his pot, seemingly surprised by its near emptiness. Watson saw that in the bar directly before the man were proprietorially carved the initials C. N.

'Could I refill that for you?'

Nutbeam slid his tankard across the bar. 'Cider. Very kind.'

'My interest is in lexicology.'

Nutbeam nodded through the separation between the bars, to two coquettish, low-bodiced women seeking custom from a group of soldiers for their place of employment further along the street. 'Don't try Betty, the blonde one. Suffers the French pox. Doreen's all right though: gone up to be the madam at twenty-eight. Understanding woman, Doreen. Knows what a man wants.'

'Lexicology is the study of language,' explained Sherlock Holmes, patiently. 'I'm given to understand Winchester College has an entire language of its own?'

'Suppose it does?' The man drank noisily and deeply.

'Can you communicate in it?' asked Watson.

'Course I can. Nothing I can't do around the college: that's my job, being able to do everything.'

'What about ziph?'

The lowered head came around sharply. 'You know all about it already!'

'*Of* it,' qualified Sherlock Holmes. 'It's the mastery I seek.'

Nutbeam went back to the inside of his

151

tankard. 'Not an easy task, by any stretch.'

'How difficult is it to become fully accomplished in its understanding?' persisted the doctor.

There was a doubtful shake of the grey head and another perplexed examination of his diminishing tankard. 'Years. It's said men – that's Notions for boy or pupil, by the way – don't truly have it all until they leave. So that's years.'

'How's it learned? asked Sherlock Holmes.

'Passed down, generation to generation. We've been here since the thirteen hundreds, you know?' The rhetorical question was posed with the pride of a man who considered himself personally responsible for the half-a-millenium survival. 'Eton's tried to match us with Notions of its own but it's a poor attempt.'

'I know your admirable history,' said Sherlock Holmes.

'There's actual examina – that's another Notion, using just "a" for "ation" – in the knowledge, set by prefects.'

'Your pot's exhausted again, Mr Nutbeam,' observed Sherlock Holmes. 'Could I invite you to another?'

'That would be extremely generous.' The tankard crossed the bar as if on greased tracks. To ribald applause and shouts of encouragement from the other bar, three soldiers departed with Betty and Doreen. Nutbeam said: 'Whoever has Betty is going to be sorely sorry...' and then sniggered at his unintended joke.

'Is there not a lex...' began Watson, correcting himself halfway through the question. '...not a written account of such uniqueness?'

'Word books,' announced the artisan, shortly.

'Word books!' echoed Sherlock Holmes. 'You mean there are dictionaries of the vocabulary!'

'Word books,' insisted Nutbeam, pedantically. 'Lists written by men, over the ages.'

'How many?' pressed Watson.

'Lots. Secure in the archives.'

'Do you have access to them?'

'Don't need to. Know it all apart from the Greek and Latin. Too clever for me, that is.'

'How difficult would it be, gaining sight of such material?'

'Impossible,' insisted Nutbeam. 'College treasure, they are.'

'A truly interested and honest person whose pastime was the study of words, as ours is, would be extremely grateful for the guarded opportunity to examine such books,' declared Sherlock Holmes.

'College never lets anyone near them. Treasure, like I said.'

'But there is no bar to you?'

'Course not.'

'Are they regularly consulted?'

'They're in the archives. Preserved.'

'As they rightly should be,' said Sherlock Holmes. 'But would it not be possible, in return for our appreciation, which would be generously shown, for you briefly to acquire them for our perusal upon our personal, deposited guarantee of absolute safety?'

'More than my future employment's worth, sir!'

'Your pot is once more exhausted.' Sherlock Holmes relieved the man of it, gesturing for a refill to the barkeep.

'I'm sorry I have not been able to help you gentlemen more.'

'On the contrary, Mr Nutbeam. You've been extremely patient and even more helpful. One hundred guineas was the sum I had in mind as a guarantee of safety.'

Colin Nutbeam once more sought guidance over several moments from the murky interior of his pot. 'The penalty, upon discovery, would be severe in the extreme.'

'And twenty-five guineas for each tome my colleague, who is well versed in both Latin and Greek, was able to examine. How many do you estimate there are?'

'Six I'd say: six at least.' Despite the continued lubrication, there was a strained hoarseness in Nutbeam's voice, which he quickly drank further to relieve.

'One hundred and fifty guineas, as well as the deposit guarantee,' enumerated Sherlock Holmes, unnecessarily.

'At the furthest end of College Street, towards the water meadows, there are the remains of Bishop Wolvesey's Palace. I shall be there at eight of tomorrow morning.'

'And so, Mr Nutbeam, shall we.'

The noise of revelry quickly receded behind them once they re-entered the Inner Close through Cheyney Court. Watson said: 'The man's an obvious villain and curmudgeon, Holmes!'

'But to our every advantage, Watson. He'll not endanger such easy profits attempting any duplicity.'

'What did you mean by reference to my knowledge of Latin and Greek?'

'Your understanding of it in duplication, of course.'

'Duplication!'

'The profession of the original monks of this cathedral was copying manuscripts, which is what I require you to do, Watson. I want you to compile a single volume, from all those that are to be made available to you.'

'Why not openly approach the college authorities yourself? Your reputation would surely gain easy access to everything you seek.'

'And prompt curiosity as to my reason for making the request, which cannot be allowed. The very essence of everything we are doing – Sebastian is doing – is the utmost secrecy, at the positive insistence of a cabinet minister himself.'

'Which opens us to the legal accusation of theft and bribery!'

'There is no intent permanently to deprive, so there's no case to answer for theft,' soothed Sherlock Holmes. 'And Nutbeam will never admit to receiving a penny piece in recompense, because it damns him out of his own mouth. He can smell a copper, I can smell a wily rascal. We were well met.'

The return of the Hemditch party to New York's Penn Station was as smoothly organized as their departure, although the private section of the platform was more crowded, not just by Oscar Lepecheron's black-lacquered and initial-identified carriage, in which it emerged Lowell Smithlane was to be carried, but by two from Julius Hemditch's stable, one to return Sebastian and Hemditch to Fifth Avenue, with a small but no less well-appointed gig to take Laura directly to an immigrant refuge she had disclosed to Sebastian during the journey from Pittsburgh that she had set up in the Battery. The parting had commenced over the final New Jersey miles with renewed assurances from Lowell Smithlane that he would secure Sebastian an invitation to the German Embassy, coupled with the demand for Sebastian to visit Smithlane's Long Island estate 'to meet like-minded businessmen such as ourselves.' Oscar Lepecheron pressed a visiting card upon Sebastian with the suggestion that Sebastian make contact within the coming week, which he undertook to do.

Awaiting Sebastian in his allocated office was Mycroft Holmes's acknowledgement of receiving – and understanding – the message he had sent on arrival, despite which Sebastian conceded they had been too quick agreeing to communicate in the language of Winchester College. As he mentally rehearsed and composed his new messages Sebastian realized that the vocabulary available in Notions alone was insufficient. There would need to be far wider use of the vowel-doubling and medial-'g'-inserting ziph slang, with the possible further addition of an even earlier word trick in the school's history, employing the suffix '-ster' to the end of a word to denote an identity or occupation. He had not ruled out, either, another obscuring variation, switching and changing vowels to render words unintelligible to anyone without the key. None of the differing methods required definite or indefinite articles, nor prepositions nor conjunctions, which improved the required secrecy, but with no way of alerting London to the cipher, Sebastian was concerned his uncle would be as confused as any eavesdropper.

Sebastian's uncertainty decided his first message and as he encoded it there was a slight relief at his being able to compose it almost entirely in the language Mycroft was expecting. 'Do you understand my messages?' was enciphered as: *Underconstumble selfsters entry task?*

'I need to know the text of Churchill's letter to Julius Hemditch' came as: *Neegeed teegxt ostiarius vessel hoststster*, with which he was far less satisfied. He did not think the ziphs were sufficiently disguised and hoped he wasn't expecting too much for Mycroft to interpret

Churchill as *ostiarius*, which in the first of two Notions definitions referred to a college prefect or doorman with commanding powers.

'I am hoping for an invitation to the German Embassy in Washington' became *Selfest hoogpee wardens om edward wickhams chamber can*. In Notions, *warden's om* was the abbreviation for *custos omnes ad carnam invitat*, or the Warden's invitation to a feast. Edward Wickham was the Reverend E. C. Wickham, a mid-eighteenth-century don after whom the room in which he taught German is named, and Sebastian's suggested phrase for Washington had already been accepted by his uncle.

Sebastian chose *Gips uupgoon pax socius wickham jupiters* for 'I have focus on a group of pro-German comrades'. In the lexicon of Notions, *gips* meant to focus or see and was named after a one-time pupil of that surname who was short-sighted. *Pax* was a particular or intimate friend, emphasized by *socius*, which defined as comrade, and Sebastian hoped *wickham* would identify the German allegiance. In Wykehamese, a *jupiter* was a notorious villain.

Sebastian's message alerting his uncle to a fuller account being aboard the *Mauretania*, which he knew from Denning's timetable was sailing for England within twenty-four hours, read: *Poll sack maauureegeetaaniiaa*.

Sebastian sat for a long time examining the embossed business card of Oscar Lepecheron, reflecting yet again upon the invitation to become part of the banker's steel-mill consortium. Without actual, final commitment he could explore it much further, both to better establish his credentials as a speculative investor in the minds of the men he had already met, and through their recommendation to gain the acceptance of others to whom Lowell Smithlane appeared eager to introduce him. It was an opportunity to be taken, which required the transference of funds more than sufficient to back up his subterfuge. Sebastian wearily pulled yet another telegraph form towards him but abruptly stopped. There was no Notions substitution for the name and business details of the Belgian banker. Nor was there the need to encode it. There was no governmentally identifiable call-back from Mycroft's telegraph address. And as a financier considering American investment it was totally understandable that he should move resources from England to where he intended to do business in the United States: *not* to do so, in fact, would arouse curiosity.

Sebastian's final hesitation was over the amount necessary for him to be accorded the proper level of credibility, but he just as easily accepted that the figure did not have to appear final, either. He demanded £4,000,000 but described it as an initial tranche which might need to be increased. He named Oscar Lepecheron, who was listed on his card as the president, to be the bank's named recipient of the funds.

Sebastian's rereading of his every message was interrupted by a light tapping at the study door and only when he responded did he realize that it was already dark outside and that unthinkingly he had put on the lights.

At the door Laura Hemditch said: 'We've been waiting … dinner?'

'This is unforgivable! I am so sorry,' apologized Sebastian, hurriedly rising. The day would be much later in England – people would be asleep – and there was little purpose in transmitting his various communiques. It was a conscious decision to leave them on the desk, the final, open request for money uppermost.

But people were still awake and working in London, although there were only Mycroft and Churchill at that night's dinner at the same, private room in the St James's club at which the First Lord of the Admiralty had first met Sebastian and Sherlock Holmes.

'I'd expected something from America by now!' protested Churchill. The meal was long over and he was on his third generous brandy.

'This was never something that could be achieved in hours or days,' defended Mycroft. He was no longer drinking, not even coffee.

'That Cabinet meeting was a parody of pusillanimity.'

Mycroft stirred with the familiar irritation at the other man's attempt yet again to inveigle him even more positively into a Cabinet-upheaving plot. 'At least it's been brought to the table.'

'To absolutely no effect! Grey should have personally gone to Washington. Russia could be stealing a march on us.'

'Our St Petersburg embassy haven't confirmed that suggestion,' reminded Mycroft. 'And if they did agree a pact, we'd be a beneficiary.'

'Not if we don't know each and every detail of that pact,' disputed Churchill. 'We've got to be in the vanguard, not trailing in the wake.'

Mycroft decided it was time to end the evening. Churchill was becoming maudlin. 'I'm sure we'll hear from Sebastian soon.'

'You're sure it's too great a risk to ask Sherlock Holmes to go, even at this late stage?'

'Absolutely,' insisted Mycroft. 'We've chosen a course of action and we've got to stick to it now.'

'Not if it proves ineffective,' insisted Churchill. 'Let me know the moment we hear from New York. And more importantly, *what* we hear.'

Eleven

Sebastian Holmes rose before six, his day firmly fixed in his mind. His abandonment of his messages the previous night had been anything but casual. He knew precisely the order and the apparent disarray in which he had left everything except the last message, in numbered order. On the uppermost remaining folio of the message pad he had left a minute, seemingly inadvertent pencil dash to identify that last page, to know at once if it had been removed for the imprint of what had been written on its preceding leaf to be traced into legibility. The pencil-marked sheet was intact and none of the messages had been moved or rearranged. There had been no incoming cables during the night.

With the benefit of overnight reflection Sebastian reconsidered each individual encipherment before eventually deciding he could not improve them without risking further misunderstanding. It took him another hour to transmit it all to London and afterwards Sebastian filed everything in his allocated cabinet.

He spent another hour composing the promised shipborne report, in which he set out in greater detail his suspicions from the voyage and what he considered relevant from the Pittsburgh visit, particularly his intention to involve himself as far as possible in Lepecheron's steel-mill consortium. He also repeated his request for the contents – an actual copy, if possible – of Winston Churchill's letter to Julius Hemditch and for any information that might be obtainable upon the banker and Lowell Smithlane from any possible English business affiliates.

Sebastian called the direct line listed on Oscar Lepecheron's card but was answered by a woman who said the banker was already in conference. She appeared, however, to recognize Sebastian's name and at once offered a 3 p.m. vacancy in the banker's diary, which left Sebastian with the entire morning personally to deliver his letter to the *Mauritania*'s captain.

Sebastian still only knew his way around the rambling mansion to a limited extent but from the previous night in the chandeliered dining room he was confident of locating the nearby breakfast room overlooking an inner, fountained courtyard. What he had not expected was to find Laura still there, although she had clearly finished eating. An assortment of silver chafing servers remained on their heated trays, flanked by matching silver coffee and tea pots.

'I said last night ... I didn't expect...' he began to apologize again, to her waved-away dismissal.

'Daddy didn't disturb you before he left

163

because you told us last night how much early business you had to conduct with London: he's very aware of the communication problems of the world's time differences.' She was wearing a full-skirted dress that in the intruding courtyard sun changed with her movements from the palest pink to white and then back again. She sat with an American confidence, with her chair pushed back from the table, one arm crooked over its back.

How was Julius Hemditch, a man far above the day-to-day commerce of selling his wares, very aware of time differences around the world? wondered Sebastian. Maybe even more importantly, why? Sebastian sat immediately beside Laura, to the matching attentiveness of the white-gloved butler who had served them at dinner. Sebastian refused anything but coffee from the buffet sideboard. 'Still no reason nor excuse for me to abuse your hospitality.'

'Of doing which you are not being accused. My father's offices are conveniently close to my refuge for us often to lunch. His invitation is for you to join us if your commitments permit.'

'Your father is being extremely solicitous.' As she was, in turn: almost claustrophobically so.

'You could scarcely have arrived with higher recommendation.'

An insistence that had been repeated to the extreme of being laboured the previous night, increasing his curiosity as to whether she had been alerted to his true purpose for being in America. 'My business today does indeed take me downtown.'

'Then everything fits. We can travel together!'

'I can be set off just short of your destination,' proposed Sebastian. 'I have but to deliver a message to partners in England. You can give me the address to which I must come.'

'I'd hoped personally to show you my refuge,' frowned Laura. 'If your business is to be so brief I can wait.'

Sebastian hesitated. 'I wouldn't wish to inconvenience you.'

'It's no inconvenience whatsoever.'

There was no alternative but inconceivably rude refusal, as inconceivable as his leaving Laura on the daytime near-bedlam of the dockside. 'Once more I have to thank you for your kindness.'

Sebastian's name was at once recognized at the Cunard offices and an officer summoned to escort them both through the liner's embarkation bustle. Laura had become animated at learning their destination and at once engaged the officer in such intense enquiry that the man offered a short guided tour which Laura at once countered with a request to see the accommodation and facilities for immigrants on the east-to-west Atlantic crossings. Sebastian assured the officer he could find his own way to the bridge.

There was a passing similarity of design and decor with the *Lusitania*, which brought his outward voyage fleetingly to mind. Would the liner on its next voyage bring from his uncle a reply to the letter he was about to entrust to the captain of its sister ship? The *Lusitania* would have reached Liverpool by now: be preparing, in fact, for yet another Atlantic crossing. There would scarcely be time for his uncle to reply by sea mail to that morning's telegrams, although relaying Winston Churchill's introductory letter to Julius Hemditch would simply require it to be securely sealed and conveyed northwards to the port.

Captain Pettit was a man so short and slight it was tempting to invoke his only just misspelled name in French as an appropriate pun. He bustled rather than moved, immediately leaving the bridge in control of his first officer personally to take Sebastian to his quarters to deposit Sebastian's letter in his private safe. Sebastian apologized for not knowing how regularly he would need the convenience, which Pettit dismissed as immaterial: Sir Alfred Booth's instructions were that his captains were at Sebastian's disposal.

Laura offered no apology for keeping Sebastian waiting for thirty minutes at their arranged rendezvous outside the purser's office, at once launching into fulsome praise of Cunard's steerage facilities compared to those of some other shipping companies she had inspected. In some the refugees were expected to provide their own food and cohabit in communal dormitories, kept behind barred and locked gates, away from any contact with higher-fare-paying passengers and with few medical facilities except in the direst of emergencies. The German and Italian ships were the worst, some so bad she had reported them to the New York port authority.

Once more Sebastian was quickly in the discordant, shouting hubbub of downtown New York, held by the distinct contrast between a polyglot society vibrantly living its life, European like, on the streets and pavements and the existence scarcely two miles distant of those who lived behind shuttered doors in the secluded gentility of Fifth Avenue and the Astor-dominated castle on Park Avenue. Sebastian was conscious, too, of the apparent recognition, sometimes even gestures of acknowledgement, of Laura Hemditch's carriage, even before the mono-gram would have identified its occupant.

That recognition became open adulation at the charity home itself. Three men stopped working in the garden to shout greetings and one hurried ahead to announce her arrival. Before they reached the buildings there were smiling faces at every window. Sebastian was introduced to the staff, a male administrator and three women, one of whom was detailed to show him the noise-filled premises while Laura and the man closeted themselves inside a ground-floor office. Some of the larger upstairs rooms on the first and second

167

floors had been subdivided, to provide more sleeping accommodation, and all were occupied by whole families. A wall had been removed on the ground floor to increase the size of a communal dining room and opposite there was a communal lounge. Next to it was a small infirmary, its three beds all occupied, two by children suffering the sort of wheezing cough associated in Sebastian's mind with consumption. The kitchens appeared as spotless as the medical provision and nowhere was there the institutional smell that Sebastian had anticipated. Every seat and desk was occupied in the adjoining classroom, adults sitting with their children, for a lesson in basic English being delivered by a fourth member of staff. Her bilingual instructions confirmed the awareness that had registered with Sebastian from the beginning of his tour.

On this occasion Laura was waiting for him. She asked the coachman to make a detour to show Sebastian a similar mansion, the garden of which backed on to that of the one he had just seen.

'The owner knows my need and is elevating the price accordingly. And even before I've made any application the city authorities have let it be known planning permission won't be automatic: they don't want the embarrassment of my having an establishment – including what could then be considered a small hospital – of the size it would be. I shall succeed, of course.'

'I'm sure you will,' said Sebastian. 'Your refuge is open to all?'

Laura turned sideways, frowning towards him. 'Yes.'

'There seemed a noticeable predominance of German. I speak the language.'

'At the moment the proportion is just over seventy per cent. I've already told you that conditions aboard German immigrant ships are among the worst. It's a scandal that should be exposed.'

It should indeed, although in Europe, not here, thought Sebastian.

Their meeting place greatly surprised Sebastian, who had firmly established in his mind Julius Hemditch – although not perhaps his daughter – to be a man so demonstrably proud of his financial achievements and power that every occasion had to display evidence of it. New York's fish market wafted its presence before they reached Fulton Street. The restaurant was actually over a wet-fish vending establishment and directly opposite a trading warehouse still hosing down after that morning's dawn business. Hemditch was already there. Their table seating put Laura alongside Sebastian, with the older man facing them. Laura was still consumed by her inspection of the *Mauritania*'s migrant accommodation and over oysters, scallops and lobster extolled the comparison with other ships in far greater detail than she had earlier to Sebastian.

Turning to him, at the end of her account,

Laura said: 'The officer who so kindly showed me the ship's facilities imagines you a man of great importance, Mr Holmes, able as you seem to be to use such a vessel, and others in the fleet, as your personal postal service.'

Damn the man and his desire to ingratiate, thought Sebastian. 'I have business associations with some on the Cunard board: it's an advantage not to be neglected.'

Sebastian celebrated the unaccustomed freedom of being alone by walking to Oscar Lepecheron's Wall Street bank, the grid streeted layout of the city fixed in his mind, and employing the time he had in hand to reflect upon what he was committed to do. It had not been until lunch that it had occurred to Sebastian that the ruse hopefully to discover more about the composition and allegiances of the steel-plant expansion consortium was likely to offend, if not positively outrage, Julius Hemditch. Laura's presence provided the excuse for his not warning the man in advance but it had been more than remiss not to have considered how a genuine business proposal might be endangered if Lepecheron guaranteed the required finance in anticipation of his falsely promised involvement. There was some reassurance in the fact that Hemditch had in the first place played him off against Lepecheron as a potential alternative backer but Sebastian suspected Hemditch would regard that as scant defence

170

if his project faltered.

Sebastian was still politely early but was admitted at once. The saturnine Lepecheron, resplendent in his frock-coated banker's uniform, was at a desk expansive enough to complete the triangle between two corner-placed panoramic windows looking out over a grassed and fountain-playing inner courtyard tranquilly gated from the outside city.

The Belgian rose at Sebastian's entry, guiding him away from the official section of the suite to a side annex in which only the seemingly out-of-place conference table betrayed the room's true function from the appearance of an opulent, velvet-draped drawing room, complete with easy chairs, coffee tables and freshly vased, long-stemmed white and red roses. Sebastian believed he saw a family resemblance to Lepecheron in two oils – one of a man, the other of a woman – in ornate gilt frames, side by side over a dormant black-marbled fireplace. The por-trayed man wore an indistinguishable but heavily bemedalled military uniform and held beneath his arm a plume-surmounted domed helmet that reminded Sebastian of the head-pieces with which he was familiar not just from French but from German art galleries and museums.

'Can I offer you anything: coffee, something more?'

'I've just lunched more than adequately with Julius.' In England he would have auto-matically referred to his host by the man's

171

surname: he was at least adapting instinctively to the familiarity of America.

Lepecheron nodded, as if he already knew. 'I was not expecting your call so soon.'

'There was little to turn over in my mind after visiting Pittsburgh and having had the opportunity of our discussions.'

'You are convinced of the expansion's viability then?'

Sebastian decided it was the moment to prepare his eventual avoidance. 'Viability is scarcely a consideration, against the financial soundness of Hemditch's corporation. I still believe, however, that there is the need for an independent cost assessment: I fear there is a substantial underestimate.'

'An independent cost assessment would surely be an agreement condition.'

Yet again he was being tested, wearily accepted Sebastian. 'One upon which my consortium would insist: I am setting out what might appear to be the obvious to avoid any misunderstanding between us. And to that end, to ensure you accept my seriousness in the matter, I have today telegraphed instructions to London for £4,000,000, which I convert to be around $19,400,000, to be transferred to an account I wish to open here, in your bank.'

Lepecheron nodded, his face impassive. 'Would such a sum represent a positive, contractual commitment on your part?'

Sebastian at once saw the way greatly to bolster his intended withdrawal. 'I have also

172

today sent a full report to my consortium colleagues, strongly recommending their approval. I obviously can't commit contractually until that formality but with the financial proof of the good faith of my group I feel during the time it will take for their response we can go much more fully into the proposal.'

'I'm afraid the situation is not as it was,' announced the banker, his face still blank.

'How has it changed?' And why, so quickly? Sebastian wondered.

'I took your refusal during our return from Pittsburgh to be a positive one. I have today expanded the bank's consortium to compensate for the additional expenditure we both agree to be necessary.' The smile was bleak. 'I considered us still to be in competition and did not wish to lose the march.'

Sebastian acknowledged it was as close to being plausible as his planned excuse of his own fictitious consortium refusing to let him proceed, but he did not for a moment believe additional finance could have been called in so quickly. Lepecheron and whomever else the banker was in association with had decided against his inclusion, most probably at that morning's uninterruptable meeting. A hard-headed but understandable business decision? Or the action of a group of men with something to hide from someone in whom there was insufficient trust? 'I am disappointed.'

'As I was by your earlier rejection,' returned Lepecheron. He shrugged. 'But such things happen in business. I am honoured that you have chosen my bank and assure you your account will be dealt with by me personally. And of course I will introduce you to any further business opportunities in which I feel you could be interested.'

After quick rejection came even quicker dismissal, Sebastian recognized. At least he was spared any embarrassment with Julius Hemditch. The requested financial bait would be as safe in Lepecheron's keeping as in any other bank and to redirect it would show petulance. 'Perhaps we will meet again socially during my time here.'

'I would enjoy that,' said Lepecheron, unconvincingly.

Once more Sebastian decided initially to walk, even more than before needing the opportunity to mull over what had occurred. It *had* to be rejection, a positive closing out of someone in whom they had insufficient trust, despite the inherent credibility of Julius Hemditch. But introduced as a potential financial rival, qualified Sebastian, objectively. So was that insufficient trust confined to business? Or did it go beyond, to the use – but more importantly the customer – to which that business was going to be directed? Too many unanswerable questions. And having been rejected, did those questions matter any more? Better, surely, to take advantage of other opportunities that hopefully remained open.

The resolve reached, Sebastian became

abruptly impatient to get back to Fifth Avenue, hailing a carriage plying for casual hire. At the Hemditch mansion he went directly to his assigned workplace, relieved that Lowell Smithlane was still in his office. Sebastian was put through at once to the freight line owner, who assured him the Long Island offer remained.

'There's a house party this weekend. By then I'll probably know whether I've been able to extend my invitation to the German Embassy to include you,' said the man. 'There's extensive stables, if you ride. And there's a lot of room: bring someone if you choose.'

'I'd enjoy a ride but I'm travelling alone,' accepted Sebastian.

'Come early, for us to talk.'

Sebastian detected the sounds of movement in the adjoining study before he emerged to find Hemditch at his desk.

'I'm glad to find you alone,' said Sebastian. 'How much of my purpose here is Laura aware of?'

'None,' replied Hemditch, shortly. 'All she knows is of Winston's introduction. Obviously I don't wish her to be in any way involved. Thank you, incidentally, for the courtesy you are showing her.'

'My meeting this afternoon was with Oscar Lepecheron.'

'I know,' disclosed the mill owner. 'Your appointment was relayed to him while he and I were still together this morning.'

The meeting that could not be interrupted, again remembered Sebastian. 'On our way back from Pittsburgh he invited me to join the expansion consortium. I'd hoped to take the discussion further, in the hope of finding its other members. Today he refused me.'

Hemditch smiled. 'This morning we signed the loan contract for the full amount I wanted.'

'In the belief that I was his competition?'

'Business, Mr Holmes!' lectured the multi-millionaire. 'It was an advantage and I took it. None of the consortium are people you seek.'

Hemditch had more than repaid himself for whatever assistance he was providing, accepted Sebastian. The man certainly wasn't owed more.

Dr Watson heard the lamenting strains of Sherlock Holmes's violin as he climbed the stairs of 221b Baker Street to the familiar first-floor quarters he had once shared with the detective, frowning at the recollection from those times that such melancholy musical reverie often accompanied the man's trifling with artificial stimuli. Watson strode into the room and was further concerned that for several moments Sherlock Holmes played on, although open-eyed, seemingly oblivious to his unhesitant entry. The eventual awareness came with the briefest impression of the man being startled.

' "Meditation", from *Thaïs*,' identified Sherlock Holmes. 'So very easy to become totally absorbed in such sad beauty.'

'I recognized it,' said Watson. 'I've heard you play it often enough. How are you?' Sherlock Holmes had left him to copy the college word books, insisting he needed to be close to his brother in London, instantly to learn of any communication from America.

'The bath chair is the deception, Watson. I am as fit today as I was at twenty.' Sherlock Holmes carefully replaced the Stradivarius in its velvet-lined case, additionally covering it in a silk kerchief before securing the lid.

The doctor had privately to concede there was no medically discernible evidence of his friend having once more lapsed. 'That's good to hear. What news from Sebastian?'

'None, as of last night. I await contact from Mycroft. You have made a Notions lexicon?'

'Which I have also independently verified,' declared Watson, triumphantly.

'How so?'

'I warned you that man Nutbeam was a blackguard.'

'And I told you I was well aware of his being one but that it was of little consequence if we succeeded.'

'I finished my copying early yesterday and engaged myself enjoying the city: visiting the cathedral as well as viewing King Arthur's supposed Round Table, which I had promised myself to do. Late in the day found me back near The Wykeham Arms, in College Street itself. There I located the school's most excellent bookshop, P. & G. Wells. And

177

discovered in it a complete and properly printed dictionary of Notions entitled *Winchester Word Book*, created by an R. G. K. Wrench, which I was able to buy for less than a guinea and which would, had I known of its existence earlier, have saved me many hours of fruitless labour. I challenged Nutbeam, of course. The scoundrel denied any knowledge of its existence, which has to be a blatant lie.'

'We now have the facility to be doubly sure of our translations,' observed Sherlock Holmes, philosophically.

'Which does indeed need to be doubly checked,' acknowledged Watson. 'I fear the villain has intruded things of his own invention, in no way connected with the true language. He was adamant I accompany him to the hostelry, where he insisted the phrase "one in" was the recognized manner in which college dons order their ale and which he had me do. Only when I failed to hear others using the expression and went back alone this morning, before leaving, did I discover from the barkeep it has nothing whatsoever to do with Notions but signifies that a drink is being purchased for later consumption, upon demand. Every time I replenished the rascal's pot I was also purchasing a second for him to imbibe later.'

Sherlock Holmes busied himself storing the violin in its regular corner space, which conveniently kept his back to his friend and so concealed his amusement. 'What with losing your wallet and your timepiece,

Watson, your sojourn in Winchester has hardly been a memorable experience, has it?'

'Visiting the cathedral was extremely pleasurable.'

'You deserve some recompense for your valiant efforts, for which I am most grateful,' declared Sherlock Holmes, taking a box from the mantelpiece and offering it to the other man. 'It's a full hunter, suitably engraved, to replace that which was stolen from you.'

Watson accepted the gift, snapping open the watch case the moment he took it from its box. ' "To J. W., my truest friend and chronicler. S. H.," ' he read aloud, looking up. 'This I shall treasure for the rest of my life, Holmes. I am truly and deeply moved.'

'Perhaps you should leave it safely at home if we have occasion again to visit Winchester,' suggested the detective.

'It is not a visit I intend repeating,' insisted the doctor, determinedly.

Winston Churchill was silent for several moments after Mycroft Holmes finished reading out his translation of Sebastian's messages, clipping and then carefully lighting his cigar. At last he said: 'I withdraw my earlier doubts. It would seem that your nephew has been most industrious.'

'We shall be better able to gauge that when his fuller account arrives,' said Mycroft. 'There are certainly some intriguing indications.'

179

'I am surprised he considers such a substantial sum necessary to establish his financial bona fides,' qualified Churchill.

'Is providing it going to be a problem?' asked Mycroft, worried at a change of heart.

'Problems will arise if he is tricked out of it without discovering what he's there to establish,' said the Admiralty supremo.

'I'll stress that in my sea-borne reply,' undertook Mycroft. 'There's also the matter of your prior correspondence with Julius Hemditch.'

'Which is an impudent request! That correspondence was a private matter between myself and Hemditch. It is sufficient for Holmes to know I recommended him in the highest terms, as a result of which he would appear to be receiving unrestricted assistance. For which he should be grateful.'

Mycroft shifted, uneasily. 'I sincerely believe my nephew would not have made such a request without good cause.'

'No copy was kept, for obvious reasons. And Hemditch was asked to destroy the original, which, knowing the man as well as I do, he will by now have done. Let Holmes judge the contents by the courtesy with which he is being treated.' Churchill straightened behind his desk. 'Let's move on! I want you to search out any diplomatic exchanges over the last year concerning Cruiser Rules and the Declaration of London upon the international laws governing naval warfare.'

'I believed we had already discussed the regulations.'

'Not any diplomatic exchanges,' corrected Churchill. 'I want to be prepared for everything.'

Twelve

Sebastian was confused – in one instance profoundly angered – by the answering telegrams he received from his uncle. Mycroft Holmes followed the precedent Sebastian set in his own transmissions, in return dividing his replies to the separate messages to ensure their clarity. All Sebastian's communications were comprehensible (*underconstumble*), re-assured Mycroft, and Sebastian's requested money (*soy*) was being transferred, although Sebastian was to restrain himself (*kept*) in its dispensation until he received Mycroft's fuller response (*vulgas*) aboard the next east–west crossing of the *maauureegtaaniiaa*, providing Sebastian with an arrival date of his first detailed communication. Mycroft's impression was that Sebastian appeared to be hopefully insinuating (*deanesley*) himself into a possible German-orientated clique (*wickham pushsters*). He was to congratulate (*junket*) himself on what he was achieving.

181

Sebastian's anger was at Churchill's refusal to disclose the contents of his introductory letter to Hemditch (*ostiarius reejgeects teegxts vessel hostster*) despite Sebastian remembering the determination of the First Lord of the Admiralty against any provable connection with his American mission. It went beyond his being sent blind into an unknown arena: he was, in addition, being pitched into battle with his sword arm secured behind his back, unsure of a host apparently intent – maybe on instructions – upon monitoring his every move and action. But to what practical purpose! There was none that made Churchill's recalcitrance understandable, apart from the man's insistence on remaining steadfastly unassociated. Which by itself, even taking into account Churchill's self-absorbed political ambitions, was surely insufficient excuse or reason? What then was an explanation even half comprehensible? Like so many other questions, it was one to which Sebastian did not have a solution. Increasingly he was coming to realize that the only uncertainty to which he did have an answer was that becoming – or more accurately attempting to become – his father's self-appointed inheritor was not proving to be as easy as he had imagined, an awareness as irritating as so much else with which Sebastian felt himself confronted.

That irritation was almost at once compounded by a telegram direct from his father's personal Baker Street telegraph, which in full read, *selfster nogo loonggeer ex trums slow carthage ferk domun entry pax nunky examina*, and which translated as, 'I am no longer unprepared or ignorant of the Wykehamist vernacular, in which we can now communicate without the need for your uncle's translation.' The combination of the ziph slang with necessarily interpretative Notions at once told Sebastian that his father had not only gained access to some word books, which he hadn't anticipated, but that by so doing – and by sending such a message – his father saw himself now capable of controlling the American investigation from afar. Sebastian supposed that, of everyone, he should not have underestimated Sherlock Holmes. In his brief acknowledgement Sebastian praised the quickness (*speedy spec*) of his father's resourcefulness but eased his initial annoyance by acknowledging his father's newly acquired understanding of the Wykeham exchanges did not require him to communicate any more fully than he originally intended. Sebastian also decided to keep for his return letter on the *Mauretania* the suggestion of using as propaganda the immigrant condition on German ships.

With time to be filled before his outing to Long Island Sebastian accompanied Laura to a performance of *Aïda* at the Metropolitan Opera House and at her request, on another day, actually acted as interpreter for a German family newly arrived at the refuge, because her normal translator was ill. On

183

another, after setting out for the Metropolitan Museum of Art – feeling uncomfortably pretentious carrying the undetectable swordstick – Sebastian changed his mind and went instead to the *New York Times* library to search for newspaper references to his host, Oscar Lepecheron or the freight line owner. What he discovered, through the library's system of cross-indexing, was a substantial file upon Laura Hemditch and her immigrant charity work. There were accounts of her long-running facilities dispute with the New York City authorities and two articles in which she was outspokenly critical of conditions aboard unidentified immigrant ships. There were also several supportive acknowledgements of what her refuge achieved. One was from an American Pan-German Association describing her as a benefactor. The Italian ambassador was quoted as calling her a friend of his country. In quite a lot of the stories Laura's father was listed as one of America's few remaining independent steel millionaires.

There were no cuttings whatsoever upon Oscar Lepecheron but a dozen upon Lowell Smithlane, the majority upon his family-history obsession. His founding of an organization named the New Americans was recorded, as well as a nationally established American Historical Association. Five of the articles were accompanied by photographs of Smithlane at social events with people described as having similar interests. Julius

Hemditch did not feature in any of them but Sebastian copied the names of those who did. He also noted that although they were described as social occasions no women appeared in any of the photographs. Few of the men were smiling, either. One picture showed Smithlane by himself in what was identified as his ancestral museum in Long Island, which Sebastian assumed to be the intended highpoint of his weekend visit.

Unbidden but not so swiftly rejected, one of his father's many dictums intruded into Sebastian's mind: *lateral thinking is often more progressive than attempting always to conjecture ahead.* What was the lateral direction from the musty-odoured newsprint on the research desk in front of him? Praise for Laura Hemditch from an organization named as the American Pan German Association connected in Sebastian's mind with her more specific criticism of German immigrant-ship conditions. Would there be any more complaints from other sources, to include in his intended propaganda suggestion to London? And what function did the American Pan-German Association have?

It only took the librarian thirty minutes to retrieve from the newspaper's archives all the cuttings on the association as well as identifying the largest proportion of those immigrant ships to be those of the Hamburg – America Line. There was no openly ascribed complaint about the conditions on the Hamburg – America Line in any newspaper coverage,

185

which was a disappointment quickly lifted when Sebastian switched to the second, manila-enveloped package. It was, again, the newspaper's index that brought up the American Pan-German Association, although not in a published article but in the withheld research material attached to it as an addendum by the writer, who had compiled what had to be at least a 2,000 word examination and identification of influence-manipulating organizations being established in the United States by Germany. The accusing analysis isolated the American Embargo Conference and the National Peace Council as Berlin-financed groups but the APGA was endorsed with the author's notation of 'insufficient documentary proof'.

The entire essay was predicated upon a demand in the House of Representatives by a Delaware Congressman named Allan G. Grant for a Congressional committee inquiry into such groups, with the man's promise to bring before that committee conclusive proof of Germany's determination to swing American public opinion in its favour in the event of a European conflict.

Yet another cross-index recorded the accidental death in a weekend hunting accident of Representative Allan G. Grant, on the eve of the investigatory committee being convened. An inquest was told how Grant had strayed from his companions, none of whom witnessed the accident, but of forensic evidence establishing that he had stumbled

186

and fallen disastrously upon his own unbroken gun. The drug-and-alcohol-induced
suicide of the article's terminally cancer-
suffering writer, Peter Pullinger, one month
after that of Grant, had prompted a half-page
obituary upon a man described as one of the
best investigatory journalists in American
newspaper history. His most recent involvement with Grant was recorded, together with
the police insistence that as well as there
being no suspicious circumstances in either
death, none of Grant's threatened exposing
material was found amongst the effects of
either man.

Circumstantial proof of nothing but coincidence impossible to ignore, decided Sebastian. So why had it been ignored? Where was
Peter Pullinger's successor, an unconvinced
investigator at least curious enough to query
two such closely connected fatalities? Wasn't
he, Sebastian asked himself, supposed to be a
determined, unconvinced investigator? There
was a flush of satisfaction at possibly finding
a way forward without any reliance upon anyone.

And initially that way was conveniently at
hand. From what he had just assimilated
Sebastian knew the offices of the Hamburg–
America Line were at 1123, Broadway. And
those of the American Pan-German Association were less than a block away, on Times
Square, which Sebastian added to his list of
curious coincidences.

Upon reaching the appropriate section of

Broadway, however, Sebastian was unsure how to proceed and so he didn't. Once more remembering – again less resistantly – his father's advice about observation and the importance of isolating trifles, Sebastian installed himself in the window seat of a cafe almost directly opposite the German shipping office and endured three cups of inferior coffee to watch the comings and goings upon the other side of the street. An immediate surprise, which he partially countered by reminding himself that it *was* a busy travel office, was quite simply at the number of people involved in those comings and goings. The main, revolving door constantly rotated and the two adjoining side doors opened and closed far more frequently than any of the office blocks or customer-reliant businesses on either side.

When Sebastian felt he could no longer occupy his place without arousing unwanted attention he left, no longer feeling pretentions with the swordstick, to walk the short distance to what had been described in the newspaper cuttings as an organization to encourage friendship between America and Germany, as well as to provide a source of contact for German immigrants. Here there was no convenient cafe. The alternative was a street bench. There was not the excuse of it being a travel-related building to account for what Sebastian again considered an unusually high number of people entering and leaving. It seemed an insufficient conclusion after less than an hour's scrutiny but when he finally quit his bench Sebastian had an uneasy feeling that there had been something else that should have registered with him but which he had failed to recognize.

Sebastian's excursion to Long Island was a black against white contrast with that to Pittsburgh and not simply because this time Sebastian travelled from Penn Station in a scheduled first-class carriage, not a private railroad car. This day's journey was through flat, barely undulating countryside dotted with original Dutch windmills and salt-box houses and at the stops at Sag Harbour and Montauk, before the train turned northwards towards the Sound, Sebastian had the panorama of the huge cutting sheds serving the Atlantic whaling fleets. Sebastian disembarked as instructed at Port Jefferson to be greeted by Smithlane's coachman with the information that the freight line owner had arrived the previous evening and was awaiting him. At first their route ran parallel to the shoreline and even before they went inland, where the size of the estates and the scale of the mansions became even grander, Sebastian appreciated that the appropriately named island was the weekend dormitory-by-the-sea for the favoured uptown inhabitants of New York.

Their approach along the tree-lined, winding drive to the square, Georgian-style house gave Smithlane sufficient warning to be on the steps, welcoming Sebastian's arrival with the same pumped, double-clasping hand-shake of their first encounter. Sebastian's luggage was dispersed between a phalanx of attendants and Sebastian escorted directly to a pagoda on a rise at the rear of the house where an assortment of drinks, including mixes in two cocktail jugs, were set out in readiness. Sebastian declined mint julep, which Smithlane admitted was a preference from his southern ancestry, in favour of martini, accepting as he sipped how lacking he personally was in their making. There was sufficient elevation for a distant sight of the sail-speckled sound and even this far inland there was a sea-clean smell in total, pendu-lum-swing antithesis to the Dantesque memory of the Pittsburgh mills: even, indeed, of the throat-clogging fog of London.

Smithlane announced at once that his German Embassy invitation had been ex-tended to include Sebastian. Count Johann von Bernstorff was regarded as the leader of Washington diplomatic society and his soirées and receptions the highlight of the social season. That night Sebastian was to meet Henry Blackmore, one of the biggest – if not *the* biggest – wheat growers in the entire state of Kansas, who was also to be an embassy guest.

'How did you introduce me to obtain the invitation so quickly?' asked Sebastian.

'As the investment-seeking financier as which you were introduced to me,' responded Smithlane, curiously.

'As a *British* investment-seeking financier?' pressed Sebastian.

Smithlane shook his head, smiling. 'I did not stipulate a nationality but don't fear that is going to be any bar. By a count I don't choose to calculate, you are not the only Englishman who considers America the honeyed land of golden opportunity precisely *because* of the current uncertainty of Europe.'

'Outnumbering Germans?' pounced Sebastian, imagining an opening.

Now it was Smithlane's moment for bemusement. 'My remark was not an accusation.'

'Nor was my response one of affront,' assured Sebastian. 'I am anxious not to cause you any embarrassment by my nationality.'

'Had I feared such embarrassment I would not have guaranteed you from the outset.'

The chance to steer the conversation was slipping away from him. Sebastian said: 'I would not wish to appear a member of any of those clandestine groupings I understand to exist.'

'*Who* are you, Mr Holmes?' demanded Smithlane, outright.

Suspicion? Or was the man inviting him to declare himself? 'I believe I have already answered that.'

Smithlane briefly remained silent. 'With nothing to add?'

'Such as?'

'A fuller explanation of precisely what opportunities you seek?'

'My consortium doesn't limit itself.' It was tempting to allow at least a hint but Sebastian held back. Legend had it that the Borgias heartily shook with one hand with a back-stabbing knife in the other.

The other man said: 'I hope you find unlimited benefit from the Washington visit.'

What Smithlane described as his hobby house was a large, specially constructed building near the stables but self-contained from them, its contents largely composed of facsimiles, reconstructions and early daguerreotype images. There were a lot of reproduction pictures and three carved reconstructions of the *Mayflower*, together with what was claimed to be an original passenger manifest, in which a Brother George Henry Smithlane, a carpenter and lay preacher from Scrooby, in Nottinghamshire, was listed. One entire wall, although still with room for additions, was inscribed with a family tree generated over the succeeding 400 years by George Smithlane. There was the glass-protected diary of George Smithlane's son, Wilfred, recounting a plague that came close to wiping out their fragile colony at Plymouth and his decision, as patriarch of the surviving family, to lead the flight south from the pestilence to Williamsburg, Virginia, where the records established their settling for the next 150 years. Pride of place was given to the family Bible recording Wilfred's birth and from which the charted ancestral tree had been created up to and including the birth of

Lowell Smithlane, his marriage to a Louise Brewer and the birth of two sons, Lowell Jnr and George. Alongside the family Bible was a book practically as thick, which Sebastian's host proudly produced as a regularly maintained autobiography, indexed and annotated to photographs in accompanying albums. That currently in use was numbered three. On a central table were arrayed an extensive and varied collection of American Indian and early settler artefacts, including tomahawks, clubs, a war bonnet, two muskets, both with Smithlane identification carved in the stock, and a similarly marked flintlock. On the wall facing the family tree were several of the photographs Sebastian had earlier seen reproduced in the *New York Times* library, the features of Smithlane's companions easier to distinguish in their originals.

Sebastian finally met Louise Smithlane upon their re-entry into the main house. She was a languidly self-assured, immaculately coiffeured and morning-dress-attired blonde woman with the first noticeably pronounced southern accent Sebastian had so far encountered. Lunch, of Maine lobster, was in a glassed conservatory on the inland side of the house and afterwards Sebastian assured Smithlane he had remembered to bring his riding habit. Sebastian's horse was a control-challenging ebony stallion upon which, to Smithlane's lead and virtually without respite for an hour, they cantered eastwards through loose forest and close cropped plain, twice

193

startling herds of deer, to a boundary post designating the edge of Smithlane's property. It took almost as long, although at an easier pace, to reach its southern limit and by the time they regained the house Sebastian's body ached from the unaccustomed exercise.

Sebastian was aware of the sound of the other weekend guests arriving as he dressed after a leisurely bath and by the time he descended most were assembled on an outside verandah. Smithlane had advised informality but Sebastian saw at once that he was not informal enough in his dark lounge suit: two of the men wore brightly striped blazers, complete with matchingly banded boaters, and white ducks that would have befitted a yachting regatta. By comparison the parasol-carrying women appeared positively subdued.

In bull-chested stature Henry Blackmore reminded Sebastian of the Russian Grand Duke, although there was no beard and the hair was blond. His companion, Jennie, was clearly not his wife and both appeared completely unembarrassed about it, as was everyone else. Unaccompanied New York Senator Jack Carson, one of the blazered and boatered guests, gesticulated so much as he talked it occurred to Sebastian that the man was almost orchestrally conducting his own words. There was the now familiar double-clasped handshake from the tall, thin-featured politician and an insistence that they had a lot to talk about, later. *New York Times*

194

political correspondent David Anderson, the other sports-dressed man, overheard the remark and pressed at once to be included in each and any discussion. His wife, Jo Marie, was a slight, fragile-faced blonde whose nervousness prompted her at almost regularly timed intervals to laugh, over loudly, without any humorous reason for doing so.

There was an hour to dress more formally after the early cocktails for a string-quartet recital of Tchaikovsky. Dinner was in the formal dining room, beneath the light of four candled chandeliers. Sebastian was seated between the sporadically erupting Jo Marie and the contrastingly languid Louise Smithlane. Neither woman had been to Europe and most of the meal was spent by Sebastian providing a verbal travelogue, although of the history and tourist attractions of various countries, not of the current political situation.

That came, however, the moment the women withdrew, encouraged by the fact that during the social conversation over dinner Sebastian's living in both France and Germany had emerged. To Carson's blunt demand Sebastian just as bluntly replied that war with Germany was inevitable. Unprompted – delighted at the opportunities presented him – Sebastian drew heavily upon his unattributable conversations with his uncle and Winston Churchill and in addition sketched the uncertainty of the Balkans and the possible weakness of a politically unstable

Russia.

'You paint a doleful picture, sir!' said Carson, finger jabbing with metronome precision. 'What of Great Britain keeping out of the conflict?'

'A serious misjudgement, according to all the opinions expressed to me,' insisted Sebastian. 'If there is aggression upon the European mainland, Great Britain will be pulled in by her treaty obligations.' Was it possible to use this man in some yet undecided way? He certainly shouldn't ignore the potential of a journalist and a politician together under the same roof after what he had so recently studied in the files of the *New York Times*.

'How influential are those opinions?' asked Anderson.

Sebastian felt no difficulty preparing himself with what he had read in Anderson's own publication. 'Sufficient for me to speak with confidence not just by having closely studied the most informed newspapers in London but also those of France and Germany. And, having conversations with politically minded people in all three countries...' The pause was for effect. '...I am also aware, as is any student of current European affairs, of the concern in both London and Berlin over the declared neutrality of this country.'

'How could such neutrality be otherwise?' asked Carson. 'America has no binding treaty obligations to bring it into any conflict. Its only stance can be that of neutrality.'

Sebastian was conscious of Lowell Smithlane studiously remaining out of the conversation, busying himself with port and brandy decanters and the cigar humidor. Henry Blackmore seemed content to sit and listen, too. Directly addressing Anderson, Sebastian said: 'In the short time I have been here I have been struck by how little coverage is given in your or any other newspaper to the daily developing events in Europe, whereas in newspapers in England substantial coverage was given to the move by Representative Allan Grant for a Congressional committee enquiry into clandestine groups – spy cells, I seem to remember his calling them – being established here by Berlin. His untimely death was also reported.'

'I am not sure of your point, sir.' protested Carson. The look directed at Sebastian was intense.

'Is it observing strict neutrality for America to permit the existence of such spy cells?' demanded Sebastian. 'I cannot call them to mind, but I seem to remember Grant actually identifying some groups or organizations by name.'

Blackmore stirred, at last. 'As I understand it, from our introduction, you are here seeking substantial investments in American enterprise. Is that not questionable?'

Perhaps the repetitive rehearsal of previous conversations was not after all to be wasted. 'Questionable by whom? I am openly here, openly meeting people such as yourself tonight. It was not people such as myself to

197

whom Grant sought to draw attention. It was clandestine caucuses, cocking a snook at American neutrality, that threatened American embarrassment.'

'Grant was someone I considered a friend,' said Carson, reflectively. 'He was someone of great integrity. I greatly mourn his passing.'

'A misfortune that such integrity has not been commemorated by his campaign being pursued,' pressed Sebastian.

'Perhaps it is,' agreed Carson, still reflective.

'I understand you are accompanying Lowell and myself to the German Embassy?' said Blackmore.

'Yes...' said Sebastian, cautiously.

'What would your response be if you were approached there, with the offer of a business investment?'

Sebastian laughed. 'I am seeking business here in America, not in Germany.'

'So you would refuse?' persisted Blackmore.

Sebastian remained smiling. 'I am not sure my curiosity would initially permit me to...' He looked to the newspaper man. 'What transpired would provide material for an interesting article, don't you think?'

'Most definitely,' agreed Anderson. 'How unfortunate it is that we are talking hypothetically. But permit me to pose a *less* hypothetical query. Is it not conceivable that Great Britain also has its people – spies according to your definition – creating similarly pro-

London groups?'

'I would be profoundly disappointed if they did not!' said Sebastian. 'Which isn't the real question either...' He looked to the politician. 'Are you, sir, content at the thought that within this country, of which you are justifiably so proud, there are possibly operating subversive organizations, be they German or British?'

'No, sir, I am not.'

'It is a situation likely to remain – worsen even – until America declares,' insisted Sebastian.

'You appear to assume that, should it declare, America would do so in support of Great Britain...' queried Lowell Smithlane, coming into the conversation at last. 'What if it saw its allegiance to be to Germany?'

'America should declare upon the evidence – or lack of it – of unjustified aggression and respect of international integrity!' declared Sebastian.

'Robustly spoken, sir!' declared Carson.

'Sincerely spoken!' insisted Sebastian.

Winston Churchill sat, head slumped, a familiar pose of contemplation, at Mycroft's insistence that there had been no recent diplomatic negotiations about the regulations of naval warfare, his only movement a meditative forefinger tap against the desk of the Admiralty Arch office. Finally he said: 'Cruiser Rules and the Declaration of London would have British merchantmen, at the demand of a German submarine upon the surface, heaving-to for a lifeboat disembarkation of passengers before the launch of torpedoes?'

'That's my interpretation,' agreed Mycroft, uneasily.

'And British merchant vessels must fly the flags of their nationality?'

'Winston!' implored Mycroft. 'For any British ship to do otherwise would turn its captain and crew into pirates!'

The forefinger tapped on, relentlessly. 'A submarine, on the surface, is a target to be rammed.'

'And beneath the surface is an unseen enemy capable of taking the lives of hundreds ... thousands...'

'There would be no cause for a vessel flying the flag of a neutral country to be asked to stop.'

'Winston, I do not wish this conversation to continue! I do not like its direction nor do I want to become part of it: you know well enough that I cannot!'

'Listen, then, to something you can hear. I've thought much about the current enterprise upon which Sebastian Holmes is engaged ... the subject of espionage and the gathering of intelligence. We know electronic communication can be intercepted: I intend establishing within the Admiralty such an intercepting facility, under the supervision of Admiral Hall.'

'*That* is a sound proposal,' said Mycroft.

'So are others I have in mind,' insisted Churchill.

On the Sunday there was a polo match in which Lowell Smithlane played for the team he sponsored and afterwards lunch in a specially erected marquee. That night, after the women once more withdrew from the dining table, the conversation was again dominated by the possibility of Britain and Germany at war. During it Jack Carson commented that perhaps Representative Grant's campaign against subversive organizations within America should be resurrected. He also suggested Sebastian should return to New York in his limousine, which Sebastian at once accepted.

Perhaps opportunities he had not foreseen were opening up to him, thought Sebastian.

Thirteen

For two men of unwavering self control and for whom any outwardly expressed emotion was anathema, their abruptly simultaneous awareness that they were actually arguing was positively startling. They both jerked to a stop, Sherlock Holmes in mid-protest, and for several moments faced each other awkwardly across the living room at Baker Street, uncertain how to continue.

It was Sherlock Holmes who did, although with his voice no longer raised. 'There has been a considerable number of messages of which I have not been made aware, hasn't there?'

'Some were judged to be sensitive, put into context with other intelligence from embassy sources,' replied Mycroft, equally subdued. Further to lessen the atmosphere of confrontation he sat, carefully choosing the seat normally occupied by Dr Watson, not that unchallengeably of his brother.

The reply brought to the detective his second astonishment in less than five minutes. 'Mycroft! Are you seriously *informing* me that I am not believed by you and the politicians you serve to be someone who can be implicitly trusted!'

Mycroft's discomfort at the scarcely needed reminder of how deeply he had become inveigled into clandestine schemes – and what he was in danger of sacrificing because of them – exceeded that earlier at realizing he and his brother were arguing for the first time in either's memory. 'Of course I am not! Knowledge of this matter is to be very positively restricted: you were made well enough aware of that by Churchill himself.'

'Restricted for the damned man's political protection and future, in neither of which I have the slightest interest. My concern is Sebastian and the mission upon which he is embarked. Which requires my knowing *entirely* what he is doing and with whom he is dealing: most important of all, my being able to gauge his interpretation. Sebastian is a man of unquestionable academic brilliance and intelligence. But on the matter in hand he is untried! Do either you or Churchill need notice of the outcome of Sebastian *failing*?'

'Interpretation is not Sebastian's function,' disputed Mycroft, although with none of the previous aggressiveness. 'That's political and for Whitehall and the Admiralty, within the fuller context of *all* the information available to it, not reached solely based upon what Sebastian provides.'

Sherlock Holmes finally took his accustomed chair, needing the moment further to compose himself from this disagreement with a man with whom he had never before disagreed: someone, in fact, in whom he had placed greater reliance – particularly in Sebastian's care and upbringing – than any other living person, even Watson himself. 'You miss my point, sir! *The* point! Consider how disastrously wrong that political inter-pretation could be if one contribution – Sebastian's contribution – were inadvertently misleading.'

The holding back *had* been urged upon him by the opportunistic Winston Churchill, accepted Mycroft. In whose integrity did he have the greater trust? An unnecessary – again unthinkable – question. Why then was he so resistant? To distance Sebastian and by inevitable connection his father from any feared mistake that would bring about public exposure? There was scarce reason or explan-ation in that. Because – even *without* public recognition – he for once wanted to orches-trate an enterprise from within the grey anonymity of his grey, anonymous life, instead of conceding to his more famous, adulated brother? In a day of the totally unexpected that unprompted conjecture took Mycroft beyond surprise into brief but positive shock. How, conceivably, could he be jealous of Sherlock?! Certainly his brother had gained international fame through his exploits but he'd never by thought or deed begrudgingly envied the man. Why then had the question emerged so readily from his sub-conscious? Why, indeed, after a lifetime of unblemished propriety and unassailable principles had he allowed himself to be seduced by Winston Churchill into a proposal that could bring about his very destruction? Sherlock was right, which he invariably was. Sebastian *was* inexperienced in the assembly of the intelligence he had been despatched to gather, which was neither a criticism nor a caveat: there were very few men anywhere with such experience. Except, of course, for Sherlock Holmes. Who very necessarily and self-protectively for them all certainly had to be allowed greater access than had so far been permitted. Mycroft's mind stopped at what *was* a caveat. Why 'greater' access? Why not total, complete, monitoring access? Because there was a valid, undeniable division between political and diplomatic expertise and Sherlock Holmes's science of analytical detection and deduction. The one should not be put into the same grist mill as the other: that would churn out confusion, not elucidation. Sherlock had virtually said as much, not minutes ago. At his brother's shift of impatience, Mycroft said: 'I heed your argument. And the warning. There's possible benefit in your overseeing matters.'

'The misfortune is in your needing to be made aware of it,' said Sherlock Holmes, unmollified by his brother's apparent change of heart. 'And I have no requirement for translation, now that I am fully conversant with this strange vernacular.'

'As you've already made clear,' reminded Mycroft. Would this episode, the first occasion on which the paths of their respective professions had crossed, create an irreparable barrier between them?

As if in answer to the unstated doubt, Sherlock Holmes said: 'This has been an unwelcome difficulty between us, brother.'

'Which is how I regard it, too. But now it is resolved.'

'Wise, though, for us to guard against our allowing such a situation to occur again.'

'I trust it won't,' said Mycroft.

At some time the remark had been made – by Blackmore, Sebastian thought, although he was unsure – that such Long Island weekends were to extend balancing perspective into their pressured concentration of weekday business. And while Sebastian did not consider himself – nor had since his arrival in America – either pressured or concentrated, the apothegm stayed with him after the intense, question-and-answer ride back from New York which had culminated in Jack Carson offering every contact facility in both New York and Washington DC, with the demand that Sebastian keep in touch, and with what Sebastian took to be the man's virtual undertaking to take over the Congressional probe into clandestine foreign infiltration briefly initiated by Representative Allan Grant.

With the arrival of the *Mauretania* so imminent – and its confirmed return to England within a week – Sebastian decided there was no urgency for a lengthy telegraphed account of his encounter with Carson, the enciphering of which, in any case, would have been overly difficult even in the now accepted bastardization of Winchester College Notions and ziphs. He restricted the alert to London to *Selfster fuulsgoomee carthage seengaatoor ostiarius wickham guilsters* – 'I have had a fulsome debate with a senior Senator upon German insinuation' – which took only minutes to encode and transmit. In contrast Sebastian devoted most of the following day to composing a tightly written report upon everything that had passed between himself and the American politician, concluding with his belief that Carson intended resurrecting the discussion – hopefully even reopening a Congressional investigation – into foreign influence organizations within the United States. In fuller detail Sebastian recounted everything he had read in the *New York Times*'s archives upon Allan Grant and Peter Pullinger and transcribed verbatim what he had painstakingly copied from the newspaper reports of Grant's complaints about the American Embargo Conference and the National Peace Council. He also included, with the addendum that it had not been publicly identified, Grant's suspicion of the American Pan-German Association, although he excluded any mention of Laura Hemditch.

Quite separately he declared his intention, because of his newly formed association with Senator Carson, to remain in Washington after the German Embassy reception. He had already taken rooms at The Willard Hotel on Pennsylvania Avenue and would communicate on open text cable any change of address from there.

Sebastian timed his arrival at the *Mauretania*'s Hudson River berth to come after the immediate chaos of arrival and disembarkation. This time he did accept the offer of coffee with the man after the exchange of their wax-sealed envelopes and was at once glad he did. Pettit recounted two debates in the House of Commons dominated by Winston Churchill and actually produced copies of *The Times* with full coverage of the second – together with two editorials – which brought Sebastian up to date with political attitudes and feeling in London, despite the newspapers being six days old. The most recently dated also carried virtually a full-page feature, date-lined Berlin, which Sebastian judged the best analysis of possible alliances in what the writer considered the inevitability of a European war. There was a secondary feature devoted to the determined belligerence and expansionist ambitions of the Kaiser, particularly illustrated in his declared intention to gain global naval supremacy for Germany. Sebastian allowed himself a moment of self-congratulation – the Notional *junket* came easily to mind – at the final article on the page, a carefully reasoned examination of the political maelstrom of the Balkans which virtually in every respect accorded with the personal assessment he had given to his father and uncle when his American assignment had first been mooted. Sebastian gratefully accepted every newspaper and urged Pettit to bring *The Times* from England on every voyage. He further asked if the request could be extended to other Cunard captains: the previously unrealized opportunity to remain as acquainted as possible with European developments far outweighed any cumbersome backlog that would unavoidably be created.

He waited until his return to Fifth Avenue before opening his uncle's package. Although he was well prepared there was still a flare of anger, unallayed by Mycroft's insufficiently explained apology, at Winston Churchill's refusal to disclose his introduction to Julius Hemditch. Sebastian thought, too, that in a failed attempt to compensate for his embarrassment, his uncle's repeated praise was exaggerated. The British Embassy at St Petersburg had failed to establish that the American expedition of the Grand Duke Alexei Orlov was in any way official but there was very definitely within the Imperial court a mystic monk who by every account wielded unacceptable – even dangerously destabilizing – power throughout the court because of his apparent ability to treat a blood disorder of the sickly young Tsarevich. Sebastian was to exercise extreme caution at the impending German Embassy reception and under no circumstances whatsoever make any approach or contact with any British Embassy staff who might, for reasons of diplomatic protocol, be present. Neither was he to allow himself to be drawn into any political discussion there concerning events in Europe. His requested £4,000,000 had been transferred to Oscar Lepecheron's Wall Street bank – which Sebastian already knew from the banker himself – but any drawing upon it had first to be approved by telegram and further delayed until a full and justifiable explanation – and final approval – had been provided via the now established seaborne link. All his other requests were being pursued and would be responded to in as much detail as possible, either by telegraph or in the next of such responses by letter.

Sebastian's irritation resurged at what he saw as his being denied any initiative, reducing him to nothing more than a performing monkey, dancing to a tune that Churchill clearly thought he could play from a distance of 3,500 miles. Sebastian's first impulse was to indicate his annoyance but it was quickly curbed. Instead he cabled *Loongdoon vulgus aarriigveed* – 'London letter has arrived' – and sent it more determined than ever to continue as independently as he saw fit.

Julius Hemditch accepted without question Sebastian's announcement of his moving to Washington, just as readily agreeing to Sebastian leaving any unnecessary belongings at Fifth Avenue. Sebastian hesitated at his locked filing cabinet before abruptly clearing it of all his incoming and outgoing messages, as well as his uncle's resented letter. Oscar Lepecheron saw him personally but assigned the formality of opening a safe-deposit facility to a personal assistant.

As Sebastian handed over the sealed communications dossier to be stored Lepecheron said: 'You appear to have been actively engaged.'

'Nothing positive. Is your consortium still closed to me?'

'Not closed,' apologized the other man. 'Completed by prior negotiation. And I've encountered nothing in which I believed you would subsequently have been interested.'

He did not return at once that afternoon to the Hemditch house but stopped short at the Plaza Hotel, where he had to wait almost an hour for his call to be connected to Washington.

'I'm being treated like a fool!' protested Sherlock Holmes, looking up at last from the desk upon which were set out Sebastian's telegrams.

'That's a dangerous error, on somebody's part,' Watson said, while in his mind thinking double damnation at his friend's recurring lapses. Nowhere in Baker Street was there visible paraphernalia to account for the staccato word delivery and twitched arm movement. Never before had Sherlock Holmes sought to hide his usage but now he apparently felt the need, which in Watson's judgement escalated the problem dangerously close to psychological if not physical dependency.

'All the worse when that person is my own brother!'

'Surely not, Holmes! That's unimaginable!' As unimaginable, he thought, as Holmes's continuing decline.

'It's quite clear, from interruptions in the sequence, that messages are still being held back from me. Some of Mycroft's responses to Sebastian, certainly. And others make little sense out of their context.'

'Inadvertent error?' Mycroft would have no conception of the pressure such treatment would impose upon his brother.

'Most definitely not.'

'Shall you confront him?' Should I? Watson asked himself.

'At a time I judge to be fitting, which is not directly.'

When would my time be fitting to seek outside additional help? thought Watson, continuing the self-questioning.

It was an afterthought, as he was making his way from the Fifth Avenue mansion, for Sebastian to make a final check of the telegraph. The telegram awaiting him was from his father and read: *Greegaatly raised sherking sconce. Sack vulgus toogtaal,* which Sebastian translated as Sherlock Holmes being greatly angered by the concealment of messages, with the instruction to send every communication that had been exchanged.

Sebastian continued on out of the house, leaving the telegram upon the machine as if unreceived before his departure.

Fourteen

By advancing his arrival in Washington Sebastian denied himself the repeated opportunity to travel by customized railcar – Henry Blackmore's this time – but considered the sacrifice to be more than worthwhile, apart from the inconvenience reminiscent of Liverpool of having to assemble his own porterage at Penn and Union stations.

In the intervening days since Long Island Sebastian had concluded that from a practical, professional point of view his primary need was to re-establish himself with Senator Jack Carson, hopefully at best to gain access to whatever official sources the man might have in addition to encouraging Carson's intimated foreign-influence inquiry. The connived visit to the German Embassy – a tiptoe into the eagle's nest rather than the lion's den – was on the face of it unlikely to produce more than the gossip of the attendance of some intriguing personalities, fully to identify whom would more than likely require him to spend more time studying the *Washington Post*'s social page archives than he had those of the *New York Times*.

Sebastian was unprepared for the contrast between America's capital and the other two American cities he had so far experienced. Unaware of the civic ordinance prohibiting any construction to exceed the 287' Capitol building atop Jenkins' Hill, Sebastian's initial curiosity was at the very obvious absence of the skyscrapers with which he had become familiar in New York and to a lesser degree in Pittsburgh. That impression was quickly superseded during the carriage ride from Union Station, from which the driver looped directly in front of the domed edifice Sebastian hoped shortly to visit, to descend Pennsylvania Avenue between the squarely large buildings presumably housing government departments. Sebastian decided the original intention to design Washington in the style of a Greek city had succeeded, even to the creation of thoroughfares – certainly the one upon which he was currently travelling – that could have accommodated rival standard-bearing Roman legions, lined abreast.

The reminders of Europe continued at the Willard. It was an ornately baroque hotel of walnut and mahogany and brass and glittering crystal and overstuffed, antimacassar-protected couches and chairs. By the reception desk – manned by frock coated clerks – and either side of the short stairway leading up to a central, dividing corridor there were even miniature forests of aspidistra and Sebastian knew at once that he would be far more comfortable and content here than living aboard Blackmore's railway carriage, which had been part of his invitation. His velvet-draped suite was on the Pennsylvania Avenue side of the hotel, with a partial view of the Elipse and the needle-like Washington Monument beyond. Sebastian unpacked his own luggage, which until recently he had been accustomed to doing himself in preference to college servants, taking particular care with the carefully packed newspapers. His accommodation to his satisfaction and with time at his disposal, Sebastian bathed and changed from his travelling clothes before telephoning as arranged the number to which he had been connected from the Plaza Hotel. An unidentified intern apologized for Carson's absence in committee but confirmed the man would be free for their appointment.

The ascent towards the American seat of government seemed to Sebastian inexplicably less impressive than his earlier descent from it and it took Sebastian several moments to decide why. Unconsciously he was comparing again, although now with the buttressed and corniced and gargoyled stone intricasies of the British Houses of Parliament and their equivalent parliamentary palaces in Paris and Berlin. Which *were* palaces, imbuing by their size and grandeur in the minds of ordinary people that their politician occupants were not ordinary but superior mortals with superior knowledge and abilities. In its virtual garden setting, the Capitol did not look imposing enough. Which was not a judgement upon its architecture but rather one of possible admiration upon its occupants. Could it be, in this new world in which he found himself, that despite their imposing administrative buildings the elected politicians of America did not feel the need to intimidate or overbear its citizens?

Sebastian's name was duly listed for admission to the private senatorial wing and a uniformed escort awaited in readiness to take him along echoing, high-vaulted corridors to Jack Carson's suite. The domain was guarded by a girdle-encased woman of both formidable body and demeanour identified by her desk plate as Edna Connolly. Sebastian thought protector of the inner sanctum would have been a more fitting description than office manager printed beneath the name.

She said: 'You're late.'

'Five minutes,' apologized Sebastian.

'Which is late. That's five minutes off your time.'

Sebastian followed her through the immaculate outer office into the total contrast of a paper and document-strewn, haphazard set of rooms in the main and most cluttered of which Jack Carson sat behind an expansive desk, proudly flanked on both sides by

216

American flags half furled from their staves. The thin-featured politician was on his feet at once but the greeting was more restrained, as was the man himself. He led Sebastian deeper into the room to an enclave of scuffed leather chairs that settled with an audible sigh when sat upon. Before Carson did so he went to the entrance from the outer offices, said something Sebastian failed to hear and then positively closed the separating door.

As he sat, to the sigh of a second depressed cushion, Carson said: 'Don't want us to be interrupted.' The restraint extending to there being no hand-waving orchestration.

'I'm glad my being in Washington makes it possible for us to meet again so soon.'

There was a bottle – bourbon Sebastian saw from the label – and two glasses on a low table between them. Carson poured, unasked, for both of them and said: 'So am I. Things have progressed since we last talked.'

'How?'

'In Long Island you introduced Allan Grant's death into our conversation. And that of Peter Pullinger,' reminded the American, ignoring Sebastian's question. 'Why?'

'It was appropriate to our discussion,' replied Sebastian, carefully. He had been curious at Carson's immediate agreement to their meeting when he'd telephoned from New York, unmonitored and unrecorded on Hemditch's telephone billing, but hadn't imagined an encounter like this. It went beyond the directness to which he believed himself adjusted to something approaching interrogation.

Carson's look was doubtful. 'It seemed a pretty detailed awareness, for someone living in England.'

Sebastian sipped his drink, thinking at the same time of guardian angels and their influence upon good fortune, although he had anticipated the usefulness of *The Times*. 'I told you it was fully reported in the British press...' He reached into the inside pocket of his discarded topcoat. '... And that foreign affairs were generally much more widely covered. I've arranged for English newspapers to reach me here. I've brought some copies of the London *Times*...' He offered them across the table. '... You'll be interested in the political coverage, which touches upon our conversation.'

Carson accepted the papers and for nearly five minutes went through the pages, not reading but scanning the foreign date lines. His pause was longest at the full-page warning from Berlin of impending war that Sebastian had admired. When he finally looked up Carson still did not immediately speak.

Before he could, Sebastian said: 'What's the progress you're talking of?'

'Can I trust you, Mr Holmes?'

Sebastian extended spread-apart hands. 'The people through whom we met are my referees.'

'And they say they know you not at all, only through an acquaintanceship with a Pitts-

218

burgh mill owner, as a wealthy Briton seeking business opportunities.'

I must stress that I am not their guarantors, recalled Sebastian: there seemed a marked reluctance of people with whom he was mixing to provide character testimonials, which was perhaps understandable in his case but not in others. 'So you have sought to learn about me!'

'Are you offended?'

'Curious.'

'As I am in a business investor with such an intense interest in politics.'

'Any London-based businessman failing to take an intense interest in European politics is a businessman doomed to bankruptcy,' responded Sebastian, smoothly. It had to be a fine balance, assured enough to gain the other man's confidence but without the glibness of someone overly rehearsed.

Carson nodded, the caution still evident. 'And intensely interested in American politics, to boot?'

'And for the same protective reason. Politics – political decisions – in any country are obviously interconnected with the business of that country.'

'Would you consider investing in a business here you suspected of trading with or having associations with Germany?' demanded Carson.

He had already answered that challenge once in Carson's presence. Within Sebastian's eyeline were the half-furled flags of a patriot, he decided. 'There would be no legal bar to my doing so and I am a believer in the free enterprise of the American way. But no, I would most definitely not. And that is why, before considering any investment, I would seek to make detailed enquiries to assure myself that I was not doing so. I will in no way aid my country's yet undeclared enemies.'

Carson smiled. 'I've had enquiries made – or rather *tried* to have enquiries made – into Allan Grant's accident. I'm not satisfied.'

Sebastian felt a stir of satisfaction, for the first time believing there might be a proper, investigative direction opening before him. Everything depended upon how carefully he followed it. 'Not satisfied that it was an accident?'

'That, among other things.'

He had to take the man beyond his enigmatic responses. 'If you're not satisfied it was an accident the obvious alternative is foul play of some sort ... Murder? You must have proof – suspicion at least – for such thinking?'

'It was an organized shoot, by Grant's campaign and office manager here. Name's Burt Williams. I spoke with him the day after I got back from Long Island,' Carson began at last, pouring himself a second drink. 'They were on their fourth drive, along the river bank of a valley where in places the trees came right down to the water. Allan had the eighth peg, which put him at the far end of the line, out of sight of at least five pegs, maybe the sixth. No one was looking at anything but the birds. No one seemed to have noticed Allan wasn't with them when they moved off for the next drive, which was about half a mile away. They were almost there when there was an emergency whistle, from the beaters collecting the dead birds. They'd found Allan about fifty yards from his peg, in thick undergrowth: entangled in it, according to Williams, who said it was crushed down all around, where Allan had fallen. His gun was there too. Both barrels were discharged. Allan got both, just below the chin. Virtually took his head off...'

The Senator stopped, sipping his drink, and Sebastian said: 'Where they found him – was it on the way to the next drive?'

Carson nodded, approvingly. 'Good question. Glad I asked it, too. No, it wasn't. It was in the opposite direction. He had no reason to be there.'

'What about the shots?'

'Williams is adamant no one – neither the other guns nor the beaters – heard any shots after the fourth drive finished. But there were a lot of birds, which meant a lot of firing while the drive was on.'

'There has to have been a police investigation.'

'I'm going to press for one now but inconceivably there wasn't one at the time. Allan's death fell between jurisdictions. In the forest it was the responsibility of the Forest Rangers, who determined it was an accident. There was an autopsy which concluded the

injuries were consistent with the man trip-
ping and falling on his own gun. That was the
inquest verdict. Williams says he asked for
police to get involved but they wouldn't cross
the jurisdiction line.'

'It beggars belief,' agreed Sebastian. 'What
explanation do they have for his being fifty
yards in the wrong direction?'

Carson snorted a laugh. 'They don't, beyond surmising he went off to relieve himself
during the shoot, tripped, and fell on his own
gun just as the autopsy and the inquest
decided.'

'But...' tried Sebastian but the American
stopped him with a raised hand. 'I've asked
that question, too. Both of Williams and of
Allan's widow, Luella, who sometimes shot
with him. They both insist Allan was a good
and careful hunter: knew the rules. Even if he
had gone off to relieve himself, which I don't
believe would have been that urgent in the
middle of a drive he knew would be over in a
matter of minutes, he would have broken his
gun precisely to avoid an accident, not
walked with both barrels fully cocked! That's
madness and totally unacceptable, like so
much else.'

'So much else?' Sebastian echoed.

'I didn't only talk to Williams and Luella
about Allan's death. Luella said he had quite
a lot of documentation about foreign infiltration, before he started his campaign and
began co-operating with Pullinger. Williams
remembers quite a lot of material, too, in the

office here on the Hill. There was no documentation about foreign infiltration among the belongings in Allan's office that were sent back to Luella after his death. She thought it had been kept in the archives here, for some official reason. Williams says it wasn't: he thought Pullinger might have been given it for his exposé but I've spoken to his wife, too. She's got cabinets of source material from which her husband worked: she was his researcher. She says it never came to them. Allan wouldn't let what he had go out of his hands. Pullinger always had to come here to talk to Allan.'

'They have to have been stolen,' accepted Sebastian. 'But from where?'

'There was no burglary from Allan's house.'

'From his office here? But how would anyone get in? My name had to be recorded, an escort provided.'

'A lot of office staff are volunteers: interns and students. It's a porous place for someone determined enough.'

'You've learned a lot very quickly,' congratulated Sebastian.

Carson smiled again, appeared to consider a third bourbon but then decided against it. Sebastian shook his head to the offer, too. Carson said: 'There's power in being a Senator that's very useful.'

'What do you intend to do?'

'As far as Allan's death is concerned, put pressure on the Delaware police to initiate the inquiry they should have begun in the

223

first place. I'm doing that through the Justice Department here and through the state District Attorney, if necessary. I'll also get the Delaware politicians here in Congress to make noises. I don't think it will be difficult to persuade them, particularly at the suggestion of someone connected with murdering a Representative possibly having spies within the Capitol itself.'

'It will still be a cold trail.'

'Depends how well I can heat it up.'

Sebastian said: 'You've questioned acquaintances about me but they were scarcely able to vouch for my integrity. And we ourselves are little known to each other. Why are you speaking to me so openly?'

There was another smile from the American. 'I have frequently to make judgements upon face value, which I have done in your case. It was you, also, who first aroused *my* curiosity about the death of Representative Grant. And, finally, because I intend to use you.'

'Use me?'

'I want to know all that you know – even if it is nothing more than gossip in England – of clandestine groups, either infiltrating or seeking to influence American business, American politics and possibly the very American way of life. I intend raising again the sort of protest that Allan Grant started, this time from the floor of the Senate. And with the already offered assistance of David Anderson, whom I've also taken fully into my confidence. But at this moment I have nothing upon which to mount that protest apart from the Congressional records of Grant's speeches and Pullinger's *New York Times* articles, all of which I will rework – together with what you hopefully can tell me – to give the impression of knowing far more than I do. Grant obtained his material – material important enough for him to be killed and for it to be stolen – from someone, and I want to attract that someone to me. We're going to do it, you and I, by playing our own version of blind man's bluff, the accent being upon the bluff.'

'I understand,' said Sebastian.

'What you don't understand is the final reason,' replied Carson.

Sebastian waited.

'I am approaching re-election,' said Carson, honestly. 'A campaign is necessary.'

Sebastian remained serious-faced. 'You have outlined sufficient circumstantial evidence to indicate that Grant was murdered: murdered because of a campaign that you intend to resume! But in so doing you are inviting your own murder!'

'I do not hunt, Mr Holmes. And if I had baulked at commenting about events and matters that might have caused me physical outrage I would scarcely have uttered a word throughout my political career, which I am anxious to continue.'

'I do not believe you should dismiss the risk so lightly.'

'Believe me, sir, I am not dismissing anything over-lightly. And neither should you. If I find that you are an agent of the very sort I am seeking to uncover, then yours will be the name I publicly denounce in the Senate.'

The interrupting demand of another committee session – Carson's chairmanship of the Ways and Means – provided Sebastian with a welcome escape from the totally unprepared encounter with the politician. Sebastian descended the hill for the second time that day oblivious to his surroundings, self-absorbed in conflicting reflections. The insistence at every briefing before leaving London had been to do nothing, risk nothing, that could result in political embarrassment. And he had minutes before parted from a man threatening him with Congressional exposure if he proved to be a British government agent. Which he wasn't, Sebastian immediately sought to reassure himself. Neither, additionally, was he working within a clandestine group as an American business or opinion-influencing infiltrator. He was acting un-officially, without any British Government authority or support, precisely to lay bare what Senator Jack Carson had just declared himself committed to uncover.

The balance came down overwhelmingly in favour of his allying himself with the American, far more so than he had anticipated possible before that afternoon's meeting. What, then, did he convincingly have to offer? Nothing that amounted to the slightest proof of cabals or caucuses or clandestine, masonic-style clubs. *Even if it is nothing more than gossip in England,* Jack Carson had said. After his sessions with Churchill and his uncle – and from his later conversations here with Hemditch and Smithlane and Lepecheron – Sebastian felt equipped enough to convey Churchill's beliefs as well as being able to indicate an awareness of American business thinking towards American neutrality.

He should advise London of the development, as soon and as fully as possible. But his means of safely doing that was several hundred miles away. Could he risk an open cable from Washington? Sebastian guessed it was not particularly unusual for public telegraph offices – or that in the Willard hotel itself – to be asked to transmit enciphered business messages. And he was sure Notions would be unintelligible. The length of what he had to pass on would possibly attract untoward attention. And even though his uncle's cable address was removed from any Whitehall identification it would ... Sebastian abruptly halted the contemplation. It was utterly impossible to consider the public telegraph! If Carson succeeded in getting the police activity that he'd described it was more than likely there would be further, even official, checks upon him. And the discovery of a coded message – timed and dated to within an hour of his encounter with the politician – to a telegraph address not beyond identifying as clandestinely that of the official secretary to the British Cabinet would guarantee everyone's public humiliation.

It was several minutes before his thoughts began to flow in time with the quickness of his pen. Dissatisfied with the strength of the envelopes available in the writing bureau Sebastian went to the front desk to choose a heavier, business document enclosure and while he was there used their flame and wax to seal the gummed flap. He had earlier identified the main post office further back along Pennsylvania Avenue and waited until he reached it, on foot, before addressing the envelope to his uncle at the Diogenes Club.

Sebastian had used Carson's words practically verbatim in his account and abruptly smiled at a recollection as he retraced his steps to the hotel. Carson had described his intention as blind man's bluff – an earlier reflection of his own – with the accent on bluff. Sebastian decided his role in the matter was to be that of performing a gigantic double bluff.

Fifteen

There had been brief times in the unique professional career of Sherlock Holmes when he had initially failed to find a path to follow. But such brief hindrances had virtually without exception been thrown in his way by nefarious villains – Moriarty the most obvious example – whose deception had been quickly dispelled. Today's – tomorrow's, the following days' and weeks' – wouldn't be. He was, Sherlock Holmes accepted, still being opposed by his previously always trusted brother and by his eventually reconciled son. For Mycroft he could countenance no excuse. For Sebastian, about whom Sherlock Holmes would always feel so much guilt, there were perhaps allowances to be made. But about his dismissive treatment from both – Mycroft far more than Sebastian – Sherlock Holmes felt a profound and hurtful disappointment.

But personal sadness was all there was. Sherlock Holmes did not waste his mental energy on pointless charges of betrayal against Mycroft nor physical effort repeating the unmet demand to Sebastian in New York for the undisclosed messages between the two of them. In Sherlock Holmes's opinion there was, in fact, sufficient in what had been made confusingly available to him after the earlier confrontation with his brother and in reluctant and piecemeal delivery by Sebastian. Very shortly they both would be taught the dangers as well as the craft of deception.

There was no visible evidence of surveillance upon 221b Baker Street but Sherlock Holmes took the precaution of despatching a well swaddled and mildly protesting Mrs Hudson in the bath chair care of Dr Watson, needing to work unfettered and at the quickest possible pace. He completed the journey to and from Liverpool in one day and spared Mrs Hudson the inconvenience of another outing by ignoring Baker Street to stay on the night of his return, under an assumed name, at a Paddington hotel catering for commercial travellers, whose company and conversation he briefly shared, his mind occupied as it was by dialect and accents. The following morning found him waiting impatiently for the opening of the reading room at the British Museum, where he was helped with the alacrity and courtesy he had met the previous day at the Cunard steamship offices. So swiftly was his research completed that in the afternoon he managed visits to both the American and Russian legations and as the result of the latter presented his card to the occupant of the fine Nash mansion bordering Regents Park.

Sherlock Holmes was sorely tempted to call unannounced that evening upon his brother at the Diogenes Club but resisted the temptation, unwilling for it to appear a direct challenge, despite what he considered his ill treatment at his brother's hands. Instead he left a message for his brother to advise by courier if it was inconvenient for them to meet the following evening and kept his own dwelling in Baker Street under observation for a full hour to satisfy himself there were no watchers to be alerted to his unsuspected absence by his return. It proved to be a precaution well taken. Awaiting Sherlock Holmes when he finally entered was a note from Watson that the doctor was sure he'd seen lingering outside the previous day the two men who had followed them during their Park Lane promenade.

Sufficiently exhilarated by what he considered an exceedingly fruitful expedition Sherlock Holmes required nothing more than the comfort of a Havana cigar, which would, he knew, have satisfied his friend so persistently – and irritatingly – critical of his other smoking choices for relaxation. It was much later into the evening, the cigar and the one generous balloon of Napoleon vintage brandy consumed, before the reflective Sherlock Holmes finally concentrated upon the benefits of his not confronting Mycroft that night. Now there was a full, intervening day, Scotland Yard and its variably efficient archives and the helpful Inspector George Lestrade at his service.

★ ★ ★

Sherlock Holmes's newly installed telegraph stood empty in the morning but, buoyed up with the hope of what Scotland Yard might provide, the detective quit Baker Street early, careless of missing a postponing courier from his brother. It required yet again the diversion of an increasingly reluctant, much wrapped Mrs Hudson and an equally disgruntled Dr Watson. Sherlock Holmes intently watched his two Baker Street sentinels emerge from their alley to take up pursuit, himself hatted and cloaked in readiness to leave unobserved practically in their wake. Sherlock Holmes, who was a man of science and level-headed practicality, adamantly refused to recognize what people commonly called luck. But had he believed in the supernatural he would have that day accepted spirit guidance or influence for his continuing good fortune. He even succeeded in identifying by name from Special Branch sketches the two by now familiar faces so often visible from the living-room window of 221b Baker Street. Still with an afternoon to occupy he took a passing carriage to the City and as a result of what he quickly learned there hurried to his third legation visit in two days, this time to the Belgian Embassy.

That evening Mycroft awaited him in green velvet smoking jacket and with a dinner table laid for two, the claret already decanted. Sherlock Holmes joined his brother in selecting beef, well aware it was the speciality of the Diogenes.

'Your note intrigued me,' opened Mycroft. 'Is there something of import?'

'More a question I should be directing to you,' suggested Sherlock Holmes. The door to Mycroft's small personal office lay open off the dining room, the telegraph plainly in view. Gesturing towards it, he added: 'I have been away from Baker Street all day. Has there been any communication from Sebastian?'

Mycroft remained frowning at his brother's opening retort. 'He has quit New York for Washington, to attend an affair at the German Embassy. I did not trouble especially to advise you, knowing you were coming here tonight...'

Sebastian's absence could account for the lack of response to his request to be sent all the telegrams. Sherlock Holmes said: 'What's come from Sebastian's information on the outward voyage? The Grand Duke particularly?'

Confound the boy for ignoring the reminder of priority and communicating to his father direct instead of allowing him to be the filter! Mycroft had categorized their knowledge of Alexei Orlov as political intelligence outside his brother's remit. There was no alternative but to brazen it out and claim an oversight upon something which had anyway proven minimally productive. 'Orlov was of little importance, apart from some gossip concerning a cleric.'

'Gregori Rasputin,' identified Sherlock

233

Holmes, at once. 'He's a drunken lecher who has gained enormous power with the Tsarina, because of what she believes to be the man's near-magical power to deal with her son's haemophilia. There is serious concern at his interference in matters of state: a suggestion, even, that he is a German agent.'

Mycroft welcomed the arrival of their meal – although the emptiness of his stomach was not hunger – for the interruption it provided for his recovery. The possibility of a German agent at such an echelon within the court of a supposed ally in the inevitable conflict ahead was beyond instant analysis: it could affect, even, Britain's ultimate decision whether to comply with its treaty obligations! He tasted and approved the wine, further to gain time. 'You are sure of this?'

'I am sure of what I am telling you. Take heed that I have only talked of a "suggestion" of this man's allegiance.'

Mycroft paused once more, his meal untouched, knowing he had to divulge what his oath of office precluded him from disclosing. 'We know from St Petersburg of this man's influence upon the Tsarina and the reason for it. But nothing more.'

'Perhaps our Russian embassy should be encouraged to give more attention to their reason for being there. What do they say of Alexei Orlov?'

The division of information – political from investigatory – was no longer a factor. 'They are unable to provide any reason for his being aboard the *Lusitania* beyond it perhaps being a Grand Tour different from the normal tour of Europe for his daughter.'

'The beef is excellent, as always: you really should attempt a little,' smiled Sherlock Holmes, feeling no sympathy for his brother's all too obvious discomfort. 'My question was what does the embassy say *of* Grand Duke Alexei Orlov?'

'He is an acknowledged member of the Imperial court.'

'That is all?' The incredulity came close to being over-stressed.

'What else is there?' Mycroft pushed his plate away.

'Grand Duke Alexei Andreevich Orlov, second son of the Tsar's late maternal uncle, Prince Andrei Orlov, is the most trusted member of the Imperial court, so trusted that since the mutinies and near uprising against Nicholas II in 1905 Orlov has headed the *Okhrana*, the Tsar's secret intelligence service. Its main and essential function is to protect the royal family against revolution and overthrow. Orlov acts as the Tsar's personal emissary in the highest but most secret matters of state, entrusted even to make decisions in the Tsar's name. Taking into account the current political situation in Europe in general and that within Russia in particular, it is absurd in the extreme to imagine Orlov's presence in America is merely an unusual vacation for his daughter.'

'How do you know all this?'

Sherlock Holmes ignored his brother. 'What of the other matter?'

'I considered it of little importance. And still do.' Which was why it was a section of Sebastian's first sea-mailed letter that Mycroft had passed on.

'Nothing is of little importance, in its particular context,' insisted Sherlock Holmes.

'What is its importance?' asked Mycroft.

'Nothing, as yet,' refused the detective. 'Just curiosity. I am greatly exercised, too, by your having been delivered of a second letter carried aboard the *Mauretania* the contents of which I have not been made aware of.'

Mycroft used the return of the club steward to clear their plates, waving away the offer of pudding or cheese, to consider this confrontation which he found far more unsettling than the raised-voice argument of the previous week. Unspeaking, he rose with the steward's departure and fetched from the safe in the tiny office Sebastian's detailed account of the newspaper-archive discovery of the death of Congressman Allan Grant so soon after declaring a campaign against foreign influence in American affairs, and the Long Island encounter with Senator Jack Carson. 'It only reached me this evening. I completed reading it not half an hour before your arrival. Winston is at this moment unaware of its contents.'

From his visit to Liverpool Sherlock Holmes knew how recent the arrival of Sebastian's second letter was: he could, he realized, have relayed it to London faster than the specially established Cunard courier service. Unhurriedly he read the document, his impassive face betraying none of his inner alarm at the details of Allan Grant's death and at the same time admiring the clarity of his son's account. Handing it back across the table, he said: 'Sebastian is of course correct in believing this to be suspicious.'

'There was a telegram, ahead of this,' disclosed Mycroft, unthinkingly. 'He's been firmly warned in the reply against involving himself too closely in political matters.'

'Something else you were waiting until tonight to tell me!'

Mycroft Holmes sighed, unable to meet his brother's gaze. Eventually, sighing afresh, he said: 'I find myself in a dilemma of my own bad judgement and now embroiled in circumstances from which I cannot extricate myself. Indeed, I would not seek to do so at this juncture, believing it essential I continue to curb Winston's wilder schemes and impulses. That said, I am unsure of the effectiveness of my restraint. I feel myself deceived and in turn to have deceived both you, my dear brother, and Sebastian, whom I consider I have every justification to regard and love as my own son...'

Mycroft was abruptly overcome by unexpected emotion, gulping to a halt, and in an instant all Sherlock Holmes's disappointments and anger at his brother evaporated. He went to speak, in an effort to cover the other man's embarrassment, but Mycroft waved him down, determined to continue.

'I allowed myself to become inveigled in Winston's manoeuvrings – and in turn involved you and Sebastian – because I was convinced Winston's impatience at the Cabinet's vacillation was justified and that there was good reason for more urgent action concerning events in America. I still believe it justified. But things have escalated since then, carrying me along with them. Sandhurst seems to have convinced Winston he's omnipotent in both Cabinet room and battlefield. He rails with equal vigour against his colleagues and our generals and admirals and takes decisions upon his own inclination, without consultation or approval from anyone...' Mycroft paused. 'If there were to be the slightest indication of what has been happening I could easily stand in a dock – with you and Sebastian by my side – accused of conspiracy and with a career and position I cherish totally destroyed.'

'A fate I think we should do everything to avoid,' remarked Sherlock Holmes, mildly.

'I admire your aplomb but these are waters too dangerously deep for my comfort. You deserve an apology, which I offer most humbly and unreservedly. And ask you to accept that there was, in my behaviour, some effort to spare you.'

Sherlock Holmes gave a dismissive flick of his hand. 'My only concern is our proper reconciliation, which I hope is finally achieved.

Everything else is of lesser importance.'

'Not to me!'

'To protect ourselves I need to know every-thing. And by everything I mean *everything*.'

'Which of course you shall. Dear God, I never thought my professional life would come to such a pass.'

'Mycroft!' protested Sherlock Holmes, conscious of the raised voice of the previous encounter but in this context unworried by it. 'What has occurred – or been allowed to occur – is past us now. We gain no advantage in self-pity.'

'Is there anything else of which I should be aware?' There was a defeatism in Mycroft's voice.

'Conundrum upon conundrums,' declared Sherlock Holmes 'Our very excellent national archives do not record a Smithlane upon the original pilgrims' voyage of 1620 to Massa-chusetts. There is, however, a Smith*bane* with a wife and two children in Williamburg, Virginia, in 1722. A Smith*lane* appears by 1744 in the historic genealogy of original settlers, and his line can be followed in that record, at the American legation, through a male line to the Lowell Smithlane who was such a generous and recent host to Sebastian. Also recorded is the marriage in 1824 of Lowell Smithlane's grandfather, a Septimus Paul Smithlane, to a Dorothea Schroeder, the daughter of German immigrants from Stuttgart...' Sherlock Holmes needed a break, to sip from his wine glass. 'Oscar Lepecheron is known to the Bank of England, and the Belgian Embassy were extremely helpful to my enquiry. The Lepecheron Bank in Brussels, of which Oscar was the smallest family shareholder, collapsed ten years ago after overly investing in what transpired to be a fraudulent mineral-extraction scheme in the Dutch East Indies: Oscar's elder brother, Hugo, was found guilty of knowing involvement in the fraud and jailed, the family prohibited by law from any future engagement in financial institutions or enterprises. Oscar was not named in the prosecution, at the height of which he left Belgium with a wife and daughter to settle in America...'

'Dear God, Sherlock!' exclaimed Mycroft. 'There is £4,000,000 from an undeclared government contingency fund deposited, with Churchill's approval but upon my authority, in Oscar Lepecheron's New York bank!'

'Then we must fervently hope that the American Treasury's A-1 rating for Lepecheron's establishment is not misplaced and that a persuasive mineral-mining salesman isn't active in New York City.'

'This is nothing to be sanguine about, sir!'

'And I am not sanguine about anything we are discussing tonight. I do think, however, that from our differing experiences of life I am at this moment better able to be objective. No dishonesty whatsoever attached to Oscar Lepecheron over the Brussels business ... And a minor matter has come to

240

my attention, through the enquiries I have been making.'

'A minor matter?'

'I have confirmed my original apprehension that my lodgings at 221b Baker Street have been under observation by two men whom I this morning identified from Scotland Yard Special Branch files to be responsible for fermenting Irish unrest against this country. There are outstanding warrants for their arrest. A watch is to be mounted at Baker Street, to effect that warrant. If they are attached to the German Embassy, which I suspect, they will doubtless invoke diplomatic immunity. But it will cause some disruption and might, temporarily at least, spare Mrs Hudson outings she does not enjoy.'

Mycroft shook his head in bewildered admiration. 'You truly amaze me. And I am glad, much relieved also, that Sebastian kept you more fully informed than I saw fit to do, to make so much deduction possible.'

The matter had fully to be aired, Sherlock Holmes decided. 'He didn't. But neither of you are good enough deceivers: you had no agreement between you upon what should be allowed me and what should not. You gave me tidbits that Sebastian withheld and Sebastian copied two messages to me that you failed to provide, which told me easily enough what was afoot. I did not, however, know anything about the Grand Duke Alexei Orlov being Sebastian's fellow passenger upon the *Lusitania* until I personally travelled to Liverpool

241

with the intention of studying the passenger list for the voyage and had the good fortune to encounter the worthy Captain Dow, master of the very liner. And learned from him of Sebastian's royal companions. It was logical Sebastian would have acquainted you with the presence of the Grand Duke. The Russian legation here were proud to tell me of the man's exalted royal position, although not of his clandestine occupation. That was provided by a nobleman of far lesser rank named Dimitri Poliakov who unwisely got himself involved in the fledgling democratic events of 1905 and now feels safer living in exile, here in London...' The detective smiled, pityingly. 'All I did tonight, dear brother, was *appear* to know of your withholding information and let you damn yourself out of your own mouth. The rest is achieved by pursuing one of the first elements of detection: knocking on sufficient doors and asking more than sufficient questions.'

'Never was a man so glad to be caught out than I. What's our way forward?'

'Sebastian must be informed of everything of which he is unaware. And perhaps more important still, of our reconciliation. Letter would be our most secure means...'

'There is something of which I fear you are still unaware,' interrupted Mycroft. 'Did your enquiries extend to Julius Hemditch?'

'Inconclusively: it's my intention to travel to Oxford to see if there is any lingering recollection of his time there. Why?'

Hurriedly, cathartically, Mycroft revealed Winston Churchill's refusal to disclose the contents of his introductory letter.

'Now there's a pot that needs to be stirred,' responded Sherlock Holmes. 'Quite clearly Sebastian is unsure of his host. Do you think there is some way in which Churchill could be playing a double game?'

'Quite frankly there are times when I doubt Winston quite knows how many games he is playing.'

'At least we have returned to the same side,' said Holmes.

Senator Carson's commitments prevented their resuming their meeting until the evening of Sebastian's third day in Washington. He occupied the intervening time orientating himself by walking the city and in doing so again felt the disappointment of his Capitol comparison at the smallness of the presidential White House against the palaces of Europe. Sebastian also spent several hours at the *Washington Post*.

He was surprised at the amount of written material there was about Count Johann von Bernstorff, despite the forewarning of the German ambassador's social leadership within the capital. There did not appear to be a diplomatic reception or gathering at which the man was not named as being a principal guest and the accounts were invariably accompanied by a photograph of the neatly bearded and moustached, autocratically featured Prussian. There were also several photographs of von Bernstorff with President Wilson. In marked contrast, references to the British ambassador were so rare it would have been possible to imagine London did not have any diplomatic representation in the city: Sebastian failed to locate a single photograph of the man with the American President.

There was what at first appeared to be extensive coverage of Representative Allan Grant's thwarted campaign but nothing more, upon concentrated reading, than Sebastian had discovered from the *New York Times*. Grant's death and the inquest were more fully reported than in New York, with a photograph of the man's mourning-veiled wife outside the coroner's court in which she had insisted her husband was an experienced hunter who would not have walked with an unbroken, cocked gun despite the contrary evidence of several witnesses described as being experts.

Their Capitol encounter had ended with Carson acknowledging the need for discretion in their future dealings, in consequence of which the politician accepted Sebastian's invitation to dine unobserved and unrecorded in his Willard suite. Aware as he was of the demands upon the man's time, Sebastian was prepared for Carson to be late – conceivably even for the meeting to be postponed – but the knock on the door came five minutes ahead of their arranged time. In Long Island

244

there had been the ritual of wine-savouring and food-appreciation. Tonight Carson served himself from the chafing dishes with scarce examination of their contents and showed a matching lack of interest in the wine. Again, there was no arm-waving orchestration of their conversation.

Sebastian ate and drank just as functionally, totally rehearsed with the benefit of the interval between their meetings. He was confident he presented as original the impressions of his business and political conversations with everyone with whom he had come into contact since his arrival in America and included the American Pan-German Association as a possible influencing organization after deciding there could be no reflection upon Laura Hemditch. He called heavily upon his railroad-car discussion with the Belgian banker and the freight line owner – as well as Churchill's insistence – of formalized clandestine groupings of American businessmen committing no legal offence by fraternizing with either European alliance. And finished by quoting, although not naming his source, Hemditch's insistence that the German Embassy in Washington was the centre of the web from which all pro-German activities emanated. It provided the obvious introduction to his impending visit to the German Embassy, which brought the first interruption from the American.

'Why should an Englishman so vehemently declared against association with his country's potential foes be so interested in attending a birthday celebration for its head of state?'

'Would you not attend, if invited?' replied Sebastian, rehearsed, too, for such a demand.

'Germany is not my country's potential enemy.'

'The inference is that you would?'

'It could be an informative event.'

'*Precisely* as I see it, an opportunity not to be shunned but rather to be seized. In view of your shortly to be declared interest I am surprised you have not weighed upon Smithlane to gain you the admission he got for me.'

'*Because* of that interest such an imposition would have seriously embarrassed the man, would it not?'

It had been an ill-considered question, Sebastian acknowledged, uncomfortably. 'You know of my purpose here: of my determination not to involve myself in any later embarrassing business dealings or associations. I regard the Kaiser's birthday reception as an essential precaution.'

'I know what you have told me of your purpose here,' said Carson, with heavy qualification.

'As I well know your intention if you believe yourself misled,' rejoined Sebastian. Double bluff upon double bluff, he thought.

Carson pushed his meal aside but remained toying with his wine glass, momentarily reflective. Then he announced: 'David Anderson is planning an article disclosing in

246

advance of my address to the Senate my intention to resurrect Grant's campaign, along with my demands for a reopened investigation to the various Delaware state authorities as well as the Justice Department and Capitol security services here.'

'Such widespread revelations will create a sensation.'

'That's the intention. How do you regard spying, Mr Holmes?'

'As a gentleman, with disdain and disgust. But the question is hypothetical.' This exchange was expanding to have more potential than he had anticipated.

'Even if it were to the advantage of your country?'

The moment for American directness, Sebastian decided. 'What is it you seek, Senator?'

'The fullest account possible of the Germany Embassy affair, in advance of my actually standing up in the Senate.'

Sebastian at once recognized the same cynicism employed by Winston Churchill. Perhaps it was a trait inherent in every politician. 'I think my conscience would square comfortably enough with that.'

Carson smiled, bleakly. 'I'd hoped it would.'

'I urge you to remain mindful of the dangers you could be attracting to yourself,' said Sebastian.

'Perhaps we should both remain mindful,' said Carson.

Sixteen

Sebastian Holmes understood why Count Johann von Bernstorff was the acknowledged leader of Washington society even before he crossed the embassy threshhold. The curving drive off Massachusetts Avenue was ablaze on either side with fiery, flame-tossed torches gathered in clumps directly in front of the mansion itself, their flickering light a burnishing illumination for the huge German flag fluttering from its masthead atop the building. The honour guard of servants between each of the approach beacons was attired in secured-to-the-neck uniforms of a severe, practically military cut and stood appropriately to stiff attention. There was military precision, too, in the way a further, matchingly dressed battalion received, disembarked and dispersed arriving carriages and occasional cars without once permitting even the suggestion of congestion or confusion.

The outside ceremony was a foretaste of the grandeur within. The vestibule was vast, more a formal reception room than an entrance hall. The floor was a marbled checkerboard of black and white and everything was illuminated by clustered chandeliers of countless lights. The first of several string ensembles were enclosed here in an artificial arbour of lilies and roses and hyacinth, all white, framed by genuine small trees and foliage with no visible support. Appropriately, the music was the first of Mozart's King of Prussia string quartets. Yet more sternly uniformed servants collected capes and canes – Sebastian had forsaken the favoured swordstick for a solid-bodied ebony – with the clockwork precision of their compatriots outside. Everything was under the iron command of a towering, rigid backed major-domo ushering arrivals towards a flowered creation even more inventive than the orchestral arbour, an arched tunnel within what normally must have been a high corridor but was now a thatched passage of tightly intertwined and plaited roses and jasmine, white again, against a deep-green background of polished-leaf ivy. Despite the smoothness of it all the crush of people made inevitable the briefest pause at the tunnel mouth. Just as inevitably, because of its commanding dominance on the lofty marble wall, everyone gazed up at an enormous portrait of the military uniformed and helmeted Kaiser Wilhelm in what Sebastian thought could easily be mistaken as a moment of homage. That thought came at the same time as his awareness that two photographers had chosen that spot and that backdrop for their pictures of the arriving socialities: as he passed he heard one address the other in German, picking up, '... *einen*

Grund erfreut zu sein...' – they have cause to be pleased.

There was an almost overwhelmingly heady aroma for the progress through the flower-bedecked avenue, which along its entire inner length had the smallest of lights in the shape of the stars they represented. Sebastian supposed the second of Mozart's King of Prussia quartets that accompanied his every step was provided by another string ensemble in the unseen outer corridor. As Sebastian neared the bower's end the whisper of sub-dued violins was lost beneath the approaching hubbub.

It was a huge, high-ceilinged and chandeliered room, dwarfing the vestibule, large as that was. Along the left side, an outer wall, ran five perfectly symmetrical French windows, all opened on to an encompassing verandah off which were regimented connecting overflow marquees. Hung from the facing wall, each with its individual illuminating bar light, were two more enormous oils of Kaiser Wilhelm, canopied by flags as huge as that on the outside masthead. Beneath and between the portraits a much larger string orchestra played. At the far end were two parallel buffet boards with a third table from which relays of waiters continuously circulated with trays of champagne flutes. Flowers, of every conceivable colour now, were everywhere in gigantic, green-fronded displays.

The ambassador and his entourage formed

a receiving group, all male, just beyond another stiff-backed major-domo who in size and demeanour could have been the twin of the other man in the outer room. Von Bernstorff was shorter than Sebastian had expected – the smallest in the group, in fact – but an ambience of authority emanated from the man like an encompassing shield. He wore his dress uniform of office, a line of miniatures across his left breast attesting to honours Sebastian assumed to have been gained in some original military career, although he supposed they could have been honorary. The beard and moustache were precise enough for each strand to have been clipped individually and the iron-grey hair was an undisturbed helmet of perfection. Sebastian guessed there to be in the region of 300 people – possibly more – already received and in the room ahead of him, but at the formal announcement of his name Sebastian was scrutinized with unwavering and totally untired intensity by everyone in the receiving line. It was composed of four men, in addition to the ambassador, with a fifth leading Sebastian through the introductions. The military attaché, Captain Otto Papen, wore the uniform of a Hussar and his miniatures row was as long as that of von Bernstorff. Both the cultural attaché, Heinrich von Strogel, and Alfred Scheele, the trade minister, bore on their left cheeks the sabre-fencing scar that Heidelberg students wore as a badge of courage and physical prowess. Both were

251

too old to have been his contemporaries but such a chance encounter – or recognition – was a possibility Sebastian had not contemplated. The handshake from each was accompanied by the heel-snapping, head-jerking Prussian formality reminiscent of his German university. Sebastian took his lead from von Bernstorff, responding to their greetings in English.

The thrust of following guests emerging from the floral walkway limited the encounter to the briefest of required officialism before propelling Sebastian onwards into the swirling crowd. He collected a conforming flute of champagne from a passing waiter but carried it with him untouched, adopting the same course as he had aboard the *Lusitania* for the captain's initial cocktail party, unwilling to have unrewarding conversation with anyone from whom he didn't imagine a benefit. His concentration was upon casually overheard conversational snippets – particularly accents – which was how, after evading three receptively smiling English-dominated groups, Sebastian eased himself into conversation with two men, one of whose cadences were unquestionably German. Ludwig Rottman identified himself as a cultural counsellor at the Austrian Embassy. The other man's German was so good that if his own ear had not been so linguistically attuned Sebastian would not have believed William Hartley to be English.

'We were discussing the unrest in Europe,'

disclosed Rottman. His English was thickly glottal.

'I am quite comfortable with German,' offered Sebastian, in that language.

'And you speak it well,' said Hartley, reverting himself.

'And so, sir, do you.'

'A German mother and the first twenty years of my life spent in the admirable city of Munich,' said Hartley. 'You?'

'The good fortune of a fine education. Heidelburg.' Sebastian judged the man now to be at least forty. Hartley's evening clothes were immaculate, without any miniatures indicating military service although the shortness of his greying hair might have hinted otherwise. He was very clear and steady-eyed, gazing almost directly and unblinking at the person he was addressing. Occasionally a tic pulled at the corner of his left eye.

'Someone well qualified to talk upon the matter then?' urged Hartley.

'May I ask what your opinion is?' said Sebastian, to the Austrian, refusing to be drawn.

The white-haired, portly man smiled, although sadly. 'I am an antiquarian first and a diplomat second. And hopefully a humanitarian somewhere in between. I've yet to be convinced from the history of any conflict that the suffering of a people and the destruction of their cultural heritage hasn't grossly outweighed any advantage of one nation's ambition over another's.'

Unusually outspoken – undiplomatic even – in such surroundings, gauged Sebastian. Or could it, on the other hand, be an enticement to an unguarded response? 'Do you fear the current situation will so degenerate?'

'I am also an optimist,' said the Austrian, although the smile was still sad. 'Wise counsel might still prevail.'

'I don't believe conflict can be avoided at this late stage,' declared Hartley, intent upon Sebastian. 'The matter's best confronted, the sides drawn up. There's no purpose in any more shilly-shallying...' He positively leaned forward, towards Sebastian. 'You, sir! How say you?'

If Rottman were a provocateur, he'd found an eager respondent in William Hartley. 'The omens were ominous immediately prior to my leaving London.'

'Sufficiently ominous for you to prefer the calm wash of these shores?' said Hartley.

Had he chosen to be offended, which at that early stage Sebastian didn't, the smiled suggestion of lightness would have failed to take away the ill grace, even outright impudence, of the remark. It would still be wrong to let it go completely. 'It is business, or rather the search for it, that brings me here, not evacuation.'

'Which I was not for one moment inferring, sir,' mollified Hartley.

'How recently were you in Germany?' enquired Rottman, with an interceding quickness belying his earlier qualification of diplomatic priorities. 'I have been away from Europe for almost two years, without an opportunity personally to assess attitudes and problems.'

'Just months,' said Sebastian.

'So you must agree conflict is inevitable!' demanded Hartley.

'I believe the risks are grave,' allowed Sebastian. Across the far side of the room, by one of the open French windows, he saw Lowell Smithlane. The shipping owner caught sight of Sebastian at the same time and gave a gesture of recognition. He was with a man and two women, neither of whom was Louise.

'How do you find the business opportunities here?' asked Hartley, in an abrupt change of direction.

'Inconclusive,' said Sebastian, prepared. 'But this is my first visit and I find myself with too few introductions. I am hopeful of an improvement.' He sipped his champagne for the first time. It had lost its chill.

'What, exactly, is your business?' pressed Hartley.

'The financing of them: investment,' said Sebastian. 'And yours?'

'Introductions,' smiled Hartley.

'That's not a commerce with which I am familiar,' frowned Sebastian.

'Linking like-minded people in shared enterprises,' said the other man. 'We could well have compatible interests.'

Sebastian decided he did not like the man

but instantly reminded himself that liking was not in any way a criterion. Rather, he supposed he should dislike the people it was his mission to uncover. Could William Hartley, seemingly so willing – anxious even – to claim Germany the admired land of his birth, be one such person? It would be wrong – inept – to attempt a hurried discovery, despite Hartley's apparent eagerness. He agreed that indeed there might be such a possibility, although a social occasion was hardly an appropriate setting for its discussion, grateful for another of Rottman's quickly timed enquiries if this were his first time in the city. It allowed the conversation to work towards an easy conclusion with talk of historical sights he should see but as he made to move off Hartley asked Sebastian if he might call upon him in Washington. When Sebastian identified the Willard, Hartley said it was a short walk from his rooms at the Army and Navy Club...

So tight was the throng of people that Sebastian occasionally lost sight of Lowell Smithlane as he edged across the room towards the open windows and the verandah. He was very close before his view was uninterrupted and realized from the man's welcoming smile that Smithlane had already seen his approach. Smithlane obviously identified him in advance from the way the others in his party turned in his direction. Sebastian was sure he had not been positively halted by not one but two simultaneous surprises, although the difficulty of making his way towards them would have covered such a pause.

Sebastian instantly recognized one of the men looking expectantly in his direction as a person he had seen enter the Broadway offices not just of the American Pan-German Association but then, within an hour, the door of the nearby Hamburg – America shipping line.

The second, quite separate surprise was the unmistakable sight at the centre of an attentive circle of men of an animated, laughing Princess Anna Boinburg-Langesfeld.

The man was a German, Hans Vogel, and was introduced by Smithlane as a member of the embassy's legal staff. His English was flawless, with scarcely any intonation. One of the women was his wife, Gerda. The other, Vera, was the new but very similar to the earlier female companion of Henry Blackmore, who had joined the group in the time it had taken Sebastian to cross the room. So had Louise Smithlane. The conversation began inconsequentially social. Blackmore insisted Sebastian had missed an excellent party ('the best steak in Kansas') by not travelling from New York in his personalized railway car, pressing Sebastian to join them in two days for their return. Before Sebastian could make an excuse, Vogel volunteered that he and his wife were eagerly anticipating the journey: it was going to be an unusual start to a vacation.

'Do you get the opportunity to go to New York often?' enquired Sebastian, presented with the opening.

'Hardly ever,' said the man. 'And never before in such style.'

'And we're looking forward to Long Island, too,' said Gerda. Her English was much more accented.

'Next weekend,' said Smithlane. 'You're welcome, if you get back from here by then.' He paused. 'Julius and Laura Hemditch are coming.'

'You're very generous but my movements remain uncertain.' Shouldn't he seize the opportunity specifically to spend time with a man who had so easily lied and whom he'd personally seen visit suspected nests of German agents?

'The offer is there if things become clearer for you,' smiled Louise Smithlane. 'We're planning a polo replay.'

'Which will be another new experience for us,' said Vogel. He almost imperceptibly touched his wife's arm, a signal to continue their diplomatic circling. They parted with the hope of seeing Sebastian in Long Island. Blackmore and his new companion moved off, too, in the direction of the buffet tables.

Louise Smithlane sighed after them and said: 'Henry is totally incorrigible. I'm really not sure we should welcome him so readily under our roof.'

'He's a good business customer,' said Smithlane.

'With the morals of an alley cat. I don't want him invited when the boys are home from school.'

Sebastian shifted, uncomfortably, and was about to use the disagreement as his excuse to move on when Smithlane ended it by nodding generally around the room and saying: 'I've been counting Congressmen. I'm up to fifteen, although I haven't spotted Jack Carson.'

Nor will you, thought Sebastian. He'd isolated two politicians from the photographs of diplomatic receptions he'd studied in the archives of the *Washington Post*. 'I appreciate now what you meant about von Bernstorff's social position.'

'Even by his own standards he's excelled himself tonight.' Smithlane more positively gestured across the room. 'And that white-haired guy talking to von Bernstorff at the moment is the Secretary of Defence.'

Sebastian said: 'You're obviously very familiar with such occasions.' Beyond the freight line owner Sebastian saw Anna was still within her group of eager admirers, although no longer so animated. She wore a long, pale-green gown he didn't remember from the *Lusitania* voyage, although it had the shimmer of sheer silk he knew her to favour. He didn't recognize the four-strand diamond choker and matching bracelet, either.

Smithlane said: 'We like Washington. It's "southern". New York is for business, Washington is for socializing.'

'And meeting the right people, which brings it back to business,' suggested Louise.

'That's what socializing is,' smiled her husband, refusing to fuel the bickering.

Both Americans took champagne from a hovering waiter and Sebastian exchanged his virtually full but now warm flute for one that was chilled.

'Shall we eat?' invited the woman.

'I'll join you in a moment,' promised Sebastian, making his escape. He shouldn't allow a personal distraction. He was there for a reason – two reasons, if he equally divided between Senator Carson and London what he believed himself to be discovering – and he shouldn't waste the continuing opportunity. *No souvenirs, no addresses*, he remembered. But not to acknowledge her, however briefly, would be ridiculous. The encounter could be over in minutes, endangering neither their parting understanding nor his further intelligence-gathering. Besides which, one of his Winchester tutors frequently dismissed his determination always to study by saying that all work and no play made Jack a dull boy. And Sebastian couldn't risk being dull.

Sebastian manoeuvred his approach to be in Anna's eye line before he reached her, to allow her a moment to collect herself from the surprise he'd experienced at finding her at the reception. He knew, from the directness of Anna's look, that she had seen him some way off but there was not the slightest recognition, although she did move slightly to widen the circle she dominated, to make it easier for him to be included. She was the only person aware of his approach. So loudly were two of Anna's three would-be suitors competing to impress that in the last few seconds Sebastian detected both the German phrasing and his way to involve himself in the gathering. The discussion was an emptily boastful attempt at intellectualism – one arguing against the assertion of the other that Heine was a more romantic poet than Goethe – and Sebastian paused, as if caught by the dispute, to suggest that Goethe spanned the classical to romanticism and was braver in experimentation with the language. The resentment at Sebastian's intrusion was palpable but Prussian mores required heel-clicking formal introductions, which Anna endured with the straight-faced politeness of a total stranger. All three men, it emerged, were on the embassy staff – two in the trade section, the other a junior cultural attaché – which reassured Sebastian that he was possibly not neglecting his volunteered role after all. Perhaps apprehensive of Sebastian's superior appreciation, the literary discussion was quickly surrendered to elaborated accounts of gunfighters still existing in some isolated parts of the American west and insistences that undiscovered gold and silver lodes of Solomon-mines proportions still remained to be found in California. Sebastian supposed the captain's-table conversations aboard the *Lusitania* with mining magnate

John Morganstein gave him a contribution to make but he remained silent, instead courteously allowing himself to appear suitably awed. It took longer than Sebastian expected for the faint English accent to be detected in his German but before the German questioning could properly begin the junior cultural attaché, clearly responding to a signal outside their group, motioned to his colleagues and all three simultaneously excused themselves.

'My trusted Porthos to the rescue again!' properly greeted Anna, at last. 'I have never met three more boring men. Nor wish to again. Gunfighters and gold lodes!'

Sebastian was watching the three, conscious of others vaguely converging towards the orchestra dais beneath the Kaiser's portrait. 'I think you were spared more by some diplomatic call than by my intrusions.'

'I prefer to be rescued by Porthos. That's how Heine would have had it.'

It was the lightness of the voyage again. 'You are the last person in the world I thought to encounter here.'

'As you are, for me.'

'How's the foot?'

There was the briefest of recollective frowns. 'Completely better.'

'I looked for you, to say goodbye the morning of our arrival.'

'That wasn't the understanding.'

'I know.'

'And now we are thrown together again.'

'Are we?' asked Sebastian. It couldn't be, if

262

he were diligently to accomplish his mission. Or could it?

Instead of answering Anna said: 'You knew on the first day of the crossing that my natural language would have been Austro-German. To make me speak otherwise when we were privately together was not the behaviour of a musketeer!'

And from this encounter potentially could have arisen a grave mistake. 'I most humbly beg your forgiveness: English and French became so naturally accepted between us...' Sebastian shrugged. '...the consideration quite simply did not occur to me. Which is a compounding of my rudeness rather than an acceptable excuse.'

'Where did you learn German?'

'Heidelberg.'

'An academy of sabre-wielding militarism!'

'A wild and unfounded exaggeration!' protested Sebastian.

Anna sniggered, too late confirming for Sebastian a playful entrapment. She said: 'This is much more amusing!'

'You tricked me.'

'Not so! You are altogether too serious, like that boring trio who reacted even more vehemently to the same accusation. I know a different Porthos.'

A justified complaint, acknowledged Sebastian. His father – according to Dr Watson's journals – was much more adept at donning the cloaks of different personae. 'You demand another apology.'

'Not demand.'

'Deserve then. And which I make.'

'Seriousness – dolefulness – easily succumbed to.' Anna looked beyond him, to the
now packed reception. 'Doesn't there seem a
determination – desperation even – to force
enjoyment here? It's all so perfect, so regimented, that it defies itself. Wouldn't it be
wonderful, although sad for the man, if just
one of those mechanical waiters dropped a
tray or a violinist or a cellist played the wrong
note?!'

'Now you're becoming serious – morbid
even – in pursuit of amusement. If indeed it's
possible to be morbidly amused.'

'*Touché!*' she accepted. 'Which I remember
you once conceding to me.'

'Along with so much else.'

Anna smiled, holding his eyes. 'I think the
concessions were mutual.'

'I am so glad we have met again.'

'No souvenirs, no addresses.'

'The carousel has turned its circle. How are
you here, why are you here, are we to part
again with some other agreement, or the
same?'

'So many demands!'

Sebastian hoped his new attempted cloak
was not as ill fitting as its predecessor. 'I have
no apologies left.'

'I arrived, as doubtless you did, with a
number of kind introductions in an unknown
land. One was to the ambassador, which I
presented. This invitation was the result.'

'A fortunate one?'

'Perhaps!'

'There were other questions.'

'I am momently in Virginia, on the estate of a widow to whom I also had an introduction...' She scanned the room. '...Mrs Amelia Becker, talking to that couple there.'

The couple were Hans and Gerda Vogel. 'Virginia is a neighbouring state, is it not?'

'Even by automobile, by which we came, it's a considerable journey.'

'It would have been pleasant if you had been staying here in Washington.'

'Where are your rooms?'

'The Willard, close to the White House.'

'I would...' Anna began but was cut off by the strident and incongruous sound of a trumpet call.

Drawn towards it, Sebastian saw the string orchestra had been supplemented by an already seated and prepared brass section. The sound was so unexpected that the demanded silence was practically immediate, complete enough for Count Johann von Bernstorff's commanding voice to be heard through the room, inviting the gathering to join him in a toast to the health of His Royal Highness, Kaiser Wilhelm. As he raised his fresh glass, along with everyone else, and echoed, *'Zum wohl,'* Sebastian saw that William Hartley was staring fixedly at him.

The orchestra at once struck up the German national anthem. The majority of the embassy staff appeared to have congregated directly in front of the dais, a virtual choir, and sang *Heil dir im Siegekranz, Herrscher des Vaterlands*, stiffly to attention. As the singing died Anna murmured: 'The sort of militaristic performance I left Europe to escape. But for the danger of too much broken glass they would have smashed their goblets to complete the ritual.' She had not joined in the singing, as a lot of people had.

The ceremony had indeed been overwhelmingly martial. 'Rare cynicism from a princess,' remarked Sebastian.

'Perhaps I am better fitted to this country, spared as it is the need for royal pomp and ceremony!' She seemed abruptly depressed.

'Can I escort you to the buffet tables?'

'I should rejoin my Virginian hostess. The understanding was of an early departure with such a return journey ahead of us.'

'Shall you get to Washington again?'

'I don't know.'

'Or New York?'

'I have no plans.'

'Goodbye again then. But this time you have my Washington address.' It was an invitation.

'Yes,' she said, failing to respond.

Sebastian watched Anna Boinberg-Langesfeld make her way through the crush, aware of her quickly changing direction to avoid the return of the junior cultural attaché. From afar Amelia Becker appeared a formidable matriarch, heavy-bosomed and authoritatively tall. There was no smile of greeting at

Anna's return.

Sebastian was uninterested in food but the buffet was the direction in which Lowell Smithlane had gone and Sebastian hoped to obtain for Senator Carson named identification of the attending politicians and maybe even of other senior government figures. But as he turned he saw Count Johann von Bernstorff less than five yards away, bearing directly towards him. The ambassador was accompanied by Hans Vogel and Captain Papen, the military attaché.

'I trust you are enjoying our soirée, Mr Holmes?' The ambassador spoke German.

'It would be a man of small appreciation and great discontent who failed to do so,' replied Sebastian, sure he had suppressed his astonishment both at the approach and at what could be deduced from it. He had, of course, been introduced by name at the receiving line but it was inconceivable it would have been remembered from that fleeting initial encounter. And he had spoken English then and again with Vogel, so someone – Ludwig Rottman or one of the group around Anna – must have specifically and unaccountably passed on his ease with German.

'Are you long in this country?' The junior cultural attaché had come up to complete the protective half circle at von Bernstorff's back.

'A matter of weeks. It is a country of great interest.' He had most assuredly been singled out. Why?

'Business or pleasure?'

267

'Business, if an opportunity were to present itself. Pleasure – although I cannot imagine an occasion exceeding this – when it does not.'

There was a grimace of a smile. 'If your business ability matches that of your diplomacy you should have great success, Mr Holmes. They instructed you well at Heidelberg.'

Only the Austrian, Ludwig Rottman, and William Hartley knew of Heidelberg. And now Anna, he remembered. But she had been nowhere near von Bernstorff since their just-concluded conversation. 'It's an admirable seat of learning.'

'I once served as ambassador to London,' abruptly announced von Bernstorff. 'I had occasion to encounter a man of great renown of the same name as yourself. Of even greater coincidence is a similarity of look and appearance between you.'

The concentration upon him, not just from the ambassador but from his three companions, was of practically unblinking intensity and the chill that engulfed Sebastian made the skin of his back physically prickle. He smiled. 'You speak, of course, of the famous Sherlock Holmes?'

'There is a relationship, then?' The German's voice was as icy as Sebastian's discomfort.

There was no more securely kept secret than that of his birth and parentage, Sebastian knew. Smiling still, he said: 'It would indeed be a kinship to be proud of but alas I cannot claim it, although the similarity of appearance has been remarked upon before. It even prompted me to enquire of my own family, who reminded me that Holmes is not at all an uncommon name and that there is no connection between us. And through his fame, it is known of course that Sherlock Holmes is a confirmed bachelor, to the extreme even of misogyny.'

In the midst of so much discordant babble there was a totally unreal moment when it seemed to Sebastian that he and the four Germans were isolated in an oasis of echoing silence. It was the ambassador who broke it. 'Of course. As I suggested, a truly remarkable coincidence.'

'Even more so as you are acquainted with the great man himself.'

The near imperceptible signal through which the embassy appeared to conduct its internal communications – the merest brushing of the ambassador's arm – came from Hans Vogel. Von Bernstorff said: 'It has been a pleasure having you with us.'

'The greater pleasure has been mine.'

The chill stayed prickling at Sebastian as the ambassador and his group moved off to continue their diplomatic progress and briefly it took the greatest effort of will to hold back from physically betraying it, shivering even. He'd confronted the spider in the very middle of his web. But had he escaped entrapment?

Without making his interest obvious Sebastian succeeded in having Lowell Smithlane point out the American Under Secretary of Trade and the senior permanent advisor at the Treasury, as well as locating twelve Congressmen whom he hoped to be able to identify later from photographs. He parted from the freight line owner with a renewed invitation to Long Island and from Henry Blackmore with the repeated urging to travel back to New York on his personal rail car. As he was threading his way through the still-thick crowd, anxious now to get away to assemble on paper all that he believed he had learned, Sebastian was confronted by William Hartley in such a manner as to make him suspect the man had laid ambush.

'You appear well acquainted with the ambassador,' challenged the man.

'A courtesy encounter,' dismissed Sebastian.

'Of the longest duration of any during his circulation.'

'You appear to pay the greatest attention to the smallest of details.'

'It is in my interest to pay the greatest attention to the smallest of details. I press again for permission to call upon you.'

The likeliest source of the ambassador or one of his acolytes learning of his Heidelberg attendance had to be the Austrian diplomat but there was, Sebastian supposed, the possibility of it having come instead from this fervent German admirer. 'You have my address here in Washington. I look forward to hearing from you.'

Slumped in his home-going carriage, Sebastian was prepared to accept that Count von Bernstorff had spent longer with him than with any other individual guest. Certainly it had seemed of extraordinary length and even more certainly anything but a politely casual diplomatic encounter. At that stage there was only one further certainty, that of his having no intention whatsoever of informing London of the episode.

The seizure of the unwelcomed observers, which Sherlock Holmes watched from the window of 221b Baker Street with Watson by his side, compensated for a totally unproductive visit to Oxford and Julius Hemditch's old college, Balliol. No tutors remained who remembered the American and the surviving records of the man's academic career reading Classics were unremarkable. He had involved himself in no extra curricula activities and Sherlock Holmes failed to find one college photograph in which the man appeared. His tutor's graduation comment upon Hemditch was a single word, diligent. Sherlock Holmes's comment to Watson upon his return was that Julius Hemditch was a man of anonymity.

The Scotland Yard arrest of the wanted men was the following day, perfectly coordinated around Dr Watson's meticulous records of their movements, which were for them fatally regular and could therefore be anticipated. Special Branch officers were already emplaced twenty yards in each direction along Baker Street when the two skulked into their customary alley, both inexpertly failing to notice that it, too, was sealed at its furthest end by an apparently disabled carriage which was, in fact, full of waiting officers. Their entrapment was achieved by tightening a screw: visibly uniformed officers – backed by companions in plain clothes – began a pincering approach along Baker Street in converging directions, forcing the two further into the alley which was an evasive manoeuvre well recorded by Dr Watson. At the alley mouth, however, the officers stopped to create a block and when their quarry turned to escape, they found the far end bottlenecked by more uniformed constabulary emerging from the broken-wheeled coach. From either end the plain-clothed Special Branch detectives closed in to make the official arrests.

From his vantage point, Sherlock Holmes said: 'So ends an irritating problem.'

'What's to stop these miserable two being replaced by others?'

'Preparation, my dear Watson, upon which all good casework is predicated. You shall accompany me this very day to the Yard, to see its benefits.'

Sherlock Holmes and his chronicler occupied an office so closely adjoining the

272

interrogation room that they were able to hear everything of Inspector Lestrade's questioning, which concentrated wholly upon the men's known activities in Dublin, which met with the steadfast refusal of either to utter a single word in response, defence or explanation. Lawyers from the German Embassy did not arrive until late in the day to invoke diplomatic immunity for both men, whose accreditation as military section support staff was confirmed by already prepared and briefed Foreign Office officials. Those same officials announced that the two detained men were to be declared *personae non gratae* for activities unacceptable to their status as diplomats. Their expulsion was to be made public, together with the strongest protest to the German Embassy at clear, although unadmitted, continuing anti-British espionage involving an Irish cell somewhere in Baker Street, which was going to be pursued until it was located.

'And there we have the preparation,' declared Sherlock Holmes, in the carriage taking them back to the lodgings. 'My name – or indication of my suspicions – does not come into it and the Germans, believing they were detected through their Irish involvement, will not in future come within miles of Baker Street for risk of further embarrassment.'

'An admirable resolution,' congratulated Watson. 'We can now operate and move unimpeded and unobserved.'

'And the good Mrs Hudson no longer has to endure her much disliked bath-chair rides.'

'Nor do I have to be the engine for such outings!'

'In fact, Watson, I think we might well consign that damnable bath chair to storage somewhere.'

'Only storage?' protested the other man.

'Always better to be prepared,' Sherlock Holmes reminded him.

Sebastian rose once more close to dawn to occupy the entire morning writing an account later to be posted to his uncle recounting in the minutest detail the events and his interpretations of the previous night. He kept to the omission he had already decided on by not including the confrontation with Count Johann von Bernstorff and also left out any mention of William Hartley. Still with time in hand before Senator Carson's arrival, Sebastian hurried to the *Washington Post* and from their archival photographs of inaugural sessions of the most recent Congressional elections succeeded from Lowell Smithlane's identification and his own recollections in naming a total of fifteen senators and House representatives who had attended the German reception.

It took Sebastian an uninterrupted thirty minutes to relay it all to Jack Carson, who at the conclusion said at once: 'Your certainty that it was Hans Vogel you saw in New York is our most vital intelligence.'

'Do you intend isolating him by name?' There was no way, Sebastian reassured himself, that he could be associated with the information.

Carson shook his head. 'There could easily be other diplomats making such calls. Leaving the identity unspecified will cause greater confusion among them.'

'When do you begin?'

'Anderson's article will appear in the *New York Times* tomorrow. I have Senate time in the afternoon.'

'I fear all the more for your safety.'

'They got away – or thought they got away – with violence once. They won't risk being so obvious again. And as I told you, I don't shoot.'

'Others do, although not at game,' said Sebastian, turning the man's remark back upon him.

Seventeen

The *New York Times* disclosure of Jack Carson's intended Senate statement was separated from the man's demand to reopen the investigation into the death of Congressman Grant but linked under a connecting headline. The combined coverage occupied half the front page and a third of page two, on to which it continued. Sebastian guessed the accompanying photograph of Count Johann von Bernstorff was from the birthday reception, while reminding himself there were few people in Washington for whom the newspaper would have a wider choice of social and diplomatic settings. A spokesman for the ambassador was quoted as saying there were no spy cells nor clandestine activities being conducted from the German Embassy and describing the claims as nonsensical and malicious fabrication. There were also photographs of the offices of the Hamburg-America shipping line and the American Pan-German Association, both of which also issued denunciations. The virtually unanimous response from the Congressmen whose identities Sebastian had supplied was that attending diplomatic functions was an essential and integral part of their political

276

life. The Secretary of Defence, who, from his photograph, had definitely been at the reception, declined to comment. In the associated story there was a picture of Allan Grant's widow alongside an interview in which she insisted her husband's death was not an accident. The late Congressman's campaign manager, Burt Williams, was also quoted welcoming the possibility of a new investigation. Directly asked if he believed Grant to have been murdered, Williams said he thought it far more likely than the death being accidental, despite the findings of the inquest.

Sebastian supposed there was a public gallery at the Senate from which he could have seen and heard Carson's speech but decided it would be unwise for him publicly to be seen there after hearing a reporter on a continuous radio news programme describe the Capitol as being under siege. It certainly sounded as if it were from the degree of background babble. Sebastian remained listening in his suite for most of the morning, during the course of which were repeated all the denials already printed in the newspaper. Sebastian was one of the few people in the hotel dining room not to be carrying or reading the *New York Times* at lunch and there was obviously very little other conversation. Sharing a table were two of the Congressmen Sebastian had seen at the embassy: one made notes in a spiral-backed jotting pad throughout the meal.

Although Sebastian believed he had made clear the unlikelihood of his taking up the invitation, politeness dictated that he formally decline in writing the offer to return to New York on Henry Blackmore's train. He was halfway through his note, a courier on standby, when he suddenly wondered if, in the circumstances, Hans Vogel and his wife would still be travelling. And decided just as quickly it was a question to be answered personally.

The cab climbed Pennsylvania Avenue by the now familiar route, enabling Sebastian a wide view of the Capitol. There were a reasonable number of people in evidence, perhaps more so around the Senate building itself, but Sebastian thought it fell far short of a siege. There actually appeared to be more people in Union Station. It took the briefest enquiry to learn that Blackmore's carriage had already been moved from its private siding, to be hitched to the New York-bound train, and even less to guess the actual car from its red and yellow paintwork before a railway inspector positively identified it as Blackmore's. Sebastian reflected that perhaps in the yellow wheatfields and sunshine of Kansas such colour schemes looked less garish.

Blackmore was at the bottom of his carriage steps and saw Sebastian from some way off, waving and shouting something back into the train, so that by the time Sebastian reached it Lowell Smithlane had also descended and was waiting for him.

'You've decided to come with us then?' greeted Blackmore.

'Alas no,' apologized Sebastian. 'That's what I've come to tell you. I didn't want you left uncertain.'

'You've seen the paper?' demanded Smithlane.

Both were equally exercised, Sebastian decided. 'Paper?'

'Come aboard,' urged Blackmore. 'There's sufficient time. The girls still have to do their last-minute shopping.'

Sebastian followed his host, with Smithlane behind. Louise Smithlane and Blackmore's current companion were seated on opposing couches, each with their individual copy of the *New York Times*, although both wore hats and had parasols at their sides. The two women seemed reluctant to interrupt their reading to acknowledge his greeting. There were other copies of the newspaper strewn about the carriage, in which the outer colour was continued for the interior decor. It appeared longer than Lowell Smithlane's, with stools at the steward-manned bar separating the dining and lounge areas. All the seats were covered in matching yellow hide and there were genuine cowboy and Native American lithographs on the wall. Sebastian imagined it was like sitting in the middle of a prairie sunset.

'See that?' demanded Blackmore, pointing to the largest lithograph on the wall. 'My grandfather. Fought against the Indians in a covered wagon all the way to where the Blackmore spread is now; no hill or rise high enough to see both boundaries at the same time.'

For a land of the future there seemed an eagerness to hold on to the past, thought Sebastian. 'It's difficult to believe.'

'Even more difficult to have achieved,' insisted Blackmore. 'You'll accept a drink?'

'Just coffee.' Sebastian didn't hurry with his apparent first reading of the *New York Times*, remaining hunched over the newspaper for several minutes after the two women began gathering up their belongings for their intended expedition.

'We were *there*!' exclaimed Louise Smithlane. 'It must have been happening all around us and we didn't know!'

'We don't *know* anything happened anywhere,' reminded her husband.

'Murder as well as espionage!' persisted Louise, undeterred and checking around her to ensure nothing was forgotten. 'Until the truth is established I think we've got to guard against invitations from the wrong sort of people.'

It had taken him a long time to establish Louise Smithlane to be a snob, Sebastian recognized. This wasn't a social visit, he reminded himself. Fluttering the opened newspaper, Sebastian said: 'These articles appear well researched; Carson and Anderson must have some well-established inside informant...'

'Or they have inherited Allan Grant's sources, after the man's death,' suggested Smithlane.

'The most obvious explanation,' accepted Blackmore, at once.

The two women announced their departure and left with specific warnings from Blackmore upon the time for their return. 'The train won't wait longer than five minutes and I won't indulge you in that.'

'Don't fuss so!' complained Louise. As the woman, talking animatedly, led the way from the car Sebastian thought how quickly Louise had lost her moral indignation at Blackmore's frequently changed partners.

'I am surprised Carson didn't make reference to what he was going to do when we were all together, particularly after you raised the subject,' Smithlane said to Sebastian the moment the three men were alone.

Sebastian experienced a stir of apprehension. He ruffled the newspaper he still held and said: 'There's a considerable difference between what little discussion we had then and the detail contained here.'

'Agents and spies!' said Smithlane, dramatically.

Sebastian decided the man saw himself as part of an adventure; the question was how much of a part? He moved to speak but Blackmore anticipated him.

'Patriots and friends afar,' said the mid-Westerner.

281

There was a deep silence with almost a palpable inference that Sebastian was expected to fill it. Sebastian did so by saying: 'I am sorry. I don't understand what you've just said.'

Blackmore made an careless movement, almost a gesture of embarrassment. 'There are stories, late-night ramblings after too much brandy, of clubs – groups of men – combining in the manner that this newspaper account suggests. Not so much spies or agents or whatever. Men engaged in legitimate commerce. But with an air of the clandestine about them.'

'About which you and I have had discussions,' Smithlane unnecessarily reminded Sebastian.

'Patriots?' pressed Sebastian, guessing the words to be titles. 'Friends Afar?'

'Drunken ramblings,' dismissed Blackmore.

'Do groups exist, by such names?' persisted Sebastian. He had an abrupt recollection of Lowell Smithlane introducing the words – patriot or patriotism certainly – in what had at the time appeared a clumsy manner, as if he were inviting the recognition of a password or code. How long it seemed since he'd had occasion to employ his own hidden language. The irony was that now, when he might be needing it most, he believed it too unsafely intriguing to use.

The two identifications had been introduced by the other two men. Sebastian decided he had every justification in pursuing the conversation. 'To whom do such groups consider themselves patriots and friends?'

Blackmore gave another embarrassed gesture. 'I've never paid much mind to such nonsense. Nor met anyone admitting to being part of such a caucus.'

'Nor I,' said Lowell Smithlane. 'I've heard the suggestions, like everyone else. But it seems to me the stuff and nonsense of cheap books.'

To the two Americans he said: 'Shouldn't you tell someone? Jack Carson for instance?'

'What is there to tell?' demanded Smithlane. 'There's no illegality.'

'It might be interesting to Senator Carson, in view of today's announcement. I assumed him to be a friend of you both?'

'I think this a matter best left to others,' said Smithlane.

'Particularly if there is murder afoot, which I personally find impossible to believe, as I find strangely named clubs themselves impossible to believe or take seriously,' endorsed Blackmore.

There was much to think about and most carefully to analyse from this encounter, Sebastian decided; probably more, at the moment, than he fully realized. The thought – and the resolve – came literally at a whistle from a trolley porter sufficient to give the obviously pre-warned car steward time swiftly to bundle and stow the dissected newspapers in his kitchen galley before descending the steps to bring on board the

Vogels' luggage. There was a trunk, as well as two suitcases.

'I had looked forward to continuing our conversation,' complained Vogel, when Sebastian told him that business prevented his making the New York trip.

'There's still the weekend,' reminded Smithlane.

'I hope to be there,' said Sebastian, still undecided.

There were two messages awaiting Sebastian when he returned to the Willard. The first was on a letterhead of the nearby Army and Navy Club, inviting Sebastian to dine there the following night and signed by William Hartley. The other was an unidentified sheet in a matchingly anonymous envelope. There was no greeting, just an address – 34 Prospect Street, Georgetown – and a time, eight o'clock. It was signed, simply, C.

There was no logical reason for Sebastian to fear he was under physical observation but for the first time since his arrival in America he set out cautiously, too easily able to remember the mistakes he had made while being tested by his father. But unlike that failed test, Sebastian's mind was now doubly occupied by his effort properly to understand the railcar encounter. Had it, in fact, been another test? Certainly there had been a definite artifice, which was difficult to analyse because his personally going to Union

284

Station had been an impromptu decision, with no forewarning to allow Smithlane or Blackmore to prepare. Or had both men doubted his German Embassy refusal to join them on the train and been expecting him, rehearsing their strange charade in the hope he would declare himself?

Washington was a difficult city in which to satisfy oneself that one was alone. Laid out as it was in the criss-cross grid fashion of New York, but without even the occasional un-planned alley or sidestreet, it was a victim's nightmare and a watcher's dream, box upon box from which a quarry could be tracked from behind, sideways or in front. Immediately around the Willard there was not even the mirroring advantage of shop windows. He walked the length of the hotel's central corridor to emerge from its rear entrance on to F Street and proceeded purposefully in the direction of the White House, the swordstick swinging easily from his right hand. He stopped, apparently to study the Andrew Jackson statue in Lafayette Square, in reality carefully scrutinizing people behind him, but did not pause again until he gained the reflective glass of the shopping area along 15th Street. There he loitered in a seemingly aimless study of window displays, failing to detect any persistent follower from the Lafayette Square check or anyone showing undue interest in him since.

He carefully calculated the hailing of a solitary cab, so none following could be taken up in pursuit, and ensured no one was within hearing when he identified Georgetown. Here he still avoided a specific address, rapping the sounding board to be set down within yards of turning on to Winsconsin Avenue from M Street. Sebastian was sure he was within the shadows of another shop doorway quickly enough to have seen any following cab in obvious pursuit. There was none. Although maintaining the grid system, the minor roads of Georgetown were narrower and easier to check, which he did over the next fifteen minutes before finally approaching the tree-shaded Prospect Street.

The door was opened at once by the tightly corseted, grey haired Edna Connolly. She beckoned him quickly inside, not speaking until she had closed the door behind him. Then she said: 'The others are already here,' and made another gesture for him to follow.

The room to which she guided him was bow-fronted, providing a view in both directions of the street along which Sebastian had just walked, although Jack Carson and David Anderson were deep within it, out of sight.

Carson said: 'Edna's offering sanctuary for our meetings: my own house is besieged by newspapermen to whom I don't choose at this moment to talk.'

'And who knows by whom else?' wondered Anderson.

'I stayed away from the Senate,' said Sebastian. 'How did it all go?'

'Not a word I enjoy using but *sensationally*

fits for once,' said Anderson. 'My own paper is making it their main lead tomorrow.'

'And the investigation into Grant's death is definitely to be reopened, this time conducted by the police, as it should have been in the beginning,' said Carson.

'Everything as you wanted it,' suggested Sebastian. How long would it be before he received something in return from the Congressman?

'Now the momentum has got to be kept up,' insisted the man. 'There's more than enough from my speech for tomorrow's papers and radio, which is why I'm laying low tonight. Tomorrow I've promised a press conference. I'll announce then the fact that Grant's original material is missing and I'm also going to demand a security check to establish how it might have been stolen from the Capitol. That should generate another Senate as well as a House debate...'

'But we need more,' completed Anderson. 'You gave a lot of stuff to Jack about the embassy reception. I want to talk it through again, pick up anything that might have slipped your mind.'

'Nothing did,' insisted Sebastian, at once.

'Let's just kick it around,' urged Carson. 'You saw the Secretary of Defence with von Bernstorff. How about any of the Congressmen?'

'Not that I saw,' said Sebastian.

'What about these secret clubs or societies?' asked the journalist.

Patriots and Friends Afar surged into Sebastian's mind together with what he just as quickly decided was the purpose of the strangely forced conversation earlier that day at Union Station. More a trial than a test, Sebastian thought. Lowell Smithlane and Henry Blackmore – at least one of them – suspected him either of involvement in some clandestine society or of colluding with Jack Carson, to whom he'd introduced the conversation about foreign influence and with whom he'd driven back from Long Island to New York. But yet again, a trial to what end? To declare himself as a conspirator in one or the other; identify a third even? Or to establish whether he was acting as Carson's source by naming both to the senator for him to in turn identify in another congressional debate or speech?

Certainly neither Smithlane nor Blackmore could be part of either group. If they were, they would know he was unassociated and would not have invited recognition. Nor would they be likely to name the groups and risk their being publicly exposed. Unless they were made up of business rivals whom they sought to denounce or embarrass. Still more conundrums but none sufficient to misdirect him. He'd say nothing yet of Patriots or Friends Afar to Carson or Anderson. Neither would he reveal Blackmore and Smithlane's travelling companions nor give any hint of the forthcoming encounter with William Hartley, about which at that moment he anyway knew too little to discuss. Sebastian said: 'I know no more than I have already talked about with you or than Grant suggested in his own speeches. I thought the hope was that you'd attract Grant's sources by what you've done.'

'Which is why I want to keep the publicity going!' said Carson. 'We can't risk everything spluttering out after a few days.'

'That's hardly likely with the reopening of an investigation into a potential murder and allegations of infiltration and theft within the Capitol,' said Sebastian.

Anderson shook his head. 'The very fact that murder is being alleged could well be the deterrent to Grant's informant coming forward again.'

'Then you've defeated yourself,' assessed Sebastian. And by so doing had closed off his chance to learn anything more than he already knew.

'That's what I am most determined not to let happen. And why I'm scratching for any forgotten crumbs.'

They talked – eventually repeating themselves – for more than two further hours, extending the conversation over a meal of what Carson's office manager called pot roast, before the senator finally declared that Sebastian had indeed told him everything from the embassy gathering.

'Is there the possibility of your learning more?' demanded Anderson.

Sebastian gave an uncertain movement. 'Not that I can foresee.'

'We'll keep in touch by phone,' announced Carson. 'Edna knows you're part of everything; she'll liase.'

Perhaps, thought Sebastian, there might have been more benefit in his taking up the Long Island invitation after all.

For want of an immediate secure and private meeting place Churchill had accompanied Mycroft directly to his Diogenes quarters from the hurriedly convened Cabinet meeting to consider the Washington Embassy telegram reporting virtually all of the *New York Times* articles.

With his Havana kindled into a comfortable glow and the brandy decanter conveniently close, Churchill said: 'There can't be any doubt that Sebastian's hand is in this?'

'There was the letter setting out his meeting with Carson on Long Island and his earlier reports of the other congressman's death,' agreed Mycroft

'Then he's done well, despite my concern at his getting too closely involved in politics,' allowed Churchill.

Mycroft sighed, irritably. 'We don't yet know the extent of his involvement, not enough to judge whether he's too close or not. The embassy talked of the American government as well as the Germans being greatly exercised. That's precisely what we want to achieve, isn't it?'

Churchill appeared oblivious to the other man's annoyance. 'Don't like being cut off from him like this. What about this code of yours?'

'Unthinkable, on an open telegraph in a public hotel.'

'What about a message in clear: something innocuous from which he'll get the proper meaning?'

'To what purpose?' dismissed Mycroft. 'He wouldn't be able to respond in anything like sufficient detail to make the effort worthwhile.'

'I think reference should be made to the matter in the House,' announced Churchill.

The man was fantasizing personal headlines again. 'What sort of reference?'

'A question asking the Foreign Office for an assessment of anti-British activities in America.'

'Carson didn't make any anti-British statement!'

'He talked about Germany and "other possible nations involved in European unrest seeking to influence American business",' accurately quoted Churchill.

'You must not do this without learning more about what Sebastian intends,' insisted Mycroft. 'It would be you, a minister of the Crown, positively identifying Great Britain. Your intervening could upset a scheme of which we're unaware.'

'I want him telegraphed, innocuously as I suggested. I want guidance.'

'We got guidance today, quite properly through our embassy!'

'We got newspaper articles relayed to us, as they'll no doubt appear in tomorrow's *Times*. Send the telegram. And congratulate your brother on his sterling work. I'm minded to speak privately to Grey about this Grand Duke business. It's monstrous our own embassy in St Petersburg was unknowing of the man's importance and possible emissary function, which Holmes was able to discover here in London!'

'How will you account for your knowledge to the Foreign Secretary?'

'Don't see why I've damned well got to,' said Churchill, truculently, adding to his brandy bowl. 'We can't afford separate, secret treaties, certainly not between Russia and the United States. We've got to know – and be able to trust – where we are with both.'

Mycroft conceded that there was no argument against. 'At least it shouldn't be difficult for our embassy to discover if Orlov has returned to St Petersburg. If he hasn't, the likelihood is that he'll still be in Washington...'

'Capital!' cut off Churchill, loudly. 'Tell Sebastian as best you can to be on the lookout. And don't pass on my congratulations to your brother. Changed my mind. I'll do it myself at dinner. Want to hear his assessment of what might be going on in Washington; how we might become publicly involved from here.'

Eighteen

Mycroft Holmes's telegraph read:

GREATLY INTERESTED TO LEARN MORE QUICKLY AND FULLY YOUR CURRENT BUSINESS NEGOTIATIONS WHICH ARE HAVING PERSONAL REPERCUSSIONS HERE STOP ALSO EVEN MORE GREATLY INTERESTED TO LEARN OF ANY REUNION WITH EARLIER GRAND TOUR ACQUAINTANCES STOP WELCOME SOONEST ADVICE STOP WITH COUPLED APPRECIATION COMMA ADMIRATION AND GRATITUDE STOP.

It was not the actual sign-off, *sodger*, that irritated Sebastian – it could easily have been a rather uncouth surname – but the use of a Notions word designating an X to draw attention to something of extra significance, as if he himself were a schoolboy who needed reminding of the importance of what he was doing.

Sebastian's initial impulse was to compose in return as scathing a reply as possible – which he most probably would have done in the early days of his time in America – but now it was a temptation at once resisted.

293

Anger begat anger, impulse begat intemperance. His first aphorism, Sebastian recognized. And though not worthy of repetition, his own. Here in Washington he was precisely where and how he wanted to be, at the centre of events into which he had successfully manoeuvred himself, beyond supervision or instruction. But still without the confidence of those in London.

What else was there to read between the lines, wondered Sebastian, collecting up the petulantly discarded telegram. Hindered by the time difference between the United States and Europe, Sebastian doubted if anything of Carson's Senate speech had been reported in that day's London newspapers, although there would have been ample opportunity for the earlier *New York Times material to have been telegraphed. But prestigious and authoritative though the New York Times* was, a repeated newspaper story would not have prompted the query he had just received. Far more likely was that, alerted by the *New York Times* articles, which had probably accompanied it, a full diplomatic account of the Senate declaration had been simultaneously transmitted to London by the British Embassy over the diplomatic electronic link. Which – again calculated against the time difference between the two countries and the hour-stamp on Mycroft's cable – had prompted immediate consideration at the highest government level, maybe even the Cabinet itself. Upon the telegram in front of him

Sebastian heavily underscored 'personally', identifying it as the clue his uncle intended. This was not an official demand; how, conceivably, could it be? The British government got its guidance from the British Embassy. This communication had been urged upon his uncle by Winston Churchill, the only influencing outsider in this covert enterprise and a man who had from the very beginning insisted upon knowing everything whilst imparting little in return. The reference to a grand tour, a phrase he had used in his first liner-carried letter naming the Grand Duke Alexei Orlov, was easily translated, as was the hint that there was some special interest in the man. Sebastian supposed there would have been a possibility – and a significance – in the Russian being present at the German reception his uncle had known him to be attending but apart from that occasion Sebastian found it difficult to imagine anywhere else their paths might cross.

Satisfied that he had not just decoded but properly analysed the telegram, Sebastian still hesitated, all annoyance gone but still wanting to include in his reply an indication of his displeasure at being called upon to justify himself. Finally, although not completely satisfied, he wrote:

CURRENT BUSINESS NEGOTIATIONS PROCEEDING UNIMPEDED IN THE MANNER IN WHICH THEY WERE ORIGINALLY ENTRUSTED STOP NO GRAND TOUR REACQUAINTANCE

He signed it *settler*, a Notions word for a crushing retort, which it certainly wasn't but was the nearest available from their chosen code.

That morning's newspaper coverage was as extensive as Carson and Anderson had predicted before their final parting the previous night. Carson's Senate performance was the dominant story in the *New York Times*, again running to the second page, and filled virtually the entire front page of the *Washington Post*, with photographs and a separate story on the reinvestigation into the death of Congressman Grant taking up most of the second page. A new development, reported in both papers, was that an official protest note authorized by Berlin was to be personally delivered by Count Johann von Bernstorff to the State Department.

Once again Sebastian remained in his suite, keeping up with the day's events on the continuous news channel on the wireless. The station initially led its coverage with an interview with the German ambassador outside the State Department, after the delivery of the Berlin note. Von Bernstorff repeated his previous day's denunciation and claimed that Senator Carson's allegations were seriously straining the hitherto friendly relations between his country and the United States. Carson was abusing both the First

Amendment of the Constitution and Congressional privilege, as had the sadly deceased Congressman Grant before him. It was to be regretted that the fundamental American democratic principle of free speech should be manipulated in such a way.

Perhaps because he knew in advance what its content was, Sebastian considered Jack Carson's radio-reported press conference a disappointing anticlimax, although with practised political adroitness the Senator turned to his advantage every question in which he saw the opportunity. Carson's cleverest move, which he hadn't spoken about in Georgetown, was to have beside him Allan Grant's widow and the man's campaign manager.

Carson had obviously heard von Bernstorff's radio remarks on the steps of the State Department and concentrated upon the penetration of the Capitol – which he perhaps too grandiosely described as the seat of modern democracy – by politically and influentially minded burglars who for the first time in American history had succeeded in criminally infiltrating and looting the private offices of a Congressman. The security system had blatantly failed but there was a register of all permanent staff, temporary interns and approved visitors. He had already filed the demand for every name on every register to be traced and questioned – including every member of the Congress security and police division itself – to discover who those infiltrators were.

A composed, quiet-voiced but obviously determined Luella Grant talked of conversations with her late husband about his not launching his short-lived campaign until he had acquired sufficient and incontrovertible evidence legally to prove his allegations: she had seen three manila folders he never risked even leaving in the safe of his Capitol office when he was absent from it. Burt Williams remembered five such binders and confirmed that Grant never allowed them out of his possession when making them available to the original investigative reporter, the late Peter Pullinger.

Asked by a Washington-based correspondent of a Berlin newspaper why he hated Germany, Carson adamantly denied hating the country or its people: his refusal was to accept the influencing of his country against its neutrality.

When he telephoned Carson's office Edna Connolly said the Senator had not yet returned but was anxious to hear anything new that Sebastian had to tell him. Sebastian said there was nothing and asked if there was any other message for him.

'Just that he hasn't heard anything from any other source,' said the woman.

The Army and Navy Club was indeed a short walk from Sebastian's hotel, as William Hartley had remarked, and by coincidence along virtually the same route that Sebastian had initially taken on his evasive journey to Georgetown. He did not, of course, follow it that night, observing his father's rule that someone believing themselves at risk of surveillance should never establish an identifiable travel pattern. Instead Sebastian struck out along Pennsylvania Avenue as if intending to climb the hill to the Capitol before abruptly striking northwards along 9th Street, pausing sufficiently to satisfy himself he was unwatched. He utilized the grid layout of the roads for his own purpose, turning back on himself along H Street to use the reflective advantage of some shop windows and although confident he remained alone continued to employ every block until he reached his destination.

William Hartley was seated in the vestibule, in a chair commanding a full view of the entrance. He started up at the first sight of Sebastian, right hand outstretched in greeting, with his other indicating to the uniformed, balding desk porter by some clearly prearranged signal that Sebastian was his expected guest.

'No cause for signing-in formalities,' dismissed the older man, cupping Sebastian's elbow to guide him up expansive, encircling stairs lined with oils of be-wigged and be-medalled admirals and generals to a first floor that continued the encirclement in a balcony of mahogany and more commemorative paintings. Sebastian counted four other gaslit, panelled corridors radiating from the observation gallery as he was bustled around it and then deeper into the building along a fifth. Like all the others it was mahogany-panelled, interspersed on either side with heavy, always-closed doors. No sound came from beyond any of them and their footfalls were soundless on the thick carpeting. Theirs was the sixth door on the left, leading into a private dining salon, the table already set for two, wine decanted, more gas lamps flickering from every wall.

'I've taken the liberty of ordering,' announced Hartley. 'Chesapeake oysters and steak. And Bordeaux. French wine travels so much better than German, alas.' At the entrance Hartley had spoken English. Now it was German.

Sebastian thought again how easily this man invited dislike. 'Excellent.' He reverted to German, too, acknowledging the flawlessness of Hartley's accent.

'Whisky or gin?'

'Martini,' requested Sebastian, as much for the awkwardness of it as to challenge Hartley's attempted command of everything. Had he made a mistake, keeping a second meeting with this intense man? There was sufficient about which to be intrigued and he necessarily had to follow every beckoning avenue, and yet Sebastian could not lose a feeling of unease. But then, he asked himself, if Hartley were in some way involved in the affairs he hoped to uncover, shouldn't he feel uneasy?

The cocktail Hartley prepared without

hesitation was better than any Sebastian had tasted so far. Hartley took Scotch, neat.

'To the success of a rightful cause!' proposed Hartley.

'*Zum wohl!*' replied Sebastian.

Hartley said: 'I fear I have to make amends.'

'For what?'

'Offending you at our last meeting.'

'I was not offended.'

'The politeness of a gentleman that I failed to match.'

Sebastian shrugged. 'The matter is forgotten.'

'With so much in the interim,' said Hartley, urgently. 'What of the furore?'

Sebastian decided it would be inept to feign misunderstanding, apart from which he saw his way to take the conversation away from the other man. 'Do you imagine it can be true?'

Hartley gave a half smile, sipping his drink. 'Carson appears to have sources: certainly he had a spy at the embassy the night of the reception.'

'So you believe him?' pressed Sebastian.

'I believe there are accusations to be investigated. The mysterious death of this man Grant, for example.'

'I am by no measure an expert in these matters but after such a delay I would imagine it difficult to reach the truth, if, in fact, truth has been concealed.' Sebastian conceded that Hartley had recovered control of the exchanges but was unworried, content for the moment for Hartley to imagine a superiority.

'What of you?' demanded Hartley. 'Do you find it credible?'

Sebastian shrugged again, surrendering his glass to be refilled. 'If there is conflagration in Europe the country with the best established commercial links with America would have a formidable advantage.'

Hartley tugged on the bell-pull as he returned Sebastian's drink. 'We can talk as we eat,' he announced, the master of every ceremony. 'If Carson can prove his allegations it could turn feelings against Germany. And change the neutral attitude of the government here.'

'Which could account for the vehemence of Count von Bernstorff's rebuttals.'

'Have you had opportunity to gauge the feeling within the embassy, since the reception?'

It was not necessary for Sebastian to force his surprise. 'Me! How – why – on earth should I?'

'I gained an impression that you were well acquainted with diplomats there; the ambassador himself even.'

How to reply, stridently in denial or to allow ambiguity? An easy choice. Smiling, Sebastian said: 'As I again recall remarking at the time, it was an encounter of diplomatic politeness.'

Smiling in return Hartley asked: 'Would you tell me otherwise?'

'Not if I was using my presence there in some private way. Which, however, I am not.'

'Are you well acquainted with the Smithlanes?'

'You strain courtesy, sir! It is not my practice nor intention to discuss one person with another!' But yet he wanted to, desperately, if Hartley could suggest what Hans Vogel was doing in the shipowner's company.

Hartley remained smiling. 'I meant no offence, sir. I offer my remark as a reference, against how this conversation may progress.'

'In what way?'

'An indication of how closely I try to establish the credentials of people – and their acquaintances – with whom I seek business dealings.'

'I have no business dealings with Lowell Smithlane. But had I, I would be even less minded to discuss them than I am to talk about my social companions.' Hartley was planning an approach!

'You are very discreet, Mr Holmes; an attitude to be admired.'

'Rather I consider myself the gentleman you so recently praised me for being. Or make every effort to be such...' Not a good enough rejoinder, Sebastian at once recognized: it generalized an exchange that needed to be focused.

'First and foremost from our brief time together the other evening I understood you to be an investor comfortable with risk,' said the over-eager Hartley, and Sebastian wondered from whom the man had gained such an understanding. He'd provided Hartley with no such evidence.

Before Sebastian could respond – before he thought of a response sufficient to draw the man further – there was a respectful sound at the door. The two men remained silent for the ocean-sized silver salver to be put between them and for Hartley's mouth-rinsing approval of the wine. It was as long as it took Sebastian to devour six oysters in aggravating silence – although total enjoyment – before Hartley said: 'We were talking, before the interruption, of your business interests here in America.'

For all Hartley's efforts Sebastian believed himself to be the ringmaster in whichever direction the conversation swung. 'Rather the search for rich opportunities that appear uncommonly difficult to find. At this juncture it remains business intention rather than business interest.'

'We also touched upon the inevitability of conflict.'

'Inevitability was your opinion,' qualified Sebastian. This was better: exactly as he wanted the conversation to go.

'And you talked of grave risks,' reminded Hartley. 'With the advantage of your being so recently in Germany as well as England, which do you believe the better prepared?'

Sebastian's pause, seemingly to consider the question, was in fact one of decision. Making it, he said: 'I have little doubt of

Germany's superiority.'

Hartley smiled once more. 'And I had little doubt that would be your opinion. Do you also think Great Britain will fight?'

'I have no doubt whatsoever. I believe it's an unfortunate fact that their going to war is a certainty.'

'Unfortunate?'

'I am a pragmatist, Mr Hartley. I have never seen good purpose in entering a contest I knew in advance I was likely to lose.'

'So you are afraid for your country.'

'I am afraid of my country's stupidity. My hope – indeed my expectation, in view of their superiority – is that the conflict will be short-lived, leaving Asquith and his crew sad times to reflect upon the error of their misjudgement.'

'May I risk impertinence once more, Mr Holmes?'

'At the risk of my rejecting it.'

The quick smile came and went. 'Given an opportunity, with which side would you cast in your lot?'

Now Sebastian smiled. 'That providing the most reward.'

'I believe we are understanding each other?'

'I believe we are.'

'In what business, precisely, would you be interested in this country?'

'An enterprise with sufficient profit to justify my travelling all the way to America to discover it.'

'That's hardly precise, sir.'

305

'I am not at all sure this conversation is precise at the level that it should be. Why do you choose to speak German, Mr Hartley?'

'It is a language more natural to me than English, for reasons already made clear. And you?'

'Courtesy, towards one who shows a preference.' Around and around spun the verbal wheel, thought Sebastian. But he was not being made giddy by it.

'No other reason?'

He had the whip and reins, decided Sebastian. 'What other reason could there be?'

'How came you to be at the embassy reception?'

A wheel had hit a rut, jarring him off balance. But again there was a saving interruption with the return of the steward, this time pushing a trolley of chafing dishes beneath which, upon entry, he lighted heating candle banks. Determined against letting the impetus drift away from him Sebastian said the moment the steward withdrew: 'An invitation achieved by a friend.'

'Lowell Smithlane?'

The recurring name isolated Sebastian. 'We have covered this ground.'

'And I have admired your integrity.'

'Then I would ask you not to press upon it.'

'Shall you be with him this weekend in Virginia?'

'No,' answered Sebastian, honestly. Nor in Long Island, either, he thought. He kept any confusion from his face.

306

Hartley frowned. 'And what of Count von Bernstorff?'

'I know nothing of the ambassador nor do I understand this turn of conversation,' protested Sebastian, again honestly. 'Is it not time, sir, that we talked to each other straightforwardly as we were a few moments ago and not in the manner of adolescents, playacting?' Sebastian took the bluntness from his sudden change of approach by cutting into his steak, which was as succulent as Hartley had promised. Sebastian couldn't name a German red wine to better the Bordeaux either.

Hartley was not taken aback. Equally bluntly he said: 'I have a business proposition.'

'Which is?'

'The insurance of a cargo.'

Sebastian's inclination was to push his meal aside, no longer wanted, but he resisted. 'There must be more shipping and cargo insurers in New York than there are hopeful immigrants on Ellis Island. I cannot see an opportunity for me in that particular line of commerce.'

'What of special cargo?'

'What indeed of special cargo?' retorted Sebastian.

'People I represent are seeking insurance for a cargo difficult to cover on more usual markets.'

A step at a time, determined Sebastian. But always dangling the hook of interest. 'What is the value of this special cargo?'

'Two million dollars.'

'A very valuable one,' lured Sebastian, betraying no surprise at the figure.

'To protect which the people I represent are prepared to pay a substantial premium.'

'How substantial?'

'The offer is fifteen per cent but it could be open to negotiation.'

No surprise, just the dangled hook, determined Sebastian. 'Its destination?'

'Germany.'

'Port of loading?'

'New York.'

'When?'

'Within the month.'

'I believe the consortium I represent would be interested in underwriting such a shipment,' said Sebastian.

Hartley smiled yet again. 'I knew I had judged you right!'

'There would, of course, be conditions.'

'Such as?'

'Quite obviously I would need to know the nature of the cargo.'

'That does not come within the terms of a pro rata fifteen per cent premium.'

'It comes within the terms of my acceptance. And not merely by my being told. I would need personally to examine it.'

There was no longer a smile. 'Surely you have an understanding of what we are discussing?'

'Mr Hartley, we are too newly met for me to

commit two million dollars to an unspecified shipment across the Atlantic, quite irrespective of any understanding between us. My condition, for a guarantee of cover, is personal inspection of the cargo. I am not going to underwrite boxes of worthless stone and then face my colleagues with a story of understandings and innuendo when something happens to make them disappear. That they would neither countenance nor accept. They would, however, have no difficulty with a cargo outside the normal scope of established insurance business. I have the finance, Mr Hartley. You have the need. And now you have my conditions.'

'I do not believe they are acceptable.'

'Then I am afraid our discussion ends over this extremely pleasant dinner, for which I thank you.' He had sufficient, Sebastian assured himself. And he had his father's unpresented introduction to the New York Police to pursue it.

'Give me time to consider!' urgently retreated the other man.

Maybe even yet there was an opportunity for more! 'Of course there should be time for consideration, perhaps on both our parts.'

'I will need the weekend.'

As so, hopefully, would he: there still needed to be time allowed for the original mystery informant to approach Jack Carson. 'You know my lodgings.'

There were three waiting carriages at the

club's rank, their snuffling horses creating the only fog in the night's chill, but Sebastian decided to walk, determined at once to reflect upon the evening and reach every possible deduction available from it. Hunched deep inside his cloak, this part of the city imprinted in his mind from his evasive wanderings, Sebastian set off instinctively southwards, oblivious to his immediate surroundings or route.

He'd found an emissary for a clandestine group. And the mystery cargo could only be weaponry. He knew it was leaving from New York, sometime within the next month, to a German port. If he were to go through even a quasi-legal pretence of issuing insurance cover, he could justifiably demand the name of the Atlantic crossing vessel, from which its sailing date could definitely be obtained for everything to be seized, on the eve of departure. So did he really need personally to examine the cargo, to confirm its contents? Of course he did. It could, even, be the confidence trick he'd suggested, not an hour earlier. But even that wasn't the full or most important reason for maintaining the insistence. Seizure of the cargo before it reached its German destination was only part of what he had to achieve. The greatest, most essential requirement was to discover and then expose the conspirators.

Sebastian was vaguely aware of passing the now empty McPherson Square and of the outline, night-darkened and solid, of the

White House far ahead. He continued down a near-deserted 16th Street, his mind switching to Jack Carson. There was the possibility of something emerging from the senator's campaign much sooner than any conclusion to what had begun this night. Was there anything from the meeting with Hartley to pass on to Carson? Definitely not, decided Sebastian, as he crossed an echoing H Street and began cutting through Lafayette Park in the direction of the Treasury block. There might eventually be something, but...

It was a reflection Sebastian never completed. He was never conscious of actually hearing their approach: no clip of a footstep against the pathway nor rustle of clothes. The awareness was of a presence, a closeness of danger, and as instinctively as he had been walking he intuitively thrust himself sideways without thinking or trying to turn, which he much later decided probably saved his life. The two whose combined weight would have borne him helplessly to the ground were made to stumble into each other by Sebastian's abrupt move, although the third man managed a glancing blow across Sebastian's left arm with a stick or a cudgel intended to crush his skull. The blow threw Sebastian further off balance. Sebastian didn't, however, fall, but exaggerated the stagger to retain his balance and take him away from his attackers. With the same movement he unsheathed from its malacca scabbard the short sword.

His balance restored, Sebastian turned to confront them. They were menacing silhouettes in the darkness, two – those who had attempted to overwhelm him – matchingly large, the third smaller. Sebastian had completely recovered now, warily retreating from their approach with the stick shaft in his half-numbed left hand and across his body, the short but narrow sword in his right, sweeping back and forth in front of him, not as a warning but hopefully to be aligned against the second attack.

He wasn't frightened! Through all the snow-flaked impressions threatening an avalanche, that one awareness repeated itself in Sebastian's mind, a ringing clarity in the confused storm. He should have been frightened – expected himself to be frightened – but instead there was total calmness, total reasoning. His wasn't a familiar épée or a rapier to keep them at bay: a sabre even, to slash and sweep. It was, in fact, a comparatively limited and slim short sword, little more than a dagger, too small effectively to distance him from three undoubted professionals.

Sebastian threw back his head and as loudly as he was able shouted: 'Help! Murder! Murder! Murder! Help!'

A voice said: *'Herrgottsack, bring ihn zum Schweigen,'* for fuck's sake silence him!

'Murder! Help!' screamed Sebastian, the short sword swinging back and forth in front of him, awareness belatedly dawning that he always had to keep them in the silhouetting darkness, not allow any of them to move into a concealing backdrop. The feeling was returning to his left shoulder and arm, although now that was a massed aching pain where before it had been numbness.

Without anything being said the three separated from being an unbroken, confronting mass against and directly ahead of him to become three separate dangers, the two larger men each moving to encircle and attack from behind, the smaller darting forwards and backwards like a medieval skirmisher to Sebastian's front, to distract and deflect him from the flanking intent.

Sebastian kept moving backwards, to keep them in sight, stiffening – physically biting at a frightened whimper – at his retreat being abruptly, solidly stopped. But there was no blow, no attack from an unseen fourth man, and Sebastian realized, almost sniggering with relief, that he had backed up to the plinth supporting the Andrew Jackson statue. And that he couldn't *be* attacked from behind. His attackers recognized it too. There was a combined rush, the taller and shorter joined in a rehearsed move for the assault to come from the third, on his right. But Sebastian wasn't drawn from his back-guard. He slashed at the small man, jabbed at the second and still kept the sword free to cut upwards before the third could close upon him. The slash connected and there was a scream and a grunt, too, when the jab penetrated.

Someone said: '*Der Scheisskerl hat ein Messer*!' The bastard's got a knife.

The voice that had emitted the scream said: '*Ich auch.*' So have I.

Sebastian screamed: 'Help! Murder! Help!'

There was an answering shout, far off, and the smaller man said: 'We've got to shut him up. Get it over with.'

They came together in a rush, although from their three different directions. Knowing who had the knife, Sebastian parried at the smaller man, with the same movement flicking up the empty scabbard to deflect the man coming at him from his left. The sword became entangled, holding him, and it was intuitive, as it had been at the beginning, for Sebastian to jerk his head away from the third, so that the blow which would most certainly have felled him instead caught him glancingly, high on his right cheek and forehead.

The plinth that had been his protection now became his trap, with the three men close to pinning him against it. With a roar of enraged defiance Sebastian threw himself at them, jabbing with the sword, flailing with its scabbard. The unexpectedness momentarily drove them back. He felt his blade sink in, to another scream, and the scabbard strike harmlessly against something, but then there was a sharp, burning sensation in his already aching shoulder and another near-crushing blow fully across his back, driving the breath from his body. Sebastian fought against

314

falling but knew he couldn't avoid it and that he was going to die. As he went down, trying to halt himself on one knee, he made one last desperate backwards thrust and felt the sword go in, to another yell of pain. But at once the blade was twisted from his grasp and he wasn't able to stop himself going fully down. He lay there, whimpering the breath back into his body, waiting for the agony, hearing the confusion of his assassins, and then there was light, from a lantern, and louder shouts and running footsteps but no pain.

Suddenly the hands upon him were comforting and he was carefully turned to look up at two uniformed policemen and Sebastian was unable to stop himself laughing from belated shock and knew at the end that he had been frightened, after all. He wasn't ashamed of it though.

Sebastian's good fortune had been where he was attacked, so close to the official presidential home with its permanent police detail, from which his rescuers had come. Sebastian endured an apologetic account of rising street crime and robbery and their congratulations at the precaution of carrying a swordstick, the blade of which was recovered, bloodstained, a few yards from where he had finally been felled. He agreed a revolver might have been a more effective provision. By the flickering light of their lanterns they examined the knife wound to his left shoulder and urged hospital attention, which Sebastian refused, insisting the cut was bleeding heavily only because of its length and was not deep enough to require professional suturing. At that stage two more policemen returned, breathless, to report that the assailants had escaped, presumably in some waiting transport, which was unusual for street gangs. All four officers accepted the impossibility of Sebastian being able to describe his attackers.

Two escorted Sebastian the short remaining distance to the Willard, where he just gained the secure solitude of his suite before stumbling into near-unconsciousness, recovering to find himself on the sitting-room floor, half supported against the low couch, his left arm and hand a dripping, bloodied mess. There was no part of Sebastian's body free of pain, the worst across his entire back, where the crushing blow had finally fallen. It took him several attempts to lever himself upwards, one-armed, and a matching effort to remain standing when he got himself upright. He grabbed, stumbling, from furniture piece to furniture piece until he reached the bathroom, sitting on the bath edge to take off his gore-soaked clothing piece by piece until he was naked. The effort to do so, slow though it was, was sufficient to break open the knife slash which extended from low on his left breast to his shoulder and most certainly should have received hospital stitching, unthinkable as it would have been to summon the hotel doctor. With no antiseptic to clean it, Sebastian improvised with shaving astringent, which momentarily brought fresh agony and more bleeding. It took a lot more time and even more hotel linen pressed against the wound to staunch it sufficiently for Sebastian to examine his other injuries. His right cheek was grazed and his right eye already discoloured, although not into a full blackness. It was difficult for Sebastian to gain the full reflection, particularly without reopening the wound, but eventually he managed to see his back, from shoulder to waist. It was one completely black, aching bruise.

Sebastian tried to remain awake as long as possible, concerned any movement in his sleep would cause fresh bleeding despite compressing a towel over the wound as tightly as possible. When he did sleep, it was fitfully, never totally losing consciousness: in his dream-like half sleep he relived the embassy reception, trying to fit men he had seen there into the shadowy silhouettes in Lafayette Park and in a moment of full wakefulness thought that perhaps he did need the protection of a revolver.

The next time there might not be the convenience of nearby policemen.

There was an ambience – effervescence was an ill-fitting description, although it came to mind – about his normally taciturn, introspective brother that Mycroft found curious, exceeding the justifiable satisfaction Sherlock Holmes deserved at discovering so much in the face of such now much regretted obstruction. Whatever its cause it was appearing to make easier their rehearsal for what was to come. By coincidence they were in the same anonymous room of the St James's establishment in which the absent Sebastian had so few weeks earlier met Winston Churchill. Sebastian's most recently arrived telegram – his openly transmitted reply to Mycroft's openly transmitted demand at Churchill's urging – lay between the two brothers on the Chesterfield upon which both sat. Despite the arrayed, opened-in-readiness bottles, neither was drinking.

Mycroft said: 'You see my difficulty.'

'Our difficulty,' qualified Sherlock Holmes. 'Irrespective of our not knowing the completeness of it, Sebastian has done exceedingly well.'

'Don't quibble with whose concern is the greater. And there's no dispute between us either over what Sebastian has apparently accomplished,' retorted Mycroft, irritably. 'What we're discussing is a potentially serious problem that has to be avoided.' So concerned was Mycroft that also between them on the Chesterfield were that day's embassy cables of Senator Carson's press conference, which Mycroft was making available with the reassurance that everything he was allowing his brother to read would be published in the following day's newspapers.

'An avoidance which you, ultimately because of your official position and the situation in which you have become en-tangled, can do nothing to affect?' said Sher-lock Holmes, relentlessly.

'No,' conceded Mycroft.

The detective stirred his elegant, musician's fingers through the papers between them and said: 'From what you've told me – and from what I've read here – I don't envisage the difficulty being as great as you fear.'

'You have not confronted Winston Chur-chill,' accused Mycroft.

'Nor, dear brother, has he confronted me.'

Ascending footsteps gave Mycroft the opportunity to restore the illicit paperwork to a prepared travelling case before Churchill's customarily flurried entry. Equally bustled, at the politician's orchestration, was the aperitif choosing, wine opening and food selection, accompanied by the apology that he had to return to the House before ten for yet another debate upon Irish home rule.

Sherlock Holmes remained relaxed, aloof almost, contentedly giving the stage to the balding politician.

'...at a time when there are far more important and demanding considerations than the confounded Irish problem!' com-pleted Churchill. 'It would seem, Mr Holmes, that your son has exceeded all expectations.' The change, practically in mid-sentence, was as abrupt as everything else about the man.

'He by no means has exceeded my expec-tations,' said Sherlock Holmes, nodding ap-provingly at the champagne that had been opened at Churchill's entry.

'Nor mine,' apologized the politician at once. 'A careless cliché. My interest now is building upon what Sebastian appears to be motivating in America.'

'What is Sebastian motivating in America?'

Churchill hesitated, his own champagne glass before him. 'A congressional debate, don't you see!'

'No, I don't see,' denied the detective. 'I know from what I've read in newspapers of the events in the Senate and of the belated investigation into what appears to be a crime of murder. But I'm not aware of a definitive account of anything in which he is involved from Sebastian himself.'

'Momentarily delayed because of the insecurity of his location in Washington,' dismissed Churchill.

'There has been this telegram,' announced Mycroft, obeying his brother's earlier instruction and handing it to the burly man.

Churchill frowned down upon it, clicking his glass against his teeth in concentration. 'What's "settler" designate?'

'A childhood nickname, to avoid his own,' said Mycroft.

'How do you read the message?' Churchill demanded, of them both.

'That he does not wish any interference from here,' said Sherlock Holmes, bluntly.

'Our interests now are to build upon events in Washington...'

'Mine are not, until I have your intentions

made clear to me,' interrupted Sherlock Holmes.

Momentarily Churchill's brow furrowed. 'In my opinion a declaration should be made in the House, categorically denying that Great Britain is in any way involved or associated with the sort of allegations being made in the American Congress.'

'Without any consultation or communication with Sebastian?'

'The moment has to be seized.'

'I will not have my son endangered,' announced Sherlock Holmes, even-voiced but very positive.

Churchill looked between the silent Mycroft and his brother. Then he said: 'I think I should have an explanation of that remark, Mr Holmes.'

'Believing, as we both believed, that we were being addressed upon a matter of possible national importance, my son and I agreed to co-operate with you and my brother upon an enterprise providing no protection whatsoever for my son, in the event of his being discovered,' reminded Sherlock Holmes. 'Indeed, much of the conversation within this very room was directed towards your complete exculpation if Sebastian fell foul of authority or foe. The claims now being made in the American Senate and in American newspapers are going to bring an investigatory spotlight with a far wider beam than that upon specific criminality and murder. They will greatly increase, in fact, the chances of Sebastian becoming the object of attention, certainly until we learn from his own hand precisely what he is doing and in which direction he is moving...' Sherlock Holmes sipped champagne. 'For your part, a public declaration that no British agent is operating within the United States further absolves you from personal culpability if my son is exposed. And by that declaration you will not be guilty of any falsehood or of misleading Parliament, because Sebastian is *not* a British agent, is he...?'

'I do not like the tone of this diatribe, Mr Holmes...!'

'I do not regard it as a diatribe, sir! I consider it a setting out of irrefutable facts. Nothing premature will be said until we hear from Sebastian. And even then further consultation between us will be necessary.'

Winston Churchill's mouth briefly opened in complete astonishment at his being told what – or rather what not – to do and he swallowed, visibly, in his recovery. The disbelieving outrage began low-voiced, flushing Churchill's face blood-red, and grew into a near-roar that took Mycroft's eyes worryingly to the door. 'Have you any conception what you have just said? And to whom you said it?'

'My answer is yes, to both questions,' said Sherlock Holmes, in total control.

'You have just issued an *order* to a minister of the Crown!'

'I have just made myself clear to someone

322

who is operating outside of any remit or authority vested in him as a minister of the Crown.'

'I am a man of profound influence, Mr Holmes!'

'And so, Mr Churchill, am I. It's my belief that it would be best for neither of us to confront the other but instead totally to direct our energies and wit towards the common cause at hand.'

Churchill thrust to his feet. 'There are other matters that prevent me dining here tonight!'

'I trust it merely to be a postponement until we receive Sebastian's communiqué,' said Sherlock Holmes.

As the door slammed angrily closed behind the politician, Mycroft said: 'I'll wager Winston has not been addressed like that at any time in his entire life.'

'You know of Lestrade, who interrogated the two Germans paying so much unwanted attention to me in Baker Street?'

Mycroft frowned at the introduction of an entirely new subject. 'Yes?'

'He speaks good German, which was thought possibly fortunate in his listening to anything the villains might say between themselves.'

'Did they?'

Sherlock Holmes nodded. 'He stayed by the peephole of their cell, before their embassy lawyer arrived. To hear one say to the other that it was going to be difficult to discover now if Sherlock Holmes had a son.'

'Does that means that Sebastian is undone?'

'I think not. Sherlock Holmes does not officially have a son, does he? But I think Sebastian should be alerted.'

Nineteen

Sebastian's bruised muscles had set from his holding himself against the slightest shift that might have reopened his wound and when he finally came fully awake it was paradoxically difficult for him initially to move at all, so stiff had he become. He did so with enforced and clumsy slowness, relying upon his uninjured right arm and side, although even that exploded pain throughout his back at every twist or turn and it took several minutes before he even managed to get himself properly upright upon the bed edge. There, panting, he remained for some time, as gently as possible trying to flex his back to unlock it. Ever more gently he bent and unbent his left arm to ease the cramp there, as well. Standing was fresh agony and he had to steady himself against the bedside table in preparation for the shuffle to the bathroom. Only there did he risk removing the hand towel from his left shoulder, to examine the cut in the mirror's reflection. The bruising had come out all around the gash but there was very little blood staining the towel Sebastian had compressed throughout the night. Now it had stopped completely, giving Sebastian the chance to clean it even more than he had been able the previous night. Sebastian first sponged the injury with water and then, inventing his own experiment, with more astringent. There was none of the stinging discomfort of the previous night, from which Sebastian knew the wound was closed. There would, he accepted, be a wide scar. He didn't risk the heat of the water by properly bathing, instead sitting on the bath rim, his feet and legs in the water, fully to sponge himself clean. He finished by administering even more cleansing astringent to his shoulder. There was still no sting. He did not feel sufficiently confident or even inclined to shave. In the mirror Sebastian decided the bruising to his face hadn't deepened but had actually worsened on his back.

The careful ablution exercises freed him of his restrictive stiffness and the sharp jabs of pain were lessening, although there was pain with the awkwardness of tenuously securing a fresh towel on his shoulder with a cravat, one edge between his teeth to allow his right hand to bandage and tie the pad in place. It felt more comfortable, held better in place, when he put on a shirt, although buttoning it, as with the rest of his clothes, was difficult.

Everything he had worn the previous night was ruined, rent by slashes and clotted hard, and Sebastian acknowledged how fortunate he had been to have escaped death as narrowly as he so obviously had. He bundled the debris into a linen laundry bag and summoned a housekeeper to dispose of it, offering a ten-dollar note and an account of an accident which had by good chance not been severe, despite so much blood.

The newspapers came with his room-serviced breakfast. There was little expansion beyond the live radio transmissions in the printed reports of Carson's press conference, although the coverage was led by the senator's later-released statement that he expected to be able to produce new and legally substantiating facts in the next few days. Against that – and balanced alongside in the presentation in both the *New York Times* and the *Washington Post* – was a new statement from the German Embassy deriding Carson's claim of evidence being stolen from the Capitol premises and the promise of new facts as proof that Carson's allegations were without substance and entirely malicious.

Sebastian tried repeatedly over the course of fifteen minutes to find an unoccupied telephone line to Carson's office, idly concluding as he fruitlessly dialled and redialled that he did not after all wish to remain all day unkempt and unshaven and that, in fact, he felt sufficiently recovered to complete the pointless but necessary police formalities, as well. He wouldn't, however, make any appointments to meet the Senator in his present restricted condition.

There was an almost immediate desire to sleep when the hotel barber reclined Sebastian's chair into a near horizontal position and wrapped soporifically warm towels around his marked face. As tempting – as demanding – as it was, Sebastian fought against the desire, with too much to consider and decide.

How all too quickly – and from whom – would the danger return? Until that soundless, unwarned and totally unexpected moment in Lafayette Park he would have sworn an oath on his own life – the life he had come too close to losing – that he was not under surveillance of any shape or fashion. So from whom – from where – *had* it come? The only established fact first. His would-be assassins had spoken German: *been* German. Could Hartley have been the instigator, galvanized by Sebastian's initial refusal into protecting himself from exposure by someone to whom he had too openly declared himself? Hartley was certainly the most obvious provocateur. But by the same token the most unlikely. They'd parted upon the clear, bargaining understanding that Sebastian might accept the insurance proposition. Hartley was cautious but it was inconceivable that the man would have had cut-throats at such instant readiness. Nor was there cause to have released them. Sebastian was sure – until now, that is – that since believing the precaution necessary he had cleared his trail, as he believed he had arrived at the Georgetown encounter with Carson without pursuit. Perhaps he hadn't been as successful as he had imagined. And how, now, did that chilling, name-recalling conversation with Count Johann von Bernstorff at the embassy reception fit?

Too many questions with too few resolutions. For which then was there an answer? Only one: that which he had no choice but to confront, as unwelcome as it was. Last night, through luck and the fitness of youth and, perhaps, his prowess with a sword, he'd avoided assassination. His luck – his would-be killers' mistake – had been their waiting until Lafayette Park and its nearness to rescuing White House police patrols. There was every likelihood of another attack and the next time rescue might not be so readily to hand. Certainly in his weakened, aching, slow-moving condition he would be in no position to resist nor fight off the most feeble of ambushes.

His chair coming upright abruptly brought Sebastian back to his surroundings.

'Well rested, sir?' enquired the barber.

'Not completely,' replied Sebastian, truthfully.

The telephone was already ringing when he entered his suite but he managed to snatch it off its rest before losing the call, at once recognizing Edna Connolly's voice.

'Have you been listening to the radio?'

'No,' said Sebastian. 'What?'

'Jack's dead.'

328

Sebastian came into the transmission in mid-report and had to wait a further fifteen minutes for its complete repetition, although it added little. Senator Jack Carson had been found dead that morning by his housekeeper in his bath at his East Side New York house. There was an extensive review of his just begun Senate campaign against foreign influence, which included the reopened investigation into Congressman Grant's death. A New York Police spokesman was quoted saying that there was no indication of foul play in Carson's death: it appeared to be a tragic accident. Further statements would be made, although no time could be given.

Because David Anderson was travelling down from New York Sebastian's agreed meeting with the journalist and Edna Connolly was not until late afternoon, which gave Sebastian the majority of the day to complete what was outstanding and to buy what he now considered essential. He made no effort to clear his trail or even seek his undoubted followers. He left the Willard with the choice of three addresses from the concierge and hired a waiting carriage for the rest of the day. The array of weaponry available at the first gunstore made a visit to the other two unnecessary, although Sebastian took his time, rejecting the salesman's insistence that longer-barrelled handguns ensured greater accuracy, preferring convenience of carrying, finally deciding upon the latest available .38

Smith and Wesson revolver. He assured the salesman he was familiar with guns – although not that particular model, which ensured its workings were demonstrated – omitting that his knowledge was limited to rifles at university gun clubs. He also purchased a box of shells. In a jacket pocket the pistol made him feel uneven and in his rear trouser pocket it protruded awkwardly and he wished he hadn't refused the shoulder holster for fear that his injury would have prevented his wearing it properly. He left it in his rear pocket, feeling obtrusively uncomfortable.

He took his waiting cab directly to the precinct house designated by the previous night's policemen and produced the docket that enabled a desk sergeant to locate the already filed report. Sebastian made and signed a statement, apologized again for not being able to describe his assailants and politely showed sufficient concern at the disclosure that his was one of six such attacks during the same period: he was in fact lucky that he alone had managed to retain all his property.

Sebastian continued to make no determined effort to detect unseen pursuers on his return to the Willard, although sitting awkwardly to avoid the discomfort of the rear-pocketed weapon made it easy for him to look through the rear view aperture of the carriage. There were five horse-drawn possibilities, apart from two automobiles apparently content to be hindered by the congestion. Although the necessary activity had loosened Sebastian's cramp there was still sufficient reminder to slow his disembarkation at the hotel. The discomfort was genuine although exaggerated for his unseen audience, but once inside the building Sebastian forced himself hurriedly along the unique and convenient central walkway, emerging on to F Street precisely at the moment that his cab rounded the block. Sebastian was into the conveyance with scarcely a pause and now determinedly looked through the small rear-view for any pursuit. He maintained the vigil for the meandering route he had designated until he hammered upon the sounding board, finally to be taken to Georgetown. He still disembarked on M Street, to conceal his ultimate destination.

As Sebastian finally paid the coachman off with a ten dollar tip, the man said: 'Husbands can be so troublesome, can't they?'

'And their investigators even worse.'

'Your avoidance is safe with me, sir. I've problems of my own.'

'Is the Willard's your rank?'

'It is, sir.'

'Perhaps we could have further business.'

'I'd welcome that opportunity, sir.'

'You're clearly aware, being a man of the world, of my problem?'

'I think I am.'

'Regard yourself as my permanent coach-man, from this moment. Will you accept

331

twenty-five dollars a day, journeys additional?'

'I will and with gratitude.'

'And ask around among your fellows. My pursuers are intent and determined. I always need to be aware of their attention.'

'She must be a lady of outstanding quality.'

'She's most definitely that,' said Sebastian. Why, he wondered, was he thinking of Anna?

Sebastian at once got off the main highway, weaving his way along the minor roads, the revolver bumping against his leg. On this second occasion he approached the house on Prospect Street from the opposite direction. Edna Connolly admitted him as quickly as before but without a welcoming smile. She was red-eyed and tight-faced. She said: 'David's just got here.'

David Anderson was in the same front-facing drawing room in which they had met two days earlier, again deep into the room. He was smoking a small cigar, the butt of its predecessor already in an ashtray at his side.

Anderson said at once: 'They killed him, just like they killed Grant.'

'There wasn't enough on the wireless,' prompted Sebastian.

It was Edna Connolly who began the account. 'There was a call, very soon after Jack got back from the press conference. A woman. She said she was Allan Grant's informant and that she wanted to see Jack, to tell him all she knew. But that she was frightened, because of what happened to Grant. She wouldn't meet anywhere in Washington. It had to be in New York and Jack had to be by himself. Just the two of them...'

'I told him he should be careful,' took up Anderson. 'Suggested I conceal myself somewhere in the house, to be a witness if nothing else. But he wouldn't hear of it. He said we had nothing else to keep the campaign going and he couldn't risk losing the chance. He'd not been given a time – the arrangement was that Jack simply waited at the house – so I was to hear from him this morning...'

'Wait,' stopped Sebastian. 'We're getting out of sequence. What about the housekeeper who found him? Other staff...?'

'No one lived-in up in New York,' said Edna. 'Jack had the house on 93rd Street, by the river, as a symbol because he was a New York Senator: he spent most of his time here, in Washington, in the Anacostia house where the staff was permanent. The New York housekeeper and the handyman are a married couple. Come in daily. Jack didn't even tell them he was going back yesterday...'

'Who took the call promising more information?' demanded Sebastian.

'I did,' admitted Edna.

'It was definitely a woman?' pressed Sebastian.

'Definitely,' insisted Edna, almost irritably.

'Was there an accent?' Hans Vogel – and his wife – were in New York, Sebastian recalled.

'There could have been. It sounded like an out of town call and it was blurred, as if she had her mouth a long way from the phone or was covering it with something. And she didn't talk at any length to me. She just said something like it was important and that she knew Allan Grant and wanted to speak to Jack, no one else.'

'I've written it, for tomorrow's edition,' disclosed Anderson. 'And told the police; I was with them for two hours, after going to 93rd Street this morning.'

'Tell me about that.'

'We'd agreed a nine-o'clock breakfast. The police were already there when I arrived.'

'How did he die?'

'Drowned, in his bath. As if he'd slipped. There was a heavy bruise, all along the right side of his head: the skin was broken. Actually cut. And there was blood on the edge of the bath, where it looked as if he'd struck, when he went down.' The man lighted another small cigar. 'It was a trap. All of it.'

'Is that what you've written?'

Anderson nodded. 'It's not simply the obvious story. It's something I owe to Jack.'

'You told the police about the phone call: the intended meeting?'

'Of course.'

'What do they say?'

Anderson snorted an exasperated laugh. 'That along with Grant's death it could be regarded as suspicious but that there's no indication of murder. There's no sign of any forced entry – which of course there wouldn't be, because Jack let in whoever did it – nor any evidence of violence. There are no marks on his clothes, which were all hung up in the closet as if he'd undressed last night. His yesterday's linen was discarded in the laundry basket, where it would have been expected to be. His robe was on the bathroom hook, his night things actually folded. I've made a point of that, in tomorrow's piece: do you neatly fold your night things before getting into your bath? I don't.'

Sebastian shifted, awkwardly, and Edna Connolly asked abruptly: 'What happened to your face?'

Sebastian had been trying to think ahead of the inevitable question, surprised that it hadn't already been asked. Everything had to be minimized. 'I was attacked last night...' He lifted his left arm, very slightly. 'I am badly bruised ... a slight cut ... I managed to get away...' The revolver was hard into his thigh.

'They know you are with us!' exclaimed Anderson. 'Where? What happened? I want to hear it all!'

'There is little to hear,' insisted Sebastian. 'I was walking back from supper. I was suddenly rushed in the darkness by a gang. It was my good fortune there were some police nearby who heard the fracas and intervened...'

'They were seized!'

Sebastian shook his head. 'They escaped. The police have it as a failed street robbery.'

335

'Which is of course nonsense! What were they like? Describe them!'

'I can't,' said Sebastian. 'There was no light, for any identification; nothing was said, to hear a voice.'

'It's obviously linked: part of it all.'

'I have breathed nothing of our connection,' said Sebastian. 'How could I have been associated?'

'Certainly not from any revelation by me,' said Anderson, defensively.

'Not from Jack,' said the woman. 'Your name wasn't anywhere in the files he was assembling: I know because I typed and collated everything. You were source A in everything that was written.'

'Where are those files?' demanded Sebastian.

David Anderson and Edna Connolly looked between each other in silence. The woman said: 'He took them with him to New York: like Grant, he was refusing to let them out of his possession.'

'The police said nothing this morning about any files,' said Anderson.

'If files that Carson was known to have created are missing you've got sufficient suspicion of foul play,' Sebastian pointed out.

Anderson smiled, in accepting awareness. 'You're right! We have!' He looked at Edna Connolly. 'New York Police will probably need a statement ... I'll call, see if they've found anything.'

'I'll make tea. Coffee if you'd prefer?'

'Nothing, thank you,' declined Sebastian, welcoming the interruption. It was right to withhold what he had. Like all the other violence, the attack upon him was most easily explained as coincidence. To connect it – and to his own satisfaction as well as obviously that of Edna Connolly and David Anderson there clearly was a connection – would be to thrust him into the public limelight and attract exactly the sort of attention that at all costs had to be avoided. What of Hans Vogel and his wife being in New York? Proof of nothing criminal and yet again not a fact he could disclose without identifying himself as the source. From sitting so long Sebastian felt his body tightening and gently started to flex his back and shoulders, unthinkingly extending the exercise by standing. He was halfway across the room, idly to look out upon the street, before quickly stopping to prevent exposing himself to view. If he had been discovered through Carson then so had Edna Connolly – and her house – which made retreating into the shadowed room pointless. But what had happened in the preceding twenty-four hours made any precaution pointless. He'd regained his seat by the time the woman returned with tea things.

Anderson was close behind. He said: 'There are no files.' He looked to the woman. 'New York Police want a statement. I promised you'd call, to arrange an interview.'

Sebastian was suddenly concerned. 'You

337

didn't say anything about what happened to me?'

Anderson lighted another of his small cigars. 'I want to talk about it in more detail. It'll go better along with the missing files for a follow-up story the day after tomorrow.'

'No!' rejected Sebastian, sharply, still feeling the hollowness. 'There's no proof of a link between Carson's death and the attack upon me: no proof of *anything*. Whoever killed Jack don't have a named source, just the initial A. There's more to learn leaving them with an impression – fear is probably a better word – that there's still material they haven't got. *That's* your story: files are missing but whoever took them still doesn't have a clue to the source that was supplying Jack Carson and before him Allan Grant.'

'You're setting yourself up as a target,' protested Edna Connolly. 'You both are.'

Sebastian shook his head. 'The way it looks we're already targets. And I am afraid that includes you, Miss Connolly.'

Sherlock Holmes was in his dressing gown and night attire, complete with his curly-toed Persian slippers, when Mycroft arrived at Baker Street to be admitted by his brother himself, Mrs Hudson already having retired.

'What's the hullabaloo?' demanded Sherlock Holmes, when his brother was seated.

'This telegram from the Washington embassy,' said Mycroft, offering the message. 'Carson's dead.' When Sherlock Holmes

338

looked up from reading it, Mycroft produced further sheets. 'And this, Sebastian's letter explaining his dealings with Carson. It arrived tonight.'

The second communication took longer for Sherlock Holmes to absorb. Having done so, unasked he poured brandy for both of them. 'Sebastian was more deeply in with Carson than I imagined. He could be in mortal danger.'

'That's why I came immediately. What would you have me do?'

'Have you spoken to Churchill?'

'Briefly. He's managed to convince himself it was his decision to withhold any statement in the House and has thus saved himself unwelcomed association.'

'I meant of Sebastian's continuance.'

'Churchill said he looked forward to Sebastian's next communiqué.'

Sherlock Holmes shook his head, despairingly. 'I'll not risk a son I've only just found.'

'I could telegraph him – we could do it now, from your machine here, in a sufficiently secure manner – to abandon his mission.'

The head shake was no longer despairing. 'But he's a grown man, Mycroft. Can I – should I – attempt to tell a grown man what to do?'

'If his life's in danger, which we both agree it could well be, then unquestionably you should.'

'You do understand, don't you, that he sees this as his initiation: his proof of natural inheritance?'

'Taking over from you, do you mean?' demanded Mycroft, surprised.

'Of course. Someone has to. And who better than he?'

'Doesn't that contribute to the argument that he should cease this current expedition?'

Sherlock Holmes spent so long with his brandy glass neglected and his head forward against his chest that, unlikely though it seemed, Mycroft thought his brother might have relapsed into his interrupted sleep. But at last the man stirred, the grey eyes anything but sleep-fogged. 'It has to be made Sebastian's decision.'

'What would you have me say?' repeated Mycroft.

'I have my own telegraph, as you so recently reminded me. I'll say it myself.'

It had taken a lot more argument to convince David Anderson that the Lafayette Park attack should not in any way be linked to Jack Carson's death but Sebastian believed he had finally prevailed, although there remained a slight uncertainty at how totally it was possible to trust a journalist. Sebastian dismissed the cab on 14th Street and despite the aching difficulty completed the remainder of his journey on foot, entering the Willard through its secondary entrance from F Street, alert for any obvious surprise from anyone in the foyer at his sudden reappearance. There wasn't any. It was a call from the concierge that halted him, crossing towards the elevators. Sebastian turned to receive the two messages, choosing the personally hand-addressed envelope first, conscious of the perfume as he did so.

In flowing script the note was addressed to Porthos and signed Anna. The coming weekend house party hosted by Mrs Amelia Becker was the social conclusion of the Virginia year, a challenge even to that of their last encounter at the German Embassy; perhaps to judge that challenge for himself Count Johann von Bernstorff had already accepted an invitation. Mrs Becker had allowed Anna to invite a guest of her choosing and she only knew one musketeer. She was anxious for his reply.

The telegram read:

RELYING UPON YOU TO DECIDE IF CURRENT BUSINESS REVERSALS REQUIRE ABANDON-MENT OF YOUR NEGOTIATIONS STOP THERE ARE MANY INTERESTING PORTFOLIOS RE-QUIRING YOUR LEADING ROLE ATTENTION IN THE FORESEEABLE FUTURE STOP

It was signed, simply, S.H.

How different would have been the wording had his father known the closeness with which the reversals had come to being permanent? wondered Sebastian. He was encouraged when he got to his rooms to find that his wound hadn't bled any further, although there was a fresh bruise on his thigh from the constant pressure of the pistol.

Twenty

The intervening days provided Sebastian with the very necessary opportunity to reflect and recover, the exhilarating conclusion from that reflection greatly contributing to his physical improvement.

Even without the repeated reading the only possible interpretation of the Baker Street message was that, having ensured his financial independence, his father, unasked and therefore willingly, had now bequeathed to him the incalculable professional inheritance as well. Quickly upon the exhilaration followed the sobering realization of the burden bestowed upon him by his father's much sought confidence. It was illogical for him to expect correctly to deduce upon initial examination every nuance, obfuscation, twist and turn of this current affair. But in this new awareness Sebastian admitted to himself there might have been more progress had he entered the assignment not just so brashly overconfident but so inanely resentful. There was consolation in his recognizing his own shortcomings rather than having them arraigned humiliatingly before him by another. Hubris begets humility, thought Sebastian, evolving another personal axiom. Overdue in coming but personally welcome nevertheless: the only embarrassment was of himself, by himself.

Sebastian occupied the entire morning not so much upon an acknowledging telegram – although he took every care in its composition – but upon the fuller letter to follow by sea. The cable read:

BELIEVE IT STILL POSSIBLE SUBSTANTIALLY TO SALVAGE BUSINESS POSSIBILITIES BUT APPRECIATE YOUR GUIDANCE AND SUGGESTIONS WHICH WILL BE ACTED UPON IF EXPECTATIONS MISPLACED STOP APPRECIATIVE AND GRATIFIED BY INDICATION OF FUTURE ROLE STOP LETTER FOLLOWING STOP

Sebastian detailed his encounter with William Hartley – so committed against disclosing the Lafayette Park attack that it scarcely entered his mind as he wrote – and told of his hope, just short of expectation, that Hartley would renew the approach somehow or somewhen during the following week. As carefully as Sebastian wrote he just as carefully omitted that if Hartley failed to take up their discussion he saw no way forward except to approach Hartley himself and drop the demand to inspect the cargo.

By the Friday of his departure for Virginia Sebastian's physical improvement was such that he could move without any pain-restricted difficulty and considered his closely

343

scrutinized face to be practically unmarked. The wound had become a livid red scar, in places more than a quarter of an inch wide, and his back, although without pain, was faded to an ugly yellow and black mottle, like the skin of some strange sea creature.

The passing days had not, however, been uneventful but, thankfully, restoratively uninvolved. David Anderson's disclosure of stolen files, quoting an unnamed member of Jack Carson's staff as to their positive existence, prompted a public commitment from the New York Police that the investigation was remaining open and being actively pursued in conjunction with detectives re-examining the death of Congressman Grant. Sebastian was briefly uneasy at Anderson's subsequent disclosure of those files failing to contain details of the mystery informant known only by the initial letter A. That revelation brought a combined appeal from both police authorities for the informant to come forward under a guarantee of complete, protective anonymity. All New York and Washington DC newspapers published a specially assigned police telephone number that could be rung, night or day, with an assurance of complete confidentiality. On the first day there were more than sixty calls, all of them eventually dismissed as cranks or mischievous. The *New York Times* and the *Washington Post* also reported receiving, in total, almost a hundred hoax approaches. The Capitol security and police departments claimed their investigations had failed to uncover, either from employment records or visitors' logs, any unauthorized or unaccounted persons gaining access to the private offices of Congressmen of either House. The German Embassy regretted the accidental death of Senator Jack Carson, at the same time asserting there was nothing more they intended to add to their already issued dismissals of the claims unfortunately made. Nor did they anticipate issuing any further statement.

Sebastian maintained daily telephone contact with both Edna Connolly and David Anderson, for his part – with nothing further to tell them – merely to ensure their safety and in return to assure them of his. During none of those telephone conversations did they have anything new or important to tell him. Towards the end of the week the stories started to be relegated to paragraphs on increasingly remote inside pages. On the Thursday Anderson demanded to be able to claim contact with Carson's source A, to Sebastian's immediate and worried refusal. To fend him off, Sebastian hinted that he expected soon to encounter a situation from which he could discover something new, promising to speak to Anderson early the following week.

Sebastian spent most of those intervening days in and around the Willard Hotel, at irregular periods during each of them specifically and very publicly embarking on outings in his now permanently retained coach, which he also employed the day after Anna Boinburg-Langesfeld's invitation to convey his acceptance to Virginia. Not once, either from the coachman's vigilance or from the man's cultivated informant network among his colleagues, was there a single report of their being hired in pursuit. Nor did Sebastian detect any from his even greater vigilance.

'Maybe we've shaken them off?' suggested the man after a tourist expedition to Mount Vernon, the historically preserved Virginia home of George Washington.

'It would be pleasing to imagine so,' said Sebastian. 'I fear, however, that they are better at their craft than we are in detecting it.'

'They won't be on our journey to Virginia,' promised the man. 'It's mostly so open we'll be able to see another carriage from a mile distance.'

The geography was accurate but the prediction was not.

Amelia Becker's Virginia estate was the most unusual and certainly the most flamboyant of any of the grand houses and grounds Sebastian had so far seen in America and with few exceptions even in Europe. The initially distant but obviously palatial principal, three-storey edifice was a combination of red brick and white clapboard, its entire verandah-encircled front supported by six enormously tall, full-height doric columns, its countless windows sparkling in the pale afternoon sun. As Sebastian clopped along the gently curving drive, long enough in itself to be considered a road, rolling, unfenced downs dotted with deer fell away on either side. It took several minutes for them to be replaced by white-railed paddocks in which arab horses with arched necks were being paced by grooms and stable boys and sometimes, unaccountably, jockeys. Closer and on the final high approach from an overlooking hill, Sebastian saw that dominatingly imposing facade, though it first appeared the colonial front was, in fact, dwarfed by the enormity of two side wings. They radiated from the main building to make an incomplete rectangle around a spectacular and verdant central oasis, which, although totally dissimilar, at once reminded Sebastian of Versailles.

The individual lawns were barbered and the low separating hedges were sculpted into intricate shapes and designs to enclose patterned displays of every flower of every colour Sebastian had ever seen and many more that he had not. It was made truly an oasis by inner water gardens of mermaids and cherubs and dolphins spouting fountain-feeding streams and pools supplying a pagoda-guarded, willow-draped lake. The lake, Sebastian guessed, would be churned by dazzling carp and burnished goldfish; maybe, even, there would be maritime creatures whose bizarre hues would match that of his no-longer painful back.

Sebastian was not the first to arrive. There were more automobiles than horse-drawn carriages already crowding the gravelled and floral-centred forecourt, and neither were being dispersed to garages and stables as efficiently as they had been outside the German Embassy. As he disembarked and stood waiting for his luggage to be unloaded and carried away by the staff of an attentive steward, Sebastian was conscious of the disdain with which other drivers, of both car and coach, were regarding his public transport.

His coachman became aware of the contempt, too. As they parted, the time for Sebastian's Monday collection decided, the coachman said: 'Beat them three times round Jenkins Hill any day, automobiles included!'

Sebastian's steward, who was black and wore deep-green livery and white gloves, informed Sebastian as they approached the mansion that his accommodation was in the north wing. Mrs Becker was receiving everyone at six. The weekend's itinerary awaited Sebastian in his rooms. His name was John and he was Sebastian's personal steward, responsible during his stay for all his needs and comfort. He would endeavour to do everything possible to ensure Sebastian's visit was pleasurable.

The house very definitely had the dimensions of a palace, its echoing entrance hall rising the full height of the balcony divided three storeys, it and the corridors along which

348

he followed his guide made light and airy by huge, single-paned windows. The corridor along which Sebastian was escorted ran parallel to the gardens reminiscent of Versailles and Sebastian became aware that in places, along the entire length of the inner walkway, there were separating conservatories, each bedecked with its own plants and foliage, with easy chairs and tables from which the outer oasis could be viewed, like opera boxes. Remembering Anna's reference to the forthcoming weekend rivalling the German reception as a social highlight, Sebastian decided that if there were a challenge his as yet unmet hostess was the floral victor.

Sebastian's brocaded, opulently furnished rooms – bedroom, bathroom and lounge – were on the third floor, overlooking the outside lake in which he was sure he could detect the flickering movement of fish. Predictably that view was through floor-to-ceiling windows and there were three separate displays of flowers. His clothes had already been unpacked and hung up, his linen folded in drawers. Against such courtesy, remembering the discovery of Denning aboard the *Lusitania*, Sebastian had carried the swordstick with him, not in his cane case. And of course the Smith and Wesson, now more comfortably ensconced – although still in his rear pocket – in a chamois holster he had two days earlier returned to the gunstore to buy.

On his lounge table an envelope was

addressed in a now recognizable flowing hand to Porthos. The note inside said, *Until cocktails at six*. There was no signature. Also there was the promised weekend itinerary, which, befitting his downstairs opera box imagery, read like a theatrical entertainment or more precisely the choice of several entertainments. On the Saturday there was even scheduled a sealed knot depicting the battle for Yorktown Heights, the final and successful engagement of the American War of Independence, freeing the North American colonies from British rule. Among the others Sebastian noticed that there was a skeet as well as a quail shoot.

As he finally took his bath, still cautious against too deeply immersing his so recently healed shoulder, Sebastian wondered if there would be any special significance for Count Johann von Bernstorff at the inclusion of the planned historical tableau of such a profound British military defeat. It was not his only curiosity. Was there not far greater significance in William Hartley's bewildering remark – *Shall you be with Lowell Smithlane this weekend in Virginia?* – when according to his understanding Lowell Smithlane was hosting his own weekend gathering hundreds of miles away in Long Island? And why, apart from a social contest with which in the current circumstances he could not imagine the German ambassador troubling himself, was Count von Bernstorff here in the Virginia countryside?

Although it didn't extend the full height
of the reception hall – the gilded ceiling
stopping at the second level – in Sebastian's
opinion the drawing room in which the
welcoming cocktail party was convened was
grander than that of the German Embassy,
which he at once conceded probably to be
due to its furnishings, which while sumptu-
ous in velvets and silks and gold inlays was
clearly lived-in, not a chamber just dusted
and aired for receptions such as this. There
were required oils upon the silk-hung walls
but side tables and crannies held family
photographs, in a lot of which he recognized
the matriarch he had seen from afar at the
Washington event. In several she was accompanied by a scowl-faced, uprightly aloof man
who in attitude could have been von Bernstorff's twin in many of the photographs
Sebastian had seen in the *Washington Post's*
archives. Nowhere were there portraits or
casual capturings of children.

Anna Boinburg-Langesfeld was conveniently near the entrance: posed was a word that
came at once to Sebastian's mind. She wore
the oyster silk with the diamond choker and
earrings he recognized. She moved towards
him at once, her face open and smiling in a
manner he found familiar and just as quickly
wished he hadn't, because it seemed intru-
sively out of place. It was the expression on
the face of the mother he had never known, in
the larger of the two photographs in his

father's East Sussex retreat.

Anna said: 'I had your address.'

'I'm glad you did.'

'I hope I am. I've risked making myself Heine's siren of Lorelei.'

Her retention of detail was remarkable, acknowledged Sebastian. Into his mind, unbidden, came *Sie hatten sich beide so herzlich lieb, Spitzbübin war sie, er war ein Dieb,* the lines from the poet's *Neue Gedichte* which uncomfortably translated as They loved each other beyond belief – She was a strumpet, he was a thief. Aloud Sebastian said: 'Why did you?'

Anna pouted. 'Because it pleased me: I thought it would please you, too.'

'It did. And has. Although it *is* unconventional.'

'I thought that's what we enjoyed being together, unconventional!'

How easy he found it to be with this woman. 'Let's not take it too far too quickly. I think I should meet my hostess, don't you?'

Instead of replying she said: 'I've learned an American word. Grouch. You're a grouch.'

'What's a grouch?'

'A spoilsport. What happened to your face?'

'Nothing.'

'Then you haven't bathed properly.'

'My hostess,' he prompted, accepting offered champagne from a waiter.

'Grouch!' accused Anna, shaking her head against the wine. She turned, leading him deeper into the room, in the centre of which, in totally unchallenged authority, Amelia Becker was holding court.

Closer she was far more the formidable matriarch Sebastian had judged her to be at first sight, tall for a woman – close to Laura Hemditch's height, perhaps – but heavier-bosomed and more heavy bodied than he'd imagined from his distanced impression. Her primped hair was completely white and he guessed her to be about sixty, although her face was youthfully unlined. She turned to their arrival and Anna's introduction, ap-praising him with an intensity that made Sebastian feel naked.

'Anna calls you her musketeer!' greeted the woman. Those grouped around her laughed.

'Were it possible to aspire to such gallantry,' smiled Sebastian. 'You're very gracious to include me in your party.'

'As you are gracious to accept. In my defence, I have to make clear the battle choice for the sealed knot was made before your invitation.'

Sebastian was not discomfited by the woman's banter, which was delivered totally stern-faced to heighten the amusement. He said: 'France fought with the Americans. How could the British hope to win a two-to-one affair?'

'How indeed?' demanded a voice, in Eng-lish.

Sebastian turned at the entry into the group of Count Johann von Bernstorff. Beside him was a thin woman of iron-grey hair, fixed

353

features and unwavering demeanour reminiscent of Gerda Vogel. The offered hand, at her introduction as Countess Eva, was hesitant, as if she was unsure of physical contact. Sebastian judged Amelia Becker's clothes-stripping examination to be quizzical. Eva von Bernstorff's sought blemishes. Sebastian was sure she hadn't been present at the German reception. At their hostess's attempt to complete introductions, von Bernstorff said: 'Mr Holmes and I are already acquainted, although I did not anticipate our meeting again so soon.'

'Which makes it for me a double pleasure,' said Sebastian. He had every reason to remember the ambassador's name but what was von Bernstorff's incentive for remembering his?

'Just imagine,' picked up the older man, 'without that unfair advantage of French forces at Yorktown the United States might well still be a British colony!'

Sebastian was uneasy at the impoliteness of the banter being taken away from their hostess, curious at the German's overstrained persistence. To retreat or do battle? A foray at least. 'What we lost as a colony we quickly more than gained in friendship...'

'Well said,' praised Amelia Becker.

'...And we still have a substantial number of dependencies elsewhere to administer,' finished Sebastian.

'Beneficence to the natives!'

'The most appreciated of which, I've always

understood, is not to regard them as such but rather as the rightful inhabitants of their own countries, whose development Great Britain can assist.'

'Such a laudable philosophy!'

This was wrong, Sebastian recognized: wrong at every level of social politeness, but worse, far worse, he was confronting the last person in Washington – in the world – whom he should even dream of confronting. 'But then I am but a fledgling in such judgements. I would always, sir, defer to your experience and authority on all such profound matters.'

'And profound matters are not on this weekend's itinerary,' came in Amelia Becker, quick to seize the opening. She cupped the ambassador's arm as she moved, bringing the countess with them, and said: 'Come! Let me show you my latest horticultural acquisition: a carnivorous plant that lives off the insects it devours!'

The gathering was broken by their hostess's departure, leaving Anna and Sebastian alone together. Sebastian said: 'That was unfortunate.'

'What?'

'That wasn't the easiest of exchanges.'

'I saw nothing untoward.'

'I hope no one else did. And that Mrs Becker has suffered no offence.'

'Amelia enjoys feisty discussion, if indeed it was such.'

Henceforth the rules of engagement had to be those of retreat, Sebastian determined: the provocation had been the ambassador's, to which he'd been foolish to respond. He had nothing to gain – possibly far too much to lose – by confrontation and antagonism. Sebastian's move for more champagne was in the direction of the doorway. William Hartley stood just inside, staring fully towards him. At Sebastian's sudden attention the man turned away, with no sign of recognition.

That night's banquet was a fully formal affair in a vast salon where the chandeliers were candle-lit and the silk-lined walls spaced with huge, gold-framed mirror panels to give the optical illusion of making it even larger. Sebastian counted thirty-five people around the elongated table interspersed with candlelabra, the odd number equated by Amelia Becker at the top of the table without a balance at its opposite end. Sebastian's unspoken curiosity was assuaged during the meal by one of his immediate neighbours, a plantation owner with a bordering estate, who disclosed that Amelia Becker's husband had died ten years earlier. The mellifluously voiced man, who shunned formal tails for an evening-tied and obviously personally tailored black frock coat, declared she had impressed everyone who knew her not just by assuming personal control of the family corporation but in those ten years expanding it to almost double its already formidable size. Sebastian waited for an indication of what the commerce was but the man didn't

356

offer and after what he still regarded as the social impropriety of the welcoming reception Sebastian judged it presumptuous to enquire. The woman to Sebastian's left was his introduction to the most pronounced and almost incomprehensible southern drawl he had imagined possible. Upon learning he was ignorant of trotting racing she took it upon herself to explain in overwhelming minutiae the finer points and art of the sport, promising further to advise him on the track the following day.

Anna Boinberg-Langesfeld was put directly opposite him but spent the majority of the meal engrossed in conversation with those around her – particularly the two closest men – exchanging little more than three or four sentences with Sebastian. William Hartley was virtually at the furthest end of the table, only two seats away from their hostess and close to Count Johann von Bernstorff.

Although there was no titular host, the women withdrew for the men to take cigars and pass port and brandy. In an obvious courtesy towards the German ambassador no discussion was broached upon the political situation in Europe, although there was an inference from a general conversation about substantial gains being possible from investing in certain unspecified commodities on the New York stock exchange.

It was von Bernstorff, assuming the role as if his by right, who led them back to the drawing room to join the women. Card tables were already set and Anna seized him as her partner in whist. Sebastian was surprised at her fierce competitiveness, relieved he played adequately enough for them to win their rubber. She moved on to show the same determination at what he recognized as bezique but which she called pinochle, at which she won again. As Anna played alone Sebastian tried, and failed, to understand the intricacies of poker, which his plantation-owner dinner companion promised to teach him before the weekend was over.

Amelia Becker signalled the end of the evening by retiring just before eleven, almost immediately followed by the ambassador and his wife. As she passed Sebastian, on her way from the room, Anna made as if to bid him goodnight but said instead: 'I'll come to you: leave your door.'

It was only at this late stage that William Hartley approached. The man said: 'I did not expect to see you.'

'An unexpected invitation. But someone you did expect appears to be absent.'

Hartley frowned. 'It was an assumption that Lowell Smithlane would be here. Are you joining the shooting party tomorrow?'

'I travel substantially equipped but I did not bring any guns.'

'Perhaps there are some in the house that would fit you?'

'I don't enjoy someone else's gun.'

'Why not walk the shoot? There might be an opportunity for us to talk further.'

Or for accidents to occur, thought Sebastian.

Anna flitted through his door so quickly and so silently that had he not been expecting her, actually looking towards it, Sebastian would not have been aware of her entry. They came together eagerly, searchingly. It was Anna who first began to undress him, but they became naked together because she wore less. He carried her, entwined around him, to the bed and it was not until she fell away from him, upon it, that she saw.

'What's *that*!' Anna came abruptly upright, straining forward towards the vivid scar and in doing so caught a glimpse of his back and stretched around him, to look more closely there, too. 'Holy Mother of all creation!'

'An accident,' said Sebastian. 'A missed footing, leaving a carriage.' It sounded weaker than he'd already known it was going to be.

'I don't believe you! It's a fight. You were in a brawl!'

'I stumbled from my carriage,' insisted Sebastian, doggedly.

'Tell me about it! Did you fight with your sword? Kill anyone?'

'I told you how it happened.'

'My poor darling! You could have been killed! Does it hurt?'

'No.'

'Can I touch it?'

'If you wish.'

Gently, a feather's touch, she traced her

finger along the scar and then came even closer, just as softly kissing the mark, trailing her tongue along it. She said: 'It arouses me,' and it did and Sebastian was impressed with himself that he could match her.

As they lay afterwards side by side he said: 'You are too demanding of an injured man.'

'It was an affray, wasn't it?'

'An accident.' Seeking to change the subject, Sebastian said: 'This weekend promises to be interesting.'

'Amelia certainly stages a spectacle.'

'Von Bernstorff's presence is intriguing. As spectacular as it promises to be I find it curious that an ambassador is a guest, unless there are political aspects of which I am unaware.'

Anna turned towards him. 'You don't know, of course! That was unthinking of me.'

'Know what?'

'Amelia's late husband, Gustav, was Prussian. It was he who founded the armaments corporation she now controls and runs. One of the biggest in America. I gather there is friendship between the two families in Germany.'

'Why a corporation here and not in her husband's native Germany?'

'Perhaps that's a question von Bernstorff would like to answer.'

Sherlock Holmes said: 'The place has gone to rack and ruin!'

'To my eye the house is immaculate,'

disputed Dr Watson, who had travelled from London to East Sussex with his friend. 'Mrs Hudson trained her country assistant admirably, in my judgement.'

'That judgement has to be Mrs Hudson's. I'm talking about my garden.' They were standing on the overlooking verandah. The taller man swept his hand out in an embracing gesture. 'An African veldt!'

'You're too harsh, Holmes. The gardener's done a splendid job.'

'The roses are not half tightly enough pruned and I can't see a flower that does not need to be dead-headed. It's good that I am back, albeit briefly for this weekend. I might even choose to remain longer, abandoning you to find your own way back.'

Watson followed the other man's lead into the drawing room with the floorboards that gave the birdsong alarm. 'My difficulty will not be finding my way back to London but understanding your not feeling the need to be there yourself in the middle of an investigation such as this!'

'Sebastian has conducted himself remarkably well.'

'I have no difficulty acknowledging that, either. I don't make a connection between the two.'

Sherlock Holmes delayed replying, pouring generous measures of whisky for them both. Watson accepted his glass, calculating that it had to be almost two weeks, perhaps longer, since he'd suspected his friend to be under the influence of any different stimulant. 'What say you, Watson, to the declaration that I am retiring?'

Such was Watson's astonishment that momentarily he could not find anything *to* say. At last he managed: 'It's beyond me to imagine you are serious!'

'Did I not buy this now miserable property for just such a reason?'

'And chafed at every minute of every day of your being here, as if in prison!'

'It is time I handed over. And who better – more qualified – than Sebastian?'

'I do not for a moment seek to question Sebastian's promise. But I do not think this current matter has progressed sufficiently to consider him qualified to succeed you. No man, not even Sebastian, will ever be sufficient for that.'

Sherlock Holmes smiled at the exaggerated praise. 'Perhaps not *entirely*. For some time in the future I foresee Sebastian needing a sounding board.'

Watson frowned. 'You envisage filling for Sebastian the role I have played for you for so many years!'

Sherlock Holmes at once saw the other man's need. 'You have a long-suffering wife from whom my demands have too often taken you.'

'Neither she – nor I – have ever complained!'

'Nor would you, ever.'

Without conceit, a vanity impossible for

him, Dr John Watson believed he knew Sherlock Holmes better than any other man, in every medical and psychological way. And psychologically he knew that the great detective could *never* have a contented, satisfied mind dead-heading dying plants. Nor pricking out hopeful seedlings. From which automatically followed, in his boredom, that he would seek that other unacceptable relaxation. 'A word, Holmes?'

'As always.'

'Apart from the lost years – for all their reasons – you have been constantly exercised in the pursuance of your craft?'

'With your acknowledged assistance.'

'Which you now, quite properly, seek to provide to Sebastian?'

'I did not imagine, old and trusted friend, that my announcement would cause you such distress.'

'It's not personal distress that I am expressing,' lied Watson. 'How can you perform as Sebastian's sounding board without keeping constantly honed and attuned the faculties developed over so many years? Do you imagine you could play your Stradivarius as exquisitely as you do without practice?'

Need indeed, thought Sherlock Holmes: far more than he had expected. 'You're right of course, Watson. I suggest a resolution. To keep myself attuned, you and I shall take upon ourselves the odd case or two. Sebastian shall exercise himself with the others.'

'So, we will still work together!'

'As we always have.'

For whose greater benefit had he manipulated this exchange? Watson asked himself.

For whose greater benefit had he allowed the manipulation of this exchange? Sherlock Holmes asked himself. At once there was another question. How was he satisfactorily to explain it to Sebastian, after his son's enthusiastic telegraph?

Mrs Hudson, at the door, said: 'I am sorry about dinner being this delayed. There was so much I had to do that the local woman had neglected.'

Twenty-One

Count Johann von Bernstorff had two gun-case-carrying escorts and two other attendants whose function might cosmetically have been that of loaders but for whom a far more apposite description was bodyguards; they would, Sebastian supposed, be housed in the separate servants' and drivers' quarters from which, additionally, would come all the backstairs gossip. There were none in the ambassador's group he recognized from the embassy reception, not even from the parking and carriage dispersal. Neither – far more importantly – did he find any resemblance in shape, size or movement to his indistinctly

364

shadowed attackers. They danced a choreo-
graphed half circle to the ambassador's rear
and sides, their performance far too obviously in Sebastian's opinion concentrated not
at all upon the shoot towards which they were
walking but far more upon potential outside
shifts and distractions, marking them as far
better and more professional protectors than
gillies.

The ambassador's party within a party was
not the only initial surprise. Sebastian conceded the greater to be the commanding
presence of Amelia Becker. She wore a
shoulder-padded and patched, speckled
green hunting suit, the ground-brushing
skirts divided into culottes. She was also
accompanied by a loader bearer but there was
only one gun case. Count von Bernstorff's
shooting attire was also and very obviously
personalized, a high-necked uniform of
military grey and green, the trouser not
knickerbockers but tailored at the knee to fit
into calf-enclosing boots, again military in
fashion.

The chief gamekeeper, supported by two
only slightly dissimilarly dressed subordi-
nates, had his own independent uniform
complete with a prominent, medal-like lapel
identification and a neck-chained whistle to
signal the end of each drive. There was a
distant view of the beaters who to Sebastian
also appeared uniformly attired estate staff,
not workers drawn from surrounding villages,
to which Sebastian was more accustomed in

Europe. The controlling huntsman betrayed little deference – not even to his employer – during the peg-position draw or the shooting stipulation, which was that nothing without clear sky beneath was a legitimate target. There were seven more in the shooting party, including William Hartley. Each who had not brought their own had been allocated a loader from the estate staff and each gun was traditionally dressed with the exception of the neighbouring plantation owner who affected a multi-pocketed buckskin jacket and droop-brimmed hat that incongruously reminded Sebastian of the voortrekkers' headgear of the Boer war.

Sebastian quite properly relegated himself to the rear for the shoot instructions, among the five others – all women – who like himself were walking. Sebastian's positioning himself as he did was more for the protection it afforded his unguarded back, but the vantage point enabled him to see one of the ambassador's protectors was directly behind the man, a physical shield. Sebastian's skin once more prickled from the intensity with which he held himself, coiled to react at the first twitch of danger or attack. For ease of withdrawal Sebastian was risking fresh bruising by abandoning his pistol's chamois-padded holster. Sebastian was embarrassed by his apprehension as well as by hiding himself beneath the folds of women's skirts: hardly, he thought, the gallantry expected from a musketeer, a pretence of which he was tiring. Anna had told him the previous night she'd join him later at the al fresco lunch. Countess Eva was not there, either.

So far there had only been the nodded and clichéd courtesies of early morning greetings, apart from which neither the German ambassador – nor his attendants – had paid him any heed. Neither had Hartley, at the furthest end of the briefing line. The only passing conversation had been with the previous night's plantation-owning dinner companion, who had generously and immediately offered Sebastian the pick of his three supplementary guns upon realizing he was unequipped – as had Amelia Becker before her neighbour, from an even greater choice of weapon – each to Sebastian's polite refusal. Sebastian equally politely endured the man's explanation that it wasn't turkeys shot on a turkey shoot but what Sebastian would recognize as a guinea fowl or pheasant.

The gun offer was repeated by Amelia Becker as they completed their walk to the first stand, at the edge of a finger-like salient jutting from the main wood.

To Sebastian's second refusal, the woman said: '*Do* you shoot, Mr Holmes?'

'With great enjoyment. But as I've explained, I did not travel prepared.' Sebastian swept an arm around him. 'All this is totally unanticipated.' Walking with Amelia Becker put him with his back to virtually everyone else in the party but he considered it safe in such a concentrated gathering of witnesses.

'What do you have?'

'Purdeys.' They had been an eighteenth-birthday gift from his uncle. At that age Sebastian had still believed himself an orphan.

'I have a pair myself. But today I'm shooting with those of my own design and manufacture.'

'*Your* own design?'

The imposing woman smiled sideways at him. 'It took America longer to emancipate its slaves than it did its womenfolk.'

Sebastian would never have grouped Amelia Becker under the banner of womenfolk unless, perhaps, she had been at the forefront of some female crusade. 'We in England until comparatively recently were privileged to serve a queen.'

'Privileged? That has a patriotic ring.'

Was this a slightly heavier banter than that of the previous evening or were there shaded subtleties to be sought? 'Coupled with that of respect.'

'To which do you respond the stronger, Mr Holmes?'

'I would hope to both in equal measure.' This wasn't banter, Sebastian determined.

'Are you a military man?'

'I have neither the ability nor the inclination.'

'How would you see yourself if events in Europe turned for the worst?'

American directness yet again, Sebastian recognized; how many more answers was he going to need for this threadbare question? 'I observe a personal as well as a business philosophy of confronting situations of significance if and when they arise, never risking ill-informed anticipation. Do you have guiding philosophies, Mrs Becker?'

The smile came again. 'Quite the contrary to your own. I anticipate the sway of events and snap up every advantage. Do you like horticulture, Mr Holmes?'

Sebastian knew it was not a change of direction in their conversation. 'I greatly admire – and share – your very obvious delight in it.'

'I must show you my *Dionaea muscipula*.'

'That which you demonstrated to the ambassador last evening?' guessed Sebastian.

'A carnivorous plant,' enthused the woman. 'The Count was fascinated by how it traps its prey: open-jawed for the unwary intruder and then...' she clicked her fingers, loudly, '...it bites shut and devours it at the first mis-step.'

'I would be as fascinated as Count von Bernstorff,' said Sebastian. What, he wondered, had been the purpose of that curious allegory – of the entire exchange, in fact? Had he been likened to the unwary intruder? Or warned of something he did not understand?

Mrs Becker had drawn the eighth peg, which Sebastian remembered to have been Congressman Grant's isolated and fatal position and which took away the protection of his remaining close to his hostess. Instead he established himself again among the other

369

women, although they automatically spread out, each behind her husband. Sebastian judged himself sufficiently back from the guns and their loaders to keep the entire party in his field of vision. As his carriers were offering von Bernstorff his choice from the two cases Sebastian saw that one held a scope-sighted rifle. The glimpse was too fleeting for Sebastian to guess the calibre but it looked as heavy as any he had ever seen on a stag or boar hunt.

The barrels of the ambassador's shotguns were intricately engraved and his chief loader wore two cartridge bandoliers, cross-slung over each shoulder, which made him look like a Mexican bandit. There was a far less ornate design on Amelia Becker's guns, the barrels of which were highly polished and reflective, not the matt finish to which Sebastian was accustomed. Hartley's guns were at first glance obviously Purdeys.

There was a distant but rising chorus of halloas and drum banging from the beaters, and the gamekeeper's whistle brought the guns to their stands. Sebastian's attention was divided between the shooting party and the smaller of von Bernstorff's porters, who retreated past the loaders and then Sebastian and the women. As the man went by Sebastian nodded and smiled. There was no response. The man carried the case Sebastian knew to hold the rifle. He halted about five yards directly behind Sebastian.

Count von Bernstorff had the fifth peg of

the initial draw, putting him next to Hartley. In Sebastian's judgement the first bird to come over was Hartley's but von Bernstorff took it with a premature but perfect shot several seconds before the Englishman. Von Bernstorff's second perfect shot brought down the following bird, which unquestionably was his, again before Hartley's move towards it. Von Bernstorff's transfer of one exhausted gun for its loaded replacement – a backwards, unlooking pass from a man assured a gun would be put into his outstretched hand – was the smoothest Sebastian had ever witnessed. The eye-blink delay gave Hartley the advantage to reciprocate the robbery by taking both the ambassador's next birds, which he did, but to level the score Hartley had to swivel for the second, overhead shot. Which brought Hartley – and four other guns, including von Bernstorff, who had also followed their target's overhead flight – directly facing Sebastian from an unmissable distance of about ten yards with unbroken and therefore potentially lethal guns if they had not fired, which the German had not. And a man behind him with a rifle capable of bringing down a fully antlered stag – or even a charging, tusked boar – from five hundred yards. The moment was frozen only for Sebastian, quickly replaced by a half-awareness confirmed by the second drive, for which Sebastian moved closer to switch himself protectively behind the turned guns.

Sebastian's recognition was of a mindset

equally shared between Amelia Becker, Count Johann von Bernstorff and William Hartley, which, in tune with Sebastian's current train of thought, he isolated as a killer instinct. All three shot at everything, never leaving a bird as impossible and frequently poaching those of others in the party, even, occasionally, ignoring the gamekeeper's insistence that there be daylight beneath a bird. What Sebastian found even more curious was that from none was there the slightest indication of their being conscious of their lack of sportsmanship. Killer or not, to behave in such a manner was most definitely instinctive in all three.

It was not until the party moved off towards the fourth drive, which automatically progressed Hartley to a dangerously end-exposed peg, that the man made the promised approach for which Sebastian had throughout always positioned himself in readiness. Sebastian later judged it to have been consummately achieved, Hartley bringing himself alongside as they descended through the trees towards an already marked valley bisected by a hurried stream opening out at the valley's far end into a more placid and proper river.

'A full day,' opened Hartley, for the benefit of anyone within hearing, for which he checked as he spoke.

'To which you are more than contributing your proportion,' remarked Sebastian, adopting the charade.

'They're bred to die,' said Hartley, dismissively.

Definitely a killer instinct, Sebastian decided. 'And are so doing, in abundance.'

'We are momently clear,' said the man.

Sebastian, who had also satisfied himself they could not be eavesdropped on, said nothing. Hartley had come to him. And could continue coming.

'I have spoken to people, since we last met,' said the man.

'I'd trusted that you would.'

'They seek their insurance in the form of a Letter of Credit, in the event of misadventure.'

'As I would seek mine for the premium. But with the condition already made clear to you.'

'They are prepared to accept that condition.'

Sebastian felt a flare of satisfaction. 'Are you in a position to discuss details?'

'Not yet.'

'When?'

'Within a week. Shall you remain at the Willard?'

'Not if the cargo I have to examine is being loaded in New York, which was my understanding.'

'Where then?'

His uncertainty at returning to the Hemditch mansion was being resolved for him: it was unthinkable after Lafayette Park to endanger Hemditch or Laura by association. 'I shall take rooms at the Plaza.' They

373

were close to the next stand now, the pegs clear against the hill, the momentarily silent beaters moving into the adjoining maize field.

'I'll reach you there,' undertook Hartley.

'With whom will I be dealing?'

'Me, of course!'

Careful, Sebastian warned himself. 'I will need assurance of bona fides.'

'As will my people.'

'Which gives us more than sufficient to discuss later.' Sebastian decided this was as far as he could safely go. It was still a slender thread that could break if he strained for a meeting with whomever Hartley was working for.

'Will you need consultation with your people?'

'That will depend upon the content and agreement of our discussions.'

'Do I need to press upon you the need for discretion?'

'I scarcely think so,' said Sebastian. 'What of physical danger?'

Hartley looked almost too sharply at him. 'I mean discretion – the greatest care – in everything!'

There was an urging about that response that did not square with any knowledge of the Lafayette Park attack. 'We must both be careful.'

'I make it my practice always to be. And so intend to continue.'

As Sebastian returned to the rear of the

guns he saw Count von Bernstorff observing him.

Luncheon gave a new definition of a picnic, an open air feast atop the highest hill upon the Virginia estate so vast that the mansion was totally lost in the distance. The hard-topped but open-sided pavilion was not a single entity but a linked circular assemblage of bubble-roofed gazebos over tables set with crystal glass and board-starched linen for either four or six settings, making up individual parts of a whole. The only unevenly numbered table was that of the unaccompanied Amelia Becker, whose place-of-honour companions were Count and Countess von Bernstorff, the table shared with two other couples. Anna was on Sebastian's table, with the plantation owner and his wife, whose deep southern accent matched that of Sebastian's previous night's dinner companion, who was on Hartley's table further around the circle. Sebastian's unpadded pistol was jammed uncomfortably against his thigh, a constant, now embarrassing, reminder of his nervousness during the uneventful shoot. Sebastian was convinced no one had detected his particular alertness but he was still relieved that Anna had not been among the walkers.

The meal was predominantly a cold collation of pâtés and salmon and beef and game pies but there was southern fried chicken from what the plantation owner insisted upon calling a chuck wagon. There was champagne as well as flat wine – pink champagne for the strawberries – everything provided by liveried servants, which further stretched the picnic definition.

The circular arrangement ensured easy conversation with every other table, although Amelia Becker tapped a glass for a moment's silence to announce the turkey shoot count to be 650 birds, which his table companion declared an average bag. Sebastian never discovered the author of the challenge, although it had either to be his hostess or the ambassador because the badinage was un-arguably initiated from where they sat, the table-hopping exchanges becoming more and more exaggerated, speculating how much greater the bag would have been had some who walked or abstained from the shoot instead participated in it. Sebastian detected no personal undertone and felt no reason to defend himself. It was Anna who took up the gauntlet, with a whispered aside about Porthos which Sebastian did not fully hear. Deftly she transformed the skeet shoot into a contest between those who had taken part in the turkey shoot and those who had not. Sebastian was still not fully minded to take part until Amelia Becker addressed him directly, insisting he choose from her selec-tion of guns, and in an aside which he did hear Anna said: 'My musketeer can now prove himself!'

By the time lunch was finished more guns

had been ferried from the far away mansion and skeet traps set up by the gamekeeper's staff on the lower slope of the hill dominated by the unusual pavilion, beneath which the women – with the exception of Amelia Becker – arranged themselves for a grandstand view.

Amelia Becker personally escorted Sebastian to the gun selection, displayed in a supply wagon like an arms dealer's mobile exhibition. There were even stocks and barrels of varying lengths; most of the barrels were highly polished, like those on the guns with which Amelia Becker had shot earlier.

'This length, I think, would suit a person of your stature,' announced the woman, picking out one of the longer-stocked guns and handing it to him. 'And there is fortunately a pair.'

Sebastian did not have time to reflect upon the apparent ease with which Amelia Becker handled the shotgun before accepting it from her and by so doing answering his own half-formed curiosity. Within millimetres it had to be the same length as his own Purdeys – certainly of every other gun used that morning – and of the same specifications, but its weight had to be at least a third less. Prepared to accept something heavier his hand actually, briefly, lifted rather than dropped. He looked up to find the woman smiling in satisfaction at his surprise.

'What is it?' he asked.

'An alloy developed exclusively by my company: never before used in shotgun or rifle manufacture.'

'Rifle?' queried Sebastian.

'Yes.' The smile had gone.

Sebastian was aware of Count von Bernstorff and Hartley approaching, in conversation. 'A remarkable innovation.'

'We think so. With great commercial potential.'

'A dazzling array!' said the German, joining them.

'Shall you choose to change your guns?' invited the woman.

Von Bernstorff shook his head. 'I prefer to shoot with what I am most familiar with.' He looked at Sebastian. 'A familiarity which unfortunately you do not have. Could we devise some handicap system to compensate for your disadvantage?'

'I can't imagine how we could: nor do I seek it,' refused Sebastian. 'A practise shot or two, to accustom myself, will be sufficient.'

'Let me at least provide you with one of my loaders.'

Perfect entrapment, Sebastian at once recognized. A malfunctioning cartridge exploding literally against the side of his head – possibly detonating its companion in the second chamber – and there would be more than forty credible witnesses to a tragic accident with an innovative shotgun with which he was inexperienced. 'That's extremely generous of you.'

'May I examine the selection?' asked Hartley.

'Shoot with one if you wish,' offered the woman.

Hartley lifted a shorter version than Sebastian's, hefting it and sighting along its gleaming barrel. Sebastian waited for a remark about the lightness, but none came. Instead the man said: 'I think, like the Count, I shall remain with what I am familiar with.'

Von Bernstorff deputed the guncase carrier who had positioned himself behind Sebastian during the turkey shoot. Sebastian was not close enough to hear the exchange between the ambassador and the man before he was introduced simply as Werner. Sebastian allowed himself four practise shots, missing half the skeets, because the lightness of the gun lured him into lifting too high. There was also less recoil than he had anticipated, to which he also had to adjust and for which he was grateful because it did not jar his fading bruises or just-healed chest ... Sebastian was unsure whether there would be any physical nervousness – the shaking of a hand, the need too often to blink – which would also have to be adjusted and was relieved there wasn't. His back still prickled, though. Werner was good, clearly as well trained as his colleague of that morning in the backwards-reaching, backwards-receiving exchange practised by von Bernstorff. It meant, of course, that now not only was there a man behind him, with a permanently loaded gun, but that Sebastian was unable to see how or with what he was loading.

Apart from Sebastian those who had not taken part that morning were those who had little or no experience of shooting and who retired, mostly laughing at their inability, after the first session. By then Sebastian had moved Werner from directly behind him to be partially to his receiving left, where he had a limited view of what the man did, although still insufficient to have isolated any booby trap. Sebastian would have liked to think the perspiration adding to his back's irritation came from the heat of the guns but in fact – a fact he made a note to add to his alert to London about the new Becker rifle – the shotgun version stayed cooler than a conventional weapon. His hand and eye remained steady, though, and by the third session the contest had whittled down to only Sebastian competing against the three whom that morning he had judged to have a killer instinct. He left undefined his own determination to win. Werner – and the man's speed of loading – was integral to that determination and it occurred to Sebastian that Werner might have a non-lethal function merely to ensure his master's ultimate victory. Sebastian added a mental timing of the back and forth switching to all the other precautions he was hopefully taking.

It was Amelia who called the halt, after five clear rounds. 'We'll be here forever! We'll speed the game up. Two traps loosing simultaneously to the call, four skeets aloft and in alternate directions at once, for a mid-shot gun change.'

'Sudden death,' completed the Count, smiling.

Each of the four hit every skeet on the first round, Sebastian's mental clock timing Werner's exchange to be unimpeded split seconds. On the next draw Hartley clipped a skeet and demanded to remain but on the third he missed a skeet entirely and retired, tight-lipped and stiff-faced in defeat. Amelia Becker missed two on the next draw. Sebastian accepted that if there were going to be sabotage from Werner it would come now. His left shoulder was beginning to ache. IIe waited, ready. The man's speed was sustained remarkably – competitive smiles passing between him and the ambassador's loader – and Sebastian and von Bernstorff remained equal for the next four pulls. The ground in front of them was black with shattered clay and Sebastian perspired now from the effort, although his newly designed guns remained surprisingly cool. Von Bernstorff tried to keep surreptitious the mopping of his brow and on the next pull Sebastian detected the vaguest slowness in the man's raising of his guns, although he still took all four targets.

He was making a mistake, Sebastian abruptly realized. The older man had goaded him but in this contest at last Sebastian knew he had acquitted himself more than sufficiently. It would be wrong proving himself better able – fitter, stronger and younger – to shoot clay discs. Far wiser – far more diplomatic – to be the loser. He hit all four skeets on the next pull but on the one that followed intentionally missed the last clay of the draw, throwing up his head in apparent disappointment.

As they climbed the hill to rejoin the others, Amelia Becker said: 'So you do shoot, Mr Holmes. And shoot remarkably well.'

'I had the benefit of a remarkable gun,' said Sebastian.

'What would you say if I accused you of throwing the game?'

'That you were wholly mistaken, madam,' said Sebastian, uncomfortably.

'Misjudging people is always a danger, don't you think, Mr Holmes?'

'Always,' agreed Sebastian.

Ahead there was a sudden, hysterical outburst, jerking their attention to the unusual pavilion. Women were trying to surround Anna Boinberg-Langesfeld but were being driven back by the violence with which she was flailing her arms around her. Sebastian ran the last few yards but by the time he reached her Anna was calming.

'What on earth...?' he said, generally.

In her distress Anna was unable to find the English and so she said, *'Die Mücke,'* and Sebastian said: 'Mosquito? What about mosquito?'

'I am allergic to their sting. They terrify me.'

'We return to the house now,' decided Amelia Becker.

Anna was very flushed and as Sebastian

decided it was embarrassment she said: 'I made myself look foolish.'

'It is nothing,' dismissed Sebastian.

'That's what people will think. That it was nothing and that I am an hysteric.'

'It's past now. Over. And you are not bitten.'

'If I had been I would have swollen up. Been ugly.'

'But you're not.'

Mycroft handed Sebastian's letter back to his father and said: 'So perhaps you were a little premature, conveying the impression that you did.'

'Not so!' refuted Holmes, indignantly. They were in Baker Street, their dinner things already cleared, cigars comfortably alight, the brandy decanter between them.

'Sebastian clearly thinks you are retiring: passing everything over to him.'

'I will apportion the majority of cases to him. But there are enquiries more than enough to occupy us both.'

Mycroft shook his head against more brandy. 'He will see it as an undertaking retracted, even as a belated indication that you have no confidence in him.'

'Which I am aware of, and that is why I seek your counsel. I cannot totally discard Watson, who has been for far too long a true and loyal friend. But neither can I risk alienating a son I for far too long abandoned.'

Never before had his brother made such an open plea: nor referred to his behaviour towards Sebastian as abandonment. 'Diplomacy, which you surely need here, is the art of compromise in which bluntness – confrontation – has no place,' lectured Mycroft. 'Let circumstance dictate circumstance. Give Sebastian his promised head: act as his discreet and unobtrusive mentor. But if he is engaged in one matter then he cannot divert himself to a second or a third. Which can be yours, faithfully recorded by the dutiful Watson. And in view of the Germans' remark overheard by Inspector Lestrade let you and I continue preserving Sebastian's anonymity, the protection under which he was despatched to America instead of yourself, someone far too well known. There is as much disadvantage as there is advantage in fame.'

'Good and true advice,' acknowledged Sherlock Holmes, supplementing his brandy balloon. 'And a well-conceived compromise, for which I thank you.'

'Sebastian's activities, after this, will remain unrecorded?'

'Until the revelation can't be avoided, Sebastian remains anonymous.'

His brother enjoyed his fame: was jealous of it even, Mycroft recognized. 'I'd like better, more secure means of contact with him at this moment over the current affair. The other contents of his letter are tantalizing but far too much stays unresolved.'

'Has something developed of which I am unaware?' immediately demanded Sherlock Holmes, ever mindful of the early attempt to exclude him.

'Rather the lack of development,' complained Mycroft. 'Winston has become obsessed with whatever mission the Grand Duke Orlov was engaged upon in America. The embassy in St Petersburg has reported the man's reappearance but they do not know how long he has been back.'

'What's the date of the St Petersburg sighting?'

'Two days ago.'

'Then he's been back in Russia no more than three days. It's clearly important for him to make his presence immediately known,' declared Sherlock Holmes.

'How can you possibly know that?'

'When I was in Liverpool I arranged to be advised if the Grand Duke and his daughter chose one of the Cunard vessels for their return. I yesterday received the communication that they disembarked there from the *Mauretania* on the sixteenth. I have not yet had sufficient time to establish if they completed their journey to St Petersburg by sea – a channel packet crossing from Dover, for an immediate train connection, would have been marginally quicker – but whichever, we should allow five days from Liverpool. Two days ago would have been the first full day in which he could possibly have made an appearance.'

'What's your deduction?'

Sherlock Holmes looked reflectively into his brandy. 'It is an enquiry they should have

385

already made – information that would have been made readily available to them if deception was intended – but have the embassy sought for any suggestion of Orlov being out of sorts, incapacitated even, to account for his period of absence from the court or from public view?'

'Deception?' queried Mycroft.

'If there was such a story, it would be confirmation for us that the man was indeed on some clandestine mission to America, would it not?'

'But leave us none the wiser what such a mission was intended to achieve,' complained Mycroft.

'And from their performance thus far there's little chance of our learning of it from our Russian embassy,' agreed Holmes.

Sebastian picked up the rudiments of poker on the afternoon of the shoot and enjoyed the element of bluff and double bluff. There was a musical recital after that night's banquet and another al fresco lunch the following day in the pavilion, now set up in another part of the estate, where the Yorktown battle was re-staged. Throughout Amelia Becker position-ed a servant with a broad fan close to Anna, constantly stirring the air to keep mosquitos away. That afternoon Sebastian learned that trotting was horse racing in which the jockey rode not upon the animal's back but upon the triangular, skeletal trap it pulled, like an American version of a troika, and he then understood the presence of the riders he had seen upon his arrival. Sebastian socialized with everyone and on the Sunday Amelia Becker announced that if Anna had not already anointed him, she would have declared Sebastian her musketeer. By then, too, his contact with Count von Bernstorff was less brittle. The Countess remained aloof, although to everyone, not singly to him. The last night William Hartley joined the poker school and out-bluffed Sebastian in every game and Sebastian conceded he still had much to learn...

Each night Anna came to him and each night seemed more passionate and abandoned than the one before. In the dark early morning of the Monday, as they lay together, finally spent, Anna said: 'And with the day, another parting.'

'I am returning to New York,' said Sebastian. 'I shall be living at the Plaza, opposite the park.'

'I believe it is an excellent hotel.'

Sebastian waited but she offered nothing more. Finally he said: 'What of your plans?'

'I have none, immediately. Amelia continues to enjoy my company, as I enjoy hers.'

'So you will remain here then?'

'Amelia has other houses. This party normally marks the closure of this estate for refurbishing, apparently. And there's California I've yet to discover.' Anna sounded quite detached.

'Safe travelling.' Their by now hackneyed

farewell, thought Sebastian.

'And you. And be careful to avoid any more brawls. That's what it was, wasn't it? A brawl?'

'An attempted street robbery that came to nothing. And was nothing.'

She kissed his healed wound. 'I'll cast a spell, to keep you from harm.'

It was not until that morning that Amelia Becker took him to the hothouses, which were decidedly hot, to show him her carnivorous plant. In such an atmosphere it was only minutes before an unwary insect strayed upon the plant, which snapped closed around it so quickly that Sebastian started slightly, even though he was expecting it.

'Beautiful, isn't it?' demanded the woman.

'Deceptively so.'

'*Dionaea muscipula* means Venus flytrap,' said the woman. 'But not Venus as the goddess of love. Did you know Venus is also the mythical patron of flower gardens?'

'Very appropriate,' said Sebastian.

'I'm planning to cultivate them,' she said.

It was when he was supervising the loading of his luggage aboard the returned carriage from Washington that the coachman said softly to Sebastian: 'There it is, the second one! Past it on its way here when I was going back after dropping you off. Recognized it right away.'

Sebastian looked in the direction of the man's gesture. Count von Bernstorff's monogrammed coach was leading the departure, ahead of a black carriage without monogram

388

but upon which there was metal-framed provision for the German insignia which now fluttered from it.

'What about it?'

'Seen it more than once, around the hotel. Not with that flag thing though.'

Twenty-Two

Julius Hemditch said: 'I won't have danger visited upon me.'

'Which is why we are speaking like this,' soothed Sebastian. One window of his corner suite at the Plaza actually overlooking 5th Avenue and standing as he was with the telephone in his hand Sebastian could see Hemditch's mansion. He supposed the older man would be in the study, next door to the room holding the telegraph machine Sebastian could no longer use.

'My concern is for Laura,' said the other man, in quick qualification.

Sebastian believed he could discern some personal anxiety, as well. 'My concern is for you both. There is no way you can be connected to me. So there can be no danger.'

'Is it to do with Carson's death and all the stories in the *New York Times?*'

There was further protection for the man and his daughter in knowing as little as possible. 'Peripherally.' Sebastian hoped the next call on his list, to David Anderson, would be easier. Perhaps he should have called the journalist earlier.

'Was Carson murdered?'

There was definitely some personal anxiety and it was understandable. But he had to be honest. 'I think so.'

'Dear God!'

'You're quite safe!'

'The police don't appear to be able to find any evidence.'

'They're not intended to, are they?' Sebastian pointed out. Would Hemditch's apprehension prevent his agreeing to the assistance for which he was about to ask?

'What do you want done with your belongings?'

The probable answer to his question, Sebastian decided: Hemditch wanted to sever all links. 'If you will permit I would have them remain. I have no immediate need for any of it.'

There was a pause before Hemditch said: 'I suppose that will be all right.'

'I have another request.'

'What?'

'I need to telegraph London.'

'That means your coming here! We've already agreed that's impossible!'

'I've devised a way. I have to visit the bank. Lepecheron is your banker, too. I will leave the telegram with him, sealed of course. My only imposition will be for you to collect it and transmit it to the London addresses I shall provide. It will be unintelligible to you. You will not even be compromised by knowing what it says.'

'I did not envisage becoming so closely involved. I told Winston that several times.'

The strongest indication yet of independent communication between the two men, Sebastian recognized. 'There is absolutely no possibility of your being jeopardized.'

There was another long silence. 'On this occasion.'

'On this occasion,' accepted Sebastian. Should he – could he – ignore Churchill's belief that the New York international exchange at White Plains was infiltrated by German eavesdropping and risk a direct telephone call to his uncle, with so much to communicate? No, he answered himself at once. One mis-step now – the slightest miscalculation – and everything would be washed away, more than probably him along with it.

'You've been very considerate,' conceded the steel magnate, at last. 'For that I thank you.'

'And I am indebted to you.' Sebastian allowed himself one final review of the account to his uncle and his father of the Virginia weekend. He concluded satisfied that the development of a revolutionary rifle by an armaments manufacturer with close German connections held equal importance with the prospect of his getting himself close to an actual smuggling group. Depending upon how long it took William Hartley to make his approach, the chances were of his having established the ring's identity and composition before his full account even reached London. He said nothing about confirming his being under surveillance.

Because it was in his mind Sebastian added to the account he intended shipping to England the possibility of events overtaking his means of telegraph communication. Composing the telegram Hemditch was to send took the remainder of the morning and early afternoon. As with his previous use of Notions, Sebastian had to draw heavily upon ziphs, as well as the expectation that his uncle would stretch his translation. Belatedly Sebastian remembered that his father had also learned the language and decided there was no danger of misunderstanding.

The final effort read:

SELFSTER BEELGILEEVEE DEANSLEY EDWARD WICKHAMS WELLS PUSH. NEGED OSTIARIUS DIBS. NEGEW RIIG FLEE DAVID'S KENNEL. EEXHOGOST EX TRUMS FIRK FUURGTHEER UURGEE OSTIARIUS TO FIELD CRUX.

Sebastian's hoped-for translation was: *I believe I have insinuated myself into a German secret clique. I need to use Churchill's contingency fund. I have discovered a new rifle here. Hemditch, no longer my host, is unprepared to send further telegrams. Please urge Churchill to help resolve the problem.*

David Anderson was clearly angry when Sebastian identified himself on the telephone, demanding to know why the promised contact had not been made and just as insistently wanting to know when and where they could meet. He only quietened when Sebastian said they were not going physically to meet because he feared himself under permanent surveillance and did not want further to endanger the other man. As he spoke Sebastian thought that the danger of observed association with the more publicly identified journalist was probably a greater risk to his safety than the other way around. Which made it even more essential that they remained apart.

'You've got somewhere then?' anticipated the man, urgently. 'That's great!'

'Not yet. I've made a contact through whom I hope to meet those involved.'

'What can I write, at this stage?'

'Nothing!' said Sebastian, urgent himself. 'Everything's on a knife edge. One mistake could bring it all to nothing.'

'The story's died!' protested the journalist. 'And the police are letting their investigation die with it: they say there isn't anything to work on.'

'Better the story dies than either you or I. Or both.'

There was a moment for Anderson to digest the reminder. 'How sure are you of being under surveillance?'

'Very sure.' The black German Embassy coach had been outside the Willard on his last day in Washington and actually followed them from the hotel to Union Station.

'It wouldn't be difficult for me to believe you were holding out on me,' accused Anderson. 'Until now I didn't know you'd moved up to New York, just that you'd booked out of the Willard, without a forwarding address. I called.'

'Personally?' demanded Sebastian, alarmed. It *had* been a mistake, not telling him in advance.

'Telephoned, without saying who I was.'

Sebastian sighed, relieved. 'I will hold out on you, unless it's all done my way. Don't forget I'm your only source.'

The threat momentarily halted the other man. 'I don't want us to fall out.'

'My way,' repeated Sebastian. Bullying was an alien experience.

'OK! OK! Your way. You sure we can't meet; really talk it through?'

'There's nothing more to talk through, not yet. I've got a possible introduction and I know myself to be under observation. That's it.'

'You're in New York?'

'Yes.'

'So it's there?'

'What?'

'Whatever the development is.'

'I just told you that if you publish anything before I agree, the co-operation ends. Don't

394

doubt me on this.' He shouldn't have told the journalist even the little he had.

'I think I should come up. Be on hand.'

'I don't want you coming to the hotel!'

'I know!'

Damn the man and his persistence, thought Sebastian, hot with exasperation. 'I don't have a New York number for you.'

'The office. Extension four-two-six.'

'Remain with our understanding, David. With me you will eventually know all: deceive me and you will know nothing.'

'I told you, I don't want us to fall out.'

'Whether we do or do not is in your hands.'

'I'll be in New York tomorrow. Call me.'

He would, accepted Sebastian. But only to keep the man silent in print. How quickly – and dangerously – an imagined asset had become a burdensome liability which nevertheless could not be ignored, as he had so wrongly ignored the man since Virginia. Sebastian was curious at his own cynicism. It had been he who had cultivated an eager senator and an even more anxious political journalist. Admittedly it had been to the professional advantage of each but the responsibility was ultimately his. And now Jack Carson was dead and Anderson was under police protection. After the blatantly suspicious death of Congressman Grant, shouldn't Carson – and Anderson – have recognized the hazards of becoming involved? No. No one, no matter what the perceived danger, imagined themselves mortally threatened. Until it had so nearly happened to him it had been beyond his conception. Responsible or not – and he tried to reassure himself there was some mitigation – Sebastian determined that he would do nothing more to expose Anderson.

That decision was the predominant determination in Sebastian's mind as he emerged without any pretence at subterfuge on to 5th Avenue, swordstick in hand, the chamois-holstered pistol conveniently pocketed. He bore the permanent scar to justify such precaution but despite his most recent reflection there was still unsettling embarrassment at the theatricality of it.

What was there to conclude from the Virginia weekend beyond what he was on his way to communicate to London? An established fact was that in Washington – and in Virginia – he had been under German observation. Which had to be with the knowledge of Count von Bernstorff. From that the logical deduction had to be that William Hartley was a traitorous agent working on behalf of an impending enemy. But why was Hartley – and presumably the German Embassy – seeking outside financial protection for a clandestine, most likely armaments cargo? An easy progression, decided Sebastian. In the event of discovery there would be no direct provable link between the cargo, its shippers and the embassy. With the additional attraction that if there were a setback the financial loss would be that of the entrepreneurs – himself and Hartley – and not the already protected embassy, whose only expenditure was the generous premium. Would that have been the deduction of his no longer resented father? Or was there a nuance he had failed to recognize? It had been his wish – his intention – to operate alone, Sebastian reminded himself. There was only his own instinct – which his father had insisted to be a prime requirement – to follow.

Sebastian walked for some distance down 5th Avenue before hailing a cab, making no effort to identify or evade his undoubted pursuers. Assuming that those watching him were associates of William Hartley, he would be expected to visit a bank, which was his first destination. And there was nothing suspicious in the second call, upon the Cunard offices, personally to deliver his recently completed letter to his uncle.

By the time Sebastian, escorted as before by a liveried attendant, ascended to the fifth floor, Oscar Lepecheron was at the private entrance to his office, gesturing Sebastian into his inner sanctum. Lepecheron said at once: 'I was relieved to hear from you. I had no way of contact.'

Surely not another oversight? 'Is there an urgency?'

'I have been approached for a credit assurance, with insufficient reason for the enquiry,' disclosed the saturnine banker.

Another piece of the mosaic slotting into

place, Sebastian decided. But why hadn't Lepecheron advised him when he'd arranged the appointment? 'Who?'

Rather than reply, Lepecheron slid a single sheet of paper across his desk. Sebastian's initial interest was more in its letterhead than its contents. Illington, Besnik and Batten, established 1882, announced themselves attorneys at law with offices at the conveniently nearby Greene Street. The partnership listing held in addition to those of the founders the names of five other partners, none of which was remotely Germanic, whatever anglicized adjustments Sebastian attempted. The letter was short, limited to three paragraphs. They were acting for clients about to enter a business enterprise with Sebastian Holmes, a visiting Englishman whom they understood to be a substantial depositor at the Lepecheron Bank. Negotiations were in progress with their clients – unnamed – which required them to establish the financial equity of the said Sebastian Holmes, before they could recommend their clients to proceed. The sum for which Illington, Besnik and Batten sought assurance was $2,000,000, to be issued, if negotiations were satisfactorily concluded, as a bank guarantee.

Sebastian said: 'I shall need a copy of this.'

'Already prepared in anticipation.'

'Excellent!'

'Am I authorized to provide such a guarantee?'

'Most assuredly.'

'Two million dollars is a substantial sum of money.'

'Already satisfactorily cleared from London?' Everything would come to nothing if a lien or second-signature authority had been attached.

'Quite satisfactorily.'

'Then we can proceed.'

'You have found your investment opportunity then?'

'Hopefully so.'

'Is there any advice or facility I can provide?'

'If my negotiations are successful, I will seek a contractual letter against a sum of two million dollars on deposit here.'

The Belgian frowned. 'A Letter of Credit to be drawn upon that amount?'

Sebastian shook his head. 'A Letter of Credit is payable upon demand, is it not?'

Lepecheron's frowned uncertainty remained. 'That's how the instrument functions.'

'I want to retain the final authority for payment.'

'You fear deceit?'

'Upon what you rightly describe as a substantial sum of money I want the final authority of release.'

'I'm not sure how that can be achieved.'

'Wouldn't a promissory note achieve the objective?'

'At the moment, Mr Holmes, I am quite unsure what the objective is.'

'I am underwriting a contract.'

'Can I ask what sort of contract?'

Sebastian shook his head in refusal. 'There is a business insistence upon total confidentiality.'

'This bank prides itself upon respecting absolutely any business confidentiality, as do I personally.'

There should have been more indignation, thought Sebastian. 'I am quite certain of the integrity of both your bank and yourself. But this is a matter of the greatest discretion.' Was Oscar Lepecheron's persistence going beyond the protective concern of a banker to a favoured client? Did he, indeed, even qualify as a favoured client?

'This bank is licensed to operate under restrictions and conditions imposed by the banking regulations of the State of New York.'

'I would imagine that it is,' said Sebastian.

'Under which I – and the bank – are required to operate at all times in the best and lawful interests of its clients.'

'I accept that to be the case,' said Sebastian, curious at the build up.

'I do not seek nor intend any offence,' insisted the banker. 'But I must ask you to furnish the bank with a signed affidavit absolving it of liability against the misuse of any promissory note issued in its name.'

Oscar Lepecheron was an extremely cautious banker, Sebastian decided, but then caution was supposedly a banker's watchword. 'No doubt your in-house lawyers can draw up such a document, which I shall be happy to sign.'

'Tomorrow?' pressed the Belgian.

'I am at your convenience.' Sebastian took the sealed packet from his pocket. 'Julius Hemditch is calling later today. I would be grateful for your passing this on to him.'

'You are no longer a guest at his house?'

'It was thought better not to be.'

The banker waited but when Sebastian did not continue he said: 'I definitely require a liability disclaimer.'

Sebastian had forgotten his request to be supplied with copies of *The Times* and the *Morning Post* but the Cunard captains had not. He needed a porter to carry the newsprint to a carriage. Also awaiting him were letters from both his uncle and his father, both of which he cursorily read on his way back uptown to the Plaza Hotel. His father's communication, which also contained a photograph, was predictably the most informative as well as in some respects compounding an already deep uncertainty heightened by an enigmatic warning against not becoming a hare rather than a hound. From his father's research into the Belgian banking fraud it was easy, at least, to understand Oscar Lepecheron's insistence upon legal indemnity.

There were two messages awaiting Sebastian at the Plaza. One was from David Anderson, from whose extension there was no response when Sebastian tried to return the call. The other was from William Hartley, proposing a noon meeting the following day...

Winston Churchill strode back and forth across his Admiralty Arch quarters, needing to vent his agitation. 'I *must* have the final say, before any expenditure of the money!'

'Then impress upon Hemditch the necessity for his continued co-operation,' said Mycroft Holmes.

'Why have they fallen out?'

'I don't know. Quite obviously Sebastian wants the conduit re-established.'

'I'll telegraph Hemditch immediately,' undertook Churchill. 'We need also to know about this new weapon.'

'There will be a letter: that's the system now established.' Mycroft hesitated, unsure whether to disclose something ahead of the entire Cabinet learning it – and its significance – but then accepted he was already too far along an indiscreet road. And he had already shared Sherlock Holmes's reasoning. 'There's been a telegram from the embassy in St Petersburg. According to the court circular the Grand Duke Alexei Orlov has been indisposed for the last month with a fever.'

Churchill stopped pacing. 'So there's something afoot!'

'It requires explanation,' said Mycroft, more guardedly.

'So does Sebastian's employment of the money,' said Churchill.

Twenty-Three

Sebastian briefly gave way to irrational anger at David Anderson's *New York Times* story, actually snatching the telephone from its rest but just as quickly stopping himself and regaining control. Much of the account, which was elevated once more to the front page, was a repetition of material already published, with every possible interpretation strained from Sebastian's previous day's telephone conversation as the basis for what Anderson described as dramatic new developments. The source from whom Congressman Grant and latterly Senator Carson initiated their campaigns had anonymously approached the newspaper, promising new revelations. The newspaper was hopeful of linking up the informant with the New York police investigating Carson's death. Unnamed spokesmen from both New York and Delaware police departments were quoted urging the person to come forward, with the promise of protection and continued anonymity. The German Embassy in Washington declined comment beyond deriding the account as a continuing effort to harm German–American relations.

David Anderson's telephone call came

within fifteen minutes of Sebastian discarding the newspapers. The man said at once: 'I tried to reach you yesterday, to warn you.'

'And weren't at your telephone when I called back.'

'I was travelling up from Washington, you knew that.'

'There was no purpose in talking to you anyway. I must go.'

'No! Wait! I haven't explained.'

'There's nothing to explain.'

'I was made to write it. I had to justify my coming up to New York to my editor. He twisted my arm into writing what I did. But I protected you: you can see that.'

'We had an arrangement. You broke it.'

'I haven't given the police your name. Anything about you.'

Sebastian felt the first stir of unease. 'What's your point?'

'They're pressuring me. Talking about withholding information from a criminal investigation: that's a crime in itself.'

'That's not very subtle, David.'

'It isn't a threat. I told you, I'm protecting you.'

'How would you describe it if it's not a threat?'

'Pressure, like I said. Upon me, not you.'

Sebastian recognized that he had to keep the journalist – and the police – at bay and wished he had a clearer idea of how to achieve either. 'Publishing what you have could wreck everything.'

'I didn't have a choice!'

'It's more than possible now that you've impeded an official investigation by premature publication. I can't imagine the police protectors being impressed by your doing that.'

'We've got to meet. Talk about things properly.'

'No! And you know why,' refused Sebastian.

'We are going to keep talking though, aren't we?'

The confounded man had bested him, Sebastian acknowledged. And hc couldn't see a way of reversing it, although he promised himself that he would, as soon as possible. 'When there's something to talk *about*. Which there isn't, not today.'

'It's still early,' persisted Anderson.

'Nothing today,' repeated Sebastian, equally persistent. 'It'll take time to recover from what you've done. People might not come forward now.' It scarcely ranked as a threat but it slightly lifted Sebastian's spirits to say it.

The telephone stopped Sebastian as he strode towards the door, anxious to conclude his business at the bank before the appointment with Hartley. Julius Hemditch announced: 'There are some messages. One's in the gibberish of your telegram...'

'The other?' queried Sebastian, at once.

'You told Winston I wouldn't co-operate any further?'

'It was obviously essential that I did,' admitted Sebastian.

'He wants me to reconsider. Called it imperative that I do.'

'Will you?' The change of heart was abrupt.

'On his pledge – and yours – that everything is absolutely essential. And strictly limited. Oscar told me you were meeting today. I've already sent your communication to the bank. It's for you to persuade Oscar to continue as a go-between, after today. I'll have no part of it unless he agrees, understood?'

'Understood,' accepted Sebastian, encouraged despite the remaining reluctance. It was far from ideal but a considerable improvement upon the man's positive refusal of twenty-four hours earlier.

The banker again greeted him at the private entrance to his office with the assurance that the banker's reference had already been despatched to Illington, Besnik and Batten. The legal disclaimer of bank liability was already prepared for Sebastian's signature and there was a sealed envelope from Julius Hemditch.

'About which I wish to talk further,' said Sebastian, determined that Hemditch would not be able to use the banker's rejection to escape. Lepecheron listened blankly to the plea, only very slightly shaking his head towards the conclusion. Anticipating a refusal, Sebastian gestured with Hemditch's still unopened envelope and said: 'This is all that is involved: an exchange of sealed notes between two customers. Surely not an uncommon facility for a bank to provide?'

'I must have your pledge that nothing we are discussing is criminal.'

'You know me scarcely at all,' mollified Sebastian. 'But that's verging upon an accusation against Hemditch, whom you do know.'

'It is not Julius to whom I am addressing the demand, Mr Holmes.'

Could he answer honestly and still maintain his integrity? Yes, he answered himself at once. His purpose was to expose people operating against Great Britain – and most likely against Belgium in the event of conflict – who were, to boot, murderers. Which put him in the position of trying to *solve* crime. Perhaps he should add an extra case to his luggage, to pack away his conscience. 'I have no problem providing you with that assurance, any more than I have signing the earlier indemnity.'

There was a moment's hesitation before Lepecheron said: 'Then I will perform the service, although I shall talk about it further with Julius. Like so many others, I am a comparatively new immigrant to this country. I do not intend behaving in any way to risk my remaining here.'

In the event of misfortune, on oath or in whatever other way it was necessary to get his word acknowledged as the truth, he would testify that neither Julius Hemditch nor Oscar

Lepecheron was aware of what he had been doing.

Mycroft Holmes's Notions communication extended just a line and a half and took Sebastian only seconds to comprehend. The message was that Churchill absolutely forbade his utilizing the contingency fund without full and prior consultation, with the intended use set out in the greatest detail. It only took Sebastian slightly longer to reply that it was impossible to operate under those restrictions but that he was taking every precaution to guarantee the safekeeping of the money.

He sealed the message in an envelope that Lepecheron provided, handed over everything he wished added to the safe deposit box and said: 'The only thing outstanding between us is the promissory note in the sum of two million dollars.' The day had not dawned well. It could only improve. He hoped.

The peremptory knock came at Sebastian's hotel door with the first strike of noon. William Hartley was inside before the chimes ended. Once in the suite Hartley looked intently, searchingly, around. Sebastian had disposed of the English newspaper backlog but made no attempt either to conceal or display that day's *New York Times*. Hartley at once jerked his head towards it and said: 'You've read it then!'

408

'Of course.' Sebastian decided that he most certainly had the other man hooked if not gaffed: the playing of the fish was over now. Hartley had to be landed and landed fast. Sebastian wondered if Hartley was thinking the same about him. Using David Anderson's otherwise irritating story, Sebastian said: 'Do you fear it affecting our enterprise?'

'It could make people nervous.' Hartley was agitated, continuing to look anxiously around the suite and at the closed doors to other rooms.

'We're finalizing an unusual business transaction,' opened Sebastian.

'Are we alone?'

It was an unexpected response. Sebastian said: 'Why should you imagine otherwise?'

'This is the moment when high stakes are laid.'

Sebastian indicated the decanters. 'There is sherry. Or madeira. Brandy, if you would prefer. Why don't I pour your choice while you satisfy yourself?'

Sebastian didn't expect Hartley to take up the offer but he did, disappearing into the bedroom, dressing room and presumably going into the bathroom as well before emerging back into the drawing room. The smile was only half apologetic. 'A small brandy. And your forgiveness, for my caution.'

'I think we both need to be cautious. But today we do put down our stakes. Don't you think it is now the moment for us to talk openly about what we are engaged upon?'

Hartley accepted his drink. 'Yes, I do think that.'

'I believe you have more to tell upon the subject than I.'

'Will you be satisfied with my explanation?'

It was another response that Sebastian did not fully understand. Frowning he said: 'Against what alternative?'

'An actual examination?'

'Most definitely not. 'You – and your people – want me to underwrite an illicit cargo without my satisfying myself that there actually *is* a cargo. We do not know each other. But you do know I am good for the money I am committing. I do not—'

'Good for the money?' interrupted Hartley.

An important admission, Sebastian instantly recognized. Could he bluff against this man more effectively than he had in the poker sessions in Virginia? 'I provided you with the details of my bank. If we are to progress beyond this uncertain moment, don't feign ignorance of the credit check and all the other enquiries that you have made.'

'The people for whom I am working: not me,' denied Hartley.

Sebastian believed the other man: believed that Hartley, stripped of the bombast, was not the instigator but rather a middleman. But then that was all Hartley had ever claimed to be. Sebastian refused to be blown off course. 'And doubtless you have enquired a lot more about me,' he persisted.

410

'Von Bernstorff believed you related to Sherlock Holmes, with whom he was briefly acquainted in London,' conceded Hartley. 'He instituted enquiries to satisfy himself there was no such relationship.'

Sebastian was sure he remained impassive. 'And had there been?'

Hartley appeared surprised by the question. 'You would have been exposed a provocateur.'

'To suffer the same fate as Carson? And Grant before him?'

'I know nothing of that!' insisted Hartley, in fresh denial.

'Yet you refer to it whenever it appears in newspapers.'

'I do not consider it my business.'

The floodgates were opening, Sebastian decided. What was there that could be isolated beyond doubt? From Hartley's own lips had come the admission that he was working for the Germans. And the man was privy to at least some of the enquiries that had been made to establish his credentials as an entrepreneur prepared, for a price, to be enticed over the boundaries of legality. And there couldn't be any doubt that the Germans were responsible for the deaths of the two politicians and could so easily have been responsible for his. Why then the attack at Lafayette Park? Sebastian supposed he owed thanks to whomever was the deity of good fortune for the successfully concealed circumstances of his birth. Impatiently he dismissed the intrusion. What else was Hartley inadvertently disclosing? That although the man might know at least some aspects of the conspiracy, he was not part of its inner core. Delay enough, Sebastian determined: he could not risk breaking the flow. 'Then I am at a disadvantage. You and those you are working with have learned much about me, most importantly that the cost of your shipment is covered. In return I have nothing: insufficient, perhaps, even to continue.'

'You can't withdraw now!'

And from that reply he'd learned of the other man's desperation. 'I most assuredly can, having been told so little.'

'What is it you want?' demanded Hartley.

He *was* literally laying out the stakes, Sebastian decided. 'I want specifically to know the cargo, its vessel of conveyance, its sailing details and its destination. And most of all I want to know with whom I am working, apart from yourself.'

Hartley drank heavily, not immediately replying. Then, soft voiced, a man reluctant with a secret, he said, 'You know full well with whom you are working.'

'No more nuance or innuendo,' insisted Sebastian.

'Germans,' said Hartley, shortly. 'And don't fake surprise at being so openly told.'

'I'll not fake anything,' said Sebastian, enjoying his own hypocrisy. 'The cargo.'

'You know that, too. Armaments.'

'Not until you tell me so. What armaments?

What quantity?'

'Mostly rifles. Two thousand in all. Two hundred sidearms. A few howitzers. And some Gatling machine guns. Ammunition for them, of course. Five thousand rounds.'

Sebastian was staggered by the size and assortment of the consignment, although he didn't betray it. He should, he guessed, have been warned by the amount of financial protection they were prepared to pay for but he had, obviously wrongly, imagined that to be an inflated figure. 'Don't stop!'

Hartley shrugged. 'What?'

'Vessel?'

'The *Freedom*.'

All the details of which – most importantly its ownership – could easily be discovered from public sources. 'Destination?'

'Hamburg.'

'Sailing?'

'Noon tomorrow.'

'You've already established my credit worthiness,' protested Sebastian. 'Such short time gives me scant opportunity to obtain a reference upon whatever financial instrument you're offering in settlement of our agreed premium.'

For only the second time during the encounter Hartley smiled, although very shortly. He took two documents from his briefcase, glancing at them briefly to establish their precedence. 'This is a pay-to-bearer Letter of Credit, against the First New York and Brooklyn Bank,' the man identified. 'This

413

is the search affidavit attesting to sufficient funds being available, issued by lawyers, guaranteeing their liability upon forfeit in the full amount of three hundred thousand dollars.'

Sebastian saw at once that the lawyers' letterhead was Illington, Besnik and Batten. 'Then all that's left is my examination of the cargo.'

The smile this time came with a headshake. 'And your providing me with an instrument of insurance.'

Sebastian picked up the contract Lepecheron had provided, and offered it to the other man. 'A promissory note in the sum of two million dollars.'

'I shall call for you at ten tonight.'

'What's our destination?'

'That has yet to be decided.'

'I shall meet the others with whom you're dealing?'

Hartley hesitated. 'That has also to be decided.'

The last time he'd had such a protracted meeting with this man there had soon afterwards been an attempt upon his life, Sebastian recalled too easily. Was he that night going to complete an investigation or be led into a trap from which he would not this time escape?

It took one telephone call to the New York Port Authority for Sebastian to learn that the *Freedom* was a 25,000-ton freighter owned by

414

the Smithlane Shipping and Freight Company Incorporated. And that it was indeed listed to sail from the Hudson River Pier Thirty at noon the following day for Hamburg, where it was scheduled to dock in ten days. Liverpool was recorded as an intermediary port of call, in nine days.

Sebastian made two more telephone arrangements, both of which met with initial protests but final reluctant agreement, before writing his alert to London. The message read:

AABOGOUUT TESTIS WELL SEEAGABOORNEE TRIGIP TIGHT DAVID KENNEL SODGER WEEAGAPOON DOMUS EDWARD WICKHAM STOP HOUSLE GRIPS FREEIGGHTEER FREGEDOOM

The translation was: *I am about to see the secret seaborne place of a formidable battle amount of ammunition and especially weaponry homeward bound to Germany. Immediately concentrate on the freighter* Freedom.

When he arrived at the bank Sebastian halted Oscar Lepecheron's renewed protest at an insufficient reason for the second visit in one day by producing the $300,000 Letter of Credit. 'It looks like a good enough reason to me.'

'I demand again to know there is nothing illegal involved,' said Lepecheron.

'You have the affidavit,' reminded Sebastian.

415

'I am increasingly unsure what protection that affords me,' said Lepecheron.

'All that you require,' said Sebastian. That was not, he accepted, an assurance that was his to offer.

'It's arrogant. And pompous to boot.' Sebastian's message rejecting Churchill's demand for approval of expenditure lay on the table between Mycroft Holmes and his brother.

'Both of those,' agreed Sherlock Holmes, mildly irritated at being summoned so hurriedly to the Diogenes Club. 'But it was not a restriction imposed upon Sebastian before he left.'

'Warning sufficiently given,' refuted Mycroft. 'I intend withholding this impudence from Churchill.'

'To what purpose?'

'A message from you,' insisted Mycroft unheeding. 'You must impress upon Sebastian that he complies.'

'We none of us know the difficulties under which Sebastian is working,' argued Sherlock Holmes. 'He might not have the time or means to consult.'

'That's bye the bye, as well you know.'

'I will—' began Sherlock Holmes but was stopped by the ringing of the telegraph's transmission bell.

Mycroft read the message as it came up on the machine, passing it wordlessly to Sherlock Holmes.

Holmes said: 'He's penetrated a cell, by the

416

look of it! Had to commit the money. But we can track the *Freedom* through Lloyds of London. And it's stopping in England before going on to Germany: if it's a cargo not listed upon a declared manifest it's contraband, liable for seizure.'

' *"About to see,"* ' quoted Mycroft. 'There's no time to consult now.'

Twenty-Four

The coach towards which William Hartley bustled Sebastian was as similarly black as the Washington embassy carriages. The driver gave no acknowledgement, a huddled, looking-away silhouette. Only the window of the open-in-readiness door was uncurtained, and with the action of following Sebastian inside, Hartley pulled it closed behind him. The slamming of the door was the instant signal for a jolted start.

'Don't!' stopped Hartley, at Sebastian's move to uncover a window.

'Why not?'

'They don't want it.'

The carriage and its snuffling, depositing horse had been facing Columbus Circle and had not thus far turned either left or right, so Sebastian knew in which direction they were initially travelling. He said: 'Which takes no account of what I want.'

'We're in their hands now,' stressed Hartley. It was barely possible to see inside the carriage, so insufficiently small were the candle-lamps, but Sebastian believed there was a sheen of perspiration on the other man's upper lip.

'Where are we going?' Sebastian had the swordstick tightly in readiness against his leg, the securing blade catch released. The pressure of the unholstered Smith and Wesson was hard against his now permanently sore thigh.

'Where you want to go.'

The coach turned, to the left, and from his earlier orientating journeying around the city Sebastian easily picked up the direction. First westwards, now southwards. Sebastian calculated they had been moving for five minutes, maybe less: certainly time to have reached Eighth Avenue, although he could not be certain. Whatever north to south artery they were on they were heading downtown, on the west side. It had – obviously, rendering the curtained-window charade stupid – to be the docks. 'Mr Hartley, where else but towards one destination *can* we be heading?'

'We have to be careful.'

'Aren't we all working, as well as travelling, in the same direction?'

'We have to earn their trust.'

Sebastian at once seized on another indiscretion: William Hartley had just disclosed that this was the first time he had operated as an intermediary for the Germans. Which made it an initiation for both of them. If there were this extreme of caution on such a baptism there was little likelihood of his discovering the true identities not just of the Germans but of their American suppliers. If he negotiated this first encounter it was inevitable others would follow. There could even be an argument for letting this intended shipment reach Germany to convince the unknown caucus of his reliability. 'My only concern is earning – and continuing to earn – their money.'

'The concern of us both,' bleakly smiled the other man.

There was a right and almost at once a left turn, which Sebastian calculated to bring them if not immediately parallel then only one avenue away from the Hudson. Although already expecting what he would find, Sebastian turned in his seat to look across the carriage, to see with the same movement if the small rear port was curtained like all the other windows. It was.

Understanding Sebastian's manoeuvre, Hartley said: 'There's a carriage in front, another behind. They are extremely careful.'

Sebastian said: 'Have you warned them I expect to meet them?'

'I've let it be known.'

'To what response?'

'None.'

'Will there be other opportunities for us to work together?'

'Would you wish to?'

'For the commission they are prepared to pay, most certainly. Would you?'

'Most certainly.'

'Then you and I are looking at a continuing enterprise.'

'Hopefully so.'

'How does it work?'

'What?'

'The operation. Do you work to order, from a provided list? Or offer what you purchase on your own initiative: a true middleman between seller and buyer?'

'It's a complicated procedure.'

'I have available considerable finance, as you know,' persisted Sebastian. 'If we agree upon a partnership there would be the where-withal for substantial independent purchasing. Our profit would be much the greater if we self-financed.'

'You are indeed an entrepreneur!' congratulated Hartley.

Further avoidance, judged Sebastian. 'You have cultivated the sources and recipients at either end of the chain. From the contacts you have already established can you imagine the sort of expansion I am suggesting?'

'Beneficial to everyone,' confirmed Hartley, without hesitation.

'Is it a deal?' How much greed could he encourage?

'I'll consider it,' promised Hartley, cautiously.

'Details would need to be agreed, of course.'

It would most definitely be necessary to allow tomorrow's shipment to reach Germany without interference: in war it was an accepted principle that small, even fatal, sacrifices were permissable to prevent greater fatal disasters. Supposedly proving himself a committed German sympathizer this first time would hopefully open the door to his learning Hartley's suppliers on the one hand and Berlin's agents on the other and enable the exposure of both, even more hopefully weakening in Great Britain's favour America's neutrality. 'There's no detail too difficult to be satisfactorily negotiated.'

'Let's hope not,' agreed Hartley.

Sebastian could hear the occasional siren of a departing vessel now, with the laboured grunt of a responding tug's hooter, in turn met with the screech of offended sea birds. From the unimpeded sharp pace of the carriage the road had to be comparatively clear, which surprised Sebastian because on every previous visit to the waterfront it had been congested by traffic to and from the harbour. But then he had never before been in the vicinity this late at night.

Sebastian felt the coach lose speed, turn to the right and then stop. He reached for the door handle but Hartley put a restraining hand upon his arm.

'Wait,' commanded the man.

Sebastian strained to hear any outside conversation but detected none. Almost at once the carriage lurched off again. It would have been a docks admission procedure, Sebastian guessed. The further halt came very quickly and again Hartley put a halting hand upon Sebastian's arm. The rap against the door on Hartley's side was very loud and unexpected and Sebastian jumped and wished he hadn't.

Hartley said: 'I am to get out. You are to stay here.'

The door was opened and closed too quickly for Sebastian to see anyone or anything outside except a wisp of fog. Sebastian could not distinguish words or even the language in which they were spoken. He timed it as a further five minutes before the door on his side opened, without warning.

Hartley said: 'You can get out now.'

They appeared to be quite alone in what seemed to be a totally deserted, black alley between two warehouses. Quite apart from the thickness of the fog, he could not see the water but gauged its presence beyond the warehouse to his right from ship sirens. Their two escort coaches were drawn far ahead, fog-shrouded. Their statue-like coachman was just as obscure upon his perch, still muffled in his greatcoat, his face completely hidden as he gazed fixedly ahead.

'This way,' guided Hartley.

Sebastian was unaware of the small side door into the warehouse until Hartley opened it. The only illumination inside came from lanterns and there were insufficient of those. Sebastian counted just six, which concentrated the light in one place, highlighting a serried array of unmarked crates, but left the remainder of the cavernous building in total, concealing darkness. Closer to the crates, Sebastian saw that six had been especially set aside, their tops unscrewed and pulled slightly to one side for inspection...

'The rifles,' Hartley announced, taking up one of the lanterns and starting at the left of the prepared examination line.

Despite a thick coating of protective grease, the metal flashed brightly in the uncertain light of the lantern and Sebastian instantly identified Amelia Becker's revolutionary alloy. The discovery fitted others communicated by his more experienced father in Sherlock Holmes's most recent long letter.

'The howitzers,' Hartley continued, moving on to the second, larger crates, trailing Sebastian behind him.

And then: 'The Gatling.'

It took a full thirty minutes for Sebastian to examine all the selected containers and as he did so he acknowledged that such a convincing display was the art of a classic confidence trick. He said: 'Is everything from the same supplier?'

'Yes.'

'How are they to be described on the Customs manifests?'

'Heavy machine parts. It's already been filed and accepted.'

There was not, after all, any reason to wait until a second consignment. He now knew Amelia Becker to be the source, Lowell

Smithlane to be the shipper and that Germans, unnamed although almost certainly under diplomatic protection at the Washington embassy, were the purchasers. But then, Sebastian contradicted himself, there was possibly *every* reason to delay. He would be the prime suspect for any disclosure to the New York port authorities or later interception.

It was not actually a cough, more a faint throat-clearing, but it came with a foot-scuff, away to Sebastian's right. Almost at once there was another sound of movement although this time to his left, and Sebastian decided it was intentional, to let him know they were unseen all around him. He said: 'And now I meet our customers.'

'They do not wish it,' said Hartley.

'Ask again,' insisted Sebastian. '*I* wish it.'

'I have already asked.'

'Ask again,' repeated Sebastian. 'If there is to be the further business we've discussed, it's obvious we have to know each other.' He swept his arm around the secured boxes. 'And let's all of us understand from this moment that I won't accept this restriction again.'

Hartley hesitated but eventually moved off, taking a lantern with him, which was what Sebastian had hoped. In the darkness the small arc of upheld light bobbed like a cork on water but always in the same unwavering line and Sebastian guessed there was little other cargo in the warehouse. From which

424

another surmise was that the warehouse was possibly privately owned by a hidden German company, assuring the total secrecy of its contents. Or, even more likely, that it was owned by the Hamburg– America line.

The cork-like bobbing stopped about twenty-five yards away. There were three outlined figures, apart from Hartley, hatted and coated into ghost-like shapes too indistinct to identify; yet Sebastian felt there was something – which meant someone – he recognized, although he could not isolate what or who it was. Certainly it could be nothing facial: he only knew Hartley by the man being the lantern carrier. No conversation reached Sebastian, unmoving beside the arms shipment. How quickly could he get the pistol out? Not quickly enough to release the safety catch before those all around would be upon him. Or before they shot him from where they stood. The light started to move once more, coming back towards him. It was very close before Sebastian made out Hartley's features.

'There is to be no meeting,' announced the man.

'Why not?'

'I told you, they don't wish it.'

'Their distrust disappoints me,' declared Sebastian, believing a muted protest was sufficient. 'Perhaps it will not be possible for us to do further business after all.'

'Let's complete this before worrying about the future. It was damnably difficult to achieve this concession.'

He had had enough, Sebastian decided. He was, in fact, his father's justified successor. In the closed and escorted carriage returning uptown, he said: 'Where are your lodgings?'

'I shall come to you.'

Sebastian turned curiously sideways. 'Is it that you now don't trust me?'

'It is not distrust.'

'What then?'

'I am considering moving and don't yet have a new address. When I do, I'll inform you. But I'll call for you tomorrow for us both to watch the sailing.'

Winston Churchill was a nocturnal person, able to satisfy his body's resting needs by cat-napping and religiously taking an after-luncheon siesta, a lifestyle sometimes imposing a heavy eyed burden upon his dinner companions. It was not, however, a problem for Admiral Reginald Hall, the reason for whose soubriquet of 'Blinker' was lost in uncertain legend, because he blinked no more than anyone else.

The dinner, of the first-shot grouse, was at the Carlton Club at a table sufficiently isolated to render any conversation unheard and now the cigars glowed and the brandy decanter was between them.

Hall, Churchill's just-appointed Director of Naval Intelligence, said: 'The War Office are insisting I work under their jurisdiction, with them as ultimate co-ordinators.'

426

'Ultimate confusers,' dismissed Churchill. 'They're building paper mountains beneath which anything of value will be hidden or lost until the Kaiser rides a white charger down the Mall to occupy Buckingham Palace. You'll work from Room forty – that is to be your code designation as well as your genuine quarters at the Admiralty – to intercept and decipher the German radio transmissions. I shall provide you with as many cryptanalysts as I can. I want daily briefings – hourly if the intelligence is of sufficient import – and the War Office can go hang if they imagine we are going to organize ourselves at their behest.'

Hall touched his brandy glass against Churchill's. 'I'd hoped to hear you say it but could never quite believe that you would.'

Churchill said: 'I don't give a damn about the Declaration of London or any nonsense about the rules of naval engagement. I intend personally to ensure no British naval or merchant ship is put at a disadvantage, particularly by these submarines the Sea Lords have so opposed me over matching, with claptrap about fair play. We've made a grave and costly mistake insufficiently acknowledging their strategic importance.'

'I'm with you there, sir, in every respect.'

Churchill stubbed out the Havana. 'You would have made a good pirate, Blinker.'

'With you, sir, as my pirate admiral.'

'It was regarded as an honourable calling under Queen Elizabeth. Let's trust we can make it so again.'

★ ★ ★

Sebastian worked until the early hours composing his longest coded message yet, pointing out the advantages of allowing the cargo to reach its destination but stressing equally that he already knew enough to wreck a German cell working with a British traitor. He could not, however, identify or connect the shadowy men in the warehouse with the German Embassy – or any German-controlled organization in America – and they were therefore denied completely revealing Berlin's espionage within the United States.

Sebastian arose shortly after dawn, anxious to scan the *New York Times* for another possible breach by David Anderson. He was relieved to find there was nothing. An increasingly reluctant Oscar Lepecheron demanded to know if he was expected to act as a conduit on a daily basis and Julius Hemditch virtually echoed the protest. Sebastian assured both he believed the arrangement was drawing to a close. Unprompted his father's letter of introduction to the forgotten inspector in the New York Police Department came to mind and for the first time since he had packed in London Sebastian extracted it from the concealed compartment of his document case. James O' Hanlan, he reminded himself from the inscription in his father's copperplate hand. Could he risk approaching the officer, in some unspecified way to circumvent the virtual blackmail to which he was being subjected by David Anderson?

Though unformed it was an idea to consider, Sebastian decided, replacing the envelope in his pocketbook, not in his document case. With that precaution in mind Sebastian collected up from his room everything he considered incriminating and took a cab to Wall Street, adding yet again to the safety-deposit box without bothering to call Lepecheron personally.

Back at the Plaza Sebastian waited with growing impatience and then increasing worry at William Hartley's failure to arrive as promised, finally leaving the hotel with only thirty minutes to spare to reach Pier Thirty, his concern at being the intended victim of a confidence trick greater now than his wish to see the *Freedom* sail.

He was initially surprised at the lack of activity around the pier before realizing that this was the sailing of a cargo ship, not a thronged passenger liner.

Uncaring of the surveillance which he accepted practically without thought, Sebastian wandered with apparent impatience one way and the other, all the time seeking William Hartley while surreptitiously checking the dockside sheds and warehouses, satisfied with the discovery of a hugely lettered Hamburg– America-line storage facility at Pier Twenty-Nine. He decided it was not sufficiently urgent to add to his already long telegram, but could form part of the Cunard-carried report still to be written that afternoon.

Sebastian watched the line attachments to the busy-body tugs, admiring the expertise of their shunting and shooing, and the ease with which the *Freedom* was freed from its moorings. Aided by its own power the vessel was quickly jostled stem first towards the open channel, the tug's job virtually completed once the freighter got under its own weigh: one line was cast off, to waves from both crews.

The explosion part-deafened Sebastian for at least an hour afterwards. The freighter visibly bucked in the water as if it was going to break in half, which it did not. There was, though, a huge balloon of orange-red flame amidships and then another explosion that took away most of the bridge and superstructure and like a volcanic eruption cast debris, some human, high into the air. That debris must have included oil or fuel, which caught alight in a spewing arc and engulfed the tug, which moved away in a separate fireball. Briefly the sea burst alight, too, although it quickly died.

There were a lot of bodies floating in the oil-smeared sea and Sebastian thought again of bobbing corks, except these didn't bob but lay heavy in the water...

Twenty-Five

For the initial minutes after the explosion Sebastian was unable to hear any response from the emergency services' telephonist and so he several times slowly repeated the berth number and that a blown-up ship was sinking. His balance was badly affected, too. He needed to lean against the side of the quay-side kiosk to remain upright, to grope along the wall of a bordering shed afterwards and to remain propped helplessly against it to look out again at the harbour disaster.

The *Freedom* did not appear to be settling in the water but was listing increasingly to port. The entire midships section was ablaze, gouting flames and smoke high into the air, and the burning tug had drifted alongside, its flames setting a separate fire aft. There were men in the water, two trying to swim towards the quay, another only able to cling to a piece of floating wood. Sebastian counted what appeared to be five lifeless bodies among a solid scum of debris. As he watched, unable physically to do anything more to help, two men appeared on the deck of the freighter, supporting a third between them. They manhandled the injured man over the side to let him drop before scrambling over them-

431

selves; one fell upon wreckage that did not sink beneath him, slipped off it, unconscious, and did not surface again. Sebastian could not see the one who had been dropped overboard to hopeful safety.

Sebastian detected the remote sounds of rescue sirens and was aware of fire trucks and ambulances and police cars arriving virtually at once and realized the impression of remoteness was the effect of the deafness. In front of Sebastian a surreal mummery of voiceless shouting unfolded, running and gesticulating figures from whom at first no sound came, just totally silent movement. It extended out into the harbour, where a tug was now attempting to get a grappling hook attached to the blazing tug, to pull it from the larger ship, on the other side of which two fire boats were getting themselves into position, water already arcing from one into the gaping inferno amidships. At last, still distantly at first, Sebastian's hearing began to return and with it, as well, he started to think beyond what was directly happening in front of him. A lot of shore-based port and office workers had also rushed to the berth but were now being herded back. Sebastian pushed himself tentatively from the wall and found, relieved, that his balance had returned with his improved hearing. He detected the 'clear the way, clear the way' from the shooing policeman when the uniformed man was only two yards distant and allowed himself to be gathered up as part of the crowd, into which he at once moved deeper, to lose himself amidst it. There was a general slow-footed reluctance to leave, giving Sebastian time to immerse himself in the densest part of the group, among some stevedores as protectively tall as himself and who stayed together when they were finally shepherded between the sheds.

Sebastian carefully chose his moment, splitting himself off at the entrance to a bustling warehouse in which work had resumed, hand-loading cases aboard wheeled pallets. He paused, drawn into the cover of a packing-case mountain, briefly to check for any followers. He detected none apart from obvious dock workers. Sebastian slipped out of the huge building through its busiest, cart-jostled delivery and collection door and believed he remained unobserved picking his way through an intentionally chosen labyrinth of alleys and passages towards West Side Highway. He was about five hundred yards from a dock gate when he saw the empty hackney carriage coming up behind and stepped into its path, determined it should stop.

By the time he settled gratefully into the carriage, Sebastian's head was completely clear, his hearing virtually restored and the necessary actions firmly sequenced in his mind. The first necessity was doubly to guarantee against honouring the two million dollar promissory note, which was why the Lepecheron Bank was to be his first call. But there was an additional, equally important reason for his going unannounced to the Belgian, which would doubtless require great persuasion but was essential to ensure he was free from unwelcome shadows.

And he had to be sure of that because what had just happened at Pier Thirty had finally resolved Sebastian's already half-reached decision to present his father's introduction to Captain James O'Hanlon, of the New York Police Department's detective division.

He had just witnessed mass murder: at least a dozen bodies had been floating in the water, with yet uncounted others still trapped in the freighter or the tug or already submerged lifeless beneath the surface. Despite David Anderson's attempted manipulation-in-reverse, which Sebastian relegated to the level of infantile, there had been nothing, evidentially, he could have provided either investigation into the deaths of the two politicians. Objectively – evidentially again – he had no proof of having witnessed a massacre. But he believed there was a way in which he could provide it.

Everything depended upon his powers of persuasion. And in the case of O'Hanlon upon how much credibility he had inherited from his father.

On this second occasion that day there was no prearranged appointment, for which Sebastian asked the ground-floor assistant to apologize to Oscar Lepecheron, but stressed the urgency. There was a wait – timed with agonizing slowness against a huge, wall-mounted clock, the hands of which jerked with plodding frustration – of thirty minutes, which Sebastian forced himself to occupy apparently relaxed in a seat with a commanding view of the front doors, without having the slightest idea of the appearance – the sex even – of an enemy he could still not be sure of having evaded.

The barrier was palpable between them when Sebastian eventually entered the increasingly familiar office of Oscar Lepecheron. There was no private-doorway greeting and even before Sebastian seated himself, uninvited, the Belgian said: 'There's a disaster, obviously! What is it?' And then sat, his face collapsing into growing horror, when Sebastian told him.

Several moments elapsed before Lepecheron appeared able to speak. 'There's no doubt about sabotage?'

'Not in my mind. It's a matter for investigation, obviously.'

'How many dead?'

'I don't know,' admitted Sebastian. 'A lot. Most of the freighter's crew, I would guess. And however many were on the tug that caught fire.'

'How deeply have you involved this bank?'

'You already know that. I underwrote a cargo which I think might have contributed to the force of the explosion.'

'Ammunition!'

'And weaponry.'

435

Lepecheron was genuinely speechless, his mouth working without forming words. 'I will sue you, to protect this bank and its functioning integrity ... your account is closed, as of this moment, with only one contract left to honour...'

'You have a legally signed and attested indemnity,' broke in Sebastian, desperately. 'And if you seek to invoke it I will give evidence on your behalf, if it's legally possible to testify against oneself. Whatever, I will ensure you – and your bank – are totally exonerated of any foreknowledge of what I have done...'

'What *are* you doing, Mr Holmes?' cut in the banker, in turn.

'Working to expose German spy rings, linked with American sympathizers, supplying Germany with war materiel,' announced Sebastian, bluntly. He had not intended such an open admission – preferring as little admission as possible – but it was necessary to prevent Lepecheron ignoring the protectively imposed bar and honouring the two million dollar promissory note. How right – essential beyond exaggeration – it had been to come first to the bank!

Lepecheron's response initially surprised Sebastian, until he worryingly recalled the Pittsburgh expedition and the association between the two men. The Belgian said: 'Do you believe Lowell Smithlane belongs to such a ring?'

'I know the *Freedom* was a vessel in his

fleet,' said Sebastian, cautiously. 'I am making no accusation. You were personally unaware of my activity until a moment ago. I am sure he is not personally aware of the contents of every packing case aboard every freighter he owns.'

There was a long pause during which Sebastian decided Lepecheron's understandable anger was dissipating. The banker eventually said: 'Why have you come back today?'

'To ensure the block is in place upon the promissory note: that you don't honour it upon presentation.'

'Despite your indemnity I – and the bank – could still be sued in a court of law.'

'The people who hold the note will not sue.'

'How can you be sure?'

'I thought I'd already made that clear enough.'

'I think I want you to remove your account, Mr Holmes. I'm no longer willing for this bank to be associated with you or with what you are doing.'

'I understand and accept that,' said Sebastian, anxious again. 'But don't impose that decision immediately. Let this run its course. And hear me further.'

'What now?' demanded the man.

'I am going to the police directly from here. To give them all the information I can.' Perhaps not all, thought Sebastian, but he didn't want to unsettle the banker with qualifications.

There was an almost imperceptible easing of the stiffness with which Lepecheron was holding himself. 'Including your use of this bank, without my knowledge?'

'A complete explanation.'

'I have your word?'

'My absolute pledge.'

'Then I'll stay my hand.'

'Knowing as you now do of my purpose, you must understand why until today I withheld it from you.'

'I still consider myself deceived.'

'Not any longer. But I ask you to say nothing of our conversation to Lowell Smithlane.'

'Quite apart from my professional discretion, which makes your request impertinent, there is nothing of this affair I wish to communicate to anyone!'

'I have another request, a practical one,' continued Sebastian. 'For a long time now I have known myself to be under surveillance. I think I evaded my pursuers in today's dockside confusion but can't be sure. It's still imperative I leave here unobserved.'

'What do you want?' demanded Lepecheron, in fresh apprehension.

'A telephone, to approach the police officer to whom I have an introduction. A public coach to be summoned and admitted past the gates to your inner courtyard, where whoever enters will be unseen by anyone outside.'

'I have your solemn pledge you will exonerate the bank in everything you tell the police?'

'I have already given it.'

Lepecheron indicated the telephone console on his desk. 'Use one of those lines while I arrange the coach.'

Broadway's 14th precinct house was quite different from what Sebastian had anticipated. The raucousness of the front hall, dominated by a station sergeant high above everyone at an elevated desk overseeing a mêlée of demanding, sometimes shouting people, reminded Sebastian of the cacophony of the downtown market stalls. Sebastian shouldered his way through, ignoring the protests, and used his height and appearance to attract the custodian's attention. But it was a waiting-in readiness policeman of whom Sebastian was initially unaware who reacted to Sebastian calling up his name, coming forward at once to lead the way out of the throng towards scuffed stairs. Before they started to climb to an upper floor another policeman moved in on Sebastian's other side.

Sebastian said: 'Does it need two?'

The second policeman said: 'Let's just keep going, buddy, OK?'

O'Hanlon's office had his name on the glass door, at the far end of an open plan office in which five shirt-sleeved, instantly attentive detectives sat at separate desks. No one spoke but each watched Sebastian's progress as he passed. Sebastian thought the pistols they wore looked similar to the Smith and Wesson bumping at his thigh. Three other desks were unoccupied. There was a heavy residue of cigarette and cigar smoke, to which two of the men were contributing. In a surprising and incongruous barred cage against one wall a totally ignored man, in sports singlet, trousers, but without shoes or socks, sat quietly crying.

James O'Hanlon was in shirt sleeves, too, behind a disordered desk. He was a large, heavy-chested man, the bulk, Sebastian decided, more muscle than fat. He was fair-haired and pale-skinned, with freckles around his nose. There were two other men with him. Both wore jackets and one, who matched O'Hanlon in size, wore a wide-brimmed hat as well. His companion was thin and bespectacled.

No one smiled. O'Hanlon didn't rise to offer his hand, either. Instead he said: 'You certainly look like Sherlock Holmes. Except that I know he doesn't have a son. So you better tell us all you know about what happened in the harbour today, which is how you got this far this quick. And then we'll talk some more to decide where you're going from here.'

The reason for the two-man police escort – which remained just outside the glass door – the attentive squad room and now this reception became abruptly clear to Sebastian. He'd talked of information about the pier explosion to get his call put through to O'Hanlon and not identified himself as Sherlock Holmes's son until they were connected.

It was a problem quickly solved. Sebastian took his father's letter from his pocketbook, handed it across the desk and said: 'Please read this.'

His father had not shown Sebastian the letter before sealing it and Sebastian was surprised – although quickly glad – it ran to three folios. It took O'Hanlon several minutes to absorb, passing each page as he finished to the other two men.

O'Hanlon was smiling, although still uncertainly, when he finally looked up. He said: 'Well I'll be a son of a gun!'

The thin man said: 'You quite sure, Jimmy?'

O'Hanlon patted the letter in front of him. 'I worked with Sherlock for a month in London, a few years back. Kidnap from their London house of a rich guy's kid: Fifth Avenue millionaire contributor to the Republican Party and buddy of the mayor. Lot of political clout all the way. Got the kid, the money and the housekeeper and her husband, who did it all, safely back here. More Sherlock's work than mine. There's five separate references in this letter that only Sherlock and I would recognize. So yeah, I'm sure...' He looked up to Sebastian again. 'Who would have believed it?'

'I'm glad you do,' said Sebastian.

'Sit down,' finally invited O'Hanlon. 'We've got a lot to talk about.'

'Starting with what happened today,' demanded the hatted man.

'Michael Patton,' identified O'Hanlon, nod-

441

ding to the large man. He nodded to his other side. 'Hank Bellamy. They're out of the 6th precinct, working the Pier Thirty investigation. That's why I got them up here, right after your call.'

Sebastian had been talking, uninterrupted, for fifteen minutes before first Bellamy and then Patton eased themselves into chairs. It took Sebastian another twenty minutes to finish. There were things he still held back, not at that moment believing them part of the direct investigation, and for which he was as grateful as he was confused far sooner than he expected.

'The emergency dispatcher recognized the English accent,' said Patton.

Bellamy said: '*When*, exactly, were you going to tell us about it?'

Sebastian allowed the surprised pause. 'I wasn't, not until the *Freedom* was sabotaged ... people killed.'

'Two congressmen died in suspicious circumstances, for God's sake. And you weren't going to say anything?'

'I've told you everything about my association with David Anderson and Jack Carson,' protested Sebastian. 'I've no positive evidence of the murder of either politician. Anderson did a clever job conveying the impression we knew a great deal more than we did, to encourage whoever was feeding Allan Grant to contact Carson. It didn't work.'

'That sounds kosher enough,' said O'Hanlon.

'We'll let that ride, for the moment,' said Patton. 'Let's get to the ship. You say last night you examined a cargo of guns and ammunition in a warehouse?'

'Yes.'

'Which warehouse?'

'I don't know,' admitted Sebastian, uncomfortably. 'I was taken there in an enclosed coach, which drew up right alongside the building. There was thick fog in the docks. We went directly from the coach into the warehouse. The only lighting inside was by lanterns and not enough of that. There were other people there but they wouldn't meet me.'

'What was the name of the weapons manufacturer.'

'There were no names on the boxes.' It wasn't a lie – there hadn't been – but Sebastian didn't yet want to divulge Amelia Becker's part.

'And you went straight back into the coach when you left?'

'Yes.'

'With William Hartley?'

'Yes.' This wasn't at all how Sebastian wanted it to be. He'd been accepted – by O'Hanlon at least – as Sherlock Holmes's son, but as far as the other two detectives were concerned he was still being treated like a suspect in a crime, not the person volunteering information. Objectively Sebastian acknowledged his account sounded unconvincing: unconvincing and amateur. But

443

wasn't that what his father was, the world's most famous amateur detective? The word amateur was unwelcome.

'What do you know about this William Hartley?' asked O'Hanlon, coming into the questioning.

'Only what I've already told you.'

'You never met him before the embassy encounter?'

'No.'

'Not friends then?' said Patton.

'Of course not. I was using him to identify the others in the ring.'

'Where's he living, here in New York?'

'The arrangement is for him to contact me, at the Plaza. And I've explained how he'll have to do that, now that I've blocked the promissory note. When he does, I'm going to insist upon meeting the rest of them.' Welcome or not, amateur seemed a fitting description.

Bellamy and Patton looked between each other. O'Hanlon said: 'We've got a few problems that don't quite square with your story.'

'What?' demanded Sebastian.

'The Customs got a tip, an anonymous letter, that there was an undeclared arms shipment aboard the *Freedom*: undeclared, it became smuggling. They put a rummage squad through it yesterday, from stem to stern. And found nothing. They're convinced – and we take their word for it – that there were no munitions aboard.'

A physical chill began moving through

Sebastian. 'I didn't get to the warehouse until after ten. It was past eleven when I left. It couldn't have been loaded until at least midnight,' said Sebastian.

'And wasn't,' insisted Bellamy. 'The Customs anticipated late loading. Put a hidden watch on the ship throughout the night. Only withdrew it an hour before it sailed. A few people, crew, went on and off, nothing else. And we know that for sure. The port authorities confirm there was no stevedore night-shift working the ship. All loading finished at six p.m. yesterday.'

'It was a confidence trick,' acccptcd Sebastian, dully. 'That's why Hartley didn't come to the hotel this morning.'

'It was something,' said Bellamy. 'We're still trying to find out what.'

'This man Hartley,' said Patton. 'You think you could recognize him again?'

'And will, when he comes for the money,' said Sebastian, bitterly.

'I don't think he will,' said Bellamy. 'There was an English passport in the name of William Hartley on one of the bodies fished out of the harbour.'

'He died in the explosion?' demanded Sebastian, bewildered.

'No,' said Patton. 'From a bullet in the back of the head.'

For the rest of the day and far into the night Sebastian's feelings ranged from disappointed despair to incomplete understanding – the

445

most illuminating aspects of which he with-held from all three detectives – with the word amateur recurring all too frequently in his mind.

It was to lessen that self-accusation that he began within minutes of being told of Hartley's murder to try to establish some credibility for his account, not knowing when he offered the suggestion how quickly that would be achieved. It was O'Hanlon who made the call to Oscar Lepecheron and said 'Shit!' when he slammed down the telephone.

'What?' demanded Bellamy.

'Two guys presented the promissory note just under an hour ago. Didn't argue when it was refused. Just left.'

'I should have thought of that,' admitted Sebastian, miserably.

'We all should have done,' said Patton.

'Descriptions?' asked Bellamy.

'We can get the securities manager in,' said O'Hanlon.

'Discreetly,' advised Sebastian, the pressure lifted by the immediate confirmation of what he had recounted. 'Don't forget the surveil-lance. The bank is an obvious place to watch to pick up my trail again.'

'You'll be the guy they'll come after,' accepted Patton.

'That was the idea,' reminded Sebastian.

'And still can be,' said O'Hanlon, to the other two detectives. 'We put guys around Sebastian and wait for the approach. When it comes...' He clapped his hands together.

'...we've got them in the bag.'

Destroying any chance of his penetrating the ring, realized Sebastian. 'For what? There'll be nothing to connect them to Hartley's murder or those of the crew who died in the sabotage of the *Freedom*. Aboard which there weren't any munitions so they can't be charged with smuggling. Attempting to defraud me out of two million dollars won't work: my dealings were always with Hartley, who's dead. You'll have my word and that of the bank teller to whom they presented the note but there's no guarantee they will be the same two men who eventually approach me. Do you think any lawyer would be satisfied to prosecute? I don't. Are you satisfied to let mass murder and sabotage stay unsolved?'

'You're making good sense,' admitted Bellamy.

'You got a better idea?' demanded Patton.

'Don't move when they come to me. Let me hear what they say.'

'You'll know what they'll say!' dismissed Bellamy.

'And what they'll use to say it, if you don't hand over,' added O'Hanlon.

'They won't use violence. They can't,' rejected Sebastian. 'They need me alive and unharmed to unblock the promissory note.'

'And then they'll kill you,' insisted Patton.

'Not until we've been back to the bank, where they can be positively identified by the simple fact of their being with me. And which

I can refuse to leave, which gives you the chance to at least follow them: discover where they are based and who they are.'

'That doesn't sound watertight to me,' said Bellamy, in unintended pun.

It didn't to Sebastian, either, but it was the best improvisation he could manage. He said: 'Then you have to come up with an even better idea.'

The three other men remained silent. The pause was broken by O'Hanlon, who said: 'I've got a debt, to your papa. If we're going to go with this, I want to be attached to the investigation. You guys any problem with that?'

Bellamy shook his head. Patton said: 'There's more than enough for everyone here so who's watching boundaries?'

It only took thirty minutes for O'Hanlon to arrange official secondment from his own precinct house, after which they all travelled downtown together in an unmarked police car for the identification of William Hartley. Only O'Hanlon accompanied Sebastian actually into the mortuary, arranging to meet the other two detectives in their upstairs office later. It was Sebastian's first visit to such a place – which smelled of chemicals and damp and an odour he couldn't isolate – and the first time he had seen a dead person so closely. William Hartley's skin looked unnaturally white and wax-like when a mortuary attendant casually pulled the sheet back, which wasn't what shocked Sebastian, although he managed to hold back any reaction. Arranged as the body was, on its back, there was no indication of the bullet's exit wound at the back of the head but the other injuries were horrifying. The chest was criss-crossed with knife cuts and there were a lot of round burn marks, which most likely came from a cigarette. The left eye was gone from its socket and there were a lot of teeth missing from the gaping mouth. Both nostrils were split the full length of the nose, where a knife had been inserted into both and drawn upwards.

O'Hanlon said: 'Looks like they gave him a going over before they killed him.'

'He doesn't have a cock or balls, either,' said the attendant.

To Sebastian, O'Hanlan said: 'This your guy?'

Sebastian supposed familiarity bred the callousness. 'That's the man I knew as William Hartley.' There was the acid of vomit at the back of his throat.

'So that's what they do,' said O'Hanlon.

'Yes.'

'You still want to go ahead with it?'

'Yes.'

'Quite a chip off the old block.'

Sebastian, relieved, followed O'Hanlon from the tiled room and up three flights of stairs into a squad room that appeared identical to that they had just left, except for Patton's name on the captain's door. There was coffee waiting, which at first Sebastian had difficulty in swallowing.

'The same guy?' questioned Bellamy.

O'Hanlon nodded and said: 'You didn't tell us he'd been worked over.'

'Wanted Sebastian to see for himself,' said Patton, unrepentant.

Before either man could ask, O'Hanlon said: 'Sebastian wants to go ahead.'

'Thanks,' said Patton. 'Thinking about it, like we have been doing up here, you're the only lead we've got. Just be careful, OK?'

'I've already decided to be.'

'What have you got from the body?' asked O'Hanlon.

'Over there,' offered Bellamy, nodding in the direction of a side table. 'I'm just going to follow up the only lead from it, if you'd like to tag along.'

The contents of Hartley's pockets seemed pitifully inadequate. Apart from the passport there was a half-filled cigar case, cutter and matches, loose coins and seventy-five dollars alongside a calf-leather wallet from which some receipts had been removed. A cloak-room ticket and meal bill from the New York Army and Navy Club and dated the previous day were separated to one side. Everything was waterlogged but it was still possible to read that the meal had cost five dollars. It was signed against room thirty-nine, which was also scrawled on the back of the cloakroom stub.

'And here's the letter: just come over from Customs,' offered Patton.

O'Hanlon read it first before handing it to Sebastian, who coughed, just managing to prevent the sickness that had been so close in the downstairs mortuary.

It only ran to three handwritten lines. It read:

THERE IS A CONSIGNMENT OF MUNITIONS SECRETLY ABOARD THE SMITHLANE LINE FREIGHTER FREEDOM IN BREACH OF AMERICA'S NEUTRALITY, SAILING FOR EUROPE ON 16TH.

The cheap paper was plain, without a watermark.

O'Hanlon said: 'You OK?'

Sebastian nodded. 'The Army and Navy Club was where he stayed in Washington.'

'Belong to one you belong to them all,' said Bellamy. 'Ready?'

Sebastian was surprised Patton was not accompanying them until Bellamy explained that an interview had been arranged with Lowell Smithlane. Sebastian's immediate concern that Patton would mention his name was met with a pained look from both Americans.

Bellamy said: 'We're in the business of investigating, not advertising.'

'Sorry,' apologized Sebastian. That was one of the occasions the word amateur recurred in his mind. He was glad the nausea and its causes were gone.

The Army and Navy Club was virtually a

replica of that in Washington, even to the balconied gallery overlooking the entrance hall. The balding, portly secretary wore a military colours tie and an air of disdainful condescension that leaked away when Bellamy announced it was a murder investigation.

Hartley's fastidiously neat room was on the first floor. Sebastian held back, deferring to the two professionals to conduct the search, which was totally thorough. Without any discussion they divided the room between them. There were three suits in the closet, with shirts and underwear in the integral drawers. The previous day's *New York Times* was neatly folded on a bedside table. On a matching nightstand on the other side of the bed there was a book, in German. When O'Hanlon held it up Sebastian translated: 'Fatherland Military Preparation: an Analysis.'

It was Bellamy who found the briefcase and document case, in the bottom drawer of the dressing table upon which Hartley's brushes and toiletries were laid out. Bellamy first examined the briefcase, exclaiming almost at once: 'Holy shit!'

'What?' demanded O'Hanlon.

Bellamy produced his discoveries from the briefcase like a conjuror bringing surprises from a hat. Flicking a pasteboard on to the bed separating them, Bellamy said: 'That's the card of a Colonel Peter Lumsden, described as the military attaché at the British

Embassy in Washington...' A red document followed. '...That's a diplomatic passport in the name of William James Hartley...' A small wallet was next. '...And that's William James Hartley's accreditation as the assistant military attaché at the British Embassy in Berlin...' The American looked directly at Sebastian. 'All the time you two guys were on the same side, trying to do the same thing. And neither of you damned well knew it!'

With the reassurance of knowing himself still free from surveillance Sebastian went personally to Julius Hemditch's mansion, persuading O'Hanlon to accompany him to convince the other American it was safe. That, initially, took longer than Sebastian had hoped. O'Hanlon had to argue persistently for a full fifteen minutes before Hemditch, anxious to distance himself even further, finally accepted that having left the Plaza that morning empty-handed Sebastian could not return with the rest of his stored belongings. And it took longer still for Sebastian to get the man to agree to continue allowing the house to be used as a telegraph conduit.

'I shall send Laura to the Pittsburgh house,' declared Hemditch.

That night's coded cable, duplicated to his father, exceeded in length all those previously sent. Sebastian had, obviously, to translate it for O'Hanlon, and after Sebastian had done so – concluding at O'Hanlon's request with the man's best regards to Sherlock Holmes and the promise of all assistance to Sebastian – the detective scrutinized the combination of Notions and ziphs and said: 'If I hadn't seen what they did to Hartley I would have thought you were taking cops and robbers too seriously. I don't any more.'

When Sebastian pointed out the Plaza was conveniently near enough to walk back, O'Hanlon said: 'We're going to rotate some people there, to watch your back.'

'You could frighten them off; I haven't been able to detect one single person watching me since I became sure of surveillance in Washington. They're damned good.'

'So are our guys.'

'Tell them to hold back from intervening until the last moment.'

'Which could be too late to prevent it being your last moment, but I know what you mean. Trust us. And we're obviously going to need to meet personally. I'll lean on Lepecheron tomorrow. Tell him that now you've put him and his bank completely in the clear it's payback time and the New York Police Department expects a room to be made available at the bank where you and I can get together away from the station. And that maybe we'll also need to use that inner courtyard trick, as well. And I'll warn David Anderson how upset NYPD are going to be if he impedes an investigation and touch base with the guys on the Carson killing, too. Could be a busy day if your guys show up.'

Sebastian walked the short distance up

Fifth Avenue with the securing clasp of the swordstick released, holding the weapon inside its scabbard by hand, his other in the right trouser pocket to which he had transferred the pistol. He took his hand out only to retrieve his key from reception, which he did with his back virtually to the desk, with most of the lobby in view. There were about a dozen people there, none of whom showed the slightest interest in him. He couldn't detect the promised police guardians, either, and was glad. He secured an elevator in which he was the only occupant and having gained the door to his suite opened it carefully, pistol in hand once he crossed the threshold. He locked and bolted the door behind him and continued to hold the gun until he assured himself all the rooms were empty. Only when he returned to the main room did Sebastian see the three separate message envelopes that had been slipped beneath his door. All were from David Anderson, demanding that he call immediately. Sebastian carefully tore the messages and their envelopes into minute pieces and flushed them away in the toilet.

Sebastian poured himself a generous brandy from the drinks tray and laid the pistol on the table beside him. There was much to digest, quite a lot of which he hadn't shared with the American detectives. How successful would he be in keeping the two matters separate? More than he had so far been with too many other things, he hoped.

★ ★ ★

The nocturnal Winston Churchill personally answered Mycroft's telephone call and listened without interruption to the complete translation of Sebastian's telegram.

'Is the money safe?' the man demanded, the moment Mycroft finished.

'For the moment. But Sebastian expects a demand.'

'It must not be handed over.' There was a pause. 'Damn Seely and his confounded War Office. Cabinet should have been informed.'

As they should long ago have been told about what you have initiated, thought Mycroft. 'The official notification will come from the Washington embassy by the morning.'

'There'll be an emergency Cabinet,' anticipated Churchill. 'We'll take breakfast. Bring your brother.'

And a lot of ideas, Mycroft mentally added.

456

Twenty-Six

O'Hanlon telephoned at 6.30 a.m. He said: 'You had a quiet night.'

'So far.' Sebastian estimated that he'd slept – and then only fitfully – for about three hours, alert to every outside sound.

'How do you read that?'

'Caution, their not knowing where I disappeared to yesterday. And I'm no use to them out of banking hours.'

'Something like that,' agreed O'Hanlon, doubtfully. 'There's a lot happening. We need to meet sooner than I thought, so I don't want you trapped in that hotel, waiting. Get out, anywhere in the open: go for a walk, get some breakfast. And we'll use the bank. Just give me time to fix it with Lepecheron.'

Sebastian was uncomfortable at the intended supervision, but accepted that at the moment he had much more to gain than to lose. 'What if they make their approach before I get there?'

'I'll know, like I knew you had a quiet night. If they do, it's all down to you. Which it's going to be at some stage anyway.'

Watchers being watched by watchers, thought Sebastian. Only the recollection of James Hartley's grotesquely tortured body prevented his likening it to a music-hall farce. He was in the lobby by 7.15 and took O'Hanlon's suggestion, striding out into Central Park and traversing the paths by the pond and the zoo as far as the Sheep Meadow before striking to his left to emerge on Central Park West. Sebastian was surprised at the number of people taking an early-morning constitutional. At no time did he feel himself under observation and began to wonder, idly, if his imagination had not exceeded his reasoning. And then he remembered Hartley again.

Sebastian had slowed and continued leisurely making his way down towards Columbus Circle, reflecting that the last time he had rounded the memorial Hartley had been beside him in a closed carriage, unknowingly on his way to an obscene death. Still literally interpreting O'Hanlon's advice, Sebastian located a cafe with pavement tables on the corner of Central Park South and Eighth Avenue and bought a copy of the *New York Times* on his way to it. He chose a table that put his back to the cafe's avenue-fronting wall. The story and photographs of the *Freedom* sabotage dominated the front page and occupied three full inside pages, although sabotage was not the word used. The cause was described as a mystery. There was no mention whatsoever of the murder of James Hartley. The death toll was provisionally put at seventeen but more bodies were thought to be missing. It took a further twenty minutes and two cups of coffee for Sebastian to scrutinize every other page to satisfy himself that David Anderson had not attempted to continue his coverage of the Congressman's murder. Sebastian had no appetite but forced himself to crumble a breakfast roll, with a third cup of coffee. Seven people – five men and two women – came into the cafe after him. The two women sat outside and left ahead of him. So did one of the men, from inside. Sebastian paid his bill but remained at his table until he saw a vacant carriage coming from the direction of the park, hailing it when it was only yards away. Until it was difficult to discern through intervening traffic he rode looking through the back port for a hurried exodus of pursuers from inside the cafe but saw none.

The room made available for O'Hanlon, more customarily an interview room, was at the rear of the bank, actually overlooking the inner courtyard. Oscar Lepecheron was with the detective and even before Sebastian was seated the Belgian said: 'It's been made very clear to me how completely you have exonerated the bank. And Captain O'Hanlon has assured me of police protection. I am grateful, to both of you.'

'Sufficiently grateful to maintain the account?' asked Sebastian, at once. One of his many sleepless awarenesses the previous night had been how vital was the uninterrupted service of an already established bank.

'We'll leave the matter open for review,'

allowed the man.

'He'll do it,' predicted O'Hanlon, when Lepecheron left the room. 'Police protection stays as long as he co-operates. He stops, we stop. Simple quid pro quo.'

'Lumsden, the military attaché, is personally coming up from Washington. We're meeting him later,' declared O'Hanlon. 'They managed somehow to fix the hull of the *Freedom* to stop it sinking, which doesn't mean it's saved as a ship, just that it isn't going to sink and jam up a harbour. Gives us time to have a look before it's towed away somewhere. Customs, too, in case they missed something and...'

'How many people died, in total?' interrupted Sebastian, irritated at the other man's priorities.

'Twenty. Two more in hospital aren't expected to make it. Which leaves five survivors ... and three unaccounted for.'

'There's nothing in the paper about Hartley.'

'Want to keep that under wraps for as long as we can. Keep them guessing whether the body was too badly hit by the explosion for us to realize that wasn't how he died. Most of the bodies recovered were badly smashed: going to make identification difficult.'

Sebastian was about to speak when the solitary telephone in the room shrilled. O'Hanlon took the call as if he had been ready for it and did not talk after identifying himself. When he put the receiver down he said:

460

'You're right. They're total professionals.'

'Who?' asked Sebastian, momentarily confused.

'We had people all the way with you through the park and down to the cafe,' said O'Hanlon. 'Two guys inside there, two gals out. They didn't make anyone on your tail, right up to the time you walked through the front door here.'

'So how do I get out again unseen?'

'Already thought out...' O'Hanlon paused, looking through the window at the arrival of a carriage in the inner courtyard. 'And here we are.'

'They'll have realized that's how I got out last time. Follow any public coach.'

'Not necessarily, but we've got to be careful,' agreed O'Hanlon, still looking out of the window. 'And here we go out again!'

Three more hired cabs came and went in the time it took O'Hanlon to tell Sebastian that not just David Anderson but his editor had been guaranteed exclusive coverage of the current case at its conclusion in return for their withholding any further speculation about the deaths of the Congressman and Senator, detectives from each investigation having been equally guaranteed full co-operation and exchange if a connection could be proved. As the fourth carriage left O'Hanlon nodded into the courtyard and said: 'Little trick I worked out with Oscar: lot of customers and bank associates are getting their mail hand-delivered today.'

461

'How do we leave?' Sebastian asked again.

'In the unmarked police car that's been parked in the inner courtyard since before you arrived and which therefore your bad guys don't know anything about. My good guys are waiting outside for us to leave. If we pick up a tail they will get in the way until we lose it. It'll work, believe me.'

It did.

Colonel Peter Lumsden was an athletically bodied man with hair greased so tightly back from his forehead it appeared to be polished. The predominant blue of his military-colours tie clashed with the brown tweed of his suit. His speech was so clipped when he spoke he sometimes bit off the end of his words. When, accompanied by Bellamy, the diplomat first entered Patton's office at the 6th precinct Sebastian guessed the ashen pallor was from just having formally identified Hartley's tortured body in the mortuary.

To no one in particular Lumdsen said: 'Horrifying. Absolutely horrifying. Bastards. Should be shot.'

'New York State has the death penalty, if we catch them,' promised Patton.

Bellamy said: 'I've brought the colonel up to date with what we have so far. And of Mr Holmes's accepted participation.

How, wondered Sebastian, could he satisfactorily explain it further without causing the embarrassment in London that Winston Churchill was so fervently determined to avoid?

Lumsden at last looked intently at everyone in the crowded office until he came to Sebastian. 'I'd like to think I would have made the family connection if we'd met. Hartley didn't. He was convinced you were genuinely pro-German...' He smiled, wanly. 'Actually called you a bastard Hun and laughed at how he was going to cheat you.'

'Someone tried to,' said Sebastian. If Lumsden didn't ask for a fuller explanation for his presence, he wouldn't volunteer one.

'That wasn't...' began Lumsden.

'Can we just slow a little,' stopped Patton. 'It's going to be a lot easier for everyone if we get the story straight from the beginning. You first, Colonel.'

'Yes. Obvious. That's what I'm here to do, help,' said the attaché. He coughed, preparing himself. 'Almost a year ago Hartley began hearing stories of arms being smuggled from here into Berlin, where he was the assistant military attaché. Warned the War Office, of course. But all he had was rumour. No proof. London decided Hartley should come to Washington, sniff around. Right man for the job: fluent German speaker, knew a lot about guns and weaponry. Top-secret mission, though. Made contact in Washington with a Congressman...'

'Allan Grant?' Sebastian broke in.

Lumsden nodded. 'Cousin of the American cultural attaché in Berlin, friend of Hartley's there. Hartley arrived here with an introduc-

463

tion, told Grant about the prevalence of the rumours in common currency in the legations of Berlin. Grant started the public campaign. Idea was to smoke 'em out...'

'Instead of which Grant was the first to get shot,' said O'Hanlon, flatly.

Sebastian accepted that Bellamy's surprised remark in the Army and Navy Club was, in fact, completely accurate. Not only had he and Hartley literally been working to achieve the same conclusion, they'd employed the same bluff. It was an unsettling possibility that he could meet the same fate, too. Unsure what Lumsden meant by smoking people out Sebastian said: 'Hartley appeared to move in high circles in Washington.'

'Grant eased him on to the circuit, to begin with,' confirmed Lumsden. 'Strategy was to let it be openly known that he wasn't averse to a shady transaction. Cultivated contacts with American arms manufacturers, dropping hints that he could act as a middleman for substantial orders, no questions asked. Hope was to start rumours of his own, get Hartley associated with weapons purchasing. Real purpose of Grant leaking those newspaper stories to that investigative journalist, Pullinger.'

Sebastian had been tensed for the positive identification of Amelia Becker but it didn't come. 'I presume Hartley was working through you?'

'Not in person. Thought to be too dangerous. Exchange of letters, if there was anything

464

specific to be detailed. Otherwise telephone calls.'

'I saw munitions on the quayside...' started Sebastian.

'Which weren't on the ship,' interrupted Lumsden, nodding towards Bellamy. 'I've been told.'

'There were other men there, besides Hartley.'

'I've been told that, too.'

'Hartley must have given you names.'

Lumsden shook his head. 'They're very cautious. And because we had to be, too, there hadn't been a letter exchange in the last week or so, just telephone calls. The only name he had was Meyer, Otto Meyer. There's no one of that name on the German diplomatic list in Washington. It's obviously an alias, even if he isn't attached. Hartley was sure Papen, the German military attaché, controlled a group: maybe more than one. And that there definitely were Americans involved. That was the purpose of your quayside examination, although you didn't know it. The Germans were insistent upon it, as much as you were, to make sure they hadn't been cheated. Hartley was convinced there would finally be someone he'd recognize: having proved himself by assembling the shipment, maybe he thought that he'd even get an identifiable introduction.'

'*He* bought the weaponry?' queried O'Hanlon.

'With money provided by Meyer.'

'Who'd he buy it from?' demanded Patton and Sebastian tensed again.

'I don't know.'

Sebastian accepted it was too late now for him to disclose the involvement of the Becker company without it being obvious he'd withheld it earlier. 'Hartley told me the shipment was to be described as heavy machine parts on the Customs manifest. Nothing was officially filed under that description.'

'We talked on the telephone an hour before he set out to collect you from the hotel: he told me about all the security precautions they were insisting upon. He said the Germans were going to file the manifest, with a copy for him so that he could make the claim against you.'

'Claim against me?' frowned Sebastian.

Lumsden gave another wan smile. 'That was the trick. The already alerted British Customs were to board the *Freedom* in Liverpool, its first port of call, and seize everything as smuggled munitions, which they have the power to confiscate. Hartley would have doubly won, getting munitions into British hands and further proving himself to the Germans by getting their money back from you. And out of pocket to the tune of two million dollars, you hopefully could not have afforded – or would have been too frightened off – to work against Great Britain again.'

'It would have been sweet had it worked,' admired Bellamy.

'You sure he believed Sebastian's cover

466

story?' pressed O'Hanlon, protectively.

'Absolutely,' insisted the military attaché, talking directly to Sebastian. 'Told me there wasn't any doubt, after the dinner the two of you had in Washington.'

'So that's what he would have told them, even under the torture we've all seen?'

Lumsden swallowed. 'No question of it. Bastards.'

'That should free up a lot of our concerns,' said O'Hanlon. 'They'll believe Sebastian is one of theirs.'

'How did they find out a British agent had infiltrated them?' asked Patton, rhetorically.

'The same guy who sent the anonymous tip-off to Customs?' suggested O'Hanlon.

That was Sebastian's belief but he said nothing.

'And who the hell can that be?' asked Bellamy.

'I've tried to answer that ever since you told me Hartley was dead,' said Lumsden. 'Only two people in America knew what Hartley was doing. Himself and me.'

'Now we know there's a third,' said Patton. 'Find him and a lot of questions could be answered.'

'One of which could be what happened to the stuff,' said Bellamy.

'It'll be on its way to Germany, in another ship,' guessed Sebastian. 'Anyone checked freighter sailings in the last twenty four hours, particularly any belonging to the Hamburg–America Line?'

'Not until now,' admitted Bellamy, as he left the office for the larger squad room.

Lumsden nodded after the departing detective. 'Officer Bellamy told me you've seen the owner of the *Freedom*.'

'Denies all knowledge of arms shipments, on any of his vessels,' said Patton. 'But says he thinks he's a target.'

'Why?' demanded Sebastian.

'When I interviewed him he told me that, within what must have been two hours, three at the most, of the *Freedom* being hit, another of his freighters was bombed in Trieste,' said Patton. 'We checked overnight with the Italians. They confirmed it as sabotage. Bomb blew the bottom right out: harbour's blocked.'

'Why does Lowell Smithlane think he – or his line – is a target?' asked Sebastian.

'He said he didn't know: that he didn't have any business enemies. Certainly none to do anything like this. We've checked him out. Nothing questionable about him, as far as we can see. Pillar of respectability.'

There was a hiatus in the conversation, each looking to the other to continue it.

'I will make arrangements for Hartley's body, as soon as you release it,' undertook Lumsden. 'Available to you, for any further help, but I have to return at once to Washington. Ambassador is asking for a meeting at the State Department. Assuring your government he was in total ignorance of it all. More than necessary, of course, my accompanying him...' The man looked directly at Sebastian. 'Officer Bellamy says you've got everything in hand here. Liaison running smoothly. Think the bastards will come to you?'

'It's our only chance,' said Sebastian. Hopefully pre-empting the conversation he said: 'I'm dealing direct with London from here, too.'

'Of course,' accepted the man militarily trained to follow rules and orders in everything. 'Separate matter. Understand. All luck.'

Sebastian at once recognized that there would have to be a diplomatic sacrifice at least privately to placate America and that Lumsden was the only logical candidate. And that, cast down by one personal career setback, the man was anxious to distance himself from the possibility of another.

There was a resignation about Bellamy's re-entry. He said: 'Two freighters operated by a Hamburg – America subsidiary: last one sailed five hours ago, so by now it'll be in international waters. Customs declarations have heavy machinery and tool parts listed on both.'

'Are either calling at British ports?' asked Lumsden, hopefully.

'Neither,' said Bellamy. 'They got away with it.'

Sebastian composed the London telegram as O'Hanlon drove him back to the bank, thinking as he wrote that the staccato combination of Notions and ziphs in which he was composing his messages matched the brevity with which the unfortunate Colonel Lumsden spoke. It read:

EEMBGAASY SLOW TEEJAY DIBS HEEGLD CRUX DAVID'S KENNEL LOOGST EDWARD WICKHAM.

It translated as the embassy being unaware of whom he represented – *teejay* was a Notions word for protégé – that the $2,000,000 was being blocked but that the arms shipment had most likely been lost to the Germans.

Sebastian omitted any reference to the embassy, translating it for O'Hanlon, who was insistent on knowing its contents before agreeing to transmit it to London from the Hemditch house.

'You got it clear in your mind how you're going to play it, if they make their approach when you leave here?' O'Hanlon demanded.

'Not positively,' admitted Sebastian. 'Everything's got to be predicated upon how they do it: I can't prepare for what I don't know.'

'I need to get somebody actually on your floor. Housekeeping, maid, something like that.'

'If you ring the cordon too tightly they're not going to be able to get through it,' warned Sebastian.

'Or out.' At once O'Hanlon said: 'Sorry! That didn't sound like it was intended to.'

470

'You didn't remind me of anything I didn't already know,' said Sebastian. 'I offered myself as the bait, don't forget.'

'So when are they going to bite?' said the exasperated detective.

It wasn't to be long.

When it came, it was by telephone. A voice said: 'We need to talk.'

'Who is this?' demanded Sebastian. He couldn't detect an accent.

'Someone you're in business with.'

'Who are you?' repeated Sebastian. 'I don't recognize your voice.'

'Do you recognize the name of Hartley?'

'You are not he. I know his voice.' He had to be careful against betraying any knowledge of the man's murder.

'Someone who was in business with Hartley.'

Sebastian isolated the past tense but decided against questioning it. 'I have a business association with James Hartley. No one else.'

'Things have changed.'

'Not as far as I am concerned. Have Hartley call me.'

'There are people at your door. Open it.' On cue there was a peremptory knock.

'I have no intention of opening my door. I intend, rather, to call the management.'

'Don't be tiresome, as you have been far too tiresome over the last days. I saw you examine the arms in the warehouse and was watching you at Pier Thirty when the ship blew up.

You're not going to call the management about anything. We will meet because we have mutual interests.'

The curt knock came again and Sebastian decided the delaying role was played out. There were two men waiting in the outside corridor. One was much shorter than the other. The taller man was bald, with no hair upon his head whatsoever. The smaller wore spectacles and when he pushed in, uninvited, he limped, favouring his left side. There was also a scar on his left wrist, as new and as lividly red as that on Sebastian's shoulder. Sebastian backed into the room, keeping them both in view, leaving the taller to close the door, which the man did, remaining in the short corridor, against the wall. The smaller man did not halt but continued on to every room in the suite, as Hartley had done. When he returned to the main room he said: 'You have been very elusive in the last twenty-four hours.' There was the distinct blur of an accent.

'I don't have to account for my movements to you. Nor permit this preposterous charade. I don't know who you are. Nor do I want to. Get out.'

The man sniggered. 'Does it make you feel brave, talking like that?'

'It makes me feel less ridiculous than the way you are conducting yourself.' Was this the smaller of the three men who attacked him in Lafayette Park, and had he got the wrist injury for his efforts? The voice wasn't familiar but the language then had been German, which would have altered the tone.

The man's face clouded, briefly, but before he could respond there was another sound at the door, for which Sebastian realized the taller man had been waiting. The third man was similarly tall with the distinctive sabre scar on his right cheek and Sebastian was at once sure he had been at the German Embassy reception, among the group proudly at the forefront singing the national anthem beneath the huge portrait of the Kaiser. He had to gain a name, Sebastian knew. It might also help to know the reason for the man's separate arrival. From the demeanour of the first two, the newcomer was clearly the one in charge. It was a command that wouldn't extend over him, Sebastian determined. 'Who are you – all of you – and what do you want?'

'My name is Otto Meyer,' said the third man. 'These are my business partners.'

Sebastian immediately recognized the voice on the telephone. Lumsden had already checked the name against German diplomatic records, so the attaché was right about it being a pseudonym. There wasn't an accent. 'I asked you what you want.'

'You know full well what I want, so let us all stop dancing around each other like virgins at a festival! You underwrote a cargo which was destroyed aboard the *Freedom* yesterday. We would like payment.' Everything was abruptly said in German, the intonation Bavarian.

Sebastian switched into German, too. 'My liability was to James Hartley, no one else. It is with him that I shall discuss the situation, no one else.' The redirection of this conversation needed to be more than just a change in the language used.

'I think we can persuade you to change your mind,' menaced Meyer.

With an exaggerated flourish the bald man went to the drinks tray and poured brandy into three snifters and distributed them, ignoring Sebastian. How easily could their exaggerated contempt be crushed by greater arrogance? wondered Sebastian. The first two were clearly thugs who would answer any opposition with violence. The man who called himself Meyer was an altogether different matter.

Sebastian got up and poured his own brandy and continued the theatricality of sniffing its aroma before speaking. 'It is extremely important that we understand each other, from this first encounter. What is most important of all is that you do not mistake me for a fool, someone whom you can bully and cheat out of a fortune as you – or other people working with you – tried to do by yesterday presenting the promissory note at the bank, who quite properly advised me of the attempt...' He made his gesture towards Meyer as dismissive as possible. 'You have already informed me I was watched by at least one of you, examining the arms cargo in the warehouse. I was also informed, by the

New York port authorities, to which I made the enquiry immediately after the explosion, that no loading was carried out aboard the *Freedom* after six p.m. the previous evening. Which was four hours *before* I was shown the arms shipment, still in its storage shed...' Sebastian gave another dismissive wave. '...watched by you. And where, I am sure, that shipment no longer remains but is instead aboard some other vessel en route to Germany. You attempted, very clumsily, to defraud me. And even more clumsily failed. How accurate are my surmises so far?'

The smaller man made as if to come forward threateningly but Meyer made a halting movement. 'Remarkably so. What are your surmises about your partner, William Hartley?'

'Part of it all, quite clearly,' lured Sebastian. 'And now skulking somewhere in the shadows, too disappointed to make an appearance: wasn't even brave enough to keep our arrangement to see the *Freedom* sail to witness the culmination of your trick. I am, I must admit, surprised you believed you had the slightest chance of success against me. Which is of little import. I am not interested in dealing with amateurs, Herr Meyer. Which you have quite clearly shown yourselves to be as confidence tricksters. I've told you before and now I tell you again. Get out of my rooms. I am no longer interested in you.'

The small man was shifting, like an animal on a leash. His taller companion was looking intently at Meyer, awaiting a signal.

'Not such a successful conjecture, particularly about Hartley,' declared Meyer, his voice level but his face tight at the condescension. 'What say you to being told that William Hartley was a British agent?'

Sebastian later believed his histrionics worthy of a theatrical award, despite his being unrehearsed. He even risked allowing a simultaneous sip of cognac, apparently to catch his breath, and sat shaking his head in refusal until he recovered himself. 'That is not possible! I encountered him at your own embassy in Washington. Was in social company with him and your own ambassador...! I cannot accept what you are telling me is true.'

'He confessed. Told us everything.'

Neither denial that they were attached to the German Embassy nor any query of his being at another social venue with von Bernstorff. He was, Sebastian congratulated himself, attaining the successful amateur ability of his father, bettering someone who clearly regarded himself as a professional. How much more indiscretion could he prompt? 'How long have you known?'

'More than a week.'

'How?'

'He was far too persistent in his efforts to ingratiate himself. He was recognized by someone far cleverer than he. It was a simple matter to get confirmation from Berlin. He was even listed on the staff there, attached to their military section.'

Meyer's sneer was justified, Sebastian reluctantly conceded: Hartley *had* been too persistently anxious to ingratiate. Would it ever be possible to bring the someone far cleverer to some sort of justice? It would be a worthy ambition, which he at that moment accorded himself. Putting the concern into his voice, Sebastian said: 'If he is a British spy he will have reported on me to London!'

Meyer frowned. 'That is possible. He firmly believed you were more committed to us than to your own people.'

'We must find out from him!' insisted Sebastian, maintaining the charade and still not challenging the grammatical tense.

There was a moment of silence before Meyer laughed outright. 'We don't like being deceived. The penalties are absolute. William Hartley has been disposed of, aboard the freighter...'

The small man made a gun out of his right-hand fingers and said: 'Bang!'

'You killed him?' demanded Sebastian.

'Eventually.'

'How?'

'Shooting, eventually. But it took a long time before I did it.'

'What did he tell you?'

'Everything we wanted to know. He wasn't really a brave man at all.'

He would bring justice, either legal or natural, upon these men, vowed Sebastian. In the totally suppressed heat of that moment he even promised himself to inflict it with the

477

same pain that Hartley would have suffered. Forcing himself on, Sebastian said: 'So, I am confronted with the prospect of being unwelcome – criminally suspect even – in my own country?'

'Something of which you have to remain aware,' agreed Meyer, believing himself to have regained command over the exchanges.

That appeared to be the impression of his two bodyguards. The smaller man stopped his animal impatience and the other moved between them with the brandy decanter, this time including Sebastian.

Sebastian shrugged. 'It is of little consequence to me, nor will it be in the future. I long ago abandoned Great Britain as anything but the accidental place of my birth.'

'What will you do? Where will you domicile yourself?'

'Neither is a concern of yours,' refused Sebastian. 'As I've repeated to the extent of boredom, I consider our association at an end.'

'There is the matter of three hundred thousand dollars advanced to you,' said Meyer.

'Against the matter of two million dollars out of which you attempted to defraud me,' retorted Sebastian. 'That was your wager, against playing a game better than me. Which you didn't. And which therefore you lost.'

The tension simultaneously came back between the three men, as if in some way they were connected to the same electrically charged wire. Meyer said: 'Are you a total fool? Or a foolish brave man?'

'I'd hoped already to have convinced you that I am not the first, by exposing your scheme for the failure that it was. Nor am I interested in debating the second.'

'You have just been told what happened to someone who tried to deceive us. He is *dead*!'

'You were the one who attempted deception, not I. And please don't imagine in *your* foolishness that there is any physical pressure or threat of harm that will induce me. The bank will not release any money without my personal authority, given and signed in the presence of bank personnel. Difficult, wouldn't you say, for a man either maimed or dead?'

'You're bluffing,' accused Meyer.

'The telephone is there,' pointed Sebastian. 'Call the bank, about the promissory note. Ask for the conditions of *any* withdrawal from my business account.' Perhaps one day he would become a good poker player.

The room was enclosed in an ominous silence, the two thugs once more straining to be unleashed by Meyer. Abruptly – so unexpectedly that even the smaller of the two physically jumped – Meyer laughed again. He said: 'You've passed.'

'Passed what?'

'Let's regard it as initiation, to my satisfaction. A lot of men would have succumbed. Suffered themselves to be robbed.'

Sebastian regarded it as something altogether different and stopped short of hopefulness, limiting himself to expectancy. 'Initiation into what?'

'A group with a common purpose. The three hundred thousand dollars remains yours, for the continuing cover on the shipment which is indeed already en route to Hamburg. There'll be contractual documents from lawyers tomorrow...' He rose, formally extending his hand, which after a moment's hesitation Sebastian rose to accept. 'Let there be no more misunderstanding between us. I am asking you to continue underwriting shipments in support of a cause to which we are jointly dedicated.'

Sebastian certainly did not have any misunderstandings but there was a legion of doubts, although he didn't think he misunderstood too many of those, either. 'I look forward to a very satisfactory relationship. How will it continue?'

'With my return here with the contract tomorrow. And an early proposition.'

'What sort of proposition?'

'One dictated by the urgency of events in Europe.'

O'Hanlon's officers would be unaware of his visitors, Sebastian acknowledged. Dare he accompany them into the lobby, to identify them by his presence for them to be put in turn under surveillance? No, Sebastian rejected. Things still hung by a thread and threads were too easily broken.

There was the predicted emergency Cabinet

480

meeting but it was postponed until the evening for further clarification during the day from Washington and to enable a meeting between the American ambassador to London and Foreign Secretary Sir Edward Grey. The delay in turn gave Winston Churchill, together with Mycroft and Sherlock Holmes, the opportunity to analyse Sebastian's assurance that the embassy were ignorant of Winston Churchill's participation and for the three of them to refine at luncheon a strategy that had defeated them at their hurriedly and earlier convened breakfast. It was near midnight before Mycroft reached Baker Street, direct from the eventual Downing Street session, slumping exhausted into a chair.

'Everything concluded satisfactorily?' demanded Sherlock Holmes, at once. He wore a smoking jacket and the favoured oriental slippers. Having gained his relaxed state in the way upon which Watson frowned, he did not join his brother in brandy.

'To Winston's satisfaction, certainly. Most definitely not to mine, being openly drawn into the affair in front of Asquith and the others. And most sincerely of all I hope not to the detriment of yourself.'

'It has the benefit of simplicity,' said Sherlock Holmes.

'To the total exoneration of Churchill but to your possible financial ruin.'

'Not ruin,' corrected Sherlock Holmes. 'More straitened resources, which I have known in the past but do not enjoy the prospect of encountering again. But as we understand the situation at the moment, Sebastian has not had to surrender his guarantee and I therefore do not yet have to reimburse Winston's contingency fund from my personal account.'

'From his shifting between us today I suspect he never intended the fund to be used, always knowing that you – or the two of us together – would do everything to protect Sebastian, covering Winston with the same convenient blanket edge.'

'Which makes him the good politician he is.'

'Which makes him the brash adventurer he is and always will be. And which makes him dangerous. I rue the day I allowed myself – and you – to become part of it.'

'No milk has yet been spilt over which to weep. Both of you are still safe from exposure and let's pray to God even more that Sebastian remains similarly protected. How did the Cabinet accept your explanation of my being the one to suspect German espionage in America after I investigated the reason for becoming the object of German surveillance?'

'Your reputation is sufficient for virtually anything to be accepted without too much examination. And Inspector Lestrade's report of those so recently rounded up outside these very premises gave it Scotland Yard credence.'

'What part did Winston play in the discussion?'

'That to which he agreed with us. Claimed personal knowledge of Sebastian and vouched he would not permit the embarrassment caused by Seely and his professional diplomats. His impudent ploy was to heap scorn upon the War Office for acting without the knowledge or approval of the government. What you seek to do is a private affair, from which the government can not only distance itself, but if diplomatically required will condemn out of hand.'

'The Americans?'

'Private complaint. The military attaché in Washington is being withdrawn, as a token. Everything possible is to be done to conceal Hartley's position in Berlin. If it is disclosed, it's to be turned – at Churchill's suggestion – as much to our advantage as possible. Hartley's absence from Berlin is going officially to be described – and to have been accepted by London – as prolonged sick leave during which we had no idea why he should have been in New York. Rumours will be spread of his becoming more friendly towards Germany than to London, which his activities in Washington will support.'

'Convincingly proposed,' congratulated Sherlock Holmes.

'By Winston,' reminded Mycroft. 'Which makes me suspect the whole episode is cleverly anticipated use of an unexpected disadvantage.'

'Let's hope it's the only disadvantage we suffer,' said Sherlock Holmes.

Sebastian was not long into the telephone conversation with James O'Hanlon when the letter was silently slid by a hotel messenger beneath his door. Believing it something to do with his most recent encounter, Sebastian excused himself to hurry to the door, recognizing the hand the moment he picked up the envelope.

'What is it?' demanded O'Hanlon.

'A query about a room-service charge, of no consequence,' lied Sebastian.

'They actually boasted of killing Hartley?' queried O'Hanlon, resuming their earlier conversation.

'The small man acted out pulling the trigger.'

'You're sure Meyer's attached to the embassy?'

'Ninety per cent.'

'I'll get as many mugshots as I can sent up from Washington,' said O'Hanlon. 'There should be some diplomatic register.'

'If he's a diplomat,' agreed Sebastian. 'How do you want me to handle tomorrow?'

'*If* there's anything to handle,' qualified O'Hanlon.

'They'll come back,' predicted Sebastian.

'You sound pretty sure.'

'I am.'

'If their legal document is from the same lawyers that made the credit check it'll give us a connection but it won't link them with Hartley's death. Or the sabotage of the freighter.'

'It's to prove their credit worthiness,' said Sebastian.

'What?' queried the detective.

'It's encouragement, for me to trust them.'

'You sure you're reading this right?'

Sebastian was eager to read the unopened letter. Instead of answering he said: 'I'll come down into the lobby with whoever makes tomorrow's approach to identify them to your people.'

'You're doing good,' praised the American.

'So far,' agreed Sebastian, replacing the telephone.

For the first time Anna's letter was in German. The season was traditionally to open in the Hamptons with Amelia Becker's house party. He'd made such an impression in Virginia that Amelia was extending another invitation. To refuse would upset both, her more than Amelia: musketeers never refused ladies.

Sebastian had determined to accept before he reached the end of the letter, and at once went to the bureau to write his own. He considered it a remarkable coincidence that the *Lusitania* was in dock when he telephoned the port authority and was impressed at the ease with which his call was put through to Captain Dow, marking it in his mind for possible future advantage. In addition to the current supply of British newspapers there was a letter awaiting him from England, advised the man. He looked forward to their meeting the following day.

Sebastian said he was, too. At last he believed he was getting more answers than bewildering questions.

Twenty-Seven

The man who called himself Otto Meyer arrived at Sebastian's suite alone at precisely the same time as the previous day, but without a theatrical telephone call or the obvious hubris. Today's arrogance was intended to be better concealed but ironically Sebastian was more pleased than offended because the indication was that they had truly accepted him as a sympathizer motivated if not blinded by greed.

'There's business to be discussed,' briskly announced Meyer, in German, choosing the same seat as before.

'So soon?'

'We have big demands to meet. You surely didn't imagine Hartley's to be the only cargo?'

'Remiss of me,' apologized Sebastian, content to play the inexperienced newcomer that he no longer believed himself to be. 'The same as before?'

'A little larger. Six thousand rifles, with bayonets. A thousand grenades. Two hundred light machine guns. Five crates of assorted ammunition and two cases of mortars.'

'Value?'

'We want cover for two million eight hundred thousand dollars. Is that too rich for your blood?'

Sebastian smiled at the goading. 'Not necessarily.'

'Depending, of course, upon the premium?'

'Of course,' agreed Sebastian, still smiling. Churchill would be alarmed at the volume of weaponry that appeared to be so readily available. It provided an additional reason for his later entrusting the letter now in his jacket's inner pocket, with an addendum, to the captain of the just-arrived *Lusitania*.

Now Meyer smiled, bringing from his pocket an unsealed envelope. 'Which is what we anticipated ... A Letter of Credit, payable to bearer, in the sum of four hundred and twenty thousand dollars. Fifteen per cent of the sum.'

Sebastian examined it with the care expected of him, seeing that it was drawn as before against the First New York and Brooklyn Banking Trust and making a mental note to advise O'Hanlon as quickly as possible, hopefully for the account name to be traced from the reference number. 'Very satisfactory.'

'And now our shipping contract and guarantee,' continued Meyer, bringing two further documents from his inside pocket. Both were upon the letterheaded paper of

Illington, Besnik and Batten. The shipping contract described the cargo as assorted heavy machinery and pig iron valued at $2,800,000. The consignees were given anonymously as clients of the law firm. Sebastian was listed by name as underwriter. The guarantee was also in the form of a contract accepting on behalf of unspecified clients Sebastian's offer to act as underwriter for the cargo as set out on the separate agreement and for other guarantees to be agreed on an individual-shipment basis, at premium terms similarly to be negotiated. A specific clause insisted that the agreement superseded all previous contracts and liens, which effectively removed the bar Sebastian had imposed on the promissory note. Sebastian went through the pretence of studying each, upon which both the names of the signatory lawyer and the person's witness were illegible. Even without legal expertise Sebastian knew the documents were legally unenforceable even if they were put before a court of law, but told himself again that was not their purpose.

Unwilling, in his newly found self-recognition, to appear totally naive, Sebastian said: 'I've been wondering since yesterday why it's necessary for us to go through this procedure. I'm content with a word-of-mouth gentleman's agreement.'

'So, of course, would I be,' said Meyer. 'Despite the necessary secrecy of what we're doing it's not, as you know, against American law. Those higher than I have a bureaucratic need for pieces of paper. Which is all these are, as we both agree.'

Just plausible, Sebastian accepted. Now it was testing time. He turned to the desk. 'Then let's satisfy the bureaucrats.'

'They naturally want the documents witnessed, as they have been on our part,' stopped the German.

'By whom?' asked Sebastian, expectantly.

'Presumably you'll want to deposit the Letter of Credit. The bank's security manager would suffice.'

'Simple enough,' accepted Sebastian. Despite the circumstances, Sebastian was close to enjoying himself. Testing still, he said: 'How shall I return them to you?'

Meyer appeared taken aback. 'Why don't I accompany you?'

'Why not?' agreed Sebastian, spared the need to create an excuse for accompanying the man into the Plaza lobby for the promised identification. 'We should alert the bank to our arrival and our needs.'

Could he risk a guarded exchange with Lepecheron? No, Sebastian decided at once. The banker was already churned with apprehension, despite the promised police protection, which made too great the risk of his making an unguarded mistake in his nervousness. Sebastian's connection to the securities manager was immediate and an appointment agreed in one hour.

'And afterwards we can properly celebrate,'

declared Meyer.

With Meyer's a remembered face, thought Sebastian. There were sufficient people in the lobby for Sebastian to contrive a brief delay, hopefully for Meyer to be identified, in handing over his key to the concierge. He did so intent upon Otto Meyer, failing to detect any surreptitious recognition by the German of people in place to ensure they were not followed. It did not mean, Sebastian acknowledged, that there weren't any. At the beginning of the journey downtown the cab followed the route he had taken with Hartley.

Sebastian said: 'When's the sailing?'

'You'll be told,' avoided Meyer.

'What's the method of contact?'

'Me.'

'Do you have a number? Somewhere I can reach you?' He had to ask all the obvious and expected questions.

'I know where to reach you. That's sufficient.'

'Why so evasive? I thought we were working together?' Sebastian believed he sounded sufficiently affronted.

'We are. This is the way we choose to work.'

'What if I am not at the hotel? I shortly have a social engagement that will take me out of town.'

'We'll try not to inconvenience your social life,' patronized Meyer.

'Have you ever lost a cargo?'

'No.'

'That's reassuring, for my part. Over what

490

period?'

'Some time.'

'Were you sent specifically to America for this purpose?'

'You're a persistently curious man, Mr Holmes.'

'For two million eight hundred thousand dollars and the very real possibility of my having been exposed as a traitor I believe I have every right and reason to be curious, Herr Meyer!'

'You are being paid an extremely large fee to provide a service that must remain known only to a very few. It is better for safety that everything between us is strictly limited.'

'It would be regrettable if I felt unable to continue providing a necessary service,' said Sebastian, in weak mock threat.

'No one is irreplaceable: the only essential thing is the need – which you already know we strictly enforce – to restrict any knowledge of what we are engaged upon,' said Meyer, in a totally real threat. 'I do not see any purpose in continuing this conversation.'

Neither did Sebastian, suddenly. 'I will, of course, want to examine the cargo.'

'Of course.'

Sebastian was relieved at their arrival at the bank, not because he feared the man – although there was every reason to do so – but because he felt he might have extended his curiosity just slightly too far. The securities manager frowned over the contracts, volunteered that he had never seen such documents before and suggested putting them before the bank's lawyers. Sebastian thanked the man for his attention to detail but declined the offer, insisting he was satisfied with the terms and conditions he had already agreed. The signing took minutes, as did depositing the letter of credit into his account. Throughout Otto Meyer ensured a highly visible presence.

Sebastian hesitated outside the bank for the benefit of the plain-clothes policemen hopefully watching him and said: 'At the hotel you talked of celebration.'

'Indeed I did,' agreed Meyer. 'Let's enjoy a little of the city's history, which is close enough to walk to.'

Pearl and Broad Streets were within walking distance and as he led the way into the Frances Tavern at their junction Meyer mentioned that the inn had been a favourite of George Washington, during America's War of Independence. Sebastian was amused at the anti-British story, reflecting that if Meyer knew enough to play the tourist guide he'd obviously been a frequent visitor if not a resident.

At Meyer's insistence they drank beer. 'Properly brewed by Germans in Milwaukee.'

'I would not have there be any ill-feeling between us from our talk in the cab,' announced Sebastian.

'I did not consider there to be any.'

'I see this as the beginning of a very fruitful relationship,' said Sebastian.

'As do I.'

'That's good,' said Sebastian. 'Your companion yesterday talked of my being evasive. I have been under surveillance?'

'I have already explained our caution.'

'I would resent it continuing,' said Sebastian. 'I have committed myself to you and your endeavours and look to you to match that commitment to me, within the bounds you've already explained.'

'You are no longer watched,' assured Meyer. 'I would not have declared myself this far if you were not trusted.'

'I'm gratified to hear that.'

They had one more schooner before Meyer said: 'Can I offer you transport in my cab back to your hotel?'

'I go to the harbour. I am expecting a communication to be brought by sea from the partners whom I am representing,' refused Sebastian. He was pleased with how he had manipulated the conversation. He did not, for a moment, believe Meyer's assurance about surveillance being lifted: announcing his destination might further convince the German the precaution was unnecessary. 'I wait to hear from you.'

'You will.'

The waiting Captain Alfred Dow warmly greeted Sebastian with a weighty pile of British newspapers – none, however, sufficiently recent to record the attack upon the *Freedom* – and a wax-sealed envelope addressed in his

493

father's hand. Over coffee the fresh-faced man embarked upon a reminiscence of Sebastian's outward journey, which enabled Sebastian to raise the enquiry that had earlier arisen in his mind and which Dow answered as he had expected. Remembering the convenience of telephoning from ship to shore Sebastian asked the favour of a call and was given the captain's office.

'We got you, all the way,' O'Hanlon announced, the moment he was connected from Patton's downtown office. 'And Meyer, as he left the tavern.'

'To where?' demanded Sebastian.

'The Broadway offices of the Hamburg–America Line. We've got it staked out now. What have you got to tell me?'

O'Hanlon listened unspeaking for Sebastian to complete his account before saying: 'Their bank and their law firm! We're doing just fine.'

'If they'll co-operate,' cautioned Sebastian.

'They want to stay in business in this city, they'll co-operate. They don't, maybe they got something to hide and we'll include them in a prosecution to find out what. We're discussing mass murder here.'

'Murder's a matter very much on my mind,' said Sebastian. 'Are you sure your people will be able to stay close to me all the time?'

Instead of at once providing the easy assurance, the detective said: 'Why?'

'They think I'm a greedy fool,' declared Sebastian. 'They don't need to insure their munitions shipments: once the weaponry is aboard a Hamburg– America ship nothing's going to happen to it. They had to go along with what Hartley imagined to be his entrapment because they wanted to guarantee what he'd provided, additionally knowing as they did by then that he was working for the British. They wanted to get him somewhere conveniently deserted to torture and then kill him. The sole purpose of the documents I signed and lodged with Lepecheron today is to get their money back, with interest. In all, they've paid me a total of seven hundred and twenty thousand dollars, four hundred and twenty thousand dollars of it today, described in the contract also lodged with the bank as the underwriting premium for a cargo valued at two million eight hundred thousand dollars. They'll invent some loss, possibly supported by further affidavits from the law firm, which will get them their two million eight hundred thousand dollars. Which recovers their total outlay and gives them a profit of two million and eighty thousand dollars, a considerable bonus with which to buy a lot more war materiel.'

O'Hanlon was silent for several moments. 'You really think that's how they're going to work it?'

'I'm convinced of it,' insisted Sebastian. 'Just as I'm convinced it is essential to the scheme to continue to keep me under surveillance, to prevent my imposing another blocking mechanism at the bank. And ultimately to get rid of my irritating presence by killing me as they killed Hartley, only this time to perfect a confidence trick.'

'You can't do this!' exclaimed O'Hanlon. 'The risk's too great.'

'I am doing it,' said Sebastian. 'That's why your men have got to remain concealed from the Germans but know at all times where I am. Their obvious choice is the docks again but they might conceivably choose somewhere else.'

'We can't possibly protect you like this!' protested O'Hanlon. 'We need squads ... plans for everyone to know what they're expected to do!'

'They've made it impossible to plan anything,' said Sebastian. 'All your men are expected to do is not to lose me. And to move quickly.'

'When?'

'When it's going to happen is another of the many things I don't know.'

'It's too risky,' agreed Patton, the moment O'Hanlon relayed the conversation.

'You heard my end,' said O'Hanlon. 'How we going physically to stop him?'

'It's his decision,' said Bellamy. 'He wants to do it, it's up to him.'

'I want personally to brief all the change-over shifts,' said O'Hanlon. 'Maybe increase the numbers.'

'For Christ's sake, Jimmy, we practically got every plain clothes cop in the NYPD on the case as it is!' said Patton. 'Any more and

Meyer's people are going to pick it up and then Sebastian's dead for sure.'

'We got to do something!' pressed O'Hanlon.

'I think Sebastian's guessing it right,' said Bellamy. 'It'll be the docks, and for that to be sufficiently quiet it'll be at night like it was with Hartley.'

'I don't want guesses,' said O'Hanlon. 'I want certainties.'

'The only certainty is that the guy's on his own,' said Bellamy.

'It's damnably complicated, Holmes,' complained Dr Watson.

'And there's still too much of which I'm unaware to attempt judgement on the rest,' agreed Sherlock Holmes. 'We've overcome Sebastian's early reticence but he's still playing his cards tight against his chest.'

'I think Mycroft is right to protest your financial commitment.'

'It was the only way in the time available to resolve the problem.'

'Is Churchill a blackguard?'

'No, Watson. He's a politician.'

'From whom, perhaps, we should distance ourselves if approached again.'

'Sound counsel, as always, Watson. I was unsure from the beginning of the enterprise but with better hindsight I fear that this was altogether too tough a bone for Sebastian to sharpen his teeth upon. But if harm befalls him I will exact an eye for an eye, tooth for a tooth retribution from each and every one who is the cause of it.'

Two technicians trailed deferentially behind Winston Churchill and Admiral Hall as they toured the operational facilities of Room Forty at the Admiralty, constantly needing to come forward to respond to the stream of queries from the First Lord. Churchill spent most of the time listening to the intercepted morse transmissions from a German warship identified to be in Bremerhaven. Three times he listened to actual eavesdropped conversations in German from unsuspecting officers.

At the door of Hall's office Churchill, the hustings-adept politician, took particular care to shake the hand of both men and to assure them that their work would be of the utmost importance in the forthcoming conflict.

Inside Churchill said: 'Fascinating! Absolutely fascinating.'

'We're fairly sure we've broken all the ciphers,' said the naval intelligence chief. 'Certainly there's nothing we haven't been able to read in the last fortnight.'

'What about these damned *Unterseeboots*?'

'We think we're OK. They need to surface to transmit.'

'Do you imagine the Germans have broken our codes?'

'I think we have to assume they can read some, at least.'

'We need to be sure,' insisted Churchill.

'How do you propose we establish that?'

498

'False messages,' replied Churchill, prepared. 'We'll use my bringing home the Mediterranean fleet. There's no way we could conceal that sort of movement, nor do we want to. Let's talk to our ships in carefully separated codes and see which ones bring their spotter vessels sniffing around our disclosed routes.'

'I like that,' admired Hall. 'Not knowing what they can read and what they can't has occupied me for some time.'

'And having discovered it, let's use it further,' continued Churchill. 'Select the code which appears to attract the greatest German response and use it to spread disinformation. When the fighting starts, I want the Kaiser's misled fleet sailing around in circles and in all the wrong directions. You think you can manage that, Blinker?'

'With the utmost pleasure, sir. I've had a lot of complaints from the War Office about delays in communication between us. The last was a reminder that they control intelligence for both services.'

'And don't know what to do with it, once it's served up on a plate for them!' rumbled Churchill. 'Damn them and their shuttered eyes. I had a close-run thing in the last few days, so Jack Seely can go on protesting as much as he wants. We go on operating as we've decided. Direct any problems to me.'

A favoured credo of Sherlock Holmes was that proof of crime had always necessarily to be absolute, but the content of his father's letter was sufficient circumstantially to satisfy Sebastian. His only remaining uncertainty was how to conclude the investigation totally. Which required a degree of patience – and an even greater degree of personal good fortune publicly to expose the activities of a German gun-running group before one or several of its members put a bullet into the back of his head.

At the Plaza, unsure of being able to secure it in his safe deposit box, Sebastian instead carefully tore the letter into small pieces, more easily to flush it away, and tried with limited success to concentrate upon the back copies of *The Times* and the *Morning Post*. Doubtless because of his long-standing journalistic association with the *Post* its House of Commons coverage of Churchill's speeches and utterances was the most extensive. There was even a leading article describing Churchill's warning statements in the House as a voice of clarity within the discordant ramblings of unimpressive politicians.

Sebastian descended to the hotel's Oak Room more from the need to fill in time than from hunger, getting a table at which he could sit with his back to the panelled wall with a full view of the restaurant. He ate beef and drank claret engrossed in the search for how more effectively to guarantee his police protection when the Germans made their move, and he finished the meal with no better idea than when he had begun it.

Sebastian sensed a presence within his suite seconds before completing his entry, preventing his showing shocked surprise at Meyer, accompanied by his two protectors, already inside. Retaining the pretence of their supposed association, Sebastian said: 'If ours is to be a continuing relationship, I will not tolerate another intrusion like this!'

'You ever pricked anyone with that little toy inside your cane?' sniggered the smaller of Meyer's bodyguards, to show off the fact that his rooms had been searched again, this time in his absence.

'Very successfully during a pitifully inept attack in Washington's Lafayette Park,' retorted Sebastian, recognizing not just the return of but an increase in the previous arrogance. 'I do hope that recently healed wound on your left hand and wrist was not too painful.'

'It's fortunate that you're with protective friends tonight and won't need to carry it,' said Meyer.

'I am to be shown the shipment tonight?' demanded Sebastian. He had to guard against their becoming aware of the pistol now familiarly against his no longer uncomfortable thigh. The face of the easily out-talked small man was mask-like and Sebastian guessed he was consoling himself fantasizing the obscene revenge he would like to exact.

'It was a condition of your underwriting,' said Meyer. 'And now your social engagements won't be upset.'

'Then let's be done with it.'

Sebastian insisted upon donning a topcoat to more effectively hide the presence of his gun. This late in the evening there were few people in the lobby and he was unable to stage a delay in handing over his key, although in the division between the three-carriage cavalcade waiting in readiness on Central Park South he got a corner seat further to conceal his weapon. Otto Meyer was his only companion.

'You could have joined me for supper rather than remain skulking in my rooms,' said Sebastian.

'I think we've exhausted all there was for us to discuss,' dismissed Meyer.

They imagined they had him totally at their mercy, Sebastian thought. Which at that precise moment they did.

O'Hanlon snatched at the telephone in Patton's 6th precinct office before its second ring, nodding as he listened. To the other two men in the room he said: 'They're on the move. It's tonight. Let's start alerting as many guys as we can.'

They were in the middle of doing that from the squad room telephones when the line rang again with an incoming call, which this time Patton took. At once Patton covered his eyes with his hands and groaned: 'Oh shit, no!'

'What?' demanded O'Hanlon.

'They ran into the home-going crowd from the Metropolitan Opera House,' said Patton.

'Our guys lost them completely.'

'They're going downtown,' said Bellamy.

'Only the harbour and half the fucking island of Manhattan to worry about then,' said O'Hanlon. 'A piece of cake.'

Twenty-Eight

About everything there was an unsettling feeling of *déjà vu*. The carriages were unquestionably the same as those in which he'd travelled with William Hartley and, as then, he was in the middle, an easy victim. The windows were curtained, the coachmen anonymous blurs high on their boxes. They set off in the same direction, towards Columbus Circle, but the left turn, downtown, seemed quicker and the following lefts and rights were more frequent. There could only be one destination and Sebastian wondered why they were bothering. To keep up, his police protectors would have to draw closer. Would they be horse-drawn or in an unmarked automobile? Both, Sebastian hoped. And in sufficient numbers. If each escort carriage carried four men, the police would be facing at least nine. Sebastian was sure that others apart from their escort had been waiting in the warehouse into which Hartley had led him.

It was wrong to journey in silence, as if he was afraid. 'Are munitions all I shall be expected to cover in future?'

'What else are you expecting?'

Sebastian shrugged. 'War materiel is a wide umbrella. It could cover foodstuffs. Raw material. A lot of things.'

'Our agreement is for individual shipments to be negotiated,' said Meyer.

Sebastian needed to remind himself that his life literally depended upon his playing out the charade of imagining he and Meyer were in partnership but he found it verging upon the unreal. 'It's worth considering, if you haven't already thought about it. Don't forget what Napoleon said about an army marching on its stomach.'

'I prefer Napoleon's remark about England being a nation of shopkeepers.' The voice was close to a sneer. The sudden slowing and then actual stopping was clearly unexpected by Meyer, who sharply pulled aside a chink in his window curtains. 'A damned theatre audience! There should be control!'

Sebastian was curious at the irritation. 'Do we have an appointment with others?'

The man didn't reply, remaining with the curtain slightly aside, looking out. Sebastian's topcoat was tailored with access through its pockets to his inner clothing and he used Meyer's distraction to put his hand through to ease the pistol into a more accessible position to transfer into the outer pocket when they disembarked. He was astonished their

504

arrogance was so great they hadn't searched him for weapons, after insisting he leave the swordstick behind. Hadn't they bothered to follow him to the gun store, believing he'd been too badly hurt in the Washington attack to move around so soon?

'At last!' exclaimed the German, as the coach lurched forward again.

'No more than a five-minute delay,' said Sebastian.

He could hear harbour sounds now, a solitary ship's siren, the throat-clearing cough of tugs. There was a further sweep of *déjà vu*. Meyer clearly expected the next halt, leaving his curtain undisturbed, staring instead fixedly across the carriage. Sebastian said: 'Are we there?'

'Soon,' promised Meyer.

Sebastian at last felt the stomach emptiness, but at once decided the fear wouldn't affect his senses or his reasoning but rather heighten them. The carriage came to a stop but then shifted back and forth, in a manoeuvre Sebastian immediately understood when the postern was opened by Meyer's smaller protector. The man's contemptuously intended hand jerk for Sebastian to get out became an ineffective, even effeminate, wave, so close were they to the side of a shed that his door would not fully open. The man had to retreat to let Sebastian get out, which he did, pointedly sniggering at the failed gesture, and the body-twisting restriction made it easy to shift the Smith and Wesson where he could keep his hand permanently upon it, his thumb ready upon the safety catch.

The comparison with the Hartley examination was now overwhelming. If anything the fog shroud was thicker, eddying in smothering, smoke-smelling clouds. The ship's siren had gone, leaving the only break in the echoing, blanketing silence the occasional grunt of a faraway tug. Once more the lonely river was hidden beyond one of the sheds cliffed and cragged all around him. To Sebastian it was a place of abandonment, a graveyard place, a thought he didn't want. Meyer was tight to his right, the smaller man to his left, both urging him towards the suddenly obvious side opening. The door slid loudly shut behind them.

There were inadequate lanterns again, like before, and like before there was the stir of movement of unseen people already there in the darkness beyond. There were boxes and crates set out but all appeared sealed.

Sebastian said: 'Why all this nonsense? Let's have some light, to look at what I'm here to see. I refuse to go on like this!'

'You're not here to see anything,' declared Meyer, half hidden in the flickering shadows, the two who always accompanied him totally lost in the gloom.

'What are you talking about! Put some lights on, this instant! I demand it!'

'This man believed himself to be clever: that he could outwit us,' announced Meyer, talking in English, his voice loud, and Sebastian realized the man was not talking to him but to an unseen audience beyond the lanterns' weak light.

'That's why he's here,' continued Meyer. 'As an example we want you all to witness and understand. So that you don't make the same mistake of believing you can change your minds: go over to the other side. What is going to happen to him will happen to any of you who turn against us. And by being here, watching, you all become accomplices. Which is something else you must never forget, your complicity. We demand unquestionable loyalty.'

'Now wait a minute,' said an American voice.

'Please be quiet,' commanded Meyer.

Sebastian's first thought was that no one was coming to help him. Then came the realization that he was going to suffer the same fate – the same obscene tortures – as Hartley, to bind his unknown audience into terrified obedience. His gun only held six bullets. They would overwhelm him but he wouldn't die alone. He needed to kill the small man, who had made too many personal promises of vengeance. He wasn't going to be able to keep his personal promise to avenge Hartley after all. The darkness was good, to his advantage. He could run, hide. They still might come.

Meyer started: 'It's going to take...' and Sebastian shot at him. Sebastian was moving as he did so, to put himself out of the light, and knew he hadn't hit but there were immediate shouts and yells all around, cries of 'Oh, my God' and 'Let's get out' and 'Let me out of here'. Sebastian collided with a wooden case and there was a shot and he cried out at the pain along the left of his face where wood splinters from the ricochet splattered into his cheek.

Other lanterns began to be lit and Sebastian took more careful aim at a pool of three, in which he could more clearly see three men, but hit a lantern instead. The oil spilled though, and ignited at once setting alight some straw and then a box and although that added to the light Sebastian didn't want, the small blaze increased the panic. A wall. If he could get to a wall there was a chance of finding a door. Getting away, like a lot of others were trying to get away. To his left then. He'd momentarily lost any sense of direction but he thought he should go to his left. Wouldn't fire any more, to attract attention. Try to lose himself as he'd lost himself in a crowd to get away from the docks the last time. Four bullets left. Only fire if he could see someone about to fire at him. A running figure came into him, grunted and ran on.

'Police! No one move! Police! Put down your weapons!'

The voice was amplified by a bullhorn and reverberated around the cavernous building and the panic worsened. Sebastian found a gap between crates and forced his way into it, careless of more splinters and of his clothes ripping, crouching completely to hide himself.

Blindingly the place was suddenly whitened with light, from the warehouse's own supply as well as from additional, hand held generator lamps. There was a shot and then more shouts, in German and English, but not amplified through a bullhorn.

'No one shoot! Stop shooting. No one to get hurt! There's no crime!'

Sebastian didn't move but there was a crack sufficient for Sebastian to make out the speaker as Hans Vogel. He thought he recognized the two men on either side of Vogel as being from the embassy, too, but the biggest surprise was easily picking out Henry Blackmore, drawn to one side with five other men. As he watched, Meyer physically reached out, pushing down the pistol his small bodyguard still held outstretched, ready to shoot.

All guns down, on the floor! Everyone on the floor. face down. Now! Down! echoed the bullhorn. Turned away from the microphone, the voice said: 'Someone put that fire out, for Christ's sake!'

Slowly, as if embarrassed, men began to prostrate themselves. From his hiding place Sebastian finally isolated O'Hanlon, then Patton and Bellamy – all carrying pistols – and at last backed out, snagging himself afresh on splinters. O'Hanlon saw him first and pointed his gun and shouted: 'Down or I'll shoot!' and Sebastian went down to the floor like everyone else. It was only when he was lying there on his face that he realized how badly he was shaking.

It took three paddy wagons to carry everyone away from the Hamburg – America-Line warehouse. In the continuing confusion O'Hanlon carefully segregated Sebastian into the police car with Patton and Bellamy, and O'Hanlon, at the wheel, took a roundabout route to the 6th precinct house to hear the warehouse story and supplement it with theirs from outside. When Sebastian finished Patton said: 'They were going to do worse to you than they did to Hartley! Jesus George Christ!'

'You hadn't fired the shot, we wouldn't have come in,' admitted Bellamy. 'We didn't have a signal. Didn't know when to move.'

'How did you find me, after losing me outside the opera house?' asked Sebastian.

'It had to mean you were coming down-town,' said Bellamy, proud it had been his deduction. 'Downtown made the docks the most likely and we managed to get guys on every gate. Our guys at the hotel described three black coaches and we saw them arrive.'

'Thank God you did,' said Sebastian.

'Sorry to put you down on the floor like that,' apologized O'Hanlon. 'Didn't know if you wanted to keep your cover.'

'I'd have probably fallen down anyway,' said Sebastian. He was glad the shaking had stopped now.

'The bastards are going to walk!' predicted

O'Hanlon. 'All the Germans are invoking diplomatic immunity – threatening *us* for arresting *them*! – and both they and the Americans are arguing, legally correctly, that it's not a crime to trade with Germany.'

'What about what they were going to do to Sebastian?' demanded Bellamy.

'You think the Germans are going to admit they were going to fillet Sebastian in bite-size pieces?' demanded Patton. 'Or that the Americans will tell us they were there to watch, reluctantly or otherwise?'

'There's weapons there! Crates of them! A Customs prosecution for false declaration would be something,' persisted Bellamy.

'No manifest has been filed with Customs: no false manifest, no smuggling charge,' said O'Hanlon. 'Tonight's little show was for the benefit of our fellow Americans, with Sebastian as the star performer.'

'This ain't fair!' protested Bellamy. 'It just ain't fucking fair. You're right! They're all going to walk. Sebastian didn't even manage to hit one of them!'

'It was dark,' defended Sebastian.

'Just disappointed, that's all,' said Bellamy.

'What are you going to do with them, right now?' asked Sebastian.

'Throw them in the cage, like the animals they are!' said O'Hanlon. 'Maybe I'll even lose the key before the diplomats arrive from Washington to prove their immunity and the American lawyers turn up waving habeas corpus writs.'

'It's going to take a while, though,' Sebastian pointed out. 'Hours even. Didn't you make a promise to David Anderson and the *New York Times*? Photographs of the whole lot in a cage...' He smiled sideways across the car. '...like the animals they are would be pretty humiliating, don't you think? And there's still Hartley's murder and torture to be investigated, immunity, lawyers or not. You wouldn't be alleging that they did it but there's no reason to hold it back from the press any longer, is there? Natural if not legal justice but it's better than nothing. And I'd like a moment, too. On the outside though, looking in.'

All three Americans laughed. Bellamy said: 'It ain't what it should be. But it's the best we got, so let's make it good.'

It was Bellamy's idea to insist upon the suicide-risk removal of shoelaces, neckties, braces and belts, so that most of them had to stand holding up their trousers. The overcrowding in the holding cage was made worse by the Americans very determinedly separating themselves from the Germans, creating a divide in the middle.

Sebastian perched himself on the nearest squad-room desk, although at least six feet away, his face temporarily padded with stinging antiseptic by the police doctor who had extracted the splinters. Sebastian said: 'I've got immunity too, to testify against you.'

'No crime's been committed,' sneered

512

Vogel, the lawyer.

'What about what you were going to do to me?'

'I don't know what you're talking about,' said Vogel.

There were head-shakes of denial among the Americans.

Sebastian looked directly at Meyer. 'As disappointments go, Otto, this has got to be the worst night of your life, hasn't it? You get exposed as the amateur you – all of you – are and it's cost Berlin seven hundred and twenty thousand dollars. I don't think they're going to be at all happy about that. I'd go as far as to say all your careers are over: over in ignominy and disgrace. Not welcome for a man proud to wear the Heidelburg sabre scar, is it?'

'We were betrayed,' spat out the small man, who had been forced to provide his name as Rudolph Weiss to claim his immunity as a German Embassy chauffeur.

'You were indeed,' agreed Sebastian. 'My guess is by the same person who told New York Customs and port authorities there were arms aboard the *Freedom* – which we know there weren't – but which made me block that first payout and stop being robbed. Who do you think it is in your embassy who knows so much and is working against you so hard? I think you've got too many spies and too much jealousy at Massachusetts Avenue. You just got in each other's way, didn't you?'

'He'll be found,' promised the German

whom Sebastian remembered from the embassy reception had compared Heine and Goethe.

'Too late to save your careers,' jeered Sebastian. He looked to the Americans. 'And what of you and your secret-society friends, Blackmore? Do you imagine you're going to be invited to so many country-house weekends after this, especially when the stories get out about what you were going to enjoy watching happen to me?'

'You spread it about and I'll sue,' declared a florid-faced man whose open document case on an exhibit table named him as Wilbur Storey and whom O'Hanlon had already indentified as a Philadelphia coal-mining millionaire.

'That's a brilliant idea,' enthused Sebastian. 'I'll definitely spread it as wide as I can and everyone in there with you can stand up in court to deny it and it'll give me the only chance there is to get what your German friends were going to do properly publicized, and how you were prepared to stand by and watch...' He went back to the Germans. 'And the police do have some idea. Hartley's body has been found. The police are going to release all the details of how he was tortured. They want to talk to you about that, Otto. You and your two minders. You think you are going to be able to help them on that?'

'OK!' declared O'Hanlon, shepherding Sebastian out of the squad room by pre-arranged signal from downstairs. 'Time to get your statement.'

Sebastian remained at the door of the interview room to watch the flurried arrival of David Anderson, accompanied by two photographers. There were instant shouts of protest from everyone in the cage, a lot trying to turn their backs or hide their faces.

Sebastian retreated further into the room, accepting a celebratory glass of what Patton promised to be the very best sour mash.

O'Hanlon said: 'You were owed your moment out there.'

'And a hell of a lot more,' said Bellamy.

'Would you do me another favour?' asked Sebastian. 'When you tell Anderson all about Hartley will you let him have that anonymous letter about the *Freedom*?'

'You've got a lot of your father's mysterious ways,' remarked O'Hanlon.

'I hope I've got all of them,' said Sebastian. 'Another favour: there's something important I'd appreciate your letting slip to Vogel.'

It was a full hour before Anderson joined them. He said at once to Sebastian: 'How we going to keep you out of it?'

'Easily,' said Sebastian.

The *New York Times* coverage was phenomenal, needing six pages in all to accommodate all the photographs as well as the separate but connected stories. The biggest photograph of the seized men in the holding cage, clutching at their trousers with one hand and a lot trying to cover their faces with the other, occupied a third of the front page. There were others inside of the back-turning and of one trying to hide behind another, but the pictures had been carefully chosen clearly to show the faces of everyone. Both Germans and Americans were named. Meyer was the alias surname for Otto von Hagel, a finance officer at the embassy. As well as individually identifying the Americans, all millionaires, their secret society title, the Settlers, was given. In print it heightened the ridicule of men desperate to keep their trousers up.

The main story confirmed that no prosecution could be brought, but given in full was a State Department communiqué that the German diplomats had been declared *personae non gratae* for activities incompatible with their status as diplomats and given seven days to leave the country. It was in this account that the reference to Sebastian appeared. He was not named but described as a material witness no longer required in the absence of a prosecution. Sebastian had not expected the newspaper to publish a posthumous photograph of the tortured Hartley – who was described as a British businessman – but they did, with a separate story quoting a police spokesman that the investigation into his murder was ongoing, as it was into the deaths of the Congressman and Senator, which were now definitely being treated as murder. There was insufficient evidence of allegations of intended torture prior to the seizure of the Germans and Americans the previous night. There was a sidebar story naming Illington, Besnik and Batten and the First New York and Brooklyn Banking Trust, quoting spokesmen from both stressing their involvement was that of a bone fide business in a totally legal activity. Also quoted were other spokesmen from New York State legal and banking regulatory authorities each stating that there would be internal professional investigations.

The newspaper was dismembered and strewn over the desk and an adjoining chair of Julius Hemditch's study when Sebastian arrived, as arranged by telephone, finally to retrieve his stored belongings.

'You're going back to England then?'

'Not immediately. Soon.'

Hemditch indicated the discarded *New York Times*. 'I'm presuming you are the unnamed material witness?'

'Yes.'

'And the intended torture victim?'

'I was very lucky.'

'Blackmore won't be acceptable after this,' declared Hemditch. 'None of them will. Socially they're dead!'

'I doubt it will stop them trading.'

'I owe you an apology,' Hemditch abruptly announced.

'For what?' questioned Sebastian, genuinely curious.

Hemditch went to a side drawer, extracted a paper and stared down uncertainly at it for several moments before offering it, without comment, across the desk. It was handwritten and at first difficult to read, because of the impatient scrawl which Sebastian turned to the end, to Churchill's signature, to identify. It was not composed as a formal letter of introduction. It urged Hemditch to consider supplying Great Britain with steel and offered secretly to underwrite the bank loan for the new Pittsburgh mill in return for Hemditch committing part of its production to England. It was only on the second page that there was any reference to Sebastian, who was introduced as the worthy son of the very famous Sherlock Holmes. Part read: 'His role is to be that of fox to the hounds of the Hun. Put him in their path if you have the means, to see where the chase leads.'

'I am ashamed now that my best warning was to refuse to give character guarantees to any to whom I introduced you. My concern was for Laura when I properly realized what these people were capable of. I did nothing to help by attempting to cut you off, I now accept.'

It was too late, too resolved, for anger. Objectively Sebastian supposed it had been his role to attract the attention of the Germans, although not as the victim he had so nearly become. 'What of Lowell Smithlane?'

'His sympathies lie with London, not Berlin.' Hemditch indicated the newspaper again. 'With a group with a far more fitting soubriquet.'

'Pilgrims?' suggested Sebastian.

'Predictable,' smiled Hemditch, in confirmation.

'Of whom you became one?'

'Short-lived,' said Hemditch. 'It became almost immediately clear you were drawing the wrong attention in upon us, not away. And then Smithlane's vessels began to be attacked. We all sought to withdraw.'

'No!' denied Sebastian.

'I am not accusing you,' said Hemditch. 'It was inadvertent, I am sure. But there could have been no one else.'

'There could,' insisted Sebastian.

Twenty-Nine

Sebastian's reservation was on the favoured side of the railway carriage, often parallel with the Sound, so that for a lot of the journey north from New York he had the waterside view he'd last admired from the opposite Long Island shore, now most often a misted smudge on the horizon. Even when it occasionally became clearer, he couldn't isolate a landmark to tell him where Lowell Smithlane's estate might be, although an historically preserved Dutch windmill, like several he'd already passed here on the mainland, looked familiar. Would the loss of Julius Hemditch's steel and Lowell Smithlane as its carrier – and as a shipper of much else – be considered justifiable sacrifice for the public exposure of the German Embassy spy ring? Unquestionably, Sebastian reasoned. Because the exposure *was* public and therefore wrecking not just to a number of expelled diplomats with the as yet incalculable political repercussions, but also to a group of American conspirators who needed the romanticism of calling themselves Settlers and who, until confronted with the threatened spectacle of seeing a man tortured to death, doubtless considered their activities a hugely profitable game, to be laughed at and laughed over in their clandestine meetings. And not everything was lost, on the British side. Lowell Smithlane appeared to have been identified, to saboteurs, but there was no indication that Julius Hemditch was. Once the man's nerve was restored, perhaps it would be possible to link him with another amenable carrier and resume the trade. Whatever, reflected Sebastian, it was no longer his concern. After today, his mission would be at an end. There was no purpose delaying the confrontation – the other public exposure – distressing though it might be to Amelia Becker. It was unfortunate after the events of the last twenty-four hours that Count von Bernstorff would be a fellow guest. He wondered who else would be. As with Henry Blackmore and the rest of the temporarily seized Americans, Sebastian wanted as big a social gathering as possible for this final act of natural justice.

Sebastian had telegraphed the time of his arrival from the Plaza and one of the matriarch's monogrammed chaises was awaiting him when he disembarked at Southampton, thinking as he did so again of Lowell Smithlane and the significance to the man of its namesake from which his long-ago ancestors had sailed to this new world. The coachman displayed no surprise at the lightness with which Sebastian travelled, instead handing Sebastian a familiarly addressed envelope. The message inside consisted of one word, *Reunion!*

Amelia's summer cottage was, predictably, a mansion, although much smaller than that in Virginia. Encircling it roof-high at eaves-level was a widow's walk from which the wives of whaling masters had watched for the safe return of their husbands, identifying it as an historical original. It fronted on to the water, into which stretched jetties for the two tethered yachts and a sleek-lined launch. The open gardens were much smaller, too, without any attempt at Versailles sculpturing or irrigation, which would obviously protect Amelia Becker's more exotic cultivations – maybe even her *Dionaea muscipula* – housed from the destructive burn of salt air and spray behind three enormous greenhouses, a separate complex by themselves. There were white-clad figures on tennis courts and a game of croquet in progress.

Sebastian was greeted by John, the same

521

major domo who had attended him in Virginia, and again there was no remark about Sebastian having what amounted to little more than overnight valises and one change of clothes. His room was as well appointed as before, with an awaiting printed itinerary that Sebastian did not trouble to read beyond establishing the time of the cocktail party, not imagining himself welcome or participating in any other activity. He wondered, even, whether he would be sleeping in the canopied bed.

He bathed attempting to rehearse what was to come, as he had tried to anticipate in New York and again during the journey northwards, but abandoned it now as he had then because everything depended upon reaction and confrontation, which was impossible to predict. Sebastian actually considered reattiring himself in his travel clothes but decided that Amelia Becker deserved the courtesy of his dressing properly. He took from his document case one of the envelopes his father had couriered across the Atlantic and which, until that morning, had been secured in the safe-deposit box at Lepecheron's bank, along with most of the other communications, two of which he also put in the envelope. Finally he picked up that day's *New York Times*.

Sebastian timed precisely at 6.15 his entry into the drawing room, his self-consciousness worsened by his carrying the newspaper, wrapped around the unseen envelope, which from her frown clearly surprised Amelia

Becker.

She said: 'Still with the crossword to complete, Mr Holmes?' and everyone laughed. Anna Boinberg-Langesfeld was at the older woman's side, her dress the usual silk, tonight in pure white, her jewellery the black pearl necklace and earrings. She laughed too but became quickly serious, matching Amelia Becker's continued frown. So, too, did Lowell Smithlane, whose presence was a benefit Sebastian hadn't expected.

'All the clues are answered,' replied Sebastian, turning the question. 'Now it's time for the solution.' He shook his head against the approaching waiter.

'What on earth are you talking about?' she demanded.

'The spy – were it not too melodramatic I would have used the word viper – in your midst.'

There was a murmured outburst, then total silence. Amelia Becker said: *'What!'*

Sebastian lifted the still-folded newspaper. 'Have you read this?'

'Of course we have,' said Amelia Becker.

'And talked about nothing else,' added a subdued Lowell Smithlane.

'In view of what happened to your freighter I am not surprised,' said Sebastian. 'The man Hartley died aboard it, shot after being tortured in a manner too obscene to recount. He was working for the British government, to bring about the exposure of the German spy ring and its American accomplices that was finally achieved last night. But before he could he was identified by someone who recognized him as an attaché, from the British Embassy in Berlin...' Sebastian hesitated, feeling again the hollowness he'd experienced going into the dockside warehouse. Then he said: 'When did you recognize him, Anna? At the German Embassy reception? Or later, in Virginia?'

Anna Boinberg-Langesfeld stood regarding him in total, wide eyed astonishment, a bewildered smile touching the corners of her mouth. 'Sebastian! What is this, this nonsense. It has no sense ... are you unwell...?'

'Confused, for too long. But the sickness that turns my stomach is disgust. And disappointment, at myself, for taking so long...' He shook his head. 'Your problem was my German. And my recognition of your German, which is hard *Hochdeutsch*, not the soft Low German of *Bairisch Osterreichisch* that a native-born Austrian would have spoken. You don't even have the vocabulary. An Austrian would have talked of *die Gelse* to explain the mosquito allergy that so exercised you in Virginia. You used the German, *die Mücke*.'

'Did it not occur to you, my darling, that my privilege of birth allowed me to be educated *in* Germany, not Austria? As I was also fortunate to study in France.'

It wasn't an endearment, so she was losing her temper, which was good. 'Of course it did. Even though at the embassy reception

524

you talked of speaking Austro-German ... It was in pursuit of your privileged birth that I had searches made, in Austria, by a man of unparalleled expertise in discovering facts. There is no Princess Anna Boinberg-Langesfeld traceable in the lineage of the Hapsburg royal family during the last hundred years. But there is in Prussia...'

'Where is this rambling getting us?' broke in a man's voice.

'I wish that I knew,' said Anna.

'To the proof, Anna, that you are a spy working for Germany, that you were the person who identified William Hartley and brought about his death and that the sabotage in New York harbour of the freighter *Freedom* was initiated by you, specifically sent here by Berlin with letters of introduction from her distant German relatives to infiltrate Mrs Becker's household and confidence and destroy a pro-British arms supply conduit operated by Lowell Smithlane...'

'Please!' pleaded Anna, turning to the people around her. 'Please spare me this attack ... fetch a doctor. Sebastian surely needs a doctor...'

No one moved or spoke.

'This is a remarkably good likeness of Anna, don't you think, Mrs Becker?' said Sebastian, taking the photograph his father had supplied from its envelope within the folds of the newspaper. 'The uniformed general with her is her uncle, Count von Buller, the head of German military intelligence and a friend of the current German ambassador to this country, Count von Bernstorff...'

'And a cousin of my late husband,' said Amelia Becker, distantly, staring down at the photograph.

The alarm was clear on Anna's face now and Sebastian hurried on, anxious not to lose the pace. He offered to Lowell Smithlane the opened-in-readiness *New York Times*, the two sheets of paper from the envelope in hand and said: 'Look again at the reproduction of the anonymous letter, claiming that your freighter was gun-running...' He offered the pages. 'And compare the handwriting with that of these letters inviting me first to Virginia and now here...'

Anna did not collapse. She turned, with a fanatic's defiance, upon the room and its occupants and said: 'I won, though! You were too trusting, Frau Becker: too eagerly ready to confide your anti-German sentiments when I feigned mine and said I'd quit Germany forever to live here. As you were too trusting of your factory staff, the first actions of one of whom when he quit your employ to return to the Fatherland to take part in the forthcoming conflict was to report the unmarked consignments dispatched so regularly to the New York docks. So regularly, in fact, that it was a simple connection to make to the timetable of Smithlane's freighter sailings...'

'Which you were too eager to disrupt with your anonymous letter,' broke in Sebastian.

'Two espionage operations getting in each other's way. And now you're all destroyed.'

'Not getting in each other's way!' rejected the woman, turning, eyes flaring, upon him. 'Vogel's group got the weapons shipment and disposed of a British spy. And Smithlane won't dare ship to England again!'

'Vogel and his group go back to Germany in ignominy,' insisted Sebastian.

'But I won't! I shall go back in triumph and to honours.'

'You might prefer to remain here in America, alive at least,' said Sebastian, in quiet-voiced contrast to Anna's stridency. 'When I was seized with your diplomats I suggested it was you who exposed everything: that you might even be a double agent, leaking German secrets to their enemies. Which they'll believe – as Berlin will – because the police told Vogel they swooped when they did last night because of another tip-off from the same source. Seemed a good idea to keep all you spies getting into each other's way.

For the first time Anna's control cracked. 'You're lying!'

'Call the bluff then. Go back to Germany.'

'Enough!' declared Amelia Becker, towering over the other woman. Get out! Get out of my house – out of my sight – now! This instant!'

Anna hesitated for a moment, laughed a jeering laugh and then swept from the room.

Sebastian said: 'I anticipate you would like me to leave also?'

'No, Mr Holmes,' said the matriarch. 'I would wish you to stay. There is much for us to talk about.'

Anna Boinberg-Langesfeld left with only three cases, announcing she would send for the rest of her luggage. Only Sebastian waited outside, by the summoned carriage. Everyone else watched silently, crowded at the drawing-room windows.

Her defiance had lessened, although there was no capitulation. She said: 'I saved you, you know. After I identified Hartley – whom I recognized from Berlin embassy receptions – von Bernstorff thought you had to be in it together: that you should be killed as well. I insisted you weren't.'

'Then I must thank you.'

Anna hesitated. 'I think I loved you ... thought...' She shook her head. 'It doesn't matter now what I thought.'

'I think perhaps I loved you, too.'

'And I have won, Sebastian. Beaten you. There's something you still haven't deduced and so I've won.'

Thirty

The venue was fittingly in the same gentlemen's club – in the very same private dining room – in St James's in which the enterprise had begun and in which it had been reviewed during its progress. Tonight Winston Churchill was not delayed at the House but was there as host to greet Sebastian, even pouring the celebration champagne to propose the toast to what he called a brilliant coup, perfectly fulfilled.

'But for the death of a brave man,' qualified Sebastian. He was ashamed at misinterpreting William Hartley's attitude, knowing now it was the man's difficulty in playing his role.

'In war there are casualties,' said Churchill. 'In that which is to follow there will, alas, be many more.'

'Some of which may hopefully be prevented,' said Sebastian. 'In our final confrontation, just the two of us, Anna boasted that she had ultimately won: that there was something I had not deduced. I didn't disillusion her: had I done so, she *would* have won...'

'I thought we knew it all,' said Mycroft.

Sebastian shook his head. 'There's a little more. My first curiosity aboard the *Lusitania* was why she should claim to be of Austrian birth when from her accent and occasional slips into hard German she clearly wasn't. But at first I did not attach any importance to it. Then – and for too long afterwards – I considered she was an adventuress choosing to invent a romantic history; that she saw me as someone perfectly suited to her plans, which perhaps might have been the case. Another uncertainty – as it was with the Russian Grand Duke – was why she should endure the difficulty of travelling to England and then halfway through an unbecoming part of the country join an English vessel when so many German liners were more conveniently available from European ports...'

'A detour that would have aroused my curiosity,' congratulated Sherlock Holmes.

'The first night she asked me to accompany her on deck. We were passing the Irish coast and she made particular enquiry about the position of Queenstown. And quickly afterwards there was an accident: she quite badly bruised her foot, against the mounting fitted to our merchant vessels for six-inch guns in the event of their being commissioned into naval service.'

'You believe she was actively spying even then?' demanded Churchill.

'I am convinced of it,' insisted Sebastian. 'I later questioned Captain Dow, the *Lusitania's* master, in the closest detail in New York. Unbeknown to me, until then, was the interrogation to which she subjected Dow when he showed concern for her injury. I do not suppose the gun mounting is a particular secret to Berlin. But I am sure her demand about Queenstown and our distance from it when we were passing – which she also enquired from Dow – was to establish the course of our merchantmen and liners beginning their North Atlantic crossings. I'm suggesting the routings be changed, to remove such vessels from interception if there is a war.'

Churchill lifted his glass in another toast, this time towards the older man. 'You have in your son a man more than worthy to bear your name, Mr Holmes.'

'And enhance its reputation,' agreed Sherlock Holmes, taking the unwitting offer to unburden himself of stored irritations at Sebastian's treatment. 'I'm sure you'll agree Sebastian's achievements should not go unrecognized. And in a way that could resolve an outstanding difficulty.'

Churchill frowned. 'I regard tonight as recognition. And I am not aware of an outstanding difficulty.'

'Your contingency fund is intact, without my needing to supplement it?'

'Yes...' agreed Churchill, doubtfully.

'But there is a surplus, is there not – the two premiums Sebastian negotiated?'

There was a moment of silence. Churchill said: 'There is. Your proposal?'

'According it to Sebastian, as his professional fee,' said Sherlock Holmes.

There was further silence before Winston

Churchill said: 'That would be a convenient resolution, for all concerned.'

Sebastian was astonished first at his father's audacity and then by the awareness of how much his fortune had increased. He said: 'Thank you. That's extremely generous.'

'But well earned,' insisted his father. 'The labourer is worthy of his hire.'

'And there's more you should know,' said Sebastian. 'Frau Becker held me at the Southampton house after I exposed Anna Boinberg-Langesfeld: I was closeted with her and Lowell Smithlane. They want to continue supplying Great Britain. Smithlane intends setting up a subsidiary company which will be unknown to the Germans. He'll ship along the Ohio River and out through the Great Lakes, which was the intention for Hemditch's expanded steel production...' Sebastian hesitated, not knowing the reason for his father's earlier intervention but wanting to vent his own irritation at Churchill. 'And I also spoke at length to Hemditch, before leaving New York. He apologized, for his hare-to-hound use of me in his financing negotiations ... found it ironic that you and I should be so closely minded about the advantages of a steel supply. Which we will have. He is prepared to supply using Smithlane's freighters, too, by the same route.'

The slight pinkness of Churchill's face was the only hint of the man's embarrassment at Sebastian knowing the contents of the introductory letter. Briskly he said: 'A total, resounding success all round. But I remain puzzled by one thing. Smithlane's support is easily understood. But why Frau Becker?'

'A question I put to her,' said Sebastian. He shrugged. 'She's made a simple choice. She's an American. She feels no allegiance to Germany, despite her marriage. She considers Germany an intended aggressor and believes America should support this country.'

'Were others so minded...' said Mycroft.

'They will be, eventually,' predicted Churchill.

The dinner stretched late into the night and afterwards Sherlock Holmes suggested they walk a while, before hailing a hackney to Baker Street, where Sebastian had lived since his return two days earlier.

'Neither I nor the police watch assigned by Scotland Yard have detected anything yet but I fear renewed German interest,' said Sherlock Holmes.

'I shall shortly move on,' accepted Sebastian.

'I can understand your wish for quiet recovery, although I wouldn't recommend a German spa.'

'I had the homeward voyage aboard the *Lusitania* to rest and recover,' said Sebastian. 'I thought I would visit Meiringen.'

Father and son walked on unspeaking for several moments before Sherlock Holmes said: 'It is some years since I've been there. How do you feel about a travelling companion?'

'Delighted,' said Sebastian.

'It would be the opportunity to discuss the future.'

'I'd certainly welcome that.'

There was a further silence. Sherlock Holmes said: 'I wish many things for you but the strongest is that you do not have to wait as long as me to find the love I did. And that you are not robbed of it so quickly.'

Sebastian continued walking, without replying. What, he wondered, was Anna doing now? And where?

Postscript

On the sunlit afternoon of May 7, 1915, twelve miles off the Old Head of Kinsale on the southern coast of Ireland and close to the port of Queenstown (now Cobh) the Cunard liner *Lusitania* was struck approximately below its bridge by a single torpedo fired from the U-20, commanded by Walter Schwieger, one of Germany's most brutally ruthless submarine captains of the First World War. One minute later there was a second, more devastating explosion slightly further fo'ard. The liner sank, prow-first and listing to starboard, in eight minutes. In total, 1,198 lives – the majority American – were lost. In Berlin there were celebrations.

The British government knew submarines were operating in the area. Their radio signals had been intercepted at Room Forty, the nerve centre of Admiralty electronic intelligence innovated by Winston Churchill. Their sailing orders from Emden had also been intercepted and decoded at the end of April. On May 1, the day the *Lusitania* sailed from New York, the German government had warned in American newspaper announcements that neutral passenger ships suspected of carrying war materiel to Great Britain would be considered legitimate targets of war. On that same day, the *Lusitania's* master, Captain William Turner, was advised he would be met off the Irish coast and escorted to Liverpool by the cruiser HMS *Juno*. On May 5, after a conference at the Admiralty chaired by Winston Churchill and attended by Admiral Jack Fisher, First Sea Lord, Vice-Admiral Henry Oliver, Chief of the War Staff, Captain Reginald Hall, Director of Naval Intelligence, and Lieutenant Commander Joseph Kenworthy, a member of Hall's staff, the *Juno* was ordered to abandon her escort duties and return to Queenstown. Captain Turner was not told he no longer had protection.

All witnesses called by the British Board of Trade enquiry into the sinking of the *Lusitania* convened on June 15 by Lord Mersey – who had earlier headed the tribunal into the *Titanic* disaster – were required to set out in writing their intended evidence before it was presented, enabling it to be completely screened by Admiralty lawyers for what they considered to be admissible. A private note to Lord Mersey from the Admiralty read: 'The government would consider it politically expedient if the captain of the *Lusitania* were promiscuously blamed for the accident.' Five days earlier, on June 10, parliament enacted a statute under the Defence of the Realm Act making it a treasonable offence for any British subject to divulge information about munitions transportation on British merchant ships. Cunard assured Lord Mersey it had submitted all relevant communications to Captain Turner prior to the sinking but that totally to disclose his orders would contravene that statute. Those orders withheld from Lord Mersey included Churchill's decision that British merchant ships should fly flags of neutral countries to avoid the German blockade, ram German submarines detected on the surface and refuse to leave-to at German submarines' insistence. All were illegal under international convention. Churchill also approved a fabricated, backdated set of supposed orders to Captain Turner, which were presented to an in camera session of the Mersey enquiry, which put the responsibility fully upon Germany for the sinking but during which Turner was branded negligent and guilty of disobeying orders. The enquiry also concluded that the second explosion was caused by a second torpedo from an unknown U-boat. It was not. The most likely explanation is that the U-20's solitary torpedo ignited the 46 tons of aluminium powder – an explosives component – being shipped contrary to American law. Also in that illegal cargo and never disclosed to the Mersey enquiry were 5,000 3.3" shrapnel shells, 4,200,000 Remington rifle cartridges and 3,200 percussion fuses.

Almost from the day of the *Lusitania* disaster, speculation began that Churchill had withdrawn HMS *Juno* and allowed the

Lusitania to become a submarine target to bring America into the war. That much-sought entry to the war did not, in fact, take place until April, 1917.

One day short of three weeks after the *Lusitania* sinking – on May 27 – Winston Churchill was forced to resign for instigating Lord Kitchener's suggestion of an Anglo-French attack upon Turkish defences in the Dardanelles channel, which forewarned the Turks of the abortive Allied invasion in April upon the Gallipoli peninsular, through which it was intended to supply Britain's Russian ally.

Churchill was to remain out of office – serving as a colonel in the Sixth Royal Fusiliers on the Western Front – until he was recalled to the government in 1917.

His first appointment was that of Minister of Munitions.